THE INTRUDER

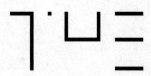

Also by Håkan Östlundh

The Viper

INTRUDER

HÅKAN ÖSTLUNDH

Translated from the Swedish by Paul Norlen

 MINOTAUR BOOKS
A THOMAS DUNNE BOOK
NEW YORK

A THOMAS DUNNE BOOK FOR MINOTAUR BOOKS.
An imprint of St. Martin's Publishing Group.

THE INTRUDER. Copyright © 2011 by Håkan Östlundh by agreement with Grand Agency. Translation copyright © 2015 by Paul Norlen. All rights reserved. Printed in the United States of America. For information, address St. Martin's Press, 175 Fifth Avenue, New York, N.Y. 10010.

www.thomasdunnebooks.com
www.minotaurbooks.com

The Library of Congress Cataloging-in-Publication Data is available upon request.

ISBN 978-1-250-02948-5 (hardcover)
ISBN 978-1-250-02949-2 (e-book)

Minotaur books may be purchased for educational, business, or promotional use. For information on bulk purchases, please contact the Macmillan Corporate and Premium Sales Department at 1-800-221-7945, extension 5442, or write to specialmarkets@macmillan.com.

First published in Sweden as *Inkräktaren* by Ordfront in 2011

First U.S. Edition: August 2015

10 9 8 7 6 5 4 3 2 1

THE INTRUDER

It was too dark to see the water, but she could hear the waves striking the side of the boat through the sound of the diesel engines. Searchlights lit up the metal deck of the ferry and parts of the yellow superstructure. There were only two cars on board—their own red Mercedes SUV and a black station wagon right behind them.

They had been gone four weeks.

They headed across the sound toward the island, their home for the past two years—if you could say that a Fårö ferry headed. It did not even have a stem, a prow, or a stern. It was a yellow sheet-metal raft with space for four rows of vehicles.

Malin never would have believed that an ugly little ferry would come to play such an important role in her life. *Bodilla*. The name as graceful as the heavy diesel-droning iron raft. They took *Bodilla* to drop Axel off at day care. It was *Bodilla* they had to board if they wanted to go to a restaurant or shop for anything besides the most basic necessities. Sometimes it was *Kajsa-Stina*, but most often *Bodilla*.

The tourist season was not over yet, but it was into the final, thin weeks. Once school had started it was mostly foreigners and retirees who ventured the whole way up to Fårö. Soon they, too, would be gone. Then everything closed except the ICA grocery store and the church.

The children were asleep in the backseat. The ferry throbbed ahead over the sound. Henrik picked the camera up from his lap and aimed it toward her.

"Just raise your chin a little," he instructed.

Malin smiled and did as he asked.

"No, don't smile," he said quickly.

She tried to resume her expression from before; perhaps she succeeded. Henrik took five or six pictures in rapid succession with small movements between each exposure.

"Don't you already have a thousand pictures of me on this ferry?" she asked.

Henrik lowered the camera.

"Every picture is a new picture," he said with a wink followed by a wide grin.

Malin looked at him, looked into his dark, alert eyes, and now she, too, had to smile. Henrik leaned forward to kiss her. She hesitated a second or two.

"What is it?" he said, looking perplexed at her.

The memory of the quarrel that morning held her back. It had been pushed aside without their really having finished it.

"Oh, nothing," she said and leaned closer.

At the same moment, the piercing searchlights went dark and the throbbing of the engines died out.

Malin gasped, tried to look out through the wide window toward the pier, but the darkness was impenetrable.

They floated quietly in the middle of the sound. They could see the lights in Broa, hear the waves more clearly against the ferry's metal plate in the sudden silence. Malin fumbled for the button on the car's overhead dome light. Before she found it, the engines rumbled into motion again and the deck was lit up. She blinked at the sharp light. No more than five or ten seconds could have passed.

"What the hell was that?" she said, looking at Henrik.

"The captain must have leaned against the emergency stop." Henrik grinned.

She laughed, but did not feel a bit amused. A heavy chill had taken hold of her body when the light and engines died. Now it would not let go.

A few minutes later the ferry landed at the pier. The ramp was lowered and the gates were opened. Malin quickly started the car and drove off.

When they left the ferry landing they also left behind the last light. She saw in the rearview mirror the station wagon turn off toward Ryssnäs. They were alone in the darkness. It was only the end of August, but still completely black around them.

They were far away from everything: from streetlights, from neon signs and display windows, from cities that spilled their light across the sky at a distance. It was as if the island were still obstinately stuck in darkness; it did not get electricity until after the war, and in practice, not until the fifties.

When the landscape that had just been lit up by the headlights of the car behind them faded out she felt worry akin to what seafarers must have felt long ago. The worry that the world would come to an end. That at any moment you might tip over the edge.

Axel coughed in the backseat. Malin peeked at him in the rearview mirror. He blinked a few times but seemed to go back to sleep.

"Hello, we live here," Henrik called in a restrained voice.

Malin braked hard so as not to drive past, and the children whimpered and mumbled in their sleep. She always found it hard to find her way in the darkness. The sign leaped out from the night without advance warning, even though the road was straight and the landscape flat.

She turned the big SUV left. Soon they were clattering across the first of the cattle guards. Their rattling under the wheels helped her keep track of how far they had gone. She counted. After the fourth one they would turn to the right.

When Malin came into the house she sensed at once that someone had been there. She shivered and turned around toward Henrik, who had Axel in his arms, but then it struck her that everything was as it should be. For a moment she had forgotten about renting out the house. Three different tenants in four weeks while they traveled around between relatives and friends on the mainland. Twenty-six thousand kronor after the agency's percentage. Money they needed.

Henrik went back out to bring in the bags from the car. Malin carried Axel up the creaking staircase while Ellen tiredly trudged along beside her.

It smelled strange in the children's room. The strange aroma of the tenants? But the smell had a rank edge. She put Axel down on Ellen's bed and set the window open with the hasp. A light wind brought with it the heavy but pleasant odor of a late-summer garden. Greenery, tomatoes and marjoram.

Ellen sat on her knees on the floor and picked among the toys she had been separated from a whole month. Malin fetched the sheets and made the bed for Axel. He was sleeping deeply, completely relaxed. Arms and legs fell loose-limbed against the bedcover as she carefully undressed him and put him down under the blanket.

Ellen held her cloth rabbit tightly and smiled broadly. Malin smiled back, while at the same time, she wrinkled her nose. The strange smell was still there, under the green.

"Are you hungry, do you want anything?" she asked.

"Don't know," Ellen answered, preoccupied.

Malin went downstairs. Henrik was sitting in the dark in the kitchen, fingering his iPhone. His right thumb traveled over the display while his left hand brushed back the dark straggly hair that fell down in front of his eyes. He had built a black mountain of baggage in the middle of the floor.

Sometimes she envied his ability to disconnect from everything around him. But usually it just irritated her. When they visited Henrik's friends on the mainland it was as if he had turned off a switch. It was just beer and talk about work, fishing, soccer, and more beer and boyish memories and long, boring discussions about house renovations. Finally she had to remind him that he had two children who needed to be taken care of and entertained and, if nothing else, at least kept track of so that they didn't wander off and drown somewhere. And then they started quarreling.

Malin turned on the ceiling light and the one over the kitchen counter.

"Do you want tea?" she asked.

"Huh?" said Henrik, looking up.

His mouth and chin were lit by the cold-blue glow from the phone.

"Tea?" she repeated.

"Sure, that would be nice, but none of that rooibos shit, please."

Malin bent down toward the cupboard where they kept the saucepans, supporting herself with her left hand against the counter. She felt her palm getting sticky and covered with crumbs.

"But what the hell," she sighed.

Henrik did not react. She looked around for the dishrag, but could not find it. Instead she opened the cupboard under the sink to take out a new one and stopped short when she caught sight of a half-full garbage bag.

"I'm getting damned tired of this."

"What is it?" said Henrik absently.

"They haven't cleaned up properly."

Only now did he look up.

"Then they'll have to pay for a cleaning company. It's in the contract."

"And who is going to see to it that they pay that bill, huh? Are you going to do it?"

"We'll have to call the agency. They'll have to take care of it."

Malin got out a new dishrag and wiped off the counter. When she had wrung out the rag and hung it up on the faucet, she had a sudden impulse and opened one of the cupboards. Her eyes passed quickly over the rows of drinking glasses and coffee cups.

"This is just too much."

She opened one cupboard after another with glasses and porcelain, even the old serving cupboard she had inherited from her grandmother that stood against the wall behind the dining table.

"There are things missing in every cupboard."

"You always have to allow for a little shrinkage," said Henrik.

"What do you mean, shrinkage?"

"Yes, we break things, too. A glass or two you have to allow for."

"But this is not one or two. Lots are missing."

She started counting, but became uncertain of how many they had of the various kinds.

"Don't you leave money if you've broken something? Or at least write a note?"

"Maybe they left a message at the agency. I'll call them tomorrow."

"Fucking shit."

In the midst of her fury she put on a kettle of water for tea, banging it down on the stove so that it splashed over. Henrik put down his phone and looked at her.

"We just brought in twenty-six thousand for this."

They had invested heavily in the move to Fårö. Money, commitment, their future. From the beginning it was Malin who insisted that they should buy a house, but then she had preferred Nacka, Enskede, or perhaps Värmdö, some place where she felt at home. Not Gotland in the middle of the Baltic. Or Fårö then. She had learned to distinguish between the two, Fårö and the "Big Island."

Malin had been skeptical, reluctant even, as they drove on board the ferry in Nynäshamn. Did Henrik really want to go back there? After seventeen years? But even before they reached the house she had been sold. The landscape that opened toward the glistening sea beyond Fårö church took her breath away.

The house in Kalbjerga had a beautiful setting at the foot of a slope, with a typical Gotland floor plan, but a little unusual with the gambrel roof. It had belonged to a colleague of Henrik who in turn had bought it from Ingmar Bergman. According to the rumors, it had served as a staff residence for a housekeeper. In the big barn, which the director used as a rehearsal space, there was even an old stage set remaining from one of the films, unclear which one.

It had quickly become a standing joke that they could auction off the set at Christie's if everything went to hell. Right now it was feeling more like a desperate hope than a joke.

They had renovated the house, rebuilt the barn into a studio, and started furnishing the big but simple wing as rooms for visiting photographers. Their plans assumed that Henrik would be able to do most of his jobs on Fårö, but also that they could entice photographers there from all around the world. Photographers and models would be housed in the newly constructed residence wing and could work in the studio, but primarily, of course, in the exotic landscape that inspired one of the world's greatest film directors.

Why not? they thought. Swedish and American photographers would make pilgrimages to India simply to take pictures of Western models in the right kind of sunlight.

They borrowed money and hired carpenters. Everything was going according to plan. Then came the recession.

The sensitive advertising industry took a nosedive as company after company reduced their marketing budgets. They had been forced to put on the emergency brake. In practice this meant sending home carpenters and paying back money they had already borrowed but not yet managed to spend.

And there they stood now. Of course everything had not gone to hell. It was not time to call Christie's—yet. But Malin knew that Henrik lay awake at night. He was calculating interest rates, calculating dream scenarios and horror scenarios, calculating where the threshold of pain was. She was trying to avoid thinking about money herself.

They managed the loans thanks to the fact that Henrik took jobs on the mainland and abroad. The exact opposite of what they had imagined. Malin's food blogging also contributed a bit. Their hope was to be able to work to get the money to finish building the guest rooms one at a time.

A couple hundred thousand left by Henrik's mother would truly make a big difference, but Malin had more or less given up hope of ever seeing that money. They did not have the means to lose a lawsuit. Then they would definitely have to sell the house. And it seemed as if Henrik's sisters would rather die than give up any of the inheritance.

She took the kettle from the stove and poured the boiling water into the teapot.

"There's a Danish photographer who maybe wants to come here for a week," said Henrik, pointing at the cell phone.

Malin nodded, not daring to hope too much.

"Fashion?"

"No, beer."

"It might as well be porn, just so we get a little business soon."

"Okay . . ."

"That was a joke."

Malin poured tea, splashed in a little milk, and went over to Henrik with the mugs. She set them down on the table and pulled out the chair.

The pain that shot up from her foot made her yell out loud.

"What is it?" said Henrik, getting up.

His eyes worriedly sought hers.

She was standing on one leg and writhing in pain, her cheeks damp with tears.

"Malin, what is it?"

"Don't know," she whimpered. "My foot, something . . ."

She sat down slowly on the chair as Henrik came around the end of the table.

"You're bleeding."

She looked down. Only now did she see big, dark red drops on the gray-painted pine floor. She held up the aching foot, her leg straight out from the seat. The pain was sharp and diabolical. It hurt so much that she was scared.

Henrik crouched down in front of her and inspected her extended foot.

"It looks like a piece of glass," he said, looking more closely. "Yes, it is. Right in the heel."

The thought of a glass shard that had cut deeply into her foot made her moan again.

"How does it look? Is it big?"

Henrik opened his mouth.

"Or actually, I don't want to know," she stopped him.

He looked at her foot, then looked up at her with a deep furrow between his eyes.

"I have to pull it out."

She instinctively pulled back her foot.

"Malin," he said, as if to a child, and put his left hand around her ankle.

"Yes, I know," she said with a sigh. "But be careful."

"You have to hold still."

She looked away and tried to relax, but it was hard. She tensed up even more when she sensed Henrik's thumb and index finger approaching her heel. The worst was when he took hold of the piece of glass and it twisted in the wound. Presumably only just barely, but it felt as if he were driving a spear through her leg all the way up to her hip. Then a brief but lighter pain and then it was over.

Malin gasped a couple of times, feeling both liberated and fragile.

Henrik held up the piece of glass. It was perhaps two inches long and slightly bent; it seemed to come from a wineglass.

"I'll get bandages," he said, setting the bloody piece of glass aside on the table.

He walked quickly toward the bathroom and came back with the green plastic first aid kit. He washed off the heel and put two bandages across the wound, according to Malin's instructions.

"It's really big. Maybe you should go to the health center tomorrow," he said when he was done and picking up the debris.

"Tomorrow it will be too late. If it needs stitches it has to be done tonight."

Henrik looked at her with an expression that she assumed meant: If you want I can go over and ask Bengt and Ann-Katrin to watch the kids, then I'll drive you to Visby.

"I don't think they would stitch it anyway," she said.

Henrik did not say anything, but looked noticeably relieved. Malin carefully set her foot on the floor.

"I hate those fucking tenants. I'm going to be handicapped for days."

Henrik was about to say something when he was interrupted by Ellen's call from upstairs.

"Mommy. Mommy, come."

"What is it, Ellen?"

"Mommy, come, there's poop here."

Malin and Henrik looked at each other.

"What are you saying?" Malin called. "What do you mean, poop?"

"There's poop here. In with the toys. Come."

Henrik tossed aside the debris he had in his hands and went up. Malin followed his heavy steps across the floor and thought that there could be more pieces of glass. They would have to vacuum the kitchen. She heard their murmuring voices up there, then Henrik's sudden outburst.

"But what the hell, this is disgusting! What is this?"

2.

Malin stared down into the big woven toy basket, holding Ellen back with her left hand.

"Could it be an animal?" said Henrik. "A cat that got in?"

"It doesn't look like cat shit," said Malin.

She felt a vague nausea sneaking up, more or less like the presentiment of stomach flu. A big black turd had been hidden under the children's toys. It was so disgusting she didn't know what to do with herself.

"A dog, maybe?" said Henrik.

"I think that some sick bastard has crapped in the children's toy basket," she said in English, dragging Ellen another few feet away from the basket.

"What is it, Mommy? What did you say?"

She was not sure herself why she spoke English. And now it had only made Ellen even more curious.

"Knock it off, it must have been some animal that got in."

"The only animal I know that sneaks into houses and poops in boxes are cats and this is not cat poop. Besides, cats don't usually place a layer of toys on top when they've done."

"But couldn't one of the tenants have done this?"

She looked at Henrik. What did he mean?

"Maybe they didn't notice anything," he clarified, "and then they were going to clean—"

"It must have smelled," she interrupted.

Henrik pondered this briefly, then he shrugged his shoulders and picked up the basket.

"I'll take this down to the laundry room and try to sanitize it somehow."

"All the toys have to be washed, too."

"Yes, I get that," he hissed, carrying away the toy basket.

"I didn't mean it as a criticism," Malin called after him.

She sighed. Good Lord. There was no reason to argue about this.

"Come," she said to Ellen, limping away with her to the bathroom.

When Ellen had washed her hands, Malin washed Ellen's face and took off her clothes. She got Ellen into her bathrobe and followed her back to the children's room, where she set her down on the edge of the bed.

"Sit here while I get some bags. Don't touch anything. We have to wash everything."

"But the rabbit," Ellen protested.

"It has to be washed, too. Don't touch anything, do you understand? Sit here quietly until I come back."

Ellen nodded.

On her way downstairs, more or less hopping on one leg, it suddenly felt wrong to leave Ellen up there. The feeling was growing stronger with every step. It was as if something strange had been there. Sure, there really had been, too, but something malevolently strange, something that left invisible traces besides the highly tangible ones in the toy basket. Perhaps she ought to have brought Ellen with her downstairs? But then Axel would have been all alone up there.

What if there was someone in the house? The thought came over her without warning, made her breathe more rapidly. She tried to force it back. Why would there be someone in the house?

Troubling thoughts. The kind of thoughts she did not usually have. Now she could not go to bed without Henrik searching through the whole house first. Malin opened the bottom kitchen drawer and quickly pulled out as many plastic bags as she could. She would have preferred to throw away all the toys that had been in any kind of contact with the poop, but that wouldn't do, of course.

"I can do that," Henrik called from the bathroom. "Rest your foot."

"It's no problem," she called back. "It's fine."

She went back up. Going up was actually easier than going down. She started packing up all the things Ellen had managed to pull out and realized that she had brought way too many bags. Three was enough. Two to pack in and one to pull over her hand to avoid touching the mess. She brought Ellen with her down to the kitchen. Happened to think that she ought to have slippers on if there were more pieces of glass. She parked Ellen on a chair and limped up and got her white rabbit slippers. When she came into the laundry room with the bags, Henrik was standing at the sink scrubbing the toy container. He looked up quickly.

"Maybe they've rubbed their privates with the tea cups, too," he said with a crooked smile.

"Do you have to be so disgusting? That was the last thing I needed."

"But . . ."

She sank down on a chair in the kitchen and sat there stiff as a poker. She did not want to lean against the back of the chair, did not want to rest her arm on the table, and had to stop herself from reprimanding Ellen, who had set her cheek against the tabletop.

She would be forced to clean the whole house from floor to ceiling before she could feel comfortable again. She smothered a sigh and reached out a hand toward Ellen.

"Come, let's get you to bed."

Malin put clean sheets on for Ellen and got her into bed. She let the window stay open to the late summer night, thought of the fresh air sweeping in and cleaning up after all the strangers that had moved in their rooms, took hold of their things, talked, laughed, and swore there between their walls.

They needed the money and it seemed so simple to rent out the house. With hindsight she did not understand how they could have come up with such a completely insane idea.

She opened both windows in her and Henrik's bedroom and took out clean sheets for the unmade bed. Before she started making the bed she shook the blankets through the window. She did her best to repress the feeling that the blankets would have to be burned along with the mattresses and the beds and it would be impossible for her to sleep tonight if they did not bring in a couple of the new beds from the guest wing.

She set aside the blankets and grabbed the pillows to air them, too. She stopped herself when she heard Henrik calling something from below.

"What? I didn't hear you," she called back.

She could hear for herself how irritated she sounded. She could not help it.

Instead of yelling even louder he came upstairs. He stopped in the doorway.

"Did you take down the pictures in the study?"

"What pictures?"

He looked at her, with the pillow in her arms.

"The pictures of us. In the study. Did you take them down before we left?"

"No."

"Are you sure?"

Malin thought for a few seconds. Not because she really needed to, but Henrik's seriousness made her uncertain. She had removed a number of things before they left and locked them in the guest wing. But she had not taken down the family portraits that were hanging in the study.

She nodded.

The worried furrow was back between Henrik's eyebrows.

"What is it?" she asked.

"They're gone."

"Gone?"

"Yes, they're not hanging on the wall, anyway."

"Huh?"

She looked doubtfully at him.

"Someone must have taken them down. I don't get any of this."

Malin tossed the pillow onto the bed.

"What kind of fucking lunatics have been here? Shit and glass and . . . Who would do such a thing? Maybe we're only going to discover more and more. They may have come up with just about anything."

A cold, dark feeling passed through her. Stealing their family portraits. That was so personal, so aggressive.

Henrik sighed deeply.

"I'll have to call the agency first thing in the morning. I'll look through the cupboards down there, too. They may have just put them away if they had small children and forgot to put them back."

"I doubt that . . ."

Malin stopped herself when she realized that she was talking much too loud. Almost shouting. She lowered her voice.

"I doubt that people who poop in other people's toys are that considerate."

Henrik made a face that meant that she was probably right. He went down anyway to look, and Malin continued making the bed.

When she was going to get the pillowcases a paper floated out of the linen closet. Malin bent over and picked it up. As soon as she turned it over she saw that it was one of the pictures from the study. It depicted the whole family together at the beach at Norsta Auren. An old friend of Henrik's had taken it when he visited them last summer. But where their eyes had looked toward the camera before, there were now only four pairs of holes. The light from the lamp on the nightstand shone right through.

This time Malin did not care that she screamed.

3.

The belt with the expandable baton clattered against the door as Fredrik Broman opened his locker in the basement of the police station. The changing room looked more or less like a changing room at a nice gym, with a tile floor and rows of birch veneer lockers. In Fredrik's locker the national coat of arms glistened on the neatly hung-up uniform. In the compartment above the uniform was his peaked cap, and the compartment to the right was stuffed with jackets for various kinds of weather.

This was clothing and equipment he almost never used. The last time was when his own clothes had been completely drenched in blood and he had nothing else to change into. The blood had come from a man who tried to kill himself with a handsaw when Fredrik and Gustav Wallin were going to arrest him.

He pushed away the unpleasant memory, took out the holster and wriggled it on. He shut the locker, went up to the gun room, and took his service pistol out of the white gun cabinet with number sixty-three on the cover. He checked the gun, inserted the magazine, and put the pistol in place in the holster. He had been meticulous about target practice, but apart from that he had not had any occasion to carry a gun since he came back from sick leave.

Fredrik went straight from the gun room and out onto the enclosed courtyard on the back side of the police station. The sun made his face feel hot. In the crown of the big elm tree migratory birds were rustling around hunting for lethargic late-summer insects.

Fredrik went past two marked police cars parked in the shade of the tree, continued out through the gate, and took a step up onto the sidewalk to the right of the entry. Now he was definitely outside the domains of the police department. He was standing in public space with his service pistol in its holster. He could maintain, if anyone was possibly interested, not only that he was employed by the Visby Police Department, but that he was in service at this very moment, right there on Avagatan in the middle of Visby, a stone's throw from the commerce of Östercentrum and another stone's throw from the medieval World Heritage City. Admittedly he was not performing any sensible task at the moment—no one had asked him to go out and stare at Avagatan—but he was in service. Patrol duty.

Fredrik put his hands at his sides and took a couple of deep breaths. He was a policeman again.

He felt relieved, excited, and slightly nostalgic. A little proud even. His little ritual would probably seem silly to an outsider's eyes, but for him it was important. What he was doing right now he had not been able to do yesterday. Today, Monday, was a workday. For the first time in almost two years he was a policeman, in every sense of the word.

The whole thing was over in fifteen seconds, but Fredrik was convinced that he would never forget that brief moment. He went back into the building. On his way up to his office he encountered two colleagues in the stairway. They said hello quickly and continued their conversation. He felt a vague disappointment and was forced to smile at himself. What had he expected? That everyone should stand and applaud and cheer under a big banner that said "Welcome Back, Fredrik"? His colleagues on the stairs presumably did not even know that this was his first day back on patrol duty. He had been back at work for six months now. Obviously they did not keep track of exactly what he did day by day.

He came up to the investigation department's long corridor of white walls, birch doors, and dreary linoleum flooring. Instead of turning right to his own office he turned left. He could just as well stop by Göran Eide's office and remind him that he had resumed patrol duty today. To be on the safe side.

On his way there Fredrik stopped by Gustav Wallin's open door. Gustav, in a light, discreet glen plaid suit and light blue shirt, was leaning over his desk browsing through a thick bundle of papers. He did not notice him. Fredrik took a couple steps closer and said hello.

Gustav looked up from the desk. The narrow edge of beard along his jawline had been shaved with the utmost precision.

"Hey there," he said absently.

He kept hold of one of the papers with his thumb and index finger.

Fredrik exchanged a few words with Gustav and thought that he ought to react to the coat of arms, but no, not a look. It was clear, they were surrounded by people who wore the coat of arms all day long. Why should Gustav react to it? For his colleagues it was just an ordinary day at work. Evidently even for his closest associates.

The disappointment came creeping again, and again he pushed it away. How could they know that he felt almost like the day he graduated from Police Academy? Proud, relieved, a little nervous, and above all full of expectation without any real target.

For almost two years he had brooded every day about whether everything would be like before or if he would never again get to work as a policeman.

Today he got his answer.

He left Gustav with his pile of papers and continued over to Göran's office. He knocked and waited until he heard a stifled murmur from the other side of the door before he pushed it open.

Göran Eide, the head of the Gotland police investigation department, got up quickly when he caught sight of Fredrik. He was almost sixty and the grizzled hair on the side of his head was all he had left. A little ways down on his nose sat a pair of cheap reading glasses.

Göran rounded the desk and extended his hand.

"Welcome back," he said with a big smile, bowing solemnly.

Fredrik thanked him. Göran made a gesture toward the blue armchair on the other side of the desk.

"Have a seat."

Göran went back and sat down behind his desk. His comfortable office chair had an extra-high back and a small adjustable neck support; in some way it made it noticeable that he was the boss.

He took off his glasses and looked at Fredrik.

"All's well that ends well, or what do you say?" he said with a smile.

"Yes, I've had worse days," said Fredrik.

Göran laughed, but then became serious.

"Twenty-three months ago it didn't look that promising."

"No," said Fredrik, moving the chair a little closer to the desk.

At last someone who understood how important this day was to him. At the same time he hoped that Göran would not get caught up in anything too long and sentimental. That was not really the relationship he had with his boss.

Strange thing about attention. First disappointment that he didn't get any. Once he got it he wanted it over with as quickly as possible.

"If I were to be completely frank," said Göran, "I didn't think you would be sitting here today. I mean, not when I was up at the hospital the first time."

He shook his head thoughtfully and looked down at the table for a moment. "Yes, you'll have to excuse me," he added with a new gleam in his eye.

"No, it's no problem," said Fredrik. "I probably didn't believe that I would even be able to sit up again myself. And to be completely honest I didn't even notice that you were there."

Göran smiled. "But now you're sitting here," he said.

"Now I'm sitting here."

"I'm extremely happy to have you back in the group. And I'm happy that it has worked so well, the whole apparatus with doctors, psychologists, the union, management, and . . . well, you know. But above all I'm happy for your sake. I know that this is what you've wanted the whole time."

Fredrik was content to nod slowly but definitely, afraid of a nostalgic quiver in his voice if he opened his mouth.

"I assume that you're anxious to get going," said Göran, changing his tone of voice. "To get out."

"That's right," Fredrik managed to squeeze out in a steady voice.

"Okay then. I have a case for you."

This was exactly the way Fredrik wanted to come back. From the first moment to feel that he had Göran's full confidence. No soft start, no hesitation at the goal. He had been soft starting for six months now. That was more than enough.

"There's a family on Fårö that—"

Göran interrupted himself, and Fredrik was startled by a fizzing sound and a strange glow right behind him. He excitedly turned around in his chair.

Two steps inside the doorway stood Gustav with a cyanide-blue

princess cake on a paper plate. From the middle of the cake a sparkler crackled. In the midst of the surprise, Fredrik could not help
wondering about the embers that floated down onto Göran's linoleum
floor.

Behind Gustav, Fredrik's immediate coworkers had lined up: Sara
Oskarsson, just as dark-haired as Gustav, today in a jeans shirt and
black pants, was standing with a heap of coffee cups and small paper
plates in her arms. Ove Gahnström was peering behind aviator eyeglass
frames, holding a pump thermos pressed against his sturdy stomach.
Even Lennart Svensson had shown up, although he had retired a month
ago. The gray curls were slightly unrulier than usual and his dress
somewhat more casual. Fredrik was very moved to see him there, which
definitely was a unique feeling.

Once the sparkler had burned out, they came forward one by one
to dole out congratulations along with hugs and thumps on the back.
Fredrik was a little worried about the cake as Gustav balanced it
with one hand and embraced him with the other.

Fredrik looked at them all and stammered out a thank you. He had
a hard time finding the words.

"What is it?" said Lennart. "You didn't get a cerebral hemorrhage
from the fireworks?"

"Lennart," said Sara, with a tired expression.

"It's okay," said Fredrik. "I would be deeply disappointed if he suddenly started choosing his words with care."

The truth was that he actually missed Lennart. The opposite of
what he had thought. Fredrik wondered whether they hadn't become a
little more boring after Lennart quit. Only in the vacuum after his bad
jokes, small provocations, and politically incorrect comments did
Fredrik realize that perhaps they did have a certain significance for the
group after all. It stirred things up. Distracted, in a good way. Kept
them alert.

Gustav put down the cake on the visitor group's round table. He
noticed Fredrik's look at the vivid blue casing.

"They hadn't had time to make any green ones yet. I was in the bakery right when they opened."

"Blue is pretty," said Fredrik, trying to mentally ignore his own words.

He still could not think of anything sensible to say.

"Here," said Ove, handing over a cake cutter. "You start."

Soon everyone had a piece of cake and a cup of coffee. There were only four chairs in the room, and Sara tried to offer Fredrik one of the chairs with the argument that he was the one being celebrated.

"No, what the hell, you sit down," he said.

Fredrik and Ove stood up, or leaned a little carefully on the furniture.

"You fooled me completely," said Fredrik. "I was starting to actually get a little—"

"You should have seen your face when I barely said hello," Gustav said with a laugh, pointing at him with the cake spoon.

"I really didn't suspect a thing," he admitted. "You seemed completely absorbed by your pile of papers. In a completely natural way."

"Hollywood is waiting," said Lennart, with a wry smile.

"They'll have to wait a little longer," said Göran. "No thinking about alternative careers until I've managed to fill the gap left by Lennart."

"That can't be too hard," said Fredrik, looking at Lennart with what he hoped was a gleam in his eye.

"Wait now," said Lennart at once. "How was it? You had some kind of blow to the head, right?"

A strange mixture of laughter and embarrassed murmuring filled the room. Fredrik hurried to say something before the embarrassment took over.

"Listen, everyone, I have to say that I truly appreciate this. This day means a lot to me. You can probably say that this day is the only thing I thought about . . . No, not the only thing," he corrected himself. "But this is something I've thought about and fought for every day for almost two years. I am grateful that you understood that! And that you did this."

They looked at him seriously. Ove nodded. Sara smiled hesitantly.

"Even though the cake was blue," he added.

They laughed with relief, and a little exaggeratedly, at the dry joke. A rescue plank under the seriousness. The conversation took off again, Lennart ate up half of Sara's piece of cake and a couple minutes later Göran came up to Fredrik and took him aside.

"Yes, as I was going to say before," he started, setting aside his cake plate, "this concerns a family on Fårö. Malin Andersson and Henrik Kjellander in Kalbjerga. They've been threatened."

4.

Göran Eide picked up a coffee mug that someone had forgotten on the shelf behind the desk. He felt slightly nauseated. It was the princess cake. He should have followed Sara's example and left half. But you don't want to act like an old lady, he thought, so instead you have to feel like you're going to throw up.

Despite the nausea, he was happy about this day. He had truly not believed that Fredrik would come back. Not as a police officer or as anything else. It had been a dreadful accident and Fredrik did not look like much as he lay bandaged and seemingly paralyzed in the hospital bed.

Fredrik did not remember much of the accident, but Sara Oskarsson had been standing only ten feet away and seen him fall from the cliff. If you read her report you might say that what happened was partly self-inflicted. Fredrik did not have to chase after the man they had arrested when he tried to flee, if *flight* was the right word to describe someone who rushed toward his own death. No one would have accused Fredrik if he had stayed standing and let the man throw himself off the cliff.

But instead Fredrik ran after him, caught up with him at the edge, and tried to stop him. The fleeing man had locked Fredrik's arm, intentionally or unintentionally, and pulled him down with him. If it was luck, or if during the brief seconds he had at his disposal Fredrik managed to get the man under him, it was impossible to say. In any event Fredrik landed on top of the man, who died instantly.

For Fredrik, the fall off the cliff resulted in a severe concussion and an extensive hemorrhage outside the hard membrane of the brain. The brain tissue itself had not been damaged directly by the fall, but was affected by the pressure from the hemorrhage. If bleeding had occurred inside the membrane of the brain, perhaps he would not even have survived the transport from Östergarnsholme to the hospital.

Göran suppressed a belch and silently cursed the princess cake. Crazy damned concoction. Couldn't Gustav have had the sense to buy a Tosca cake or an ordinary Danish braid? The nausea made him almost dizzy. He pulled out the top drawer in the pedestal drawers and searched in the back among paper clips, business cards, and pens. He found two Maalox, wiped the dust from the package, pressed out one of the tablets, and swallowed it.

5.

The wind came in gusts through the rolled-down window, smelling of seawater and diesel. Malin was sitting in the car on *Bodilla*'s deck, the children belted tight in the backseat. To the north Hau rävlar and Lansaholm reached out to each other, leaving only a glimpse of sea in the narrows. To the south, on the other hand, the view opened out toward the Baltic. The sun-glistening surface of the sea was subdued into darker, dull patches when the wind picked up.

Malin had been worried that it would be hard to drive with her injured foot, but it went fine. It hurt more when she walked, even though she limped along on the toes of her right foot.

"Mommy, can I play with Lisa today?" Ellen asked from the backseat.

Malin turned around and smiled between the neck rests. Axel was sitting with his nose pressed against the window, staring at a big yellow-beaked gull that was following the ferry.

"I'll have to call her mom, then we'll see."

Ellen cheered and tugged on the seat belt.

"Ellen, it's not for sure. We'll see, I said."

It was complicated to have friends in Fårösund when you lived on Fårö. If Ellen wanted to go home with someone after school it had to fit more or less with Axel's schedule, otherwise Malin had to spend the better part of the day driving and taking the ferry back and forth between Fårösund and Kalbjerga.

When they moved to Fårö the municipal day care center was in the process of being shut down and the new parents cooperative only existed on paper. They chose Fårösund instead. In the first place, because Henrik refused to share a parent cooperative with Elisabet and Alma, secondly because it had seemed so vague. If Malin had more faith in the new day care center maybe she could have convinced him. But considering what happened later, with the inheritance and the lawsuit, it was probably best as it was. Sometimes they got sour comments from parents on Fårö who thought it was treachery to choose the day care in Fårösund. But they didn't have the whole picture. They didn't understand.

Sure, day care on Fårö would have been easier. They would have saved a lot of time. On the other hand if they overslept and missed the school transport, like they did today, they could console themselves that they had to go into Fårösund anyway.

Just think that they ended up here. Malin was actually more surprised that Henrik had wanted to than that she herself said yes. When she met Henrik he was still on his way to Los Angeles. He would go out into the world; was already out in the world, just not a hundred percent there yet. All that was left of that today was that awful picture that David LaChapelle had taken of him. The one he proudly hung up in the workroom. Why hadn't the tenants stolen that instead? Henrik happily grinning, in Las Vegas, on the one side entwined with an almost-naked photo model who was at least a head taller than him and on the other side being hugged by an over-the-hill Elvis impersonator of the overweight variety.

Malin realized, of course, that the picture was not just awful. She understood its ingenuity and that Henrik wanted to display it. If only to impress his clients. It was also on his website, of course. But how did you get from that picture to Kalbjerga, Fårö? What had happened? She could not completely understand it.

Malin settled back in the seat again and looked over toward the ferry pier that was slowly growing larger. In the fishing harbor was a small, light blue fishing boat with the black flags of the fleet fluttering in the wind. Behind it the tugboat could be glimpsed as a speck of bright orange.

They had made a police report. A detective would come up and talk with them and look at the picture this morning. Malin could not stop thinking about the portrait with the eyes poked out. For brief periods she managed to think of something else, but before long the image was back. She was seething with discomfort. She had a hard time sleeping. After the first night they had replaced the beds with two from the only finished room in the guest wing. She could not make herself lie in the same bed one of those crazy people had been in. The poopers. The glass trap-setters. The eye poker-outers.

She had cleaned the whole house, scoured the floors, wiped down cupboards and woodwork, gone over every cranny, and almost scrubbed the enamel off the bathtub. Now she was satisfied. It felt like her house again. Almost. The uneasiness was still there, even if the sticky disgust had subsided.

Bodilla glided in between *Kajsa-Stina* and the old lime kiln that bluntly pointed toward the sky. Malin drove off the ferry, turned left at once onto Strandvägen, and continued toward the school. The large stone buildings that stood closely along the first two blocks always made her feel secure. They were presumably built in the mid-nineteenth century or perhaps even in the late eighteenth century and could just as well have been on Södermalm or in Old Town in Stockholm. They were city buildings. It made her feel at home. She assumed that the majority around there thought exactly the opposite. The city made them uncertain, while the countryside stood for security.

After the first blocks, more modern apartment buildings and single-family houses took over. Along the shore pleasure boats large and small were bobbing. They passed a few of Ellen's classmates on the sidewalk and Ellen waved frenetically through the rear window.

Malin stopped the car on the street outside the red, barracks-like building that housed Axel's day care. Ellen gave her a quick hug and scooted off toward the white school building a hundred feet from there.

"Shouldn't I go in with you?" Malin called after her.

"No, that's not necessary," Ellen called back.

"I'll call Lisa's mother."

Ellen waved to her before she disappeared behind the big school building.

"You have to go with me," said Axel.

He looked worriedly at her.

"Yes, of course I will," she answered.

She took him by the hand and started walking toward the day care entrance.

"You should pick me up early."

Axel's lower lip pushed out a little extra, but she knew he wasn't sad for real. He had learned to play on her feelings, little as he was.

"Are you sure of that? Don't you want to be with your friends at day care? You haven't seen them in a really long time."

Axel's eyes moved back and forth under lowered eyebrows. That was evidently something for him to think about.

"No, you should pick me up early," he then said.

"Okay, I'll do that."

The sun warmed pleasantly during the brief walk. The last week in August. And September was one of the best months on Gotland, she had learned. Still summer, sunny and nice for swimming and empty of tourists. With a little luck October was almost as nice. Two long months to make the most of before the drudgery with overalls and rain pants started up.

School had actually already started last Thursday. Ellen had a couple extra days off. Otherwise they wouldn't have managed the whole mainland tour. And they couldn't have rented out the last week, either. What if they hadn't bothered about that anyway? Then they would have escaped that lunatic who had been there and . . .

She stopped the thought. It could not just be by chance, not so simple that none of this would have happened if they had simply not rented out their house. Or what? Her head just got more and more jumbled.

They came into the day care center. Malin talked awhile with Jenny, one of the aides, and left things in Axel's cubby that they had brought home over the summer. Raingear, stuffed animal, the photo album with pictures of the family and relatives. Her relatives. Henrik had none, other than on paper. Then it was time for the waving ritual in the window. Malin had been worried that it would be drawn out and tearful, but it went surprisingly well. She avoided leaving with the anxiety of being a bad mother, which to her was like a spear in the back.

She had six hours to herself before she had to return to pick up Axel.

Minus travel and lunch, this meant four and a half hours of actual time. She had to plan the week's menus for the blog, but suspected that it would be hard to concentrate before the police had been there.

Malin had started up Malin's Table right after they moved to Fårö. She had done it mostly to heal the loss of Kakan, the café she ran on Borgmästargatan in Stockholm. And to maintain contact with her friends on the mainland.

Her long-term plan was to start up a little restaurant during the summer in connection with the guest operation. But that would have to wait, of course. When things started getting difficult financially she had been quite prepared to take a job at a café or restaurant in Visby. Not because she was sure there were any jobs to be had. During the winter, Gotland's restaurant and café life shriveled to a small flickering flame compared with the fiery, at times crazy outdoor life during the summer months.

But then came the blog. She had thought that in the best case she might get a few hundred readers, friends and old faithful café customers, but word had spread and after only a couple of months she had thousands of readers every day. She got additional publicity when she was awarded a blog prize, and soon they were calling from Coop, asking to have her on their website. There was not much to think about. Coop offered her more for blogging about food on their site than she would earn at a café in Visby. She avoided commuting besides.

Malin looked toward the day care center one last time to make sure that Axel had not come back for a final wave, but the window was empty. She unlocked the SUV and had climbed up with her left foot on the running board when a sense of being watched made her stop. She looked back over her shoulder. About fifty feet behind her a light-haired woman stood watching her. Or was she looking at something else? Malin looked toward the day care again to see whether there was someone or something there that could have made the woman so curious.

There was not a person on the street and no one was visible in the windows.

Malin pretended to fish for her car keys in her jacket pocket, but at the same time studied the woman in the side mirror of the SUV. She was dressed in jeans and a short military-green jacket and was partly hidden by a small white car gray with dust. The light, slightly reddish hair shone in the sun. She was glaring right in Malin's direction. Malin stood a long time and studied her in the rearview mirror. The woman did not move so much as a finger.

Malin turned around and looked straight at the blonde, and then started calmly and unmistakably walking in her direction. It took five or six steps before the woman reacted. Malin noticed how her facial features changed, but she was too far away to be able to see what they expressed.

When Malin had come a little closer, so close that she could see that the woman was her own age, the woman turned around abruptly, hurried over to the driver's side, opened the door, and slipped in. The next moment the engine started and the car drove off. Malin could only watch while it disappeared, the woman a dark silhouette behind the wheel.

Malin started feeling cold out in the sunshine and noticed how her field of vision narrowed as if she were in a tunnel. She closed her eyes and felt the hairs rising on her arms. There was a metallic taste in her mouth. She wasn't about to faint, was she?

She took a couple of deep breaths.

Someone stood and stared at her in Fårösund. What about it? Maybe people were curious about strangers. Maybe it was someone who read her blog? Maybe it was a fan?

But, she thought as she got in the car and closed the door, who was it? She had never seen her before. It could not be the mother of one of the children in the school. No one new had started that she did not already know. And why the sudden flight? Even if you overlooked the curious staring, it was definitely strange to take to your heels when the person you had been looking at tried to make contact.

She should have taken down the number on the license plate. But she had not even thought about looking at it.

August 24

I was there in your house. It felt good. It was like I was living there. Sat in the armchairs, turned on the TV, opened the refrigerator, slept in your bed. Looked at everything that was yours. Like the child in the fairy tale about the bears.

I hardly remember what I did. The days passed. I didn't dare go outside. Thought that someone might see me and that their eyes could burn right through me. Expose me. They would despise me. Because I care. You shouldn't care. Not care at all. Whatever people do to you. You have to go on. Get a life, like.

But I'm not like that. Maybe I wish that I was. How easy everything would be. Or would it? What is it like to live that way? Don't you run around at last and smile, full of wounds, like a leper who doesn't feel it when he injures himself?

No point in thinking about it. That can never be me, anyway. You are who you are. And I'm the sort who never forgets. My wounds heal slowly. And they hurt. They torment me. They made me come here—to you. No, that's wrong. It was you who made me come here. You.

6.

Fredrik took the keys to the car he had reserved and wrote his name on the whiteboard. He and Sara continued over to the garage. After five years in the renovated building, the corridors and fixtures had acquired, in Fredrik's eyes at least, an attractive patina. A bit worn, a bit used, in a pleasing way. It was no longer like working in a furniture store display.

Take Sara with you up there, Göran said. Fredrik had not really seen the interview with the possibly threatened Fårö family as a job for two people. He had nothing against riding with Sara, on the contrary, but he had a definite feeling that Göran wanted her along more to keep an eye on him than to do police work.

They found the car almost at the opposite end of the dusty garage, by the door, and got in on either side.

"I don't know if he was being nice to me to send you along as chaperone or if he was being mean to you to have you sit alongside and wait for me to have a stroke and drive into a ditch," said Fredrik as he adjusted the rearview mirrors.

Sara looked at him and seemed almost a little wary. "Can you have one?"

Fredrik laughed. "No, of course not. Then I wouldn't be sitting here."

Sara followed his movement as he put the key in the ignition.

"Maybe I should drive anyway," she said.

This time she was joking, he heard that.

"Is that what everyone thinks? That at any moment I'll have a cerebral hemorrhage or collapse in an epileptic seizure?"

He turned toward her with his hands on the steering wheel.

"Don't ask me," said Sara. "You were the one who started talking about strokes."

"More like Lennart."

"Yes, but Lennart . . ." Sara said with a sigh.

Fredrik started the car and backed out.

"The risk, in any event, is no greater for me to have one than for you when you're sitting behind the wheel."

"Can we stop talking about strokes now? If you really are healthy, I mean. Or are you going to be an old retiree who always harps on his infirmities?"

He should stop thinking about it. Göran no doubt had his reasons to have Sara ride along. With a little goodwill it was probably a good idea even apart from the accident. He had not been on patrol duty in two years. Maybe he needed a mentor.

Sara brushed her black hair behind her ears and looked toward the garage door, which had quickly opened. The light from the cloud-free late-summer sky made Fredrik blink. This time it was not only symbolic, like on the sidewalk just half an hour ago. This time it was for real. He was a detective on his way out on a mission.

Two years earlier he never could have suspected that one day he would feel fortunate about a routine job on Fårö.

He drove toward Route 148, turned left, and stepped on the gas, headed north through the flat landscape. Patches of forest alternated with fields and pastures and scattered houses whose front steps almost crept up on the asphalt edge. After a couple miles they caught up with a tractor with a trailer full of light green sacks of silage. The driver, in burgundy-red ear protectors with mandatory antenna, moved politely over to the edge of the road so that Fredrik could drive around him.

With the ferry transport and a wait at the ferry, it took one and a half hours to make their way up to Kalbjerga on Fårö. Quite the trip, for being on Gotland. It was not so strange that Fredrik himself, who lived at the far southern end of Gotland, seldom went up there. It was mostly when he and Ninni had visitors from the mainland that they took the trouble with the long trip. And when they took their guests to Fårö they infallibly followed the same pattern every time. Bought raspberry pie from Sylvi's Daughters and swam in Ekeviken.

He knew that one of the bakery's daughters lived at the farm in Kalbjerga, but he could not remember how he knew that. Presumably heard it from someone at work. The police station was an information and gossip center that did not miss much. You never knew what might be useful to know as a police officer.

Henrik Kjellander's and Malin Andersson's house was almost at the top of Kalbjergahobben, a little rock hillock that made itself known as a slight rise in the landscape. A dizzying height by Gotland standards.

Fredrik could see the Kalbjerga farm straight ahead, just over a half mile away, before he turned right. Kjellander's and Andersson's house was partially concealed behind a big barn with a sheet metal roof, but stood out more and more as they approached. The lot was enclosed by a wide-meshed barbed-wire fence stretched between rusty iron posts. He slowed down as he caught sight of two cars right in front of the gate, on either side of the road. An older model red Mercedes SUV and a new black Honda. He turned in and parked alongside the Honda.

They got out of the car and crossed the road, which was actually not much more than two separate ruts over the hillock. Fredrik held open the gate for Sara and closed it behind him. They continued down the slope toward the house. A few crows were squawking on a meadow farther away. The house sat open in the terrain, but the entry was protected by an overgrown lilac bush that was starting to thin out at the bottom. Fredrik stepped onto the lichen-covered limestone landing and knocked.

The door was opened by a dark-haired woman with a light suntan. She had freckles on her nose that spread moderately across her cheeks. Her hair was put up like Sara's, but she had bangs that ended right below her eyebrows.

"Malin Andersson?" asked Fredrik.

"Yes."

Malin smiled warmly but modestly as she invited them to come in.
As soon as they entered the hall they heard steps from the next room.
A short man rounded the doorpost. He was thin and fit and his
medium-blond hair was a little unruly. He looked at them with curiosity as he extended his hand. Henrik Kjellander looked happy. Despite
the threat against his family. Perhaps it was not as serious as the report
made out, thought Fredrik.

"I guess we can sit down, or how do you want to start?" said Henrik, looking at them inquiringly.

"Of course," answered Fredrik. "We would like to hear more about
what has happened."

Henrik led them back into the living room. The room was furnished
with a large gray couch with a protruding part at one end, a kind of
cross between sofa and divan. It seemed to be the prevailing fashion in
couches. Gustav and Lena had bought one like it a few years ago.

Around the low coffee table there were also three black armchairs
with oak arm supports that resembled oars. On the floor evidence of
small children could be seen. Colorful plastic toys. Henrik and Malin
sat beside one another on the couch. Fredrik and Sara each took an
armchair. On the wall behind the couch three black-and-white photographs were hanging, big as posters. One of them depicted Malin on a
street in a big American city. The other two depicted two small children, the couple's own children, Fredrik assumed. They were pictures
full of life, taken on the go, with crooked horizon line, blurred movement. Fredrik had developed a certain eye for photography thanks to
Joakim, and picked up a concept or two.

"It's best if you start from the beginning," he said. "You came
back home Saturday evening and then you discovered some kind of
threat? A picture?"

"It was more than that," Malin said seriously.

Henrik and Malin looked at each other. The brief, wordless deliberation ended with a nod from Henrik.

"Okay," she said, leaning forward on the couch before continuing. "We came home from vacation. It was already dark. We had the house rented out, so of course you wonder a little how it went. The first thing I notice is that it is not cleaned and there is garbage. Then I discover that things are missing. Glasses and cups in the cupboards. Our family pictures in the study."

Fredrik could hear in Malin's voice that she was still upset by what had happened. Her voice transformed as she progressed farther along in the story. The glass she got in her foot. The excrement in with the children's toys. And then the picture that floated out of the linen closet. When she was done, she put her hands in her lap and stared at them.

"We would like to look at the picture," said Fredrik.

"I'll get it," said Henrik.

He got up and hurried off to a room that faced the back side of the house. He came back with a photograph in a transparent plastic folder, which he handed over to Fredrik. Fredrik set it down on the table in front of him.

"I've tried not to touch it," said Henrik. "I thought that . . . well, fingerprints and such."

"Exactly the right idea," said Fredrik, leaning over the photograph.

It was a fine picture. Malin, Henrik, and the children were in swimming suits on the beach. They seemed to have just unpacked something to eat. The smallest child, a three-year-old boy, was holding a shovel and seemed more interested in digging in the sand than in a picnic. Everyone was looking right into the camera—the boy, too. But his and the others' eyes were missing. They were poked out of the cardboard-like paper. Fredrik studied the faces of the two children. A strong feeling of discomfort swept through him. The feeling surprised him and he coughed involuntarily, as if to distract himself.

He held the picture up toward one of the windows. The light from outside shone right through in eight defined points and he thought he could hear the sound of a sharp pencil or the point of a compass being pressed through the paper.

Not until he became aware of the others' perplexed looks did he realize that he had been sitting a little too long, staring at the picture. He handed it over to Sara.

"I understand that you were scared," he said.

"I don't get who could do something like this," said Malin. "It's creepy."

Her voice got fainter and she stroked her hand across her arm as if she were cold.

"But it wasn't just this that was gone?"

"No," said Henrik. "All the pictures that were hanging in the study were gone. Six of them. This is the only one we've found."

"And you've looked everywhere?"

Malin nodded. "I've looked through everything."

"But those are still hanging up?" said Fredrik, pointing at the pictures of Malin and the children on the wall behind the couch.

"Yes," answered Malin curtly to the rhetorical question.

Sara set the picture down on her lap.

"We need to take this with."

"Sure, of course." Henrik made a gesture as if he were handing the picture over again.

"These various persons who rented your house, how did you find them?" asked Fredrik.

"Through the Gotlands travel agency," said Henrik.

"So you've had no contact with the tenants yourself?"

Henrik shook his head. "No, everything has gone through the agency."

"But perhaps you have their names and addresses?" Fredrik asked.

"Yes, we do. They sent copies of the contracts."

Henrik leaped up off the couch, sprinted across the floor, and was soon back with the papers.

Fredrik quickly skimmed the three sheets. Two of the families came from the Stockholm area and one came from Gothenburg. The one from Gothenburg was the last.

"Have you tried to contact any of them since you came home?"

"I actually called the ones from Gothenburg," said Henrik. "I got so mad when we found the picture. I couldn't help it. But I didn't get an answer."

He shrugged his shoulders dejectedly.

"If it is one of the tenants behind this, it's likely one of the ones who were here last," said Fredrik.

"Yes," said Henrik. "That's what I thought."

"But if we overlook the tenants, can you think of anyone who might have done this? Who would want to frighten or threaten you?"

"What do you mean?" said Malin.

"Well, that is, you can't rule out that someone may have been here after the last tenant left the house, but before you made it back."

There was silence from the couch. Henrik moved back against the back support. Malin looked at him.

"Well," Henrik began. His hand scratched nervously back and forth through his hair. "I have relatives here on Fårö, two half sisters that I've actually never had any contact with—"

He interrupted himself, looking from Fredrik to Sara and back again with an embarrassed smile.

"I don't want to point fingers at anyone . . ."

"But, really!" said Malin. She straightened up and looked at Henrik with irritation.

"To begin with, this is not about pointing fingers at anyone," Sara intervened. "Simply think about whether there is anyone who could conceivably want to get back at you for something, even if it feels improbable. Then it will be our job to find out whether that person actually has anything to do with this picture or not."

"Okay, I understand," said Henrik.

Malin nodded at him encouragingly.

"I have two half sisters here on Fårö," said Henrik. "In principle I've never met them, except at my mother's funeral. Or not in principle. I've never seen them except then. The little contact we have had beyond that has been by mail and telephone. But all in all we're talking about a few occasions."

Fredrik listened attentively. Instinctively he felt that there was something important in the story, despite so far having heard only the beginning.

"It's a long story but I'll try to make it fairly brief," said Henrik.

"Take the time you need."

Henrik rocked his upper body almost unnoticeably while he thought about how he should continue.

"My dad was actually never in the picture. He left Mother before I was even born. I don't even know if they had a steady relationship. Well, she knew who he was and that, but . . ."

He lost the thread, got stuck with one hand raised in a gesture that was never completed.

"Anyway, then my mother met this Ernst Vogler from Fårö when I was one. After a while he proposed to Mother, but set as a requirement, or his family set as a requirement, that I would stay with my grandmother in Fårösund. That was where we were living then, Mother and I."

Fredrik nodded thoughtfully and then looked very briefly at Malin. She was looking intently at him with a determined expression, as if she wanted to underscore every word that Henrik uttered.

"Evidently Mother thought it was a good idea, because that's what happened."

Was Henrik's mother already pregnant with one of the sisters? thought Fredrik. In that case it could make it a little easier to understand such a drastic decision. That ought to be easy to figure out.

"To tell the truth, I don't know much about why it turned out the way it did. What I know is what my grandmother told me."

"You haven't had any contact at all with your mother?" asked
Fredrik.

"Sure. None when I was really small, but from the time I started
school sometimes she would come to visit Grandma and me. Not often,
but . . . well, maybe when I had a birthday and similar occasions."

It sounded like a guess, but that was the sort of thing you remembered, pictures that made an impression. Packages on the breakfast
table, cake and lit candles. Someone ready with a camera.

"I know that it sounds very nineteenth century," said Henrik. "I
actually have no idea how these people are constructed."

These people. Did that also include his mother?

"But to get to the point," said Henrik. "When my grandmother
died . . ."

His gaze wandered off and no longer seemed as lively and happy.
Henrik closed his eyes.

"First you got the letter," Malin prompted him.

"Exactly. I got a letter from my grandmother," he said, opening his
eyes again. "She wrote that she wanted me to inherit the money when
the house was sold. Not all of it. I would get half and my mother half.
When Grandmother died a few years later I pointed this out to Mother
and I guess she said that . . . well, something along the lines of, that if
that was what Grandmother wanted . . . But then nothing happened
and I didn't want to pressure my mother. And somewhere maybe
I hadn't expected either . . ."

He fell silent.

"I don't know," he added.

He sounded resigned.

"This letter you received," Fredrik said. "Was it a will?"

"No, it wasn't. It was just an ordinary letter. But that was what Grandmother wanted. It didn't concern that much money, but it still felt . . ."

"Viveca didn't have a chance against Elisabet and Alma," Malin said
sharply.

"More likely against Mr. Vogler, if you ask me," said Henrik.

"Against all three."

"Maybe so."

Henrik sighed quietly and looked at Malin before he continued his story.

"Then Mother died just a few years later. It was two and a half years ago now. In connection with that I brought this up about Grandmother's letter again. First I called Elisabet, but it was not even possible to talk with her, so I wrote a letter to the lawyer who was taking care of the estate inventory, but was dismissed with the excuse that the letter had nothing to do with Mother's estate."

"They were actually really awful," said Malin.

Henrik sighed through his nose with a resigned look.

"I wrote another letter and disputed his view of the matter, but you don't have much chance against a lawyer. I got another negative response, but this time it was full of a lot of legal terms and references that were completely incomprehensible. So I contacted an attorney myself and got help in writing another response."

"And this attorney, what did she say, or he, about your chances to get the inheritance from your grandmother?" Fredrik asked.

"She said that it wouldn't be easy, but that I might have a chance. The letter from Grandma could be of use, even if it wasn't a regular will."

"But we had to be prepared to sue for the money," Malin added.

"Yes, exactly."

Henrik sank against the back of the couch as if the story tired him out.

"Did that happen?" asked Fredrik.

"They completed the estate distribution without paying any attention to our viewpoints," said Henrik.

"So you got nothing?"

"Yes, I did get my lawful inheritance. A third of half of Mother's assets. But that was only a few thousand she had in the bank. All property was registered either to Ernst or to Elisabet, and the personal property . . . well, I had no desire to go in and root around in that. As you can see I was not exactly welcome."

"And where do you stand now?" asked Fredrik.

"For a while I thought about forgetting about it all. I hate these sorts of conflicts. The risk is that you lose more than you gain, even if you win the case in the end. It takes so much energy . . . But in the end I decided to sue them. And, well . . ."

He slowly raised his hand in a tired gesture.

"There we stand now."

"So at the moment it's open?"

"Yes, you might say that," said Henrik.

Malin leaned forward over the coffee table and looked firmly at Fredrik and Sara.

"The money is only one side of the case. They have a guilty conscience, and they would rather not be reminded of Henrik. And now they are trying to scare us away from here."

"We don't know that," said Henrik.

Malin turned argumentatively toward him, but did not say anything.

Fredrik was prepared to agree with Malin. At least in her suspicion. The Vogler family would surely heave a sigh of relief if Henrik moved away from here with his family.

"We will have to check up on this, then we'll see what it leads to," he said. "Elisabet and Alma Vogler, was that right?"

Henrik nodded.

"And the dad's name is Ernst," Malin added.

Fredrik wrote down the names and addresses.

"There are no other names that come up when you think along these lines?" Sara asked. "Any ex-boyfriend or ex-girlfriend, perhaps someone you've quarreled with about money?"

"No," said Henrik. "We've thought along those lines, of course—"

"Really," Malin chimed in.

"Customers, colleagues, models . . . No, nothing like that. And we've been together for thirteen years, so a jealous ex doesn't feel quite relevant," said Henrik, quickly stroking his hand over Malin's knee.

"And you haven't witnessed any crimes?" asked Sara. "Or a traffic accident? Sometimes people get threatened in such contexts."

"In that case, we were witnesses without having realized it ourselves," said Malin.

"You can think some more, and if you come up with anything then give us a call. We will start following up on the tenants and this inheritance dispute with your sisters in the meantime, then we'll see."

"And the photo?" Malin asked, nodding toward Sara.

"Our technicians will have to look at it," answered Sara. "But it's rare that you find fingerprints on threatening letters."

"I see," said Malin, looking a little disappointed.

She brushed back her bangs. The forehead that was glimpsed was paler than her suntanned face.

"Do you feel worried?" asked Fredrik.

Malin and Henrik looked quickly at each other. Malin tipped her head a little and wrinkled her nose.

"Of course you get worried," she said, "but I don't think some lunatic is going to rush in here and . . . well, I don't know."

Fredrik moved a little forward in the chair, took hold of the rental contracts with both hands, ready to conclude the interview, but Malin continued.

"It's so personal, so aggressive to go after our private family pictures," said Malin. "I can't stop thinking about it."

"I understand that," said Fredrik. "And we take this extremely seriously. At the same time, it can't be ruled out that the person who did this perhaps sees it as a kind of joke."

"Strange sense of humor, in that case," said Henrik, sounding a little offended.

"I really don't mean to trivialize this," said Fredrik, "but it may have been some bored teenagers on vacation with their parents."

"Fine by me," said Malin. "It would make everything feel a lot better if it turned out to be pure stupidity. But I have a feeling that this is something else. Something much worse."

7.

Malin watched through the kitchen window as the two police officers walked up the rise toward their car. For a moment she felt silly. Could it be so simple that everything was a twisted joke? Some young people egging each other on to cross a boundary?

No. They had been threatened. They had come home after a four-week vacation and been met by a family portrait with poked-out eyes. No one could blame her for doing what she could to find out who was behind it. They lived isolated and unprotected, a slow-moving ferry between them and civilization.

It would have been easier to shrug and blame foolish adolescents if they were still living in Stockholm. In a building full of neighbors who heard and saw things. The police a few minutes away.

She felt Henrik behind her. He put his hands on her shoulders and pulled her backward. She let herself fall into his cautious embrace and got a different image in her head, a different family portrait: she and Henrik proud outside the new studio; the photographer's fill flash on a tripod part of the picture, to underscore the subject.

"Do you think this could have anything to do with the article?"

"This?" said Henrik.

"Yes."

A reporter from *Gotlands Allehanda* had interviewed them early in the summer: the entrepreneurs on Fårö who would attract photographers and models from all over the world. The article had been published while they were on the mainland. Besides the picture that had been taken in front of the studio, it had also been illustrated with the picture of Henrik together with the model and the Elvis impersonator.

"That might have provoked someone," she said. "Someone who got an image of sin and naked photo models in their skull."

Henrik made a face as if she was out on a limb.

"No, but seriously," said Malin, with an edge in her voice. "Think about the production of *Macbeth* by the limestone pillars in Ljugarn. Some lunatic severed their electrical cable with an ax during the premiere. In the background there was a story about a porno film being made by the pillars ages ago."

Henrik laughed again. "What the hell, I've never heard that."

"It's true. I even know someone who was there."

"And wielded the ax?"

"Really nice."

She felt a growing irritation.

"Okay," said Henrik, turning serious. "But there is still a difference between running around in a nature preserve and running a company at home on your own property."

"Yes, but there is also a difference between a porno film and Shakespeare. Who knows what goes on in people's skulls when they read that photo models are going to come here."

Henrik sighed.

"Well?" said Malin.

"No idea," he said.

"I intend to tell this to the police anyway. Anything against that?"

"Not really. I think you should."

Malin saw that their car had already left.

"I'll have to call them."

Henrik's hands slid down over her breasts. Heat spread quickly from his hands further into her body.

"I have to go to Barcelona for a job," said Henrik, letting one hand slip in under her blouse.

"What? So for how long?"

"It's a two-day job plus travel, so I'll be gone for three nights."

The heat that had filled Malin abruptly vanished.

"So when is that?"

She tried to sound unperturbed. That was fairly successful, even though she felt completely empty and abandoned.

"The thirtieth," he said.

"The thirtieth? But that's this Sunday."

Henrik playfully swept his hand down toward the edge of her jeans. But Malin's desire was gone. She could only think that she would be alone in the house for three nights. She carefully slipped out of his grasp.

"We need the money," he said. "Besides, I can't say no to this client."

"I know."

He did not need to say that. She knew what it was like with the big, recurring customers. If you said no once, maybe they would call someone else the next time.

Henrik reached out a hand and tried to draw her in, but she slipped away.

"I have to get the week's menus ready," she said. "I should have done that yesterday."

Malin set a course to the study without turning around. She heard Henrik sigh behind her.

8

Fredrik and Sara managed to find the nearest neighbor, which was also the only one if you didn't count the farm over a mile away. The house was behind a carefully stacked stone fence only a few hundred yards from Malin and Henrik's house.

"Do you think Henrik Kjellander has any chance with that lawsuit?" said Sara as they got out of the car.

Fredrik shut the door and shrugged his shoulders.

"Not the foggiest. It sounded farfetched with that letter, but I really have no clue."

"We'll have to check with Klint."

They walked slowly toward the opening in the stone fence.

"But maybe it's as Malin said, that the conflict is much bigger than the inheritance," said Fredrik. "The suit was only the last straw."

"That made relatives start pooping in toy baskets?" Sara looked anything but convinced. "But what a story," she said.

"Only on Gotland," said Fredrik.

Sara laughed and put a guilty hand in front of her mouth. "But isn't it a bit strange that he wanted to come back here after all that? It almost seems like he was looking for a confrontation, doesn't it?"

"Who knows," said Fredrik. "People do strange things when their parents die."

They continued up the stone-paved path to the house, and Sara pressed the doorbell.

The woman who opened the door was named Ann-Katrin Wedin. She was in her fifties, tall and thin with a raven-black braid that went far down her back. Dyed, Fredrik assumed. She lived in the house with Bengt Wedin, who was at work.

Ann-Katrin Wedin knew that the neighbors' house had been rented out over the summer. After some discussion back and forth about dates, she decided that the first tenants had been a family with a boy and a girl of elementary school age. They had a big black SUV parked outside the house, not so different from Malin's Honda. After them had come a group of five or six people in their thirties. As far as she could tell they did not have any children with them. A thin, blond woman had passed the house several times—on her way down to Tällevika to swim, she presumed. The others she had not seen close-up. The last week she had not seen anyone at all. Then her vacation was over and she had been gone during the days, so that might be the explanation.

Sara asked her in particular about observations on Saturday, but she had not seen anyone then, either. Possibly she had heard a car, but she was not quite sure that it was on Saturday.

"Shall we try the sisters?" said Sara when they were in the car again.

"Yes, we can go and take a look at them anyway," said Fredrik.

They drove slowly the same way back, passed Henrik and Malin's house, and came out on the better, but not much wider gravel road that led up to the main road. Fredrik increased speed and rolled over the first cattle guard.

"So what do you think?" said Sara.

"I believe more in the sisters than the tenants. If you want to threaten someone, there must be much simpler ways than renting a house for eight thousand kronor. Would you even pay eight thousand to someone you dislike that much?"

"No, you do have a point there, but if you want to conceal your identity maybe it would be worth it anyway."

Fredrik slowed down and stopped completely. A dozen lambs had lain down in the middle of the road. He honked at them, without result.

"That usually doesn't work," said Sara.

Fredrik rolled down the window.

"Usually?" he said. "Does this happen to you often?"

He stuck his head out the window and hollered at the lambs.

"Not anymore. But when I was little we had a summer place in Häls-ingland. They had a lot of sheep there."

Sara unbuckled her seat belt.

"I'll take care of it," she said, getting out of the car.

She only needed to take a few steps toward the lambs before they quickly got to their feet and toddled away from the road. Sara got back in the car.

"So you don't think it's one of the tenants?" she said when they were on their way again.

"No, not if it really is a threat. If it is one of the renters who's behind this it's some teenager who did it."

"Sure," said Sara. "Maybe it is some adolescents after all."

They continued out on the eastern part of the island where Elisabet Vogler lived. She ran a farm along with her husband and they hoped to find her there. Her sister, Alma, on the other hand, worked at the technical college in Visby as an IT technician. They would have to question her when they were back in town.

After fifteen or twenty minutes, they turned right and stopped in front of a big white stone house with a pantile roof and pink corners. It was an archetypal Gotland farmhouse with a low ceiling on the bottom floor, and an upper floor with more space, added on much later. It would not surprise Fredrik if a Vogler had hauled the first cornerstone there sometime in the fifteen hundreds.

Right on the boundary between the yard and the garden two stately maple trees were growing. The house had dense forest at its back and a smaller, ochre-colored detached wing on the right side. On the left side, but farther away than the wing, was a big barn. In front of the two buildings, the landscape opened up in an expansive meadow where two horses stood completely still in the sun like bronze statues.

The main building lacked a back addition and did not appear to have any other kitchen entrance, either, so Fredrik and Sara went up to the double door and knocked. There was a pair of child-size red rubber boots tossed in the gravel alongside the steps.

There was movement behind a curtain, and shortly after one half of the door was opened by a man in his thirties dressed in gray work pants and green T-shirt. Probably Elisabet Vogler's husband. He was shorter than Fredrik, broad and sturdy like a wrestler. His face under the sun-bleached hair was also broad and square. Fredrik asked for Elisabet and hoped that he could avoid further explanations, but that was obviously naïve. The man looked at him suspiciously.

"What's this about?"

"It concerns her half brother, Henrik Kjellander," said Fredrik.

The man stood silently and looked at him a little longer than was completely natural.

"One moment, I'll go see," he mumbled, shutting the door in Fredrik's face.

It did not sound obvious that they would get to see his wife. Fredrik stepped down from the big piece of limestone that served as a landing and looked out over the well-tended yard. A short distance away was a machine shop. The door stood open and you could make out the outlines of a tractor.

The farm was too big to be on Fårö. The majority of the island's farms were small, part-time operations.

After more than a minute the door opened and Elisabet Vogler came out accompanied by her husband. Elisabet was not at all like Henrik. She was blond and a good bit taller. Her eyes were beautiful but cold, her cheekbones high.

Elisabet came down and took a couple of steps in the direction of Fredrik and Sara. Her husband remained standing, right by the door.

Fredrik heard a sound behind them and glanced over his shoulder. An older man had come out from the detached wing, leaving the door ajar behind him. He stood looking at them, but made no attempt to come closer. Fredrik assumed that it was Ernst Vogler. Father and daughter each lived in their own house on the same property.

"Yes?" said Elisabet when Fredrik and Sara had introduced themselves.

She had crossed her arms, all claws out.

"We need to ask a few questions in connection with an investigation that concerns your half brother Henrik Kjellander," said Fredrik.

Elisabet Vogler looked at Fredrik without saying anything. He assumed this meant that the ball was in his court.

"What did you do last Saturday?"

She made a surprised face and glanced over toward the older man outside the other building.

"What was I doing? Do you want me to tell you what I did?"

"Yes, just very briefly," said Fredrik politely.

"Why is that?" She laughed. It sounded scornful, or possibly nervous.

"Unfortunately I can't go into that right now."

"I see."

She shook her head almost imperceptibly, but then at last she answered.

"I worked in the morning. We had lunch together, all three of us. In the afternoon I was at home with the kids."

"And in the evening?"

"Yes, then, too. We watched TV with the kids."

"During the morning, when you were working, did you leave the farm then?" asked Fredrik.

"No, I was here the whole time."

Both the younger and the older man nodded in agreement from their respective front steps, but said nothing.

"Henrik Kjellander moved here to the island two years ago," Fredrik continued.

"Yes, I'm aware of that," said Elisabet Vogler.

"What did you think about that? That he settled down here with his family?"

Elisabet looked at Fredrik, her mouth like a narrow streak.

"I don't understand what business he had here and I didn't like it. But I'm not getting involved in that. This is a free world."

Fredrik took notes. Elisabet impatiently followed the movements of the pen across the paper.

"Your mother died two years ago," he said. "As I've understood it, there were a number of questions about the inheritance."

Elisabet shook her head firmly.

"No, there were no questions. All that was arranged long ago. There was a prenuptial agreement."

"But isn't it the case that Henrik has questioned the distribution of the estate?" asked Fredrik.

"He does have certain ideas and that's his business, but as I said, everything was arranged long ago. If you want to know exactly how, it's best that you read it yourself."

"So the fact that Henrik has filed a lawsuit is not something that worries you?"

Her eyes narrowed when the lawsuit came up.

"No, not in the slightest. He doesn't frighten me. If he wants to fight about that, it's fine with me. I'm the one who has the law on my side."

The high cheekbones became even clearer when she angrily clenched her jaws hard.

9.

Fredrik and Sara stopped in Fårösund and had lunch at a place with solid pine furniture, blue drinking glasses in a display case, and a little opening where you ordered your food. Fredrik's stomach was growling. It was past one o'clock. There was fried herring with mashed potatoes. Good and well-prepared, not too much butter in the potatoes, just the way he liked it.

"What do you say about the evil stepsister?" he asked Sara.

She looked at him with amusement.

"Eyes poked out, yes," she said quietly. "Poop in the toy box, doubtful."

"People can do the strangest things."

Fredrik took the last bit of herring and set aside his utensils.

"Dad and her husband give her an alibi," Sara pointed out.

"Yes, but she had just shouted that alibi out over all of Fårö, so I don't think much of it."

Sara folded up the napkin.

"Are you done?" she asked.

"I'm done."

They said thanks to the woman behind the opening and went out into the sharp sunlight.

"Maybe Alma Vogler is the toy box type," he said.

Sara squinted toward the sun.

"Can we go back to the station before we do the interview with Alma? There are a few things I want to check."

Fredrik had no objections. It might be worth digging a little before they spent more time on an intractable half sister.

* * *

Back at the office Fredrik pulled out the rental contract they had received from Henrik Kjellander. The last tenant was Inger Kvarnbäck from Gothenburg. Fredrik made a few quick registry searches. Inger was sixty-seven years old and married to Thomas Kvarnbäck, born the same year as she was. They were registered at Prinsgatan 8.

Fredrik tried calling their home number, but got no answer, not even an answering machine. There were two cell phone numbers, one for Inger and one for Thomas. He tried both. Thomas's cell seemed stone dead, and when he called Inger's the voice mail started immediately.

He decided to continue with the two other tenants. Even if it was unlikely, it could not be completely ruled out that it might have been one of them who slipped the picture into the linen closet and pooped in the toy box, while the last ones were simply unusually messy and inconsiderate.

The first tenant was Jörgen Malmqvist from Bromma in Stockholm. He was thirty-seven years old, married to Eva Maria Malmqvist. They had two children, age seven and nine.

Tenant number two was Emma Dahlberg, age twenty-nine. She was registered at an address in Vasastan in Stockholm and was neither married nor living with anyone. Her income suggested that she was a student. It was not probable that she rented the house for two weeks to stay there by herself. She must have been one of the five or six thirty-year-olds that the neighbor noticed. This meant then that there were three or four individuals about whom it was hard to find out anything unless he called Emma Dahlberg and asked.

Fredrik picked up the receiver and called the agency that had arranged the rental of the house.

"Maj-Lis Eriksson, GotlandsResor," a cheerful voice answered.

"Hello, my name is Fredrik Broman and I'm calling from the Visby police—"

"I see, oh my. I haven't done anything crazy, have I?" came out of the telephone.

"No, no," he assured her, and explained why he was calling.

Maj-Lis promised energetically to do what she could to help out.

"I was wondering if you have more personal information in your system than appears on the contract."

"You mean whether they rented through us before?"

"I actually would like to know that," said Fredrik, "but I was thinking about whether there are more names. If, for example, several people are renting, do you enter all the names in the system?"

"No," answered Maj-Lis. "We don't usually do that. Sometimes, if there are two families who will share a house, it happens that both want to be on the contract. To share the liability. If they want to that's fine, but it's not that common. The majority book on the Internet and there it's not possible to have more than one name on the contract."

"And you can see after the fact what bookings have been made on the Internet and which ones you've taken over the phone?"

"Of course."

Fredrik went through the three tenants with Maj-Lis. Malmqvist, the family with children, had rented through GotlandsResor before. Two years in Hellvi, but this time Malin and Henrik's house on Fårö. Emma Dahlberg rented for the first time. Maj-Lis could see that she requested a house for at least four people. The Kvarnbäck couple were also renting for the first time. It did not show how many people they were applying for, only that they requested lodging on Fårö and north Gotland, which was a single region in the company's system.

"How do they get the keys to the house? Do they pick them up from you?"

"If you haven't arranged otherwise with the landlord, you pick up the keys here at the office, that's right," said Maj-Lis.

"How about with this particular house, can you see that?"

"Well, now, let's see here," she said. "All of them picked up here."

"Can you see who gave out the keys, too?"

"Just one moment, then I have to go in . . ."

Maj-Lis fell silent and Fredrik could hear her fingers against the keys like faint whispers.

"Indeed. I must have been the one who handed out the keys to the first ones, Malmqvist. Elin did the other two. She's not still here. She was a summer temp."

"Do you remember anything about the Malmqvist family?"

Fredrik could easily picture Maj-Lis's broad smile.

"No," she laughed. "July is when we're busiest. The majority change on Saturdays and then it's on the verge of chaos. People stand in line out the door. You barely have time to look them in the eyes."

"I understand," said Fredrik, but asked for a telephone number for Elin anyway.

"Nothing else that you recall about these customers?"

"No, I can't think of anything," said Maj-Lis after thinking a moment.

"The last ones, Kvarnbäck, must have turned in their keys as recently as Saturday. Nothing in connection with that?"

"There's nothing noted."

Fredrik thanked her for the help and hung up. Then she called both Jörgen Malmqvist and Emma Dahlberg. He asked for the names of everyone who had stayed in the house or visited them during the rental period. Had anything out of the ordinary happened? Did they possibly leave the house earlier than planned so that it stood empty a few days?

Both Jörgen Malmqvist and Emma Dahlberg had used all of their rental days, and they gave an honest impression when they said that nothing special had happened. Emma was accompanied by three persons. Two men and a woman. They had also had a visit from a fifth person for three nights, a woman. He took down all their names.

At last he tried calling the Kvarnbäck couple again, all three numbers, but without result. Why didn't they answer?

10

The Gotland police shared a building with the public prosecutor's office, and the investigation department was next door, so it was almost simpler to look up a prosecutor in person than to call. Especially if the line was always busy for the prosecutor you wanted to get hold of.

Sara heard Peter Klint's melodic, slightly high-pitched voice far off in the corridor. The door to his office was ajar and she carefully stuck her head in. He waved to her to come in and sit down. The telephone conversation continued; it seemed to be something of a personal nature. Klint laughed and continued an enthusiastic account of a vacation memory.

Would she have to sit here long? Klint smiled apologetically and made a gesture toward the phone, even though he was mostly the one who kept on talking.

The fifty-four-year-old Klint had a fresh haircut and was casually dressed in a striped shirt with rolled-up sleeves. He was going to be a father again. The rumor had been confirmed for a week. Two years earlier he got a divorce and met a woman sixteen years younger. Not necessarily in that order.

Sara wondered whether he knew what he was getting into. Personally she thought it was demanding enough to have a long-distance relationship with a man in Stockholm. And no children. But that was the price a man had to be prepared to pay if he wanted to trade up for a newer model. Sixteen years younger. The same age as Sara.

She sighed, not overly explicit, but loud enough so that it would be noticed.

"Listen, I have a meeting here," Klint said into the phone. "Of course, let's do that, bye now. Bye."

He hung up.

"Okay," he said. "What can I do for you?"

"How are you at inheritance law?"

"Well, so-so. What's this about?"

Sara briefly described what Henrik Kjellander had told about his half sisters, the letter from his grandmother, and what followed after his mother's death.

Peter Klint sat awhile and nodded to himself.

"I'll have to double-check, but I don't believe that a letter from the grandmother has any great weight in this case. If it had been a regular will it would have been a different story, but without one of course it's the mother who inherits."

"I checked with Lantmäteriet," said Sara.

"Yes?"

Peter Klint laced his hands together and leaned back in the chair.

"Four years ago Ernst Vogler transferred most of the property to Elisabet, but nothing to the other daughter, Alma. Alma on the other hand bought a smaller property on Fårö, a single-family house on an ordinary lot, about the same time the farm was signed over to Elisabet."

"It sounds like Grandmother's money went to compensate the daughter who didn't get any share in the farm," said Klint.

"Yes, that would be my guess anyway."

"You can think what you want about it, but the mother does as she wants with the inheritance from the grandmother, that's how it is."

Klint threw out his hands symbolically and let the money fly away. "The letter is not enough, I would say. An individual may have a number of different thoughts and intentions about what she leaves behind, but it is always possible to maintain that the person in question changed their mind between the time she expressed them and when she actually died."

"So Henrik Kjellander doesn't have much of a case?"

"Probably not. But this does not rule out him suing them anyway. If he's lucky they'll be frightened enough to give in and propose a settlement."

It had not sounded as if Elisabet Vogler had any settlement in mind, thought Sara. More likely the contrary.

Gotland University College was housed in a beautiful old factory building that was attached to a newly constructed part with a glass façade facing toward Cramérgatan. GOTLANDS MALT FACTORY AB could still be read at the very top of the façade on the older part. Something that surely had given rise to many tired student jokes.

The sea breeze swept in from Hamnplan and blew sand in the eyes of Fredrik and Sara as they got out of the car. Squinting, they turned toward Almedalen and the library, where the swinging doors let out a group of students who were done for the day. The students stopped briefly on the sidewalk and spoke with large gestures before they separated. Perhaps plans for the evening.

Fredrik and Sara passed through the college's can-like metal and glass entry and asked at reception for Alma Vogler.

Alma worked at the college computer support department on the second floor in the factory building. She was blond, like Elisabet, but in contrast to her sister, she looked much more like Henrik. Especially the curious, inviting gaze and the kind, almost childish face. She was thirty, according to the census records, two years younger than her sister.

"We can go down and sit in the mezzanine in the restaurant. There probably aren't too many people there this time of day," she suggested.

They went one flight down to the restaurant to immediately go one flight up to the balcony that hovered in the middle of the glass wall facing Cramérgatan.

Alma had guessed right. A few students were sitting at the tables on the ground level, but the balcony was empty.

"What we mainly want to know is where you were on Saturday," said Sara as soon as they sat down.

"Yes, I heard that you've been at my sister's, but I don't really understand why you're asking."

It was clear, Elisabet had presumably run to the phone as soon as they left. They looked at Alma, waiting for her answer.

"Excuse me, I should answer the question. I was out shopping right before lunch, otherwise I was at home all day. You can ask my husband."

"So do you mean you shopped on Fårö?" asked Sara.

"Yes, at Nyström's."

"Were you alone or did you have anyone with you?"

"I went alone; it usually goes quicker that way. Nisse and Marta were at home with Krister."

"Krister is your husband?"

"Exactly."

"Can you estimate how long you were gone?"

"Oh, this is getting precise. It sounds like I've murdered someone at the very least," Alma said with a smile.

"No, it isn't that serious," said Sara. "We just want to check some information."

"Okay, well, it took about an hour in all. You can ask at Nyström's. I'm sure they'll remember that I was there."

"Yes," said Sara, making note of the most important items.

Alma was the exact opposite of her sister. Happy, open. Did not seem to have anything to hide, at least.

"Have you lived your whole life on Fårö?" asked Sara.

"Yes, except for two years when I was studying on the mainland."

"But there can't be many jobs for someone with your education here on the island?"

"One is enough," she said.

"Yes, of course."

"No, I understand what you mean," said Alma. "It's not really that easy to find challenges here. The work at the college is actually a little below my level, but I think it's worth it."

"To be able to live on Fårö?"

"Yes. I've sometimes thought about moving to the mainland for a while, but right now I'm content with my job and my house on Fårö. We'll have to see."

"Your sister owns a good deal of land, but not you," said Fredrik. "Did she buy you out?"

Alma made a slight grimace, smiled quickly toward Sara, and then looked out the window. Two young men were unlocking their bikes at one of the many bike stands on the sidewalk just below. One of them was wearing a hat that made him look like he had escaped from another era.

She turned back toward Fredrik and Sara with a distant look in her eyes.

"I have no great desire to talk about this," she said, fingering a button on her shirt.

"I see," said Sara cautiously. "Is there a conflict behind it?"

Alma responded with a tired smile.

"I guess that's why I don't want to talk about it."

Sara nodded that she understood.

"What did you think about your half brother Henrik Kjellander moving to Fårö?"

Alma lowered her eyebrows and wrinkled her nose slightly. She seemed to take the question seriously and had no ready answer like Elisabet.

"I guess I was mostly surprised," she said.

"Because?"

"I didn't think . . ."

She fell silent, thought awhile longer.

"If I were him I probably never would have set foot here again. Really. Especially not after Grandmother died. I would probably just want to escape it all. I don't understand how he has the energy to mess with this."

"You're thinking about the lawsuit?" said Sara.

Alma sighed, produced another tired smile, but no reply.

"Is that also part of what you don't want to talk about?"

"Yes, thanks."

"You bought a house on Fårö four years ago," said Fredrik. "How did you finance that purchase?"

Alma turned toward Fredrik, but did not answer.

"Well," said Sara at last. "We can't take the right to remain silent away from you."

Then Alma sighed. Deeply and heavily.

"It was Dad's idea to sign over the property to Elisabet. He wanted the farm to stay in the family, and that was his way of resolving that. He saw an estate distribution as a threat. That we would sell, or be forced to sell because neither of us would have the money to buy out the other."

"But you got no compensation?" said Fredrik.

"Yes, we got help for our house," she said reluctantly.

"But not the corresponding value on the land?"

Alma stretched.

"I don't know. I love Fårö, but I'm not interested in running a farm."

"How is your relationship with your father and Elisabet?"

"It's good, but we don't see each other as much since Mom died."

"And Henrik? Do you have any contact with him?"

"No."

"Not at all?"

"No, I've only met him one time. It was at Mom's funeral."

"You've never been curious? He is your half brother, after all."

"He was never mentioned at home. I was pretty grown up before I even found out that he existed. And why they did what they did with him, that's perhaps—"

She paused and searched for words.

"You'll have to ask my dad about that. I wasn't even born. I've decided to let that be."

Alma clearly pushed away from herself with both hands.

"I just want to live my life. Can I do that?"

Fredrik looked at Alma and saw a young woman who had made a decision, very deliberate and perhaps also wise. But he also saw something that resisted that decision inside.

"Be my guest," he said, making a gesture with his hand toward the stairs.

Alma hesitated a few moments, as if it could not be that easy, then she got up and left with a quick good-bye that almost sounded disappointed.

"But we may be in touch again," Fredrik called out after her.

She gave him a glance, but then continued down the stairs without answering.

11.

Malin made a quick trip to Nyström's. She was out of garlic. And she needed to get milk.

The little store with yellow paneling was a lifeline. If it didn't exist she would not have been able to live on Fårö. True, the assortment was limited, and true, she had to drive to Visby anyway at least once a week to get everything she needed. But to have to take the ferry even to shop for simple things like milk and flour would have been much too claustrophobic. She could not have handled that. At Nyström's you could also mail letters and order from the state liquor store and the pharmacy. Which also made existence on the island a bit simpler.

Malin was at the back of the store searching in the corner with organic products when she heard it.

Go home.

A hiss behind her back. She turned completely cold, stood stock-still with a package of crushed linseed in her hand. Had she really heard right? Go home?

She recovered her ability to act, put the package of linseed back on the shelf, and rounded the store shelves behind her just in time to see the outside door to the shop shutting with a firm swoosh.

She set her shopping basket right down on the floor and rushed toward the exit, grazed a stand with paperback books, which swayed worrisomely, and had to squeeze past a sportily dressed tourist who was poking among the foreign coins in the palm of her hand.

The doors refused to open. She had been too quick, was forced to back up a few feet and slowly go forward again. This time they slid open and she was outside.

Malin stopped outside the entry. Not a soul. But a little over a hundred yards away on the road south a car was leaving. She could hear the driver putting it in higher gear. It was too far away for her to see either the license plate number or what model it was. Even so, she tore her cell phone out of her pocket and took a picture. It was only an idiotic spot on the display.

She remained standing on the concrete landing outside the doors. Looked around again, a little more thoroughly this time. But no one was visible. Was it really possible to make it outside, start the car, and get that far away in the time it had taken her to get out of the store? The more she thought about it, the more convinced she was that the driver of the car could not be the same person who whispered to her. Whoever it was, she, or he, had gone in a different direction. Malin thought the voice had sounded like a woman's, but she was not completely sure.

Could the person who ran out be hiding around the corner or crouched down in one of the cars in the parking lot, and was now just waiting for Malin to leave?

Go home.

Was it even a whisper she had heard? Was it perhaps only the hissing of the door as it closed? *Go-ohm.* Did it sound like that?

Malin went back into the store and found her basket. Berit, at the checkout counter, looked at her inquisitively.

"You were really in a hurry."

She could, of course, ask Berit who had just gone out the door. But wouldn't that sound strange?

"Excuse me," she said. "I thought I saw someone I knew, but I guess I was mistaken."

She thought that Berit was about to say something, but seemed to purse her lips at the last moment. Or was that just her imagination, too?

12.

Fredrik rolled onto the grass-covered farmyard in front of his family's stone house at five thirty. After several years of renovations and puttering they had got it into really good condition, even if the work, of course, was never ending. Many times he had cursed the idea of buying an old Gotland farmhouse that needed renovation. On the other hand, he had felt grateful just as many times that the house was no more than a hundred and fifty years old.

The mere thought of acquaintances who wrestled with shale and grass roofs on, practically speaking, medieval houses left him in a cold sweat. They were forced to gather a whole neighborhood council and at least one wise old man as soon as anything had to be repaired. People to whom they then owed return services for all eternity.

Fredrik got out of the car with a pike in a plastic bag. Out of nowhere he had gotten the idea to fix quenelles for dinner. He had stopped by the fish market in Hemse on his way home and asked if they had pike.

The man in the fish market opened a door to the nether regions of the store, pulled a pike out of a plastic tank like a large garbage can, more or less wrestled the fish down onto the floor, and killed it with a wooden club.

Fredrik had almost recoiled behind the glass counter. He was aware in principle that the animals he ate had been killed at some point and had no problem either with fishing or then killing and taking out the catch. But when he stepped into a fish market he didn't really expect to witness an execution.

Now, in any event, he was at home with a very fresh pike and hoped that he could transform it into quenelles before it got too late and Ninni and Simon were too hungry.

The pike in the bag aroused no enthusiasm from Simon. Fredrik's explanation that quenelles were like fish balls although much tastier did not make things any better. But he felt sure of himself. Once the quenelles had melted in their mouths, along with a mousseline saba-yon sauce, not even Simon could complain.

Food had been an important part of Fredrik's rehabilitation after the accident. He refused to look in his old cookbooks. Convinced that it must be possible to coax the know-how out of the reluctant convolutions of his brain, he had cut loose in the kitchen without any guidance other than feeling. After a few initial catastrophes, it was as if his senses showed him the right way: tastes and aromas, the color of the raw materials, the very feeling of an avocado against his fingertips or the sound of a pepper being slapped down on the cutting board. The tears in his eyes from a finely chopped onion.

Sometimes he wondered whether the fall and the injury had affected his sense of taste. That it had become more sensitive. Or just different. It was an interesting, slightly strange thought. That what tasted one way for most other people tasted completely different, or at least more, in his mouth.

He quickly filleted the fish and assembled the meat grinder. That was the trick. An ordinary food processor would mercilessly transform the pike into a tough, unappetizing mess.

When, a short time later, he was whisking the sauce over a water bath, Joakim called his cell phone. Fredrik decided to answer and somehow managed the sauce with one hand.

"Hey, how's it going?" Joakim said happily.

"Fine," he answered. "How's everything with you? You sound upbeat."

Joakim had been accepted to the Nyckelvik School's photography program, and today had been the first day at school. His boisterous tone of voice sounded promising.

"It's going fine."

"Cool. Any decent classmates?"

Fredrik felt divided, had a bad conscience because he couldn't really concentrate on the call.

"Yeah, they're really nice," said Joakim. "But I've already met most of them."

"You have?" said Fredrik with surprise.

"One guy, Johann, set up a Facebook group when the admissions were done. We went out a couple of times last week."

"That's great," said Fredrik. "Then you don't need to have acclimatization, where you roll around on the floor in sweat suits and hug each other for two days."

Joakim giggled into the receiver, then he briefly cleared his throat and his tone of voice became more serious.

"Well, I was wondering . . . Could I borrow a thousand for rent? It's just temporary, until my student loan arrives. That will take about a week."

"Of course," said Fredrik without even thinking about it. "I'll transfer the money to your account after dinner."

"Thanks. That's really nice."

"I'm happy to do it, but now I have to go before I completely destroy this sauce."

"Okay, but we'll be in touch," said Joakim.

Fredrik ended the call and removed the water bath and saucepan from the stovetop.

Photographer. Fredrik didn't know whether that was something Joakim saw as his future, or just something he wanted to try out. Considering what he had seen today, it seemed to be a profession that a person could live on. But perhaps Henrik Kjellander was an exception. Like all artistic professions it was certainly tough.

Joakim had truly changed. It was as if a kind of castling had occurred in the family. Only a couple of years ago Joakim was always sitting in his room in front of the computer with the door closed while Simon was the happy and outgoing one, still with a focus on Ninni and Fredrik. Now it was the other way around. Joakim had suddenly become a responsible, talkative, and independent adult. Perhaps not so much with focus on his parents, but in any event present when they met. Simon had taken over Joakim's old role and closed the door to the boys' room.

"How's it going?" asked Ninni.

She rounded the table, picked up a magazine from the pile on one of the chairs, and was about to sit down.

"Almost ready," said Fredrik, "I'm just going to simmer the quenelles. It would be great if you could set the table."

Ninni tossed the magazine aside on the table with a mock sigh. She opened the cupboard and took out three of the light yellow plates.

"Could we use the white ones instead?" said Fredrik. "The sauce disappears on those."

"Yes, boss."

She put the yellow plates back and took out the white ones.

"So it was fish balls you thought of to celebrate?"

"Listen, this is culinary art of a higher school," said Fredrik, pointing to the quenelles waiting to be put into the pan. "Ask anyone at all who knows a little about food."

"And I don't?"

"Okay, ask anyone at all who knows a little more about food."

Ninni put the plates on the table and took out glasses and silverware.

"Wait till you taste them," he added.

"How was it then, the first day?" said Ninni while she put out the three place settings.

"Good. It was really good. Not a remarkable job. Sara and I were on a quiet tour to Fårö."

"Sounds like a real vacation. And female companionship besides."

Fredrik made a face.

"That was a joke."

"I hope so," he said.

There was silence. Why did she have to say that? Today of all days.

"It really was just a joke," she repeated. "I'm happy that you're back at work. It will do you good. You can see it already."

"Okay, I believe you. Anyway it felt really good."

Fredrik removed finished quenelles from the pan with water and put in the last batch. He observed the pile of newspapers on the chair while he waited for the quenelles to float up. He did not like that pile, it had started since Joakim moved to Stockholm. He did not like the pile of newspapers and he did not like that the table was only set for three. There was something gloomy about that. In one stroke the house had become much too large and quiet. They had barely managed to get their existence in order before conditions changed again.

At the same time that Joakim was accepted at the Nyckelvik School's photography program, his girlfriend of two years had been accepted in the general studies program at the same school. They had arranged for an apartment for themselves in Stockholm. A microscopic studio at Gärdet, only one subway station from Ropsten where they took the bus to school. He did not doubt that Joakim would manage in Stockholm. Besides, both his grandmothers were in Gustavsberg and his paternal grandfather in Nacka. It wasn't that. But it was sad not having him at home. Sad above all to have him so far away that he could not even come home on weekends. More than occasionally. It made him feel old.

Or did it have nothing at all to do with age and the empty fourth chair? Perhaps it was in his head, something to do with all the shit. The hell of Östergarnsholme. The accident.

"Simon," he called out to the second floor. "Time to eat."

He got no answer. One who moved out and one who closed the door.

"Simon," he called again.

Louder this time. The scraping of a chair being pushed back was heard faintly through the ceiling.

The first day. Maybe she should have made dinner, not him. At least she ought to have thought of a little surprise.

Instead she had reminded him about that old infidelity. Completely unintentionally, she could swear to that. Or not old. It wasn't really all that long ago. It only felt that way. The accident and the long period Fredrik had been on sick leave were like a boulder of eternity between the present and everything that happened before.

When Ninni tried to think back to what it had been like before the accident, it was like peering out over the sea in dense fog. It was as if it had lost its significance, vanished somewhere far away, and was something you could barely get hold of any longer. And yet that stray comment. Today of all days.

She was clearing up after dinner. There were never many dishes when Fredrik was cooking. During his training at cooking school, which he dropped out of after three months, he had learned to do dishes and clean up in the short breaks while you waited for something to be done. When the food was on the table the kitchen was often just as sparkling clean as when he started. She was the exact opposite. Left behind an explosion of saucepans, sticky beaters, and peelings.

She was happy for his sake, she really was. But if she were honest the feeling was mixed. Back on patrol duty. That meant risks, you couldn't ignore that.

Fredrik had been checked up and down by doctors, psychiatrists, and psychologists, and they had taken their sweet time. There was no one who said okay, let's test and see how it goes. She understood that. She was not worried that he wasn't ready. But there was a different worry. That he would stretch the limits a little too much, not think enough about himself, and for that reason something would happen to him again. The danger was just as much him, the person he was, as the risk the job entailed.

Of course he ought to have learned something from what had happened. Ninni had spoken with him about it countless times. His memories from the accident itself were incomplete and his conclusions not completely clear. Not to her anyway. She had even talked with Sara about it on several occasions and she could not really get the pictures to fit together. Sara had hinted in some way that Fredrik had done more than he really needed to. In the heat of the moment, of course, there were difficult considerations, but if Ninni understood Sara correctly she thought that Fredrik could just as well have let the man they arrested at Östergarnsholme get away. He could have let him jump off the cliff if that was what he wanted. It involved an unreasonably large risk to try to stop him. No one had demanded that of Fredrik. No one would have held him accountable.

Ninni dried her hands on the linen towel with Grandmother's monogram. She looked out the window. August. It was still light. And then a darkness opened below her without warning. That accursed anxiety.

She took a few quick steps across the floor, as if she could get away from her inner darkness through a quick maneuver in the kitchen, and it actually worked. It usually did.

13

Little puffs of fog were creeping across meadows and fields when Fredrik peered out the kitchen window on Tuesday morning. They looked beautifully elfin as they hovered in the blue light of dawn. The light Charoles cattle stood motionless in the ribbons of fog, the calves still with the cows. It would be a few months before they would become beef for twelve hundred kronor a pound.

Fredrik showered, got dressed, got the newspaper, and set the table for breakfast. Ninni came in as usual just as the last drips of coffee ran through the filter.

"Is anything going on?" she said, pointing to the disarray of newspaper supplements on the table.

"Doesn't seem like it," he said. "It was an unusually quick read today."

Ninni sat beside him on the kitchen bench, as close as possible without sitting on his lap. She looked at him, smiled broadly, and then gave him a kiss. A friendly morning kiss.

He could not help but wonder how she had endured these two years. The last year perhaps had not been so bad, in and of itself. Perhaps even better than a normal year considering that he was home so much. But those first six months. How did she manage?

When he was in the car on his way into Visby a little later, the fog was gone, burned off by the sun.

Yesterday had been a long day, his first on patrol duty in almost two years. Back and forth to Fårö, then intensive work at the computer and on the phone, and then straight home to the stove with the newly clubbed pike. Yet he had not felt the slightest bit tired, more like the contrary. Presumably it was the kick of being a policeman for real again that kept him going.

He drove north without really seeing the landscape he was passing. He must have driven this same stretch more than a thousand times, back and forth. Hemse, Linde, Lojsta, Hejde, Väte . . . What he actually saw was a mixture of memories that were stored on one another like double exposures. A black-tarred church steeple; a big lifeboat that, according to rumor, belonged to someone who was waiting for the Flood; the closed shops, of which there were more and more; the military-green back loaders rusting alongside the road; and the sign with the tennis court that pointed right into the forest. And after what sometimes felt like two hours, sometimes ten minutes, the sign with VISBY 8 showed up. Then he was there. He did not even notice the last few miles.

Fredrik had parked the car and was rounding a corner in the corridor on the ground floor when he almost ran into Eva Karlén.

"Oh, hi," she gasped, backing up.

She nervously stroked her blond shoulder-length hair and flashed a smile that she immediately tightened up as if she wanted to take it back.

Since Eva had put an end to their brief relationship during a dinner at the harbor restaurant in Herrvik four years earlier, their interactions had been strictly professional. With the exception of some unexpected spontaneous necking at a crime-scene investigation in Levide a couple of years ago. But that was an isolated incident. He assumed that these were things that could happen with a former lover as a colleague.

When Fredrik returned to work six months ago all his feelings for Eva were gone. True, the memories were still there: their passionate encounters for a couple of intensely shimmering spring months, the crash with Ninni, the time in exile in Johan's house in Nore where Eva had spent a few nights with him before she suddenly broke it off. But he felt nothing. She was like any other colleague. That was strange.

That is, purely intellectually he felt it was strange, but because the feelings were lacking it was not something he gave much thought to.

But a few months later he had suddenly felt a strong attraction when he caught sight of her at a table in the café. It came over him like a wave of heat from nowhere. But the most bewildering thing was that the next time he saw her he was completely indifferent again. No wave of warmth, no desire. And it had gone on like that ever since. On, off, on, off. It was not that he didn't feel a little crazy on those occasions when it was on, as if he was a container for emotions without proper anchorage that could float up to the surface completely by chance. He tried to ignore those attacks of attraction as much as possible. Actually, he had wanted to ask his doctor about it, but it never happened. The threshold was a bit too high. He had never mentioned his infidelity to her. Perhaps it would have been easier if the doctor had been a man.

He looked at Eva, met the light blue gaze under the sun-bleached eyebrows. Nothing happened inside him. This was evidently one of the calm days. His emotions were dormant.

"Have you had a chance to look at the photo?" he asked.

"Yes, there are some fingerprints, but there were no hits."

He looked disappointed, but he had not really expected anything else.

"It's a shame they threw out that turd." She grinned. "It doesn't get better than that."

"No," Fredrik said, laughing, and then stupidly wondered what his colleagues would think if they saw him standing and laughing with Eva Karlén in the corridor. "No, I guess they were in a hurry there."

Eva smiled and looked down at the floor for a moment. She was very good-looking, there was no denying it, even when viewing it from a somewhat neutral perspective.

"Nothing else?" he said.

"The hole was made with a pencil, but that's hardly any help to you."

"No, not directly."

"It's a nasty thing in any event," said Eva. "I would sleep with a shotgun under the bed, if I had one."

Fredrik came up to his office. Standing by the desk, he picked up the phone and tried calling the last tenants again, the Kvarnbäck couple from Gothenburg. This time he got an answer. From Thomas Kvarnbäck.

Fredrik introduced himself and explained why he was calling. There was silence on the other end.

"Hello?" said Fredrik.

"Yes, I don't really understand," said the man.

"You rented a house on Fårö," said Fredrik. He tugged copies of the rental documents out of a plastic folder on the desk. "From the sixteenth to the twenty-first of August."

"Uh," came out of the phone. Then more firmly: "We rented a house in Spain, two weeks."

The man seemed confused. Perhaps he had Alzheimer's, or suffered from some other form of dementia. True, he was only sixty-seven, but it could happen early in certain cases.

"Spain?" said Fredrik.

"Yes. Where are you calling from?" asked Thomas Kvarnbäck. "I didn't really get that."

If you suffered from Alzheimer's you could do strange things without really meaning to. Fredrik recalled when Sven Wollter played a man suffering from Alzheimer's. He peed in a flower pot in a restaurant. But it was only a film, of course.

Fredrik did his introduction again, clearly and a little more expansively.

"The homeowners have had a number of problems connected with these rentals, and that's why I am contacting all the renters," he concluded.

"Then you must have mixed things up somehow," said Thomas

Kvarnbäck. A hint of a laugh was bubbling behind his words. "Is it the same travel agency?"

"No," said Fredrik, "this was booked through GotlandsResor. They only book houses on Gotland. It says Inger Kvarnbäck on the contract. That is your wife, I assume?" he said, although he knew that perfectly well.

He thought it was unnecessary to reveal that he had checked up on them.

"Yes, it is," said Thomas Kvarnbäck, "but she was with me in Spain."

"I see," said Fredrik. "She couldn't have helped a relative or acquaintance make a booking, and then her name ended up on the contract by mistake?"

"No, I have a hard time imagining that."

"Is Inger there?"

"Yes, she's at home."

"May I speak with her?"

"Yes, of course, if you think that will make you any wiser."

Thomas Kvarnbäck called to his wife without first taking the receiver from his mouth. Fredrik had to hold the phone away from his ear to spare his eardrums.

After some crackling from the speaker and some explanations at the other end, he had Inger Kvarnbäck on the line. Fredrik went through the whole procedure one more time, now with some additions.

"I don't understand this at all. We rented a house in Spain for two weeks together with our youngest daughter and her family. We came home yesterday. We haven't been to Gotland in I don't know how long. It must have been in the seventies."

"So you can't think of any explanation that your name ended up on the rental contract for the house on Fårö?" said Fredrik.

"No," said Inger, pausing. "No, how could that have happened?"

"You didn't book a trip earlier that you canceled?"

"No, no," she said firmly. "We discussed various different alternatives before we decided on Spain, but Gotland never came up."

The possibilities seemed undeniably exhausted. And he thought that Inger and Thomas sounded trustworthy. As far as he could judge they were not lying. They had not been in Gotland. The only thing he could think was that they booked the house for someone else, a child or a sibling, and now they were trying to protect that person. But that was farfetched. It was more likely that someone had made use of their names.

"There must have been some misunderstanding," he said. "I apologize for troubling you."

"Don't worry, it's no problem," said Inger.

Fredrik sat down, dialed the number to GotlandsResor, and asked for Maj-Lis Eriksson, who he had spoken with the day before. She remembered him. He asked a few questions about the booking procedures.

The majority of GotlandsResor's customers made the reservations themselves on the Internet, but there was still about 30 percent who booked by phone.

"Or else they call to ask questions and then complete the booking on the Internet. Many want that personal contact. I guess it feels more secure. Maybe they want to be certain that we exist," Maj-Lis concluded with a little laugh.

"How does it work, do you check the identity of the ones who rent in any way?"

"The person whose name is on the contract has to provide their civil registration number, but we can't ask for any identification or the like because the bookings are done via the Internet or by phone. So we don't really do any checking. But they pay by credit card so that becomes a kind of identity control."

"And if they don't pay by credit card," said Fredrik, "then you have to send out an invoice."

"Yes, then we do that."

He asked her to see how Inger Kvarnbäck's bill was paid.

"It was paid by PlusGirot."

"Then she must have received an invoice," he thought out loud.

"Yes, as I said, we e-mail it if someone does not want to pay by credit card."

"E-mail? You don't mail the invoices?"

"No, only if the customer doesn't have an e-mail address."

Fredrik peered down at the contract he had in front of him: inger .kvarnback@gmail.com.

Of course. Anyone at all could create a Gmail address without giving out their real identity.

"Okay, I follow you there," he said. "Can you see if a transfer was made or if it was paid directly at a bank?"

"Not here on the computer, but I can get that information if you want."

"It would be really nice if you could do that."

"But I can't do it right now. I have to call the accounting firm."

"I understand. When do you think?"

"Have to see, it's already three o'clock. If I get hold of them it can happen in ten minutes, otherwise tomorrow. I'll do what I can."

"Excellent, thanks so much for your help."

Fredrik gave her his cell phone number in case he had left for the day by the time she produced the information.

He put down the receiver and stood up. He would be extremely surprised if it was possible to produce a sender from the payment. That is, someone besides the borrowed address to the Kvarnbäcks. Someone had chosen to hide behind Prinsgatan 8 in Gothenburg. Why that particular address? Did it mean that the actual tenant was also in Gothenburg? Or was it Alma or Elisabet Vogler, and they made a completely random selection from the Swedish phone directory?

14.

They had coffee after eating in the little bower in front of the entry. It was a mild evening; the sunlight was fast disappearing, and the shadows of the fruit trees in the high grass reached almost all the way up to the gable.

The taste of strong coffee, and strong alcohol, lingered in Malin's mouth. Henrik had a weakness for odd, local types of liquor that he dragged home from his travels, but which unfailingly lost their charm as soon as they were put in the liquor cabinet on Fårö. Metaxa, Raki, Vietnamese coconut schnapps. Now, in any event, they had decided to drink from those bottles in small, two-centiliter portions in the middle of the week to get rid of them. And that way it was even a little bit fun.

Henrik gathered up the coffee cups and glasses and carried them all into the kitchen. He started doing the dishes while Malin checked on Axel and Ellen in the living room. They were sitting quietly and stock-still in front of the TV, close to the screen on the shaggy IKEA rug. Axel had his thumb in his mouth and was leaning his head against his sister's arm.

Malin slipped down next to them. When she felt their warmth and the odor of children, tears suddenly started running down her cheeks. It was not because they were so sweet or because she loved them so much. She was crying because she could not escape the feeling that everything was so unbelievably fragile and somewhere also the feeling that everything was not as it should be.

She could not explain it any better to herself. Did it really need to be explained? Nothing had been as it should be since they came home from vacation and Malin stepped through the front door with Axel in her arms.

She did her best to hold back so that they wouldn't notice she was crying. Luckily the animated film had a firm hold on their attention. The characters on the TV screen were blurry through her tears. She didn't like herself when she was like this. Anxious and full of emotions. That wasn't her. She was the efficient, courageous one. The one who started her own profitable café in Stockholm and then risked taking the leap to a small island in the Baltic and, without really understanding how it happened, was supporting herself as a food blogger.

Exactly. The thought reminded her. She had to post a recipe.

She carefully dried her tears behind the backs of the children and gave them a hard squeeze before she stood up. They rocked absently without taking their eyes from the screen as she pressed herself against them.

Malin uploaded a recipe for truffle mayonnaise and French fries that she had swiped at an American restaurant forum and adapted for Swedish households. Creative reuse. Then she wrote an entry about pears, that they were better suited in flan than on a cheese tray, and a lyrical outburst about the Greve Moltke pear tree they had in the garden. It went quickly. She was probably the only one who would think it sounded strained. The readers didn't know, of course, that someone had been in their house busy symbolically poking eyes out.

When she was through blogging she took off on the Internet and completely lost track of time. It was only when Ellen came in and asked whether they shouldn't go to bed that she realized what time it was. She had spent over an hour reading about various alarms. Axel was asleep on the floor in front of the TV. Henrik was talking on the phone in the kitchen and had not noticed anything.

When Malin came down again after putting the kids to bed, Henrik was sitting on the couch looking at the news. They went from screen to screen, it struck her. The TV, the computer, the cell phone, and then the TV again.

"Do you mind if I turn it off?" she said, reaching for the remote control.

"Not at all," said Henrik with a yawn.

She turned off the TV and nervously brushed her hair back with both hands.

"I think we should install an alarm."

"Is it because I'm going to Barcelona?" said Henrik.

"No, that's not why," she said. "I've really thought through this. We can't just sit here. We have to do something."

"The police are doing something."

"I know, but that doesn't change the fact that we are sitting on a little island seventy miles and one slow car ferry from Visby. It takes an hour to get here."

"I see, okay," he said tiredly. "But how would an alarm help us?"

"A modern alarm, that doesn't even cost all that much, can tell us whether anyone has been inside the house while we were away. It can warn us if someone is trying to get in while we're at home. Besides, it works as a fire alarm and signals water leaks. Well, that's not the main thing, of course, but I mean if we were going to install one anyway."

"That sounds advanced," said Henrik, and she understood that he was thinking what it would cost.

"It's only a couple of thousand," she said quickly. "Maybe five or six if you want something more advanced."

"Boy," said Henrik, rubbing his chin.

"I know that we have to keep track of money, but it's not really that much and it will be paid for by the business anyway."

"You've got to take in money, too. It's not enough to just deduct."

Henrik's favorite objection when Malin pointed out that something was deductible. She sat silently looking at him.

"I guess I'll have to check on that," he said at last with a little sigh.

"A camera can be installed, or several, and they can be connected to the alarm's motion detector. Then we can know if someone is sneaking around outside the house, even who is driving past on the road."

"Really?"

Malin saw a curious gleam in Henrik's eyes. She knew that the camera monitoring feature would do the trick.

"The alarm can even send pictures to your cell phone. Or you can call the alarm and ask it to send pictures."

"But you have to be extremely polite." Henrik grinned.

Malin grimaced.

Henrik laughed. "It sounds like *Mission Impossible*."

"I know," she said. "But it only costs a few thousand."

"How many of these just-a-few-thousand-kronor bills are we up to now?"

"I mean in total. And you can install it yourself."

"Hm, sure."

She was starting to get tired of arguing, wanted him to just say yes. This was on a completely different level than a new appliance for the home, whatever it was. It was about safety, theirs and the children's, being able to feel secure. Her eyes were drawn to the two windows where the evening sun was shining in on the red plastic Pastil chair. The children loved to play on it. Malin was just as afraid every time that they would get hurt when they transformed it into a seesaw.

Henrik had also fallen silent, sitting with a clenched fist against his mouth and pondering what Malin had said. She could easily imagine that he was thinking about how pictures from the house would show up on his cell phone. How he might show customers and associates.

If he didn't go along with buying an alarm she would order one anyway and take the money from her own business. Maybe that wasn't quite fair. Somehow he should also be included and pay because her contribution to the household would be less. But in just this case she didn't care about that. She had to have that alarm. The sooner the better and definitely before Henrik went to Barcelona.

"Who installs that sort of thing?" he asked. "Is it a locksmith, or what?"

"Locksmiths and security companies, but I don't know what there is in Visby."

"We'll have to check that out and then we'll drive into town and talk with them."

He smiled at her and she smiled back. She felt a warm, pleasant feeling spreading from her abdomen and out into her body. It was bizarre, but the thought of installing an advanced alarm and monitoring system made her happy and calm.

15.

Malin coasted down the hill to the mailboxes and the big pile of logs. An early morning with an intense blue sky over the green meadows always made her feel that life was a lot easier. It was as if the world was smiling at her. The headwind was blowing nicely as she rode her bicycle, bare-legged under the dress she had put on, to retrieve the newspaper.

She thought about the work she had neglected the past week. She had written her posts, but thought they had turned out dry and unimaginative. Boring food. But today felt different. She was inspired and eager to get started and work. Perhaps it was because they had decided to buy the alarm? It made her feel active. She hated being a victim of circumstances. There was almost always something you could do so that things would get better. It wasn't enough to sit and wait for someone else to do it for you.

The hill leveled out and Malin pedaled the last stretch over to the mailboxes. It was a motley collection of mailboxes, sheet metal, and plastic in various sizes. She braked in front of the carmine metal mailbox they had inherited from the former owner.

With both feet on the ground and the bicycle leaned against her leg, she stuck her hand down in the dark interior of the mailbox. The newspapers from Stockholm and Gotland were lukewarm against her hand from the sun shining on the metal. Before she got the newspapers all the way out of the mailbox something glided away under her fingers. It fell back down into the mailbox. Malin squeezed the newspapers under her left arm and fished again with her right hand. She was certain that it was an advertising brochure that came with one of the newspapers.

She saw with surprise that it was a letter. No mail should have come this early in the day. When she turned over the brown envelope she saw that it lacked stamps as well as an address.

For some reason, she raised her eyes and looked over toward their home. The house, the studio, and the guest wing. Then her hands started shaking. Soon she was shaking all over. She held the anonymous envelope with both hands. The morning papers fell to the ground. She hardly noticed. She only cared about the taped envelope that she did not want to open, but that she had to open. She took a deep breath and tried to force back the presentiment of what the letter contained. There was a good chance it was only a mailing from the local historical society or the parish or another one of the languishing but stubbornly struggling small associations on the island.

Malin stuck her thumbnail in the opening and tore open a bit of the flap, then got her thumb in and tore open the rest, quickly and carelessly.

She immediately recognized the photograph that was in the envelope. Only she and Henrik were in that picture. It was an amateur photo taken one morning at Kakan three and a half years ago. Malin had on a black apron and striped sweater, the same uniform as all the employees. She was sitting with Henrik at one of the round mosaic tables in the corner in the back. Henrik often stopped by in the mornings when he

had left the day care, if he had time. They sat with their heads close together over the table. A slightly silly, but nevertheless romantic gesture.
Even before Malin pulled out the photograph into the light with
trembling fingers she knew what she expected. Even so she could not
stop herself when she finally saw it. She screamed. Right out loud.
"Henrik!"
Loud and cutting. Over and over again.
"Henrik . . . Henrik."
He did not hear her. No one heard her.
The sun was shining right through the four holes that had replaced
their eyes.

16.

Fredrik left the car in the parking lot facing Birkagatan and took the
opportunity to slip in through the garage as a patrol car rolled out.
One of his colleagues in the car shouted something through the open
side window, but he could not make out what. He was about to turn
around but at the same moment felt his cell phone vibrate in his back
pocket. He continued into the garage. It was a Fårö number.
"Yes, Fredrik Broman."
He pressed his key card against the reader, entered the code, and
put away the keys to get one hand free to open the door.
"Hello," said a voice in the phone. "This is Henrik Kjellander.
We've received another photo with eyes poked out."
Fredrik felt a chill run from his temples down over his neck. This
changed the situation. They could completely erase the possibility that
this concerned an ill-willed tenant or someone with a strange sense of
humor.

"Received?" he said.

"Yes, it came with the mail. Or not with the mail. It was in the mail-box. Malin found it when she went to get the newspaper."

Henrik's voice sounded calm and collected, but the almost panting intake of breath in the pauses told of something else.

"Just one moment."

Fredrik had to use the key card again to get from the corridor to the cloakroom. When he reached the patrol officers' debriefing stations he sat down on a vacant chair.

"You mean that someone other than the mailman put it there?" he asked Henrik.

"Yes. There was no address, no sender, nothing."

"Is this also one of the photographs that was gone when you came back?"

"Yes."

"You haven't noticed anything else? No one driving past yesterday evening or during the night?"

"No."

The newspaper carrier, thought Fredrik. It might be worth checking with the newspaper carrier. As a witness, that is.

He looked up toward Göran Eide's window, which faced the glass-covered courtyard where he was sitting. One of the building's nodes with a stairway up to investigation, administration, and the prosecutors. Right behind the curved staircase the on-duty commander and the radio communications operator were moving soundlessly in the bulletproof aquarium.

"Where are you now?" he asked. "Are you still at home?"

"Yes. We're going to drop off the kids, then we're going into town to . . . Yes, we have an errand."

"It would be good to be able to see this photograph. Can you come by the police station? Then I'll talk with my boss in the meantime."

"We can be there around eleven."

"Good. Ask for me in reception."

He heard Henrik breathing into the receiver.

"Are you still there?" asked Fredrik when there was no answer.

"Yes, excuse me. It was Malin. We were wondering about something. . . ."

"What?"

"No, nothing like . . ."

Henrik fell silent and Fredrik heard a faint mumbling in the background. Something about the children.

"At eleven then," Henrik's voice was heard again.

"Was the photograph lying loose in the mailbox?" Fredrik asked.

"No, it was in an envelope. What about it?"

"Bring the envelope, too."

"If we find it," said Henrik. "I don't really know where it went."

Fredrik felt his irritation rising. It wasn't fair, he realized. You could not make police-related demands on someone who wasn't a policeman. But still.

"Malin was extremely upset," Henrik added.

"Take time to search. It may be important."

Henrik Kjellander handed over a plastic folder with the picture and the envelope to Fredrik.

"We found the envelope," he said. "Malin put it back in the mailbox without thinking about it."

"Good," said Fredrik. "I'll take it down to tech as soon we're through here."

He looked at the photograph. In contrast to the picture they found in the linen cupboard, it depicted only Henrik and Malin. Whoever it was who wanted to frighten them, the person in question had chosen an effective way to do it. Seeing yourself with eyes poked out, that went straight to your emotions. It was considerably stronger than threatening letters or telephone calls. And the eyes in particular . . .

The photograph in the transparent folder changed form when he looked at it. Malin and Henrik became Ninni and himself. They stood in the yard outside their big Gotland house, smiled at the camera, with their eye sockets gaping empty, paper chads and pencil remnants around the edges. Then a third picture that was not only an image but reality, admittedly created by an out-of-control imagination, but still so real. He and Ninni without eyes, not smiling and black-and-white, but bloody, dead, and with terrified, distorted facial features.

Fredrik pushed away the images, tried to forget the fantasies by treating them drily and professionally. Who would he suspect if he had received a similar picture of Ninni and himself in the mailbox? Presumably someone he had put away.

He looked up from the photograph, met their worried gazes. Malin leaned quickly over the table.

"It feels damned unpleasant," she said. "It feels as if anything at all might happen."

"Someone obviously wants to frighten you or threaten you," Fredrik said carefully.

That anything at all might happen was perhaps going too far, but this was not the right moment to argue.

"Have you talked with Henrik's sisters?" asked Malin.

"We have," answered Fredrik. "And it does not seem as if they would have had an opportunity to get into the house on Saturday."

He did not go into the fact that Elisabet's alibi was solely based on the testimony of her immediate family members and therefore naturally could be perceived as less credible than if it had been confirmed by an outsider. It was nonetheless an alibi.

"So then it must have been one of the tenants?" said Henrik.

"Yes and no," said Fredrik, pausing.

Henrik and Malin looked at each other, perplexed.

"It appears as if the person who rented your house last week gave a false name and address."

Malin clenched her fists and moved them down to her lap.

"The persons who are on the contract exist," Fredrik clarified, "but they were not the ones who were in the house the last week it was rented out. They were not even in Sweden."

Malin stared at Fredrik with her eyes wide and mouth half open. She turned toward Henrik.

"Henrik," was all she could get out.

"This means, obviously, that we have to look a bit more seriously at this, but I still don't think—"

"It's just—" Malin started but stopped short.

She sighed deeply.

"This is so damned unpleasant. This person, whoever it is, was standing down by our mailbox last night. The one who put that in there," she said, reaching out and pointing at the picture, "must still be here on Gotland. Perhaps on Fårö."

"Yes. It is very possible, but not completely certain," said Fredrik.

"Are there any leads to who it might be?" said Henrik. "I mean, to who really rented the house."

"Not directly, but for some reason the one who rented the house gave Inger Kvarnbäck at Prinsgatan 8 in Gothenburg as the name and address. It's not altogether unusual that someone who uses a false address chooses an address from a place or an area to which he or she has some type of relationship. If you think along those lines, does that address say anything to you?"

They sat quietly a long time but then shook their heads.

"Think about it some more. It doesn't have to concern just Prinsgatan. Is there anyone in Gothenburg, an old acquaintance, colleague, or whatever that might be worth taking a closer look at?"

"I hardly think I know anyone in Gothenburg," said Henrik.

"Perhaps you know someone, or have worked with someone, who moved there?"

Fredrik looked at both of them.

"Don't worry if it seems farfetched. Anything that in the slightest way might seem to be a breeding ground for a conflict is interesting. And that applies whether or not it has a connection to Gothenburg."

17

Malin turned out of the police station parking lot. It could not be more than a mile to the locksmith on Södervägy. She had checked on the Internet.

She made a jerky start when the light turned green and took a left onto Norra Hansegatan. She felt like she was trembling all over, but her right hand was steady and firm as it moved between the steering wheel and the gearshift. The trembling was inside.

When she took the photograph out of the envelope and saw what it depicted it was as if someone had struck her full force. It made something inside her start vibrating, and the vibrations were still going on. A little core of weakness that threatened to spread. She was surprised that she could still think clearly, make decisions, drive a car, talk with people, as if everything was almost normal.

The shaking, the fragility, was a tone, a kind of warning that only she could hear.

She did not want to wait; the alarm should be in place today. She hoped they could install it themselves. If it required an installer coming up from Visby it would surely take several days, maybe a week. It said on the Internet that the alarm was easy to install yourself, but she was not sure that this locksmith sold that one in particular.

"Just so we don't have to wait for delivery, too," she said. "Then who knows how long it will take."

"Maybe we shouldn't count on them having any in stock," said Henrik, looking out over the Östercentrum shopping center.

"Do you have to be so negative?"

She drove faster.

He sounded like her dad.

"I'm not negative. I just mean that maybe it's not an item they have in the store."

"Why not? A TV dealer has a lot of TVs in stock. Can't a locksmith have an alarm in stock?"

"Yes, of course."

"If they don't have any in stock, we'll order it on the Internet. Then we can get exactly what we want and it will presumably not take more than one or two days. The only reason to buy here is that we'll get it right away."

"Why don't we take one thing at a time?" said Henrik.

"What do you mean?"

"I just mean let's start by seeing what they have and then take it from there."

"There's nothing wrong with having a Plan B, is there?" she said, irritated.

"No, sure."

Henrik looked away. Malin realized that she was doing seventy in a fifty zone and let up on the gas.

It was hard for her when Henrik got so rigidly reasonable like that. Like a bloody anchor slowing them down. What bothered her most was that it wasn't even particularly like him. He was never like that with clients or with his friends. Not with her friends, either, for that matter. It was as if she was the one who brought out this side of him. When she got eager and enthusiastic, it kicked in like a brake in him. Sometimes maybe it was good that both of them didn't fire on all cylinders, but today it was almost making her furious.

She turned left across the street and carelessly parked at a diagonal outside Gotland's Glass & Locks. There was plenty of room on the big asphalt lot in front of the store.

She studied the display window while they walked from the car. Heavy chain locks for bikes and mopeds were crowded in with cash registers and an advertising sign for wrought-iron gates.

False name. It sounded so ugly. And serious. Someone had really exerted themselves to be able to get into their house without leaving any traces. To scare them, get revenge, mess with them? Malin had felt certain that it was one of Henrik's sisters, or one of their husbands or relatives who was behind all of it. But now . . . Of course it could be one of the sisters who rented the house and called herself Kvarnbäck, but Fredrik Broman sounded as if they were not suspects at all. Or almost, in any case. So who was? A wild strange lunatic from Gothenburg who had chosen them for God knows what reason? No, that sounded too crazy.

She had not said anything about the woman who was standing outside the school staring at her. Nor about the whispering inside Nyström's. She could still not say for certain whether it really was a whisper or if it was just the sound from the doors.

Shouldn't she tell the police about it? Yes. In any case, about the woman by the school. As soon as they were home again with the alarm she would call Fredrik Broman. What if it was that simple? That it was her.

But why?

18.

Ellen was good at finding her way, although she was only seven. Mommy had said so. Of course she knew where the ferry pier was. It was really close. Just go straight from the school, out onto the big road past the ICA grocery store, and then a little bit more and then there it was.

Even so, the lady in the car did not understand when Ellen said how to get there. Maybe she wasn't so good at explaining, even though she was good at finding her way. Or else it was the lady in the car who was not good at understanding.

When Ellen explained for the third time the lady asked whether Ellen couldn't ride with her in the car and show which way she should go instead. Then she would be sure to find it.

Ellen did not know whether she would have time before lunch period was over and looked around for Lisa, who had just been with her. She could not see her anywhere.

"It's not that far, is it?" the lady asked.

She smiled broadly at Ellen and brushed back the long light hair from her face with one hand.

"No, it's super-close," said Ellen.

"But then you might as well ride along and show me. Then I'll drive you back."

Ellen did not know whether she wanted to. She looked around toward the school.

"I can't ride to the ferry," she said. "We're starting soon."

"No, you don't need to. I'll drive you back at once. Just show me, then I can drive myself to the ferry."

Ellen thought about it. That would work, of course, but she was still not sure she wanted to.

"I'm going to buy a kitten," said the lady, "but I've gotten lost. I'm a little worried that they'll sell it to someone else if I get there too late. Does the ferry take very long?"

"No, not very long," said Ellen. "The ferry goes slow but it's not very far."

"So you can show me then?" said the lady, opening the door for Ellen.

Ellen thought that she could. It would not take long and she would get a ride back. She thought about the kitten. It would be sad if it was sold when the lady got there. And then in some way it was as if the lady thought that she had already said yes, so it was strange to say no, too.

Ellen got into the car.

"Don't forget the seat belt," said the lady.

"No," said Ellen, reaching for the seat belt.

"Do you need help?" asked the lady.

"No, I know how," she said.

The lady drove off before Ellen clicked the belt into the buckle. Mommy never did that.

Ellen looked at the lady while the car drove away from the school. She had fine long hair that the sun shone in. She was more like a big girl than a lady. Ladies didn't usually have long hair, not fine like that. And then she didn't have a ladies' name. Her name was Ellen, just like her. That was strange and a little exciting. When she stopped the car and asked about the way to the ferry, she had asked Ellen what her name was. When Ellen said it, she looked at her with big eyes and said, "You don't say, that's my name, too." "Is your name Ellen?" Ellen had asked. "Yes," she said, and Ellen laughed and then the big Ellen in the car laughed, too.

"Are you hungry?" big Ellen asked.

"No," said Ellen.

"Would you like some gum then?" said big Ellen.

She put her hand in her jacket pocket and took out a little plastic container that she handed over to Ellen. Ellen looked at the container and understood after a while that there must be gum in it. She opened it, but then she happened to think, "I only get to have candy on Saturdays."

"But this is sugar-free. That doesn't count as candy. It's good for your teeth."

Big Ellen took two pieces herself and put them in her mouth. She held out the container to Ellen again. Ellen put her index finger in and poked up two pieces of gum. It crackled a little when she started chewing. It tasted different, not bad, but a little more boring than regular gum.

Big Ellen smiled at Ellen. She had fine, white teeth. Maybe it was because she chewed that kind of gum.

"Yes, where should we go now?"

Ellen looked out over the road. It was strange, but she didn't recognize it at all. She didn't understand. They drove there every school day, the road straight from school, then to the right on the big road past ICA and then you got to the ferry. Ellen knew right and left. She didn't even need to think the hand you shake with or the hand you hold your pencil with when you write. But now she didn't know her way around at all. Had she forgotten the way over summer vacation? How could she have? She did not understand and did not know how she should answer the question.

She looked at big Ellen, at the lady. Ellen no longer thought that she looked as much like a big girl.

"Okay, my friend, where shall be go? Last chance now."

Ellen lowered her eyes. She felt empty and hungry, even though she had just eaten. Her head was completely empty, too. She had no idea how she should respond. The sun was no longer shining in Big Ellen/ the lady's hair and her cheek was chapped. She was no longer as pretty. Ellen sobbed.

"What do you mean, last chance?" she peeped.

"No, excuse me, I didn't mean it that way at all," said the lady. "It was just a game I played when I was little. A computer game. There was a little troll that drove a train. He used to say that. Excuse me. I'm sure you'll find the ferry. You'll get as many chances as you want."

Ellen snuffled and wiped away a tear. It felt a little better, but still not good. She wanted to go back to the school, but she did not dare say that. She had promised to show the way to the ferry.

"What do you think? Shall we turn here?"

Big Ellen had stopped the car at a road that went to the right. Ellen did not recognize it, but in any case it was to the right. She nodded twice without saying anything.

"Then that's what we'll do."

Big Ellen turned onto the road.

"Have you ever played that game with the troll?" she asked.

"No," Ellen answered quietly.

"Maybe it doesn't exist anymore," said big Ellen. "Too bad, it was fun."

Ellen tried to imagine a troll driving a train. It sounded fun. Big Ellen turned the car onto another road. This time she did not ask Ellen whether she thought it was right or not, but Ellen did not know the way here, either, so she thought it didn't matter.

"There's a DS in the glove compartment," said big Ellen.

Ellen did not answer. She did not know what a glove compartment was.

"If you open that compartment," said big Ellen, pointing at a small handle right in front of Ellen.

When Ellen did not move, big Ellen opened the compartment herself. She took out a white Nintendo DS and handed it to Ellen.

"I thought maybe you would want to play."

Ellen took it, but held it without opening it.

She thought that there was no point in starting to play during the short ride to the ferry. Besides, she was going to show the way. She did not understand how she could show how to get to the ferry if she was playing. Although it was obvious, she had already lost her way. She had no idea how they would find the ferry from where they were now.

"Do you think they're selling the kitten now?" she asked.

"I hope not. No, they probably won't. I think it will work out."

She no longer sounded worried. It was almost as if she no longer cared about the cat. Ellen felt empty and hungry again. Everything was constantly changing. The lady wanted to go to the ferry, then she didn't seem to care whether they made it there or not. It was the same with the kitten. She asked about the way, wanted Ellen to help her find it, but then she should chew sugar-free gum and play Nintendo. Everything felt wrong and strange and she realized that she was the one who had made a mistake. Every conceivable mistake. That was the sort of thing she had heard, like both Mommy and Daddy had said. Many times for sure. Don't ride in a car with someone you don't know. Don't take candy from someone you don't know. The lady had said that it wasn't candy, but maybe she was being tricked.

Ellen fingered the DS game. Big Ellen smiled at her. They came out of the shadow, the sun hit her hair, and she almost looked like a big girl again. Ellen opened the game and started it. The empty feeling disappeared a little when she heard the familiar melody. The game was one of her favorites. Nintendogs. She chose Chihuahua and started to play. She knew that she would not be able to find the way to the ferry if she sat there and played, but thought that even so it was best that way. That it was the point. She sensed that the lady would be pleased if she played.

19.

They were en route with *Bodilla* across the sound and in the backseat were parts for an alarm for six thousand five hundred kronor. It was wireless and would be easy to install themselves. The locksmith had shown them the brochure with instructions and said that they could just call and ask if there was anything they didn't understand.

Malin rolled down the side window and set her arm in the open window. She squinted toward the sun. She had gotten what she wanted and Henrik's misgivings had been unfounded. *Bodilla* puffed out diesel steam and her yellow plates shone brightly in the sunlight. Malin felt relieved, actually really satisfied. Whoever was behind this would see that they could take up the fight. It was not that easy to chase them away from the island. And if this lunatic tried anything else they would have him or her downloaded on the alarm's hard drive.

The alarm monitored that the outside door was closed and locked;

four motion detectors let you know if someone was trying to get into the house any other way. Malin had sketched the floor plan and the locksmith determined that four should be enough. If more were needed it was easy to add on. They had bought a video surveillance system with three cameras that were also controlled by motion detectors. When the cameras were activated they sent images to the alarm's own hard drive and to one or more cell phones. You programmed the numbers yourself into the server, which should be concealed in a wardrobe or cabinet, preferably on the top floor. The locksmith had demonstrated it in the store. It was like science fiction, but just as easy as changing channels on the TV.

Malin placed her right hand on Henrik's thigh and ran her fingers along the inner seam of his jeans. There was an odor of newsprint from the newspapers that Henrik bought while they were there. They were in a thick pile alongside the plastic bags with the parts for the alarm.

Henrik leaned over and bit her lightly on the neck while he quickly touched her breasts. A little flash of heat fired off from her abdomen down between her legs. For the first time since she came home from vacation she was really turned on.

First the alarm, she thought. Henrik stroked his index finger against her nipple. Malin's cell phone rang. She reached for her bag in the backseat and Henrik sank slowly back in the seat with a vague sigh.

"Yes, Malin," she answered.

It was from the school, Ellen's classroom teacher Anita Frisk. Anita got caught up in a detailed account of what the children had done during the lunch break, which finally ended in a question.

"You didn't happen to pick Ellen up early today?"

Malin had a hard time understanding exactly what she meant.

"No, we haven't picked her up," she said, making a face to herself. "Why do you ask?"

It was only when she looked up at Henrik and saw his worried facial expression that it occurred to her what the teacher's veiled question actually meant. Could mean.

"What is it?" whispered Henrik.

"What do you mean? Isn't Ellen there?" asked Malin.

"She didn't come into class after lunch."

Anita Frisk's voice sounded wobbly, but it could be poor coverage.

"Didn't come in? What do you mean, is she gone?"

Malin held Henrik's gaze firmly. He sat rigidly in the seat beside her.

"Yes, that is, we went out and looked in the schoolyard, but she wasn't there and nowhere in the school, either. So then we thought that—"

"But good Lord, what time is it now?"

Malin looked at the instrument panel. Twelve thirty.

"When did lunch break end?"

"Ten after twelve," said Anita.

"Ten after twelve. That's twenty minutes ago. Twenty minutes. Why haven't you called?"

Her voice was shrill. She was almost crying.

"Why the hell haven't you called?"

"We've been searching and talking with the children who were with her at lunch. . . ."

"But that doesn't make any sense. My daughter is missing and you only call me after twenty minutes. Don't you understand how serious this is?"

Malin had leaned forward in the seat so that the belt was taut. She stared out the windshield at the blue sky, but saw only one thing. The family portrait where Ellen's eyes had been replaced by two gaping holes. She felt sick.

"What's going on?" Henrik hissed beside her.

"Malin, I'm happy to talk about what we ought to have done and when," said Anita. "But right now it's probably better if we concentrate on finding Ellen."

A devastating wave of nausea almost paralyzed Malin. She wanted to kick and scream, but could not move. Fucking idiot. Fucking Anita Frisk. Then it subsided.

"Have you called the police?" she asked.

"No, we called you first. We thought she might be with you."

"I'll call the police. You have to go over to the day care and make sure that Axel is there. We've received threats. I haven't said anything about it, but we have been subjected to threats and this may—"

She was not able to say the last words.

"We've already been there," said Anita Frisk. "We thought that Ellen might have gone there, but she didn't."

"I'll call the police," Malin repeated. "We're on our way. We're on the ferry now, in the wrong direction. We're on our way. Call if there's anything."

Then she ended the call without saying good-bye.

"What is it?" said Henrik, looking worriedly at her.

"Ellen is gone. She didn't come in after lunch break."

Malin held up the cell phone and tried to enter 911.

"Has something happened? What do you mean, gone?"

"I don't know. No, nothing has happened. Not that anyone knows anyway. She's just gone. I'm calling the police now."

Henrik sat mute while she tapped on the green phone.

"What did they say about Axel?"

"He's there. They were in the day care searching for Ellen. We have to go there."

She turned around and looked up toward the bridge of the ferry, which was elevated on a frame above the car deck.

"We have to get them to turn around."

"We're already there," said Henrik.

The ferry rocked as they made contact with the pier. Malin dropped the phone, which slipped in under the pedals. She leaned over between her own legs, turned double to get at it, but the seat belt made it difficult.

"Damn it shit shit shit," she screamed and sobbed.

Then she got loose—Henrik must have undone the seat belt for her—and she could pick up the phone. The call had been interrupted. She entered the number again and pressed SEND, put the cell phone to her ear.

The gate opened with a buzzing sound and the signal for their lane was green. Malin moved the cell phone to her left hand and tried to turn the key in the ignition. Nothing happened. The car just stood there.

"But what the hell," she whined.

Henrik reached out a hand. He wanted to take over the call. Malin waved his hand away and fussed with the key until she saw that the gear selector was in drive. She must have moved it without thinking about it.

The cars behind them were honking and she wanted to rush out and scream at them that her daughter was missing, kick the cars and scream at them to go to hell with their fucking worries about not getting off the ferry fast enough.

Everything collapsed and the whole time four pairs of eyes were staring at her. Four pairs of eyes that were not eyes but holes in a photograph.

20.

It was silent in the car. Gustav was driving, Sara sat beside him, and Fredrik was in the backseat. He looked out through the side window at the sun-drenched landscape rolling past. The same trip he and Sara had made three days earlier, minus the last bit on Fårö. That time it had concerned something small that might have been almost nothing.

Now it concerned something big that could prove to be the worst imaginable.

Had they taken the threats against the family too lightly? Fredrik would answer that they had done what they could with the information that Malin Andersson and Henrik Kjellander had provided. They had questioned Henrik's half sisters on Fårö. They had checked out the tenants. And these were good answers, not bad excuses. Even so he could not help thinking that they should have done more.

"It's been such a short time." Sara broke the silence. "It can be just about anything, that she had a falling out with one of her classmates and ran away."

Fredrik hummed in response. Gustav remained silent behind the wheel. Of course she might be right, but Fredrik was certain that they were all mentally preparing themselves that they were on their way to a catastrophe. He had not met Ellen, only seen a picture of her, and it had lacked eyes. Even so he could easily visualize her. She was playing in the sand at Norsta Auren. His imagination even added a look full of life and delight. He tried to hold onto those thoughts. They might as well remain there on the idyllic sandy beach, not rush off to something else, something terrible.

He was feeling very ill at ease, and quite selfishly he hoped to be spared that. He hoped that he would not be the one who had to stand before a dead seven-year-old in a forest clearing somewhere, if it turned out badly after all. That he would not be the one who would have to sit with the devastated parents and with his awkward sympathy coax out information in a situation that was completely inhuman.

But he would not be spared, he knew that. It was his job. Taking care of it. Managing it. Coping.

He tried to concentrate on the view, more or less like a carsick person who fixes his gaze on the horizon.

He was not normally pursued by unpleasant thoughts like this. Not when he was on his way to a crime scene. He could usually concentrate on the task, keep his head cold and close out his emotions until later. But this time it was clearly different. Or was it simply that he had become a different person?

Gustav looked grimly resolute behind the wheel. Were his thoughts moving along the same lines as Fredrik's?

Sara looked at her watch, took her cell phone out of her pocket, tapped on it a while, but then put it away again.

"Is Micke coming over the weekend?" Fredrik asked.

"Yes," she said, turning away.

Fredrik sensed the trace of a contented smile. Sara was the secretive type where her personal life was concerned. There was a guy in Stockholm she had met last Christmas. That was basically all he knew.

"I was thinking about whether I should phone, but it's probably a little too soon."

"Wait on that," said Fredrik. "He won't be getting here until late, right?"

"No, the twelve-twenty boat," she said.

"All right," said Fredrik. "Then there's no problem."

But of course there was. If the worst had happened. If the girl was dead.

21.

"What car are you talking about? Do you mean someone saw Ellen drive off in a car?"

Malin was staring at Anita Frisk.

"No, a girl in the class said she saw a car stop in front of the school right before the bell rang."

Ellen's teacher brushed aside the silky blond hair from her face with a trembling hand. She was short and slender, small even compared with

Malin. How could this little person protect a whole class of seven-year-olds from all the dangers that were lurking out in the world?

Malin had never thought along those lines before, but now when she did it seemed completely absurd. The women with whom she entrusted her children did not have a chance. And the school itself. It just sat there completely open with its playground where the children ran free as if nothing bad could happen to them. It was only a matter of stepping in and stealing a child. As easy as anything. There should be walls and guards.

"So who, who saw the car?" she asked, taking hold of Anita's arm.

Malin had a definite feeling that more than anything Anita would like to slip away from there. Leave her in the ugly room in the school office that smelled of throat lozenges and body odor.

"It was Matilda, but . . ."

"I want to speak with her."

"Of course you can speak with her, but . . ."

"I have to speak with her now," said Malin, squeezing Anita's arm.

Anita brushed back her hair again and shaded her eyes.

"I'll get her," she said curtly. "Wait here."

She stopped in the doorway. The glow from a fluorescent light in the corridor ceiling outlined a long dark shadow under her nose.

"Just take it easy with her. She saw a car. That's all. The children . . ."

"What the hell have they been doing here?" Malin burst out to Henrik as soon as the door had closed behind the teacher.

Soon they would probably appoint a crisis committee to take care of the children who were left. Perhaps this was more important than calling the police when her daughter disappeared.

"I can't just stand here staring," Malin continued before Henrik could answer. "I'll take the car and go out and search."

Henrik came closer, put his arm around her back.

"They didn't know," he said.

"No, but they know now. Even so, they're like sleepwalkers."

She backed out of his embrace and shook her fists in front of his face. "Our child is gone. Isn't there anyone who can do anything? Who at least can pretend like it means something?"

How could they have been so dense that they left the children out of sight even for a second after what she found in the mail this morning? She ought to be shot. She thought it was good for the children that everything was normal, thought they would be safe in school, that it was the house in Kalbjerga that was the target. She could not imagine that anyone would go after the children.

She sobbed, but took a deep breath and snuffled back the crying attack before it had time to start. This was not the right moment to be weak.

22.

"If Ellen were to have gone off by herself somewhere, where might she have gone? Can you imagine any place? Any place where she feels at home?"

Fredrik Broman looked seriously at Malin and Henrik.

If she had gone off by herself? Why was he even asking that? thought Malin. Nothing had happened that would have made Ellen run away from the school. No trouble. They had already gone through all of this. Actually she felt confidence in Fredrik Broman, in Sara Oskarsson, too, but right now it was as if everything around her was wrong.

"We don't spend much time in Fårösund. Ellen has a couple of friends here, but they're in school now."

Malin threw out her hand toward the building behind them.

She had to exert herself not to sound angry and hostile. That was important. She could not get on the wrong side of the police. They had to like her. They had to want to do their utmost when they were searching for Ellen. Her life might depend on it. That little extra effort. The second that determined everything.

"No classmate who's home sick?" asked Fredrik.

Malin looked quickly at Anita, who shook her head.

"No, everyone's here."

The first police officers had arrived before Malin had time to ask Matilda about the car she had seen. There were four of them and they came in two regular police cars. Malin thought that everything was going frightfully slow. They had come sauntering into the school as if they had all the time in the world. As if nothing in particular was at stake. Leisurely and cumbersome, loaded down with guns and apparatus around their waists. Shouldn't they have been running? Shouldn't they already be out looking, calling in the national guard for a search party, sending out a missing person bulletin?

Only a few minutes later Fredrik Broman and Sara Oskarsson came along with a third detective. When they found out that Matilda had seen a car outside the school when Ellen disappeared they walked over to speak with the girl—just as Malin wanted, but didn't have time to.

Malin had been present at the conversation. The only sensible thing they got out of Matilda was that the car was white. However they twisted and turned the questions, it ended at that. A white car. Matilda seemed shy and mumbled her answers to the questions. Malin could not help feeling that the girl knew more than she was saying. That for some reason she could not spit it out. Because she was shy, afraid, a little dense, or perhaps did not understand that she ought to tell.

Several times Malin had to restrain herself from taking hold of Matilda, shaking her and yelling at her that she should tell what she knew.

After they had spoken with Matilda, they went out on the playground to see where Ellen had been the last time anyone had seen her. That was where they were standing now, or to be more precise, on the sidewalk outside: Malin, Henrik, Anita, the four police officers in uniform, Fredrik Broman, Sara Oskarsson, and the third plainclothes officer. It felt a little more secure in some way that Fredrik and Sara were there. After all.

"No other place?" Fredrik continued. "Any store where you stop?"

"That would be ICA in that case," said Henrik. "But we don't shop there that often."

"And she couldn't have taken the ferry because she wanted to go home for some reason?" Sara Oskarsson suggested.

"Perhaps she could have," said Henrik. "But I have a hard time imagining it. It's much too far to walk; she probably understands that."

"Okay," said Fredrik.

One of the uniformed policemen, the one who was named Knutsson and appeared to have no hair under his blue cap, turned to Fredrik.

"We'll drive down to the ferry landing and stop at ICA on the way, then we'll check the nearby blocks."

Fredrik nodded at him and they exchanged a few brief words that Malin could not hear. Finally something was happening, she thought. Anita had printed out copies of Ellen's school photo on the school's color printer. Knutsson was holding them in his hand.

"I know it hasn't been very long, but I think we should get a search going," said the plainclothes officer; he was in a suit and had a well-tended beard.

Knutsson looked at him, pressing down on the edge of his cap over his neck.

"Considering the threats," the officer in the suit added.

Knutsson answered, but Malin was no longer listening to him. Something quite different had caught her attention. Two hundred feet away along the road a small figure approached with tired steps. She was too far away to say for sure who it was, but Malin felt her heart almost stop in her chest, and then immediately beat so fast that she was afraid it would be torn loose from its moorings. She placed one hand against her chest and took a long step in the direction of the child who came tramping along the road. Could it possibly be . . . surely it was . . .

She stood completely still and waited, sharpened her gaze. The child came closer and closer, a little girl with dark hair, jeans, and a red-checkered top with short sleeves.

Malin could not hold back a loud howl.

Henrik, the police officers, and Anita stared at her with fright. She did not care about them. She was quite certain now and started running in the direction of Ellen. She felt the tears running down her cheeks, her chest felt hot and painful in a strange way, and when she wanted to shout Ellen's name her throat tightened up and not so much as a whisper came across her lips.

She saw how Ellen stopped and then the next moment came rushing toward her.

"Mommy."

Ellen ran with her arms outstretched, leaning forward in a way that seemed to defy the law of gravity. Malin saw how she fell. Again and again her daughter lost her footing, whirled forward through the air and struck the ground headlong. The soft, unspoiled face against the rough asphalt. But it was only in Malin's mind that Ellen fell. As if it was too good to be true that she was back, that something had to happen at the last trembling moment. All the emotions she had been forced to hold back to be able to be nice to the police, to be able to function at all during the last half hour of her life, rushed ahead and played out the terror in brutal fantasies.

But Ellen did not fall. She ran and Malin ran, and she heard Henrik's voice calling Ellen's name. Now he had understood, too, everyone understood.

Then she threw her arms around her. Leaned down toward the little body and enclosed it in her arms.

"Ellen."

The tears were flowing out of her. Floods. She sobbed and snuffled and emitted a crazy laugh.

"Mommy."

The little fingers that groped and squeezed on her back.

"She said she would drive me back."

The white car. So it was true. Malin felt her legs getting very soft below her and she sank down on her knees on the asphalt with her arms around Ellen.

"She said she would drive me back, but she didn't," Ellen sobbed.

Someone had lured her daughter into a car and taken her away. Right under the noses of teachers and schoolmates. A female. Ellen had said she. And now she had brought her back. Right under the noses of her parents and seven police officers. She could not be far away. Had not been far away.

"I had to walk super far."

Ellen sobbed against her neck. Malin heard steps behind her, felt a hand on her shoulder. It was Henrik. He sank down on his knees beside them. Placed his other hand on their daughter's head.

"Ellen," he said gently.

Malin did not understand how he could sound so controlled. Emotional, but still controlled. She herself had just died and been born again. She tore her eyes from Ellen briefly to meet Henrik's. She felt calmness coming back when he looked at her. This was her life. This was for real. Henrik, Ellen, and Axel. She never wanted to let them go again. She wanted to go into the day care right now, pick up Axel, and go directly . . .

There the thought ran into resistance. Go where? Home to the house in Kalbjerga? The house where some strange person had struck out their eyes on the family portraits, the house where a stranger used the children's toy box as a toilet and intentionally scattered broken glass over the floor. A stranger.

Malin looked at Ellen. *She said she would drive me back*. She.

Malin looked over her shoulder toward the police. Anger flared up in her when one of the uniformed officers rolled his eyes at Leif Knutsson. She did not actually see more than the last part of the movement, but it was more than enough. She understood exactly. Everything was already clear to them. Ellen had sneaked off to buy candy at the ICA store where they were customers and seven police officers had driven all the way from Visby for no reason.

She could not stop herself anymore. She stood up abruptly with Ellen by the hand and walked quickly toward the police officers.

"Malin?" Henrik asked behind her.

But Malin kept walking.

"She was taken away," she said loudly in the direction of the police. "Ellen was lured away by a woman in that car. She was kidnapped, damn it, so don't stand there and sneer at us."

All seven police officers looked at her with stern expressions.

"Damn it, she was kidnapped," she repeated.

Fredrik Broman said something to the others and started walking in her direction. Only then did she realize that she was too far away for them to be able to hear what she said.

23.

It was like Malin said, thought Sara. The woman in the car had dropped Ellen off right under their noses. They might very well have met her on their way up.

Sara sat with Ellen and her parents while Fredrik and Gustav talked with the teachers and the schoolchildren. Sara was the only one who had both training and experience in questioning children.

Leif Knutsson and the others were searching for witnesses who might have seen a white car with a blond woman and a dark-haired girl moving around in the area. There was not much to go on, but on the other hand there were not many cars on the road in Fårösund on a Thursday at the end of August. With a little luck Fårösund residents might have noticed a strange car sneaking around in the neighborhood.

Ellen's teacher had shown them to a room in the school office. It was stuffy in there and Malin opened the window after the teacher left.

Ellen and Malin were sitting across from Sara at the narrow white table. Ellen seemed to have recovered after the excitement. The first thing they had done, naturally, was to make sure that Ellen had not been subjected to any type of assault. Ellen seemed mostly shaken up by the fact that the lady in the car promised to drive her back to the school, but then left her off by the big road all the way up by the Statoil gas station. It had been a long walk.

Henrik Kjellander sat at the short end of the table in a wrinkled black cotton suit jacket and a long dark blue shawl wrapped a couple of turns around his neck. His eyes oscillated nervously between Ellen and Sara. In a display case behind him were three table-sized Midsummer poles, a countless number of small yellow chickens, and two gnomes.

Sara turned to Ellen.

"Do you remember anything else from the car? I mean, whether there was anything on the seat, was there anything hanging on the rearview mirror, maybe there was a sticker somewhere. That sort of thing. Do you understand what I mean?"

Ellen nodded and her gaze wandered off while she thought.

"I got gum."

Sara saw how Malin winced. She appeared to want to say something to Ellen, but held back.

Ellen glanced at her mother as she continued.

"I said I couldn't, but she said it was healthy. Sugar-free."

Malin forced a smile toward Ellen, but seemed about to burst into tears at any moment.

"I see," said Sara. "And the lady in the car, did she also have some gum?"

"Yes," said Sara, nodding exaggeratedly. "She had some gum, too."

It seemed as if that information calmed Malin. She leaned back a little and her shoulders lowered an inch or two.

"You said that the lady seemed young. Do you think, like your mom, approximately, or how old do you think she was?"

Asking children about the age of adults was tricky, not to say borderline meaningless.

"I don't know," said Ellen. "At first I thought she was a girl. I know that she was big, but I still thought that she was a girl, but then after a while I didn't think that anymore. Then she was more like a regular grown-up."

"Like me?" Malin asked.

"Hmm, but still a little more like a girl," said Ellen.

"Younger than me?"

"Yes, maybe."

What did that mean? Was this a very young person, or someone who tried to make herself childish to ingratiate herself and get close?

"You said she was blond with hair down to here." Sara imitated Ellen's gesture from before with a hand a few inches below her shoulder. "Was there anything else you can think of about how she looked?"

Ellen ran her fingers along the neckline of her checkered top.

"She was thin and had a green jacket."

Sara waited. It appeared as if Ellen was searching for something in her memory.

"Her name was Ellen."

She sounded almost excited as she said it, wriggling on the chair and kicking her dangling legs.

"Her name was Ellen just like me."

Sara and Malin exchanged a glance over the girl's head.

"I see," said Sara. "Imagine that, her name was Ellen, too."

"Yes."

"Do you remember who said their name first? Was it her or you?"

"She asked me what my name was. Then I said it and then she said that her name was Ellen, too."

Ellen lowered her eyes, talked down to her lap.

"But I don't know."

"What do you mean?" said Sara.

"I think she was fooling."

"About that her name was Ellen?"

"About everything. She was strange."

"In what way was she strange, do you think?"

"Tricky."

"Tricky?"

"Yes."

Ellen turned abruptly toward Malin, threw her arms around her, and pressed her face right into her flower-patterned blouse. Malin stroked her hair and looked in anguish at Henrik.

"I think that will be enough," said Sara.

Malin leaned over and kissed Ellen on the top of her head. Sara could not decide whether Ellen was crying or if she just wanted to hide.

"It was nice that you could answer all my questions," she said to Ellen's neck. "We're done now. I won't ask anything else."

Ellen peeked carefully at her, still with her head pressed against Malin.

"If you think of anything else, you can tell your mom. Shall we say that?"

Ellen nodded.

They stood up. Malin left first with Ellen, Sara and Henrik right behind them.

"Yes, one thing . . ." said Sara, stopping in the corridor.

Henrik stopped, too. Malin turned to look at them.

"You two go ahead," said Sara. "We'll be there in two seconds."

Henrik looked at her, perplexed, and nervously ran his fingers through his shiny combed-back hair.

"It's good if you talk with Ellen about what happened. You don't need to torment her with it, but if she brings it up herself it's good if you follow along and clarify things. Call me if anything new comes out. All details are important."

"I understand," said Henrik.

He ran his hand through his hair again and again. His fingers were trembling slightly.

"Do take notes of what she says, too. Write it down as literally as possible."

"I'll keep that in mind," Henrik promised.

He was pale, his face almost gray, and he looked as if he had already forgotten what she said.

Fredrik had just finished the questioning of Anita Frisk and was on his way back to the car when Malin, Henrik, and Ellen came out of the school. Malin caught sight of him, said something to Henrik, and set a course toward Fredrik. Henrik remained standing with Ellen.

"I thought of something," said Malin. "I have to talk with you."

"Of course. Shall we sit down," said Fredrik with a gesture toward the school, "or is here okay?"

"No, here is fine."

She looked down at the ground and took a deep breath.

"There was something that happened last Monday, when I was dropping Axel off at day care. Over here."

She quickly pointed at the day care center that was on the other side of the school building.

"When I came out to the car I caught sight of a woman who was standing a short distance away staring at me."

Malin held her hands completely still now, concentrating on her story.

"She really stood and stared at me, but didn't say hello or anything, just stood there. At first I thought about getting in the car and driving away, but when she kept looking at me that way, well . . . Yes, this was just a day and a half after we came home and found the pictures. It's possible that I was a little oversensitive, I don't know, but in any case I started walking over to her. I thought about asking whether she wanted something. But then she jumped into her car and drove off."

"And you're sure that you were the one she was looking at?"

Malin looked mutely at Fredrik. He understood exactly what she was thinking. But as a policeman he was forced to try to see everything from multiple viewpoints, take some kind of neutral position.

"I'm not questioning your story," he said. "I just want to rule out that she was standing there looking for a child."

"She was looking at me. I even turned around to see whether there was someone behind me. I know she's not a mother of any of the children. Then I would have recognized her."

"Okay. What did she look like, this woman?"

"That's just it. She was slender, had a green jacket and blond hair; it's possible that it was a little on the strawberry blond side. But I think that Ellen perhaps perceived it as blond, especially in the sun. And the car was white."

"How old did she appear to be?"

"Hard to say. I didn't get that close. Somewhere between twenty-five and thirty-five, up to forty maybe."

"You didn't recognize her at all? I mean, you were close enough to see that it wasn't someone you knew, or in any event knew by appearance?"

"Yes, I didn't recognize her."

"And this was on Monday?"

"Yes, Ellen's first day in school. The same day you and Sara were at our house."

"Can you say anything else about the car? Model, type of car?"

"It was a smaller car, with a hatchback. I didn't get that close, as I said, and when she took off she drove away from me."

"In what direction?"

"That way, up toward Stuxvägen," said Malin, pointing straight ahead.

"It may have been a relative or acquaintance that had dropped off a child. That might explain why you didn't recognize her. I'll check with the teachers."

"But what would she be doing . . . I mean, what if it was her? The woman who carried her away. It could be her."

"First and foremost we have to see about finding this woman," said Fredrik. "As I said, we can talk with the teachers and the other parents. If we get that far we can arrange a lineup with Ellen."

"Now Ellen did actually say that she was blond, and I perceived this woman more as strawberry blond, but not much . . . Ellen may have thought that it was blond. Or else I was the one who was mistaken."

She smiled nervously at Fredrik.

"The light can be deceiving sometimes," she added.

"Sure, that's a possibility. We'll investigate it, then we'll see where we end up," said Fredrik.

Malin sighed faintly. She seemed disappointed.

24.

"I'm not going back home," Malin hissed at Henrik as soon as the car started moving.

"Huh?"

He stared at her in the rearview mirror.

Henrik had taken the car keys when they left the school to drive down and pick up Axel. Right then it had felt good. She wanted nothing more than to sit in the backseat with the children and keep them close beside her. But now she regretted it. With the keys she had given away control. If she was sitting behind the wheel she was the one who decided where they went.

"And where should we go then, were you thinking?" said Henrik.

"We'll have to stay at a hotel."

"Do you think that's so good for . . ."

Henrik fell silent, guided the SUV toward the sidewalk, and stopped in front of a brick house with brown roof tiles. He got out without saying anything and closed the door behind him. Malin sat silently staring ahead, did not want to get out of the car, did not want to leave Ellen, but then reached over Axel and opened the door.

"Where are you going, Mommy?" said Ellen.

"I'm just going to talk a little with Daddy. It won't take long."

"Can't you talk in the car?"

"I'll be standing right outside the car, you'll see me," said Malin, squeezing out past Axel.

She smiled at Ellen and gave Axel a pat on the cheek. He closed his eyes as her fingers touched him. Happily unknowing, she thought, reluctantly closing the door.

She hated this. Standing and arguing outside the car with the children in there like in a protective jar. A young mother came walking with a stroller on the sidewalk. They stood quietly and waited for her to pass. Malin thought that she glanced curiously at them as if she saw right through them.

"Isn't it best for Ellen to go home? Staying at a hotel will only be a source of worry," said Henrik when the mother with the stroller was farther away.

Malin had to go up to the hood of the car to be able to see him properly.

"So you think that we should go home and pretend like nothing hap-

pened? Wait for the next letter with poked-out eyes? Or until someone comes and pokes our eyes out for real?"

"Stop it," said Henrik.

"Or sets fire to the house."

Henrik did not reply. They stood on either side of the red hood of
the car without speaking. It was a lovely day. Blue sky, small tentative
waves in the sound. A mild breeze against their bare arms. But inside
her there was chaos. She wanted to get away from there, far away from
Kalbjerga and Fårö. Away from Gotland.

"The worst thing is not understanding," she said quietly. "Why is
someone doing this to us? Have we done something? Or is it just some
lunatic who totally randomly . . . I don't get it."

Ellen knocked on the side window and made an impatient face. Both
of them smiled at her and waved happily.

"We'll be going very soon," said Malin with exaggerated mouth
movements, nodding encouragingly.

She turned back to Henrik.

"I know," he said. "I agree with you. But can't we go home now, so
we can talk about this in peace and quiet. We do have to install the
alarm."

"I'm not sleeping there tonight," she said, looking him in the eye.

"Can't we talk about this when we get home?"

She was about to protest, but he interrupted her.

"I'm not going to force you to sleep there if you don't want to. I
promise. But can't we go home now? I don't want to stand here like an
idiot having a discussion. If you feel the same this evening we'll go to
Visby and check into a hotel. Okay?"

Malin looked away, stood awhile staring out over the water. Her
daughter had been carried off from her school by a strange woman. It
was like a nightmare that would not end.

"I wish there was somewhere you could go and buy a pistol," she
said without looking at Henrik.

"I know what you mean," he said.

The question was simply who she would shoot at. The one who was doing this to them always seemed to be at a safe distance. Too far away to even be seen.

"Okay then," she said. "Let's go home."

Maybe they would be safe there anyway. Everything that had happened so far had happened as if behind their backs. The one who was doing this did not seem to have the courage to meet them face-to-face. She acted in secret. In that case, what was the next step? Burn down the house, as she had just blurted out? But in that case, when they weren't at home. Wasn't that the most logical? It fit the pattern. Or was that over now? Would there be no next step? Malin had a hard time believing that.

25.

The ferry reduced speed and landed gently at Broa. It only took a few seconds before the ramp was lowered and the gates went up.

"The question is whether this woman carried off Ellen and then changed her mind and released her, or if it was the plan right from the start," said Sara as they rolled off the ferry on the Fårö side.

"That she just wanted to scare them?" said Fredrik.

"Yes."

An unknown woman, thirty-ish, blond, coaxed Ellen into her car under the pretense of getting directions to the ferry, mixed in with a cute kitten and that they were both named Ellen. That was basically what they knew.

"I'm thinking that the schoolyard is right by the road," said Fredrik. "That means it's easy to stop a car and make contact with a child, but on the other hand, it must be hard to get someone to get into the car without one of the other children noticing it. The person who took Ellen with her must have waited for the right moment."

"Either that or else it has nothing to do with Ellen at all," Sara answered. "It was just a lunatic who drove past and happened to be lucky."

"Well, if it was an ordinary sexual predator then that would have been highly probable," said Fredrik. "But now we have the threats from before plus that it's a woman who carried off Ellen and that Ellen came back."

"You're right," said Gustav from his place behind the wheel. "It was planned."

This was the first time he had opened his mouth since they left the school in Fårösund.

"Yes, presumably," said Fredrik. "My point is that if the woman truly was after Ellen in particular, she must have been at the school a number of times. Sat in the car waiting."

"And in that case someone ought to have noticed her," said Sara. "Or the car anyway."

"Another possible thought is a deranged person who moves in tighter and tighter circles," said Fredrik. "First distance with the pictures that are left in the house when they're gone, and then in the mailbox after they've come home. And now one of the children."

"Someone who is coming closer?" said Sara.

"Yes, that is a documented pattern. First threats or violence at a distance, then the perpetrator gets braver and comes closer. So far there is no violence, but it can escalate from threat to violence just as the distance shrinks."

"Well . . ." said Gustav without taking his eyes off the road.

He was truly unusually taciturn.

"Henrik Kjellander said that they were going to install surveillance cameras in the house," said Fredrik. "That's good."

Sara nodded.

"We can always hope I'm wrong, but I think the risk is great that this person will come back to mess with them one way or another. Presumably while they are asleep, or when the house is empty. They must make sure that the images from the cameras are stored somehow."

He took out his notebook.

"I'll have to call them about that."

They drove on. Long, tired stone fences wound through the landscape, dividing off pastures from forest and fields. They looked like petrified dragons from an old saga.

"Everything that has happened points to someone trying to frighten them," said Sara.

"The only ones who have anything resembling a motive are those sisters," said Fredrik.

Sara turned toward him.

"But if it is Elisabet she is taking a really great risk of being recognized. A confrontation with Ellen can of course be disputed in court, but it's hardly something you count on."

"No, that's true. You probably have to be a little crazy to take that risk."

Gustav mumbled something to himself and passed the car ahead of them when there was a stretch with a clear view.

They still had to check Elisabet's alibi. Alma was already freed from suspicion. She was having lunch with a colleague at work when Ellen disappeared from the school.

"I'll call GotlandsResor again," said Fredrik. "If the last tenant scheduled the house under a false name, she or he must have left some kind of trace anyway."

"Are you thinking IP number?" said Sara.

"Yes. Whoever booked the house must have been sitting at a computer somewhere."

Gustav stopped the car on the farmyard right in front of the two big maple trees and the opening in the wall. All three of them got out. An

unintentional show of force. Sara and Fredrik started walking toward
the house while Gustav went over to the short end of the barn where
three cars were parked under a canopy. A green pickup, a silver-colored
Volvo, and a white Peugeot. Gustav placed his hand on the hood of the
white car.

"Cold," he said quietly when he was back. "But she must have had
at least an hour's head start."

Sara knocked with the help of the door knocker. Along the steps
where the red rubber boots had been tossed last time there was now a
yellow toy bucket full of pinecones.

The lock clicked and the door opened.

"Oh, what an entourage," said Elisabet Vogler when she came out
on the steps.

She extended her hand and politely greeted Gustav, who she had
not met before.

"What might this be about this time?"

She looked at Fredrik but it was Sara who answered.

"We have to ask a few more questions."

Elisabet Vogler smiled stiffly and nodded, but said nothing more.

"Where were you today between eleven thirty and twelve thirty?"

"I was having lunch with my husband."

Sara was about to ask a follow-up question, but Elisabet Vogler got
there first.

"Here in the house, that is."

"What did you have for lunch?" said Fredrik.

Elisabet Vogler looked surprised.

"You mean seriously?"

"That I want to know what you had for lunch? Yes."

"But what is this?"

Elisabet Vogler smiled and sought eye contact with Sara and Gustav in turn, but met no signs of sympathy.

"This concerns a serious crime so I must ask you to answer the question," said Fredrik.

"Of course," she said with exaggerated willingness. "We had cod with dill sauce and potatoes. You're welcome to come in and look in the trash. There was a little left over that I thought about giving to the chickens."

Fucking hag, thought Fredrik, we ought to take her along to Visby.

26.

Malin was sitting on Ellen's bed, with Ellen and Axel on either side, reading from one of their favorite books, *Children in the Water*. It had been Malin's favorite book, too, when she was little. The pages were well thumbed and the cover was torn.

Henrik was downstairs unpacking the alarm system she had convinced him to buy. She had a somewhat guilty conscience for having first argued for an alarm that cost almost seven thousand kronor and then not wanting to be in the house at all. But the circumstances had changed. To say the least.

Now as she sat with the children in bed it felt good anyway. You could see that they felt secure. But she could not keep from thinking that it was a false sense of security. There was someone out there who knew where they lived. Who had been inside their house. Who had lured their daughter away in a car. A blond woman. The same woman who had been staring at her by the school?

Axel squeezed closer to Malin and pointed at the nursery troll Ture in the book.

"He's pulling out the plug."

Axel always said that when they got to the pages with the sharks with mean eyes and mouths full of razor-sharp teeth. As if to reassure himself that everything would be fine.

"Hmm," said Malin, to confirm but still not completely give away the ending.

Malin looked at him before she continued reading. Axel's eyes were fixed on the book. He had slept through the commotion on Saturday evening and he had no idea what had happened to his sister today. Or did he? Had Ellen told him anything? Should she ask her not to say anything to Axel, or was it best to let it be? She felt uncertain.

"Read," said Axel.

He made a little drum roll with his legs against the edge of the bed.

Malin continued to read. The nursery troll Ture pulled out the plug, all the sharks and the entire ocean ran out through the sewer and the story was over. She shut the book. Axel immediately jumped down from the bed, ran over to the turquoise secretary, and pulled out paper and crayons. The once drab brown piece of furniture had been left in the house when they moved in. Malin had re-painted it.

Ellen stayed sitting beside her.

"Can't you read some more?" she asked.

"No," Axel protested.

"You don't need to listen if you don't want to," said Malin. "You can sit there and draw."

"No," said Axel.

"But stop," said Ellen.

Ellen had not mentioned the woman in the car at all since they left the school. Unless she had said something to Axel when Malin was not present. Didn't she think about what had happened? Perhaps it was nothing more to her than the immediate, the very surface. Someone had asked her to show the way to the ferry and promised to drive her back to the school, but then did not keep the promise so she was forced to walk almost a mile.

Could it be that simple? Malin was doubtful. If nothing else surely Malin's, Henrik's, and all the other grown-ups' worry had spilled over on her and made her wonder what she had really been involved in. The police. That they went home before the school day was over. A night at a hotel would only add to that.

"I have to ask you about something," she said quietly, placing one arm around Ellen's back.

Ellen did not say anything.

"That lady in the car that you rode with, what color hair did she have?"

Ellen looked at her.

"Light-haired. I already said that."

"Yes. But I was just thinking that you can be light-haired in different ways. Take Lisa, for example. She's blond, but not all of her hair has the same color. Here and there it's almost like strands—"

"I know. Like light brown," said Ellen with sudden fervor.

"So I was thinking whether you remembered how this lady's hair was. Was her hair completely even in color, or was it more like Lisa's? Or perhaps it changed in some other color?"

Ellen seemed to lose interest again when Malin brought the conversation back to the woman in the car. She looked down and rubbed her nose.

"Do you remember that?"

Ellen sighed.

What was it Sara Oskarsson had said to Henrik? You don't need to torment her with it. Was she doing that now? Tormenting her?

"It was light hair," said Ellen. "Lighter than Lisa."

Malin stroked Ellen across her back with her palm.

"Sometimes blond hair may have a little red, too, without anyone thinking about it. That is, you say that it's blond, although actually it's a little bit red, too. It doesn't look really red, more like pale orange, but we usually say strawberry blond."

Malin smiled at Ellen, who had slithered forward a little so that she could dangle her legs over the edge of the bed.

"She wasn't red-haired."

"No, I understand, but that wasn't really what I meant, either. If someone is red-haired, you see that right away. But some . . ."

Malin interrupted herself when Ellen glided down from the bed and went over to the secretary desk where her little brother was sitting with his head bowed over the paper and the crayons poised. Presumably he was drawing sharks and Ture. Ellen stood quietly and followed the movements of his hand across the paper.

Malin decided that there was no point in asking her more right now. She would follow the police officer's advice and wait for a suitable moment, but she could not wait too long. This was serious. They had to find out what she knew.

Five minutes later Ellen was sitting on a stool alongside her brother and drawing, too. It was tempting to sneak up and see what was appearing on the paper, but Malin chose instead to leave her in peace. She could look at the drawings later. The wadded-up and discarded ones as well as the proudly displayed ones.

27.

Gustav did not have much to say on the way back to Visby, either. They left the car in the garage and Sara hurried off to make a call.

"Is there something?" Fredrik asked.

"No, no, nothing in particular," Gustav replied quickly.

They went up to the crime unit and Gustav slinked into his office, sat down heavily behind his desk. Fredrik remained standing in the doorway.

"I was just wondering. You've hardly said 'boo' the whole day."

Gustav looked at him with surprise, as if he did not understand why Fredrik hadn't gone to his own office.

"Sometimes you just have other things to think about. That's not so strange."

"Sure," said Fredrik.

He tapped awkwardly on the doorpost and was turning around to go when he heard a deep sigh behind him. It was a little too demonstrative not to mean something. That he should stay, for example. He turned around slowly, prepared to quickly leave if he had interpreted the sigh wrong.

Gustav was looking down at his right hand; he clenched it and opened it.

"It's Lena."

"Lena?" said Fredrik.

"Yes," said Gustav, and continued in a low voice, almost absently, "she has some suspicious symptoms."

Fredrik took a step into the office and closed the door behind him.

"Suspicious symptoms? That doesn't sound good."

He thought that the words were clumsy, but he had to make some kind of response.

"Yes," said Gustav. "She has had strange prickly sensations and numbness in her legs. And she has felt—"

He interrupted himself and swallowed before he continued.

"This has been going on for a while. It doesn't hurt or anything and she . . . Well, you know how it is. You think it's nothing, it will pass. But this has just continued. Pricking, numbness, strange creeping sensations in her legs, plus she has felt tired. She called her sister; she's a nurse."

Gustav looked out the window, up toward the roof of the police station, as if he wanted to assure himself that no one was in flight from the jail's exercise yard.

"She started crying," he continued. "Her sister, that is. When Lena told her she started crying."

Fredrik felt himself turning completely cold. Gustav had not even said what it was Lena might conceivably be suffering from, but he sensed it. Parkinson's, MS, ALS.

"Well, that was really cheerful," said Gustav.

Fredrik hummed in response.

"They suspect MS."

"Do you know that?"

"They've taken samples and then there are a number of other tests. It's clearly not easy to make a diagnosis."

"But you don't know. She can still turn out to be okay?"

"Yes, but after her sister's crying spell the mood is pretty low, as perhaps you understand."

"Yes," said Fredrik.

He sought desperately for something sensible to say, but the more he exerted himself, the more blocked he became. During the eighteen months he had been away from the job after the accident Gustav had been the colleague who supported him most. Not so much through words, of course, but by stopping by and visiting. At least once a week he had stopped when he had been out on some errand anyway. Sometimes on the weekends he rode his bicycle. That made Fredrik feel that he was not completely cut off from work, that there really was a way back. It would be too bad if he couldn't repay that in some small way.

"When will you find out?" he was finally able to say.

"We have an appointment, or Lena has an appointment, for a return visit next Monday, so I assume it's then that—"

"And Martin?"

"We haven't said anything yet. We thought it was just as well to wait."

Martin had moved to the mainland to study, just like Joakim, but had chosen a completely different path. He was studying to be a psychologist in Lund. Fredrik was both surprised and fascinated by these occupational choices that seemed to come out of nowhere. One year the kids were sitting in front of a video game, the next they were going to be a psychologist and a photographer. Where did that come from?

"It could be a false alarm."

"We have to hope so," said Fredrik.

Gustav got up and wriggled out of his jacket.

"But you can keep this to yourself," he said. "Lena doesn't want rumors to start before we know ourselves."

"No, of course. I won't say anything."

28.

Henrik was standing on a ladder, mounting a motion detector up by the ceiling, when Malin came into the kitchen.

Their large kitchen was more practical than charming. After seven years as a café owner she wanted it to be functional. Normally she got inspired when she came in there, started thinking about new recipes to try and write about. But today was different.

"How's it going?" she asked.

"Not bad," said Henrik. "How are things with Ellen?"

"It seems okay. Or it seems good. Listen, there's one thing; I haven't said anything about it before but . . ."

She came closer, stopped alongside the ladder. Henrik lowered the screwdriver and looked at her.

"I spoke with Fredrik Broman today. I thought it was best."

"About what?"

She told the whole story about the reddish-blond or possibly blond-haired woman outside the school and the idea that Ellen had perceived the hair color as blond, or light-haired. That it could be the same person.

"Are you sure?" said Henrik.

"Yes. There was something about her. She stood there much too long. I'm completely sure."

"Why didn't you say anything?" he asked.

It was not that she hadn't wondered about that herself. But it was always easy to second-guess.

"It was right after we found the first picture. I felt completely paranoid. I thought I was imagining things."

"But you did see what you saw?"

"Yes, of course, but thought that I overinterpreted. I thought that maybe she was just a little off or was thinking about something, or what do I know."

"But now you're sure?"

"Yes. Sure enough to say that there was something about her. What happened yesterday puts things in a slightly different light, doesn't it?"

"Sure," he said.

"Every incident about which there's the least little question is worth mentioning."

Henrik slowly rotated the screwdriver in his hand, his gaze lost somewhere at the other end of the room.

"What is it?" she said, looking up at him.

He did not answer.

"What is it?" she repeated.

"Nothing," he said, and now he met her gaze.

"Sure there is. I see that there's something," she said.

He shook his head.

"It's just a little . . . I mean, I understand that you thought it was unpleasant, but . . ."

He threw out his arms, waving the screwdriver a little.

"But what the hell, Henrik. There is something. You're thinking about something."

"I'm sure it's nothing. It was just something that occurred to me."

"But you can say what it is, can't you?"

"Of course, it . . ."

He climbed down from the ladder, put the screwdriver down on the counter, and looked seriously at her. Malin felt the hair rising on her arms. She did not like that look.

"But say it then," she almost roared.

"It's probably nothing," he repeated. "But there was something about how you described her and . . ."

"Yes?"

He swallowed.

"It reminded me of a girl I was with a long time ago. It was in Stockholm, but she was from here, or from Fårösund, that is."

"What do you mean? Why haven't you told me about her?"

Malin put her hands on her sides.

"I have told you about her," said Henrik.

"I see. What's her name?"

"Her name is Stina Hansson. It was a long time ago, but I have mentioned her."

Malin had never heard about her, but she was bad at names. She might have forgotten it.

"And you were together in Stockholm?"

"Yes. It was when I was at the photography school. We met through some common acquaintances from Gotland. I knew her from here, but we didn't really socialize then. It lasted less than a year. We broke up, or I broke up with her. It got really messy because she didn't want to let go, kept on calling and that. But then suddenly she moved back to Fårösund and then . . . Well . . . Then we weren't in touch anymore. She must have quit school. Or that was what they said anyway."

"So what do you mean? That this Stina has carried off our daughter and stuck needles in our family pictures because you broke up with her . . . what will it be, fifteen years ago or something like that?"

Henrik looked at her in dismay. His hand was trembling as he brushed back the hair from his forehead.

"Good Lord, I don't mean anything. You're the one who saw someone staring at you outside the school. It's probably not even her. I only said that I happened to think of her when you described her."

Malin's head was spinning. One moment she thought she was decisively on the trail, the next it seemed like paranoid fantasies. Nothing that had to do with reality.

"But you know that she still lives in Fårösund?" she said.

"Yes."

"Have you seen her?"

"I've run into her a few times."

"A few times . . ."

Malin fell silent and looked at him, felt cold and strange.

"Why haven't you said anything?"

"Said? I've run into her a couple times in Fårösund. What should I say?"

Henrik's voice had acquired an angry tone and one eyebrow was raised as if the question was a little stupid. Malin thought he looked like a liar.

"So where in Fårösund?"

"At the Bungehall grocery store."

"And those are the only times?"

"I saw her once in town, but that was at a distance and she didn't see me. Does that count?"

There was that ironic expression again, as if it was Malin who had done something wrong. She ought to get angry, but felt that instead she was sad. He remembered that he had seen her in town, even though they hadn't even spoken. Extremely quickly he remembered that. It seemed like he was counting the times.

"I don't understand that you didn't say anything," she said flatly.

"It's not like we went out for coffee or anything. I've seen her at ICA and we stood and talked a little while."

"About what?"

Henrik sighed demonstratively before he answered.

"What are you doing nowadays? Married, two kids, blah blah blah. You know. That kind of thing."

"Is she married and has two kids?"

"No. I'm married and have two kids."

He smiled a little, tried to get her in a good mood again. But it was too late now for that type of cheap charm.

"But not her?"

"No. She's not married."

"No husband, no children."

"No."

"Damn."

"What do you mean, damn?"

Malin tried to look at him from a place far away, distant and superior, but was uncertain whether it succeeded.

"Was it nice with Stina?"

"Huh?"

Henrik tried to look offended, surprised.

"Yes. Did you have a nice time with her? Was it nice sleeping with Stina?"

"What the hell are you saying?"

"It's not so strange that I wonder what she means to you, is it?"

Malin hoped that it would sound factual and a little cool, but to her disappointment heard her voice quiver a little on the final syllables.

"Malin, that was fifteen years ago. It lasted less than a year. I broke up with her. I hardly remember it."

He walked slowly over to the table, sat down at the short end with his arms crossed.

"This is ridiculous."

Malin did not reply.

"Excuse me, but it really is."

Was it ridiculous? Was *she* ridiculous? She tried to think about how the conversation ended up where it did. One thing had led to another. She had followed her emotion. Had it really ended up completely wrong? An old girlfriend from fifteen years back. That was three years before she and Henrik met. Surely he had mentioned Stina Hansson in one of their childish run-throughs of old exes. She had forgotten that. She forgot names. She forgot a number of other things, too. Henrik used to say that it was practical. Every three years he could reuse old jokes and she would still think he was the most amusing guy in the world. That joke she remembered anyway.

"I'm from here," he said. "I know people."

"That's not really the same thing."

"Isn't it?"

"No."

Henrik sighed as if he was right and she was just silly to let her emotions run away with her. He looked at her seriously.

"Can't we just concentrate on ourselves and get this alarm going?"

Malin swallowed. She did not intend to apologize anyway. Perhaps she had gone too far, but she still thought it was wrong that he hadn't said anything. He ought to have told her that he had seen this Stina Hansson the same day he did. That was the kind of thing you did when you were in a relationship. Just to avoid suspicions and outbursts of this type.

"Sure," she said. "But you have to call the police and tell them."

"Yes, of course. I'll do that."

"Do it now."

29

Stina Hansson lived in a two-room unit in an old villa that had been divided up into apartments. The house on Kalkugnsvägen in Fårösund was slightly shadowed behind a row of tall willows with ungainly root suckers. Stina Hansson normally worked at the register at the college restaurant in Visby, but today she was out sick.

In other words, Stina worked in the same building as Alma Vogler. Fredrik wondered whether they knew each other. At least by appearance they ought to. Stina Hansson must have taken payment for Alma's lunch numerous times.

He had nothing against driving up to Fårösund again. After six months behind a desk he was just happy for any opportunity to get out and move around. Sara, on the other hand, had groused a little when Göran asked them to go. Not in front of her boss, of course, but in the corridor on the way down to the garage. Fredrik could understand, but unless something completely unforeseen were to happen, they ought to be back in Visby before Sara's long-distance boyfriend got off the ferry.

Their first impression of Stina Hansson was of a healthy thirty-three-year-old woman. Beautiful blond hair fell down a little over her shoulders, and she met Fredrik's gaze with a smile and determined ice-blue eyes when they met.

He explained briefly that they needed to ask a few questions due to an incident earlier in the day, and at Sara's suggestion they sat down at the kitchen table.

She turned on the light over the table. The kitchen was dark, even though it was still completely daylight. It was presumably more pleasant in the mornings when the sunlight shone in through the crowns of the trees outside.

"You're on sick leave," said Fredrik. "Is this the first day?"

"Yes. I started feeling poorly last night."

"In what way?" he asked.

"What do you mean? Did the insurance company send you?"

Stina smiled a little provocatively at Fredrik.

"No," he answered. "Unless we discover some serious insurance fraud we aren't going to coordinate our information with them."

Sara gave him a look. Perhaps he had let himself be too sarcastic in his response. He made a more correct addition.

"No, we haven't been sent out by the insurance company."

The smile disappeared from Stina's lips. She seemed to have liked the first answer better.

"I felt cold, I had pain in my joints. Typical flu symptoms, so I called my boss last evening."

"Have you been at home in the apartment the whole day?"

"Yes."

Stina's eyes moved between Fredrik and Sara before she continued.

"Why are you asking me this? I don't really understand."

"If we ask our questions first, then perhaps we can answer yours later," said Fredrik.

Stina raised her eyebrows and gave a barely perceptible nod.

"If that's what you say."

Fredrik had noticed a faint odor of cat pee when he came into the hall. Now he seemed to see a pair of yellow eyes gleaming under the couch in the living room.

"What were you doing between eleven thirty and twelve thirty today?" he asked.

"I was here," Stina answered, as if she thought he was a bit dense.

"And doing what?"

"I was reading."

She made a gesture toward a four-inch-high pile of newspapers and magazines. In the middle of the pile the edge of a book peeked out. Fredrik had noticed several piles of books and newspapers around the apartment.

"Did you read anything in particular?" asked Fredrik.

"No, I read the local paper and browsed in a few magazines. I got up really late."

"I see, when was that?"

"Nine thirty."

"And you sat here at the table?" he asked. "Between eleven thirty and twelve thirty, I mean."

"Yes," Stina answered, and with each question she got a more and more confounded expression.

"Are there any neighbors in the building or in the buildings nearby who can confirm that you've been at home here today? Someone who may have seen you?"

"Don't think so," said Stina Hansson. "But you can always ask. But can't you at least tell me what this is about?"

"These are routine questions," said Sara Oskarsson. "We're questioning a number of people here in the area."

"I see."

Stina Hansson did not look convinced.

"Do you know Henrik Kjellander?" asked Sara.

There was silence for a moment. Stina leaned against the back of the chair.

"Yes," she said lingeringly. "Or knew, at least. We went to the same school here in Fårösund. And one year at Säve."

"You had a relationship? Is that correct?" asked Sara when Stina did not continue.

Stina laughed.

"Good Lord," she sighed. "Yes, we did. But that was ages ago. I must have been nineteen or twenty and had just moved to Stockholm."

The initial image of a healthy young woman was somewhat changed when Fredrik had been sitting across from her at the table for a while. For some reason he got a feeling that Stina Hansson did not go out much, or that in any event she kept to herself. He was not sure whether it was the dry skin, the piles of books, the cat odor, the complete seasons of *Friends* on the bookshelf that made him think that, or whether it was something completely different.

"Did you live together?" Sara continued the questioning.

"Yes, but only a few months. It was more for practical reasons. I had nowhere to stay for a while."

"How long did the relationship last?"

"A year, approximately."

"Who ended it?"

"He did. Henrik."

The name sounded so domestic in her mouth, as if she was talking about someone close to her, thought Fredrik.

"Did you live with him then?" asked Sara.

"Yes, but I had just gotten a student apartment. Sometimes I wonder if he waited to break up until I had somewhere to live. To be nice." Stina laughed lightly and looked at Sara with clear, unperturbed eyes. "Are you really interested in my relationship with Henrik Kjellander fifteen years ago?"

Sometimes I wonder, thought Fredrik.

They heard the ferry departing. The metallic scraping from the ramp, the diesel engines picking up speed. It was five thirty.

"We are interested in Henrik Kjellander and everything that concerns him," said Fredrik. "He is not suspected of anything, but for various reasons that we can't go into right now this may be important."

Stina looked at him with a curl on her upper lip.

"I guess I'll have to be content with that," she said.

"I guess you will, for the time being."

It would probably not be long before the village gossip reached her, or she read about it in the newspaper.

Sara Oskarsson continued to probe into Stina Hansson's relationship with Henrik. As they had already understood from the phone call with Henrik, she had taken it very hard when he broke up with her.

"In some way I got the idea that it had nothing to do with me as an individual," she said, stroking her fingers over her cheek. "Instead it was that I didn't fit into his life because I came from Fårösund."

"But Henrik is from here, too, isn't he?"

"Exactly," said Stina with a crooked smile. "But he wanted to get away. Not only away from Fårösund and Gotland. He wanted to become a different person: successful photographer, someone who moved out in the world among significant, glamorous people. Something like that. Then he happened to meet me. I think he really liked me, got attached to me, but then it was like he suddenly thought that he was stuck in the past, in Gotland—through me. I became part of what stuck firmly to him and that he had to get rid of in order to get where he wanted. I had a hard time letting go. I was probably pretty annoying. But that was because I thought it was such a shame. I don't really think he was tired of me, it was that other stuff that got in the way."

She fell silent and looked out into the dark garden. Two pale roses were seen on her cheek. She had spoken calmly and collectedly, but it was still a revealing harangue to be about something that had ended fifteen years ago.

Fredrik wondered whether there really could be something in what Stina had said. Three years later Henrik met a waitress and started a family with her. Not exactly glamorous.

"And now he's back. It did come as a surprise," said Stina. "Especially that he chose Fårö."

"What do you mean by that?" said Sara.

"I think it's extremely strange after everything that happened with his family. Everyone probably thinks that."

"How did you react to the fact that he was back here?" said Fredrik. "Besides being surprised."

"Isn't that enough?" she answered in a joking tone.

"If I were to put it a little more clearly," said Fredrik, "how did you feel about running into him here in Fårösund?"

Stina's eyes wandered off; she thought before she answered.

"Of course it felt a little strange after not having seen him for years, but . . . Well, I don't know what I should say. It wasn't really a big problem. I was more curious about what made him change his mind."

"Did you stop your car outside the Fårösund school on Monday morning?"

Stina looked in amazement at Fredrik. She waited to answer.

"Yes . . ."

"What were you doing there?"

"Is she the one who said that? Malin?"

Fredrik sat quietly, waiting for an answer to his question.

Stina sighed.

"I caught sight of the car when I was on my way to work. Their red Mercedes SUV. They're the only ones who have a car like that here, so . . . It was far away on Strandvägen. I suddenly had the desire to talk with Henrik, I thought it was him who . . ."

She stroked her hand across her cheek again, slowly and meditatively, stopped with the nail of her middle finger on a flake of skin.

"When I turned up from Strandvägen the car was parked outside the day care. I stopped a short way from there and got out and waited."

"Why didn't you stop next to Henrik's car if you wanted to talk with him?" said Fredrik.

"I don't really know."

"What happened then?"

"Yes, then she came out. For some idiotic reason it's like I took it for granted that it was Henrik in the car. I was at a total loss. I just stood there staring for a long time before I thought of getting in the car again. I assume it seemed strange. Did she say that? That I'm strange in some way?"

Fredrik ignored the question.

"What was it you wanted to talk about with Henrik when you decided to follow the car?"

"I don't remember."

"You don't remember? That sounds strange, I think. If you took
the trouble to follow him in order to talk with him, there must have
been something you wanted to say, right?"

Stina Hansson squirmed worriedly in the chair and looked out
through the window.

"I don't remember," she repeated.

30.

Malin hung up the phone. Her sister had made up her mind at once
when Malin told her what had happened. She would come down and
stay at least until Henrik was back from his trip.

Malin looked out toward the big ancient sundial that was squeezed
between the treetops and a dramatic cloud formation to the west. The
apples shone green and red in the warm glow and the pears had started
to turn yellow. It was time to harvest. It surprised her that they could
grow at all there in the stony ground.

Far away Kalbjerga's metal roofs glistened above the pines. The
family on the farm and Ann-Katrin and Bengt were their only neighbors. Then nothing. Just forest and meager meadows with bleating
sheep. When the sun went down they were alone in the dark.

That thought was easier to bear since Maria said that she would
come.

Everything that was whirling around in her head quieted down
enough that she could think. She and Maria had always been close.

From the very start it was mostly Malin who pitched in and took care of her little sister. But with every year that passed the three years between them meant less and less. Not even when Malin was fifteen or sixteen and should have thought it was awkward to have a little sister hanging at her heels did she push her away. That probably made Maria a little precocious, but also secure and self-confident. Confidence that Malin could lean against when she needed it.

Maria was the only one who had been on Malin's side when she quit medical studies to open a café instead. Stubbornly, she had wrangled with Mother and their big brother, Staffan, who thought she was an idiot. Say no to becoming a doctor. How stupid can you be? She had probably never completely recovered from those quarrels. *Superficial* and *bourgeois,* Maria's words echoed in the dining room during the family's Sunday dinners.

Mother and Staffan had become a little more conciliatory when they saw that things were going well for her, anyway. The third year with Kakan she had received an award from the *Entertainment Guide.*

Maria would arrive on the eleven o'clock boat tomorrow. She would be on Fårö before four o'clock. Malin counted the minutes. It would feel so nice to have someone there who understood her one hundred percent and who made her feel safe.

She thought about Stina Hansson. As if it was not already bad enough as it was, perhaps this woman who carried off Ellen in her car had some sort of connection to Henrik. Had even had a relationship with him. Fifteen years ago, to be sure, but only three years before he met her. Malin had a hard time believing it was true. That he could have slept with that woman. Whispered that he loved her. Or maybe he hadn't done just that. She hoped it wasn't the case.

When Henrik had told about her it was as if she was suddenly there in their home. Moved in with them. Stina Hansson. Why hadn't he said that he had seen her? Didn't you do that? Would she have done that herself? She thought so anyway.

Maria had dismissed all such thoughts. Why should he have said anything about it, an old ex from when he was twenty? Knock it off. Malin had Googled Stina Hansson. She wanted to see what she looked like. But she was nowhere. No Facebook page, no sports club, nothing. The slender figure with the light long hair, jeans, and military-green jacket who stood staring at her outside the school had etched herself in her memory. But the image was incomplete. The piercing, cold eyes continued to stare at her from a face that was no more than a light speck of skin.

Henrik must have pictures of her. Without a doubt. But Malin was reluctant to ask him. She was not sure she wanted to see Stina Hansson smiling lovingly at the man behind the camera.

31.

Simon swore at a setback in the game and yelled out a comment via Skype to a classmate who was sitting at home with his computer taking part in D-Day, or was it the Ardennes offensive? Fredrik had learned to interpret the sounds that penetrated the closed door to the boy's room. He had also realized that Simon had quietly learned to set the router so that his own computer was prioritized. With both Web games and Skype with images it ate up all the bandwidth. Fredrik's and Ninni's computers just sat and churned when they tried to get on the Internet.

He knocked on the door and heard a mumbled yes between the considerably more emotionally charged shrieks.

Simon gave him a quick look over his shoulder as he came into the room.

"How's it going?" asked Fredrik.

"Justfinehowaboutyou," mumbled Simon in a single long, hard-to-decipher string of words.

"It's fine," said Fredrik. "How are things at school? Have you gotten started for real?"

"Yes."

Simon tossed a hand grenade, changed weapons, and advanced, quickly shooting four Germans who were trying to hide behind a burned-out tank.

"You don't have any homework you have to do?"

"We have a theme week."

"So you don't have any homework then?"

"No!" shouted Simon as a red half-circle became visible on the screen.

He had been hit, lost power. When the circle was complete you were dead. Now it turned pale instead.

"You didn't answer," said Fredrik.

"No. Or yes, but I've done it."

"So what's the theme?" Fredrik asked.

"Marie Curie," said Simon.

"That sounds like a narrow theme."

"No, but women in history, that is. I'm working on Marie Curie."

Simon sounded irritated. He hammered on the keyboard. Fredrik could not say for sure whether he was irritated at being disturbed or because the game was going poorly.

"Speak up if you need any help."

His dreary questions about homework were not much to offer compared with defending Bastogne. But Fredrik had a strong feeling that he would have no chance against the game whatever he had to offer.

"Listen," he said. "I have to get on the Internet. Can you think about taking a break?"

Simon took a deep breath, but held back the sigh.

"Sure," he said, sounding surprisingly cooperative. "Just five minutes."

* * *

It took more like fifteen minutes, but finally Fredrik managed to capture a little space on the family broadband. "Malin's Table," which was under Coop's home page, showed Malin Andersson in the kitchen at home in Kalbjerga. She stood smiling behind a small marble table that was loaded with vegetables and fruit, carefully arranged with a metal can of Greek olive oil. On the kitchen counter in the background a large loaf of bread and a couple bottles of red wine could be seen.

Fredrik had been to the site before, but only in haste to get a sense of what Malin did. Now he studied it more carefully. He clicked through the registry of recipes. Many were simplified variations on familiar dishes, primarily from French and Italian cuisine, mixed in with some Swedish home cooking.

Fredrik clicked through the blog. He was surprised when he saw that the most recent entry had been made only a few hours before. It was about an Asian cucumber preserve, an obvious side dish for every conceivable Asian entrée, but which could also add a surprising zest to moose steak with cream gravy and lingonberry jam. The entry was brief, but it was still hard to understand how she managed to sit and blog about cucumber after what had happened earlier today. He guessed that a professional blogger had an archive of more or less general entries that could be tossed in if you were short on time. Or even when your daughter was kidnapped.

He heard steps behind him. Then Ninni was standing there resting her hands lightly on his shoulders.

"Are you planning dinner for tomorrow?" she asked.

The thought of lying flew momentarily through his head, but then he said what it was.

"No, it's work. It's connected to the girl who was taken away."

He pointed at the screen.

"This is the mother's blog."

He leaned his head back and looked up at Ninni.

"I probably shouldn't be sitting with this now, but . . ."

Ninni looked skeptical.

"But it's not impossible that I'll find something good," he continued. "There's quite a bit here."

"Okay," she said with a smile, stroking him across the neck. "Just don't sit there too long."

He heard her steps disappear out into the living room and tried to ignore the guilty conscience that made itself known like a little weight between his shoulder blades.

Dutifully, he selected desserts in the menu, clicked around at random, but soon settled on pear pie with gorgonzola on the side. Malin Andersson suggested, no, almost required that you should have a glass of the strong Portuguese wine Setúbal with it. That didn't sound bad. He downloaded the recipe and went back to the blog.

Fredrik started by looking at the entries from last spring, the months before the house was rented out. He hoped to find something provocative, a critical statement about a colleague, a panning of a restaurant, anything at all that might arouse bad blood in a twisted mind. But Malin's entries were completely uncontroversial and the little criticism that was presented was rather modest and aimed at vague groups such as "meat producers" or "the global food industry."

The comments he read extra carefully. In the undergrowth a lunatic or two might show up. There were a couple of comments that were a bit sharp, that maintained that Malin ought to embark on a completely different career. Another stated bitterly that of course it was more important to be good-looking than a good cook. But none of them exactly made any warning bells ring.

He went on to the summer and quickly skimmed through the entries of the past few months. Besides those that were about food there were a number of comments about more personal matters. Who had been to dinner at Malin and Henrik's, where they had partaken of Malin's magnificent picnic basket, and what restaurants they had been to. Sometimes there were even entries about things they would do. Restaurant visits she looked forward to, that she would look for truffle oil at some place in Visby, and so on. And the whole time Malin's broad smile in the border at the top of the page.

After Saturday the comments about personal matters ceased. No places, times, or names. Wise, he thought. Until then the blog had been a gold mine for anyone who wanted to keep track of Malin Andersson.

Ninni was sitting slumped on the couch in front of the evening's reality show. Fredrik was certain that she was deeply dependent on those programs. Perhaps she was, too. But she was not really interested in how they turned out, who won or was voted out. It was a few minutes of emotional involvement completely without demands on any deeper thoughts. And that was exactly the way she wanted it. She could not rule out that it might work just as well with a CD of birds twittering and a calm voice saying things like "Your whole body feels heavy. You are completely relaxed. You see a beautiful summer meadow. You feel calm and harmonious."

She wished that Fredrik could do the same. Not necessarily watch reality shows or listen to hypnotic voices, but that he could let go of work when he came home. She understood that it was hard. Someone carried off a little girl and it was his mission to find out who. That was not something that was easy to simply turn off at a certain time of day. But still. He was not alone in that and the girl had come back. And Ninni was certain that no one had asked him to spend the evening snooping through the mother's blog.

She reached for the remote control and turned off the TV. The program did not seem to have any effect this evening. It did not clear away her thoughts the way it usually did.

Two years since the accident. The first year had been heavy, the second easy. All her apprehensions had come to naught. Step by step their life had returned to normal. Perhaps that was just what weighed her down. That they were back in the everyday.

For a long time she had been happy simply because the catastrophe she had prepared herself for had not arrived. When she went up to the hospital the first time and saw Fredrik lying there motionless with an empty gaze she had been completely convinced that she would not cope with it. She had returned to Gotland, driven around blindly in the car, wept and screamed, thrown things around her. She had thought about their children, who would have a dad but still be fatherless, she had tried to imagine needing to spoon-feed a grown man with purées like baby food and listen to mentally incapacitated babbling and try to convince herself that she loved him.

Not always such lovely thoughts, but she had not escaped them. She had not tried to pretend, either, that she was better than she really was. In any respect, not to herself. When she realized that it would not be as bad as in her fantasies everything got easier. But the kind of musings that used to take up much of her time—how much did she really like her job at the Högby School, would she even keep living on Gotland when Simon, too, had graduated from high school and perhaps left the island to study on the mainland—there was no room for at all. Her thoughts circled around whether Fredrik would be completely restored or only almost. If he would be able to work as a police officer again. If they would ever have a sex life again. If he could. If she would want to.

Now all that was sufficiently far back in time so that she could not automatically feel happy that it hadn't turned out that way. They were sleeping with each other again. He could. She wanted to. It was perhaps not the world's best sex life, but had it always been before the accident? Hardly.

They had been well on their way to healing again after the separation when the accident happened, but she was not certain that they were completely done. The accident had come as an interruption. It was only now that she felt that they could pick up the thread again in earnest, continue where they had been.

When she read about similar incidents in a magazine, people who managed by the skin of their teeth, they always sounded as if they had been changed forever, became better people, learned to accept things and be grateful for life. Every second of it. Ninni did not recognize her-self in those stories. A year ago perhaps she felt that way, she could go along with that, but no longer. Sooner or later the old normal life al-ways caught up with you.

32.

Malin looked at the blond woman through the window opening, then at her daughter. Ellen was standing on a stool to be able to see prop-erly. They were at the far back of the police station's assembly hall that happened to be dubbed FÅRÖ. Sara Oskarsson had shown them past the rows of chairs and narrow tables up to the short wall and the burgundy-red drapery that she had just pulled back.

On the other side of the window six women were standing. They were of approximately the same height and figure. Two of them were blond, two reddish-blond, one medium blond, and one red-haired. One of the two blondes was Stina Hansson.

There was no doubt that this was the woman who stood and stared at Malin outside the school that morning. There was no doubt, either, that she was blond. Not the least bit reddish-blond. So she must have been mistaken.

Malin looked at the blonde again. The blonde. It was easier to think of her that way than as Stina. A hair color kept her at a proper distance.

Malin observed her and thought she was smiling in a strange way as she looked right at Ellen, almost in a kind of mutual understanding. Malin knew that this was not possible. The other side of the glass was a mirror. The blonde could not see them. Not Ellen, not her or anyone else. Sara Oskarsson had explained that very carefully before she pulled back the drapery.

And yet. Malin was certain that something was going on between them. Not mutual understanding perhaps, but more like a kind of contact. This silent communication through the glass frightened Ellen into silence, reminded her of an agreement that had been made in the car. Words that Ellen never mentioned, just because it was part of the agreement not to mention them. You may never say that you recognize me. I'll only let you go if you promise that.

That was nonsense of course. Fantasies. And yet. It drove her to madness that she could not know for certain what had happened in that car. What had been said. What if Ellen had been threatened? Frightened into silence. Perhaps she had given them a completely false image of what had happened because she didn't dare do otherwise.

"Think about it," said Sara Oskarsson. "We have lots of time."

Ellen turned around and looked with uncertain, pleading eyes at Malin. She smiled at Ellen and it hurt inside when she realized that she could not help her. Was not allowed to. Thought about what she had said earlier: Sometimes reddish-blond hair almost looks like blond, you can actually think that it's blond. . . . Perhaps she had confused her with that. Perhaps she had ruined everything. Perhaps Ellen recognized her, but was uncertain because Malin was always talking about hair color. Should she say something to Sara?

She wondered what was going on in Ellen's head right now. What did she see in the blonde's eyes? She could see a faint reflection of Ellen's eyes in the glass in front of them, see them moving jerkily between the six individuals.

She regretted going along with this. She had wanted it, actually pushed for it when Sara Oskarsson brought it up as a possibility. She had been careful to point out that doing the confrontation was completely voluntary.

Ellen whispered something she could not make out. Sara Oskarsson leaned down.

"What did you say?"

"I don't know," whispered Ellen.

Malin could hear in her voice that tears were not far away.

"It doesn't matter," said Sara to Ellen. "If you don't recognize any of them that's fine. Then just say that. You don't need to feel the slightest bit compelled to recognize anyone. Do you understand that?"

Ellen looked at Sara, but did not answer. She stood a long time completely silently, then she quickly looked at the six women.

"Ellen," said Sara gently. "When you say you don't know, do you mean that you don't know for sure, or do you mean that none of them are the woman you rode with in the car?"

"I don't know, I don't know," she sobbed, extending her arms toward Malin.

Malin crouched down and put her arms around her. She hated herself for this. Hated herself because she hadn't thought about it and said no. Good Lord, weren't there other ways? Couldn't they check whether Ellen's DNA was on the passenger seat in Stina Hansson's car? That must be easy as pie these days. She would call them later and ask. Now she didn't want to say anything. Not while Ellen was there.

She raised her eyes toward the window and looked at the blonde one last time before Sara Oskarsson pulled the drape.

33.

They timed the ferry departure wrong, would have to wait for more than twenty minutes. But the boat from Nynäshamn came when it did, there was not much to do.

Maria had brought presents with her for the children, which she gave to them as soon as they got in the car. A picture book for Axel and a diary for Ellen. *You can already write so I thought maybe you want to try to write a diary. I started doing that when I was your age.*

Oh well, Malin thought, that was probably not really true, but she didn't say anything. Their relationship was free of annoying jabs and status markers. She had never felt that she needed to compete with her sister. It was almost strange. Many of Malin's friends could harp on their siblings with sternly squinting eyes. There seemed to be constant elbowing for parental attention far into adult age. Not to mention tear-filled battles about some old lopsided oak table the parents tried to give away with the best of intentions.

"I'm so happy you're here," she said to Maria while they sat and waited in the stuffy car.

She undid her seat belt and rolled down the window. It was quiet and peaceful at the ferry landing, not a person was in sight. Malin's Honda was the only car in front of the boom. The ferry had not even left Broa yet and in the sound barely a ripple was seen on the surface of the water.

Maria leaned over to her and whispered, "Ellen seems to be doing fine."

Malin glanced at her daughter in the backseat. She was reading Axel's book while he drew stick figures in Ellen's new diary.

"Yes," she whispered back. "I don't think she really understood what happened. And that's probably just as well."

Maria nodded in agreement.

"But I don't know," she added.

Maria fanned herself with her hand.

"Shall we get out a minute?" Malin asked. "It's really hot."

They opened the doors and got out of the car, asked whether the children wanted to come with, but they just shook their heads. During the summer season the line to the ferry was a given occasion to beg for ice cream or a piece of candy, but this late in August the kiosk and souvenir shops in the old fishing sheds were closed up. They left the car doors open anyway so that Axel and Ellen got a little breeze.

"I was hoping for a dip, but that doesn't look promising," said Maria, pointing across the sound.

The sun was broiling over the main island, the traffic authority's flag was hanging limply alongside the Swedish flag, but over Fårö a low, blue-gray bank of clouds had settled like a kind of gloomy whipped cream over a scanty cake bottom.

"I think it will blow over. It's already starting to break up over there in the east," said Malin, pointing.

Maria laughed loudly and suddenly bowed. "Two years out here and you're already a weatherman." She stroked Malin over her shoulders, down along her arm, and kissed her on the cheek.

"Fortune-teller," Malin corrected her. "I have actually learned a thing or two. You have no choice when you live on a little island in the middle of nowhere. I think there may be swimming."

"I hope you're right."

The ferry came pulsating across the sound, and a short while later they were on board. The children had been extremely patient where the ferry was concerned. It had not been that way at first. The children and Malin sat fidgeting in the car and thought it was almost the end of the world to have to waste all that time in front of a boom on the dreary end of a pier. Now it was part of their lives, no stranger than waiting at the subway, a time when you could browse through the newspaper or write a shopping list. Besides, she had gotten good at keeping track of the departures.

They came home to Kalbjerga. Maria threw herself around Henrik's neck as usual. They had always liked each other. She thought Henrik was a keeper and Malin was happy that she did. Because she liked her sister so much it would have been a disaster if she hadn't gotten along well with her husband.

Maria got the whole sitting room to herself. It mostly stood empty during the summer. As winter approached it might get a little cold down in the living room. Then they moved the TV up to the sitting room and left it there until Easter.

Just as Malin had predicted, soon the dreary cloud cover disappeared. They packed into the car again, without Henrik, who had to get ready for his trip, and bumped down to the beach.

"I love this place," said Maria when she was standing before the glistening, deserted bay in a pair of borrowed flip-flops.

"Me, too," said Malin.

Malin often rode her bicycle down there, alone or with the kids, sat down at the water's edge, and looked out over the sea. After a few minutes in the stillness and with the meditative lapping of the waves in her ears, it was easy to get the feeling that you were the only person in the whole world. But it was not frightening like the feeling of being abandoned in the dark, far from civilization and the nearest neighbor. This was something completely different. Here there was no civilization. On a sunny, pleasant day like this, she was the first human. It was just her, the sun, the sea, and perhaps God. There was no time. Everything was eternal.

On a cloudy, gray, windy day, on the other hand, the stony beaches were gloomy and hard, as if burned to ash, the sea dark and threatening. A low-pressure system turned the pages from the creation story to the Book of Revelations from one day to the next. Then she was the last person on Earth, eternity was over, and she got a heavy lump in her throat from thinking about it. Soon there would only be stone, ice, and darkness left. No sun. No life. No God. But the landscape was still beautiful.

She looked at Maria. They were so ridiculously alike. It was even more noticeable when they changed to swimming suits. Their bodies were similar, they were almost the same height, less than an inch apart, to Maria's advantage. Their eyes were frighteningly identical, Henrik liked to say. Malin's face was a touch rounder. She did not have Maria's defined cheekbones, which she thought gave Maria's eyes an extra speck of sharpness. Then Henrik could say what he wanted. What set them apart the most was their hair color. Maria's medium blond and her own dark brown, almost black.

They followed the children down to the water's edge. Maria kicked off her flip-flops and put one foot down in the water.

"It's really warm," she panted.

Malin stayed with the children in the shallows while Maria waded out among the stones, threw herself headfirst into the water, and swam a couple of quick strokes. Ellen and Axel splashed water on each other, but it was warm enough that it would be fun. Malin sat down on the bottom with the water to her navel and closed her eyes. She heard the sound of the waves, saw the glistening of the sun right through her eyelids, and felt the aroma of suntan lotion that was not there. Her whole body relaxed. All that bad stuff would blow over. Whoever left the pictures and picked Ellen up outside the school must realize that it was over now. The police were involved, all of north Gotland was keeping their eyes open for the blond kidnapper in the white car.

Maria came back into the shallows with water splashing around her legs. Malin opened her eyes when Maria sank down beside her.

"Do you want to swim a little?" she asked, brushing back wet strands of hair from her face.

"Later maybe," Malin replied.

"It's Sunday that Henrik leaves, right?"

"Yes."

Malin leaned her head against her knees and looked at her sister. Small drops of water were glistening in her eyelashes.

"I don't get that he can go now," said Malin, but just as she said it she felt that it no longer disturbed her as much.

"But knock it off, of course he has to go," said Maria. "You've complained yourself about how tight money is for you."

"Sure, but—"

"And I'm here. You can't start letting that lunatic control your lives. Then she's won. Right?"

"Yes. You're right."

Maria was with them now. Nothing could happen.

34

A message from Eva Karlén popped up when Fredrik logged onto the computer. "IP number Fårö." That was it.

Couldn't she have written what she had come up with? He reached for the phone.

"Eva Karlén, Visby police," she answered, in other words not bothering to see where the call was coming from.

"Hi, it's Fredrik," he said. "I saw that you came up with something."

"Yes," she said. "The hardest part was getting them to give out the information."

He heard that she was moving around while she was talking to him. She usually worked with a headset to avoid interruptions when the phone rang.

"Preferably you should have a paper from the intelligence service saying that the security of the realm is threatened."

"Did you get one?" he asked with amusement.

"No, but they finally gave in. Wait, let's see here, then you'll get the exact address."

There was a short pause. He could sense Eva's breathing.

"Uppsala," she said.

It was silent again for a while.

"The IP number belongs to a computer at the Uppsala public library, the main library on Svartbäcksgatan 17, in the middle of town."

"Staff computer or public computer?" asked Fredrik.

"Nice and easy, then you'll get everything you need."

"Okay, sorry, I'm listening."

"It was a public computer. I assume that you want me to call the Uppsala public library and ask whether any of the librarians made any particular observations around the public computers at one forty-five on the fourth of June?"

"It sounds like you've already done that."

"Yes. They thought I was completely crazy."

"No results, in other words?"

"No."

"So someone books the house on Fårö from a computer in Uppsala and provides a false address in Gothenburg," he reasoned. "There goes the local idea."

"It may, of course, be someone who lived in Gothenburg previously," said Eva. "Someone who moved to Uppsala."

"That's true," he admitted.

Fredrik was not a frequent borrower, or user it must be called nowadays, but he recollected a visit to the Älmedal library during the spring. He had sat down at an available computer on the upper level to quickly Google something, but the computer had been blocked.

"Don't you have to schedule a computer if you're going to do something other than search in the catalog?"

There was no cheering from the other end, but he understood the pause for thinking as a kind of acknowledgment.

"I'll check that. With a little luck we'll have a list of everyone who sat at a computer at Uppsala public library at quarter to two on the fourth of June."

35

Maria paid no attention that Malin's hand signaled stop at the edge of the wineglass, but instead filled it almost to the brim.

Malin had tried to teach her numerous times that you did not fill a wineglass more than a third, but it never stuck. The same with the cheese, which should come before dessert. Maria had already stopped listening when Malin tried to explain that it had nothing at all to do with snobbery, but instead was about getting the most possible out of the taste. That was an aspect of Maria that did actually irritate Malin. Not that she poured too much wine in the glasses, but that she dismissed Malin's professional knowledge as uninteresting rules of etiquette. On the other hand she always listened when it really counted, like now, so she could live with the rest.

Henrik had left at eight o'clock that morning to fly to Arlanda and then on to Barcelona. Only now when she and Maria were alone in the house and the children had gone to bed did she feel that she could talk freely about her worry and about everything that had happened. In particular, it was only now that she could let loose about Stina Hansson. She knew what Henrik would have thought and maybe he was right. It was probably silly of her to dwell on an old girlfriend and that he saw her in Fårösund without saying anything, but somehow she had to get that out of her mind. Otherwise it would stay there and gnaw at her, bringing out jealousy and uncertainty.

Maria also thought her reaction was a little exaggerated, but she listened with an expression that was anything but dismissive. More like curious.

"I'm sure that Henrik has pictures of her somewhere. At first I thought I didn't want to see them, but I think I have to look for them. Otherwise I can't stop thinking about it."

"Are you sure that's a good idea?"

"No," Malin said honestly.

Maria almost laughed right into her wineglass, but held back at the last moment.

"I think I have to."

"But what if you regret it?"

Malin looked at her. It was not like Maria to be so cautious.

"I thought that maybe it would be awkward," said Maria when she saw the look.

"Presumably."

Malin got up suddenly. "And you're going to help."

"Now?"

"Yes."

"If you say so."

Maria removed her feet from the footrest of the couch and turned toward the study.

"Does he keep them in there?"

She set down her wineglass.

"No. All the negative binders are in a cabinet up in the sitting room. It's been years since he went over to digital."

Malin took a couple of steps in the direction of the stairs.

"Come now."

Maria got up and went with her. After only two days, it was as if Maria had taken over the entire large sitting room. Some of her clothes were hanging up here and there where it was possible to hang them, others were tossed over the backs of chairs or wedged into shelves. When Malin saw her sister's clothes she realized how much her own had changed during the past two years. She dressed simpler, more practical. It was unavoidable, it crept up on you whether you wanted it to or not when you lived the way she did. If Maria was pop, Malin had become more conventional.

On the table in front of the window, Maria's computer was parked between two unstable piles of papers. She had worked a couple of hours both yesterday and today. That was how it was possible for her to come rushing to Malin's without notice and with no planned trip home.

Entrepreneurship they had in common, but while Malin kept to food, Maria jumped from one thing to another. She had started as a sales and marketing person at a small record company, then studied to be a real estate agent, started her own company, but shut down the business after a failed attempt to sell it. Now she was selling furniture and home décor items on the Internet. None of her businesses had made her rich, but she paid the rent and seemed to have a lot of fun. Just like Malin, in other words.

"Here," said Malin.

She put her hand on the heavy oxide-green cabinet that dominated the one long wall. Along the worn edges an older reddish-brown layer of paint was visible.

"He has thousands of old negatives, tens of thousands. There's a lot to search through."

"Okay," said Maria.

Malin turned the key and opened the doors to the upper part of the cabinet. At the very top was a pile of photo paper cartons that she knew contained selected copies of Henrik's best and most noteworthy pictures. The kind that had been displayed and which appeared in newspapers now and then in various retrospective contexts. The rest of the shelves were full of binders.

Maria eyeballed the spines.

"Here there doesn't appear to be anything before '97," she said.

"Then it's probably down there," said Malin.

Malin quickly closed the upper cabinet doors, leaned down, and opened the lower ones. She crouched down in front of the binders.

"It must be '93 or '94?" she said, running her eyes over the spines.

Maria sat down beside her.

A tingling sensation made itself known right above her navel. It was a strange mixture of discomfort and curiosity that drove her forward, drawing her eyes toward the spines of the binders marked '93 and '94 followed by a numerical code that presumably were the numbers of the negatives.

"If I start with '93, you can go backward from '94," she said, pulling out the first of the nineteen binders.

She felt how the tingling above her navel almost became painful as she opened it. The acid-free negative pockets rustled with a brittle sound.

"There are contact sheets and everything," said Maria. "I thought it would only be negatives."

Malin's gaze swept quickly over the thirty-six images on the contact sheet before she turned to the next one. The first ten or fifteen rolls were product images that she could quickly browse past, then came almost half a binder of photo models in studios, Henrik called them catalog images, but after that finally were some that seemed more personal. Party pictures, a sheet from an outdoor concert, then something that must be Paris, two women and a man who kept recurring, but none of them could be Stina Hansson.

"Here," Maria exclaimed. "Is this her?"

She handed the binder over to Malin. A light-haired woman about twenty assumed various poses at a café table. It did not seem to be a job, more like play. But it was not Stina Hansson.

Malin realized that she had no idea what Stina Hansson looked like fifteen years ago. Longer or shorter hair? Made-up in a completely different way? But considering that she still looked so young, she ought to be quite similar in the pictures.

"That woman has a much narrower face. And smaller mouth," she said, thinking about the face she had observed through the mirror glass at the police station.

Maria took back the binder and continued to browse. Malin took out the next binder and opened it. The last square on the contact sheet depicted a disheveled little head between two lit candles on a kitchen table. She recognized her at once and the tingling in her belly was transformed to a worried flutter in her chest. Stina Hansson smiled broadly at the camera and before her on the table an ample breakfast was spread out. She recognized everything: the scrambled eggs, the crisply fried pieces of bacon, the oven-baked cocktail tomatoes, the glass pitcher of grapefruit juice, the pastrami, the Appenzeller, the neatly arranged slices of avocado and cucumber, and of course the bread from the Riddar bakery and the cappuccino cups. That was exactly how Henrik used to set the table on her birthdays, but sometimes also on a normal Saturday or Sunday morning just to surprise her. Since they'd had kids it didn't happen as often, but at least a couple times a year he arranged it.

She could see no cake or any packages on the table, so perhaps it wasn't Stina's birthday. Unless they were on the part of the table that wasn't visible in the picture.

The next roll no doubt contained more pictures from the same occasion, but she dragged her index finger hesitantly along the edge of the contact sheet. Did she really want to see more? She turned the page. As expected there were more pictures from the cozy breakfast. Still no packages, so presumably it was not a birthday. She browsed ahead. And there . . . Malin stared down at the contact sheet, her body suddenly completely weak.

"Maria," she said and surprised herself by how strange her voice sounded.

Maria leaned over the binder.

"But . . . What is this? Is that her?"

"Yes."

"Holy shit," said Maria, her eyes nailed to the open binder.

Malin cleared her throat.

"Okay, maybe that was a little thick," said Maria.

It was Stina Hansson, a whole contact sheet of Stina Hansson. On the first row of pictures she was sitting in an open car, some kind of SUV. She had pulled up her shirt to right below her chin and displayed a pair of perfect, drop-dead gorgeous breasts to the camera.

Malin looked at her sister. Maria shrugged her shoulders with a wry smile.

The rest of the pictures were taken indoors, presumably at Stina Hansson's home. Malin did not recognize any of the furniture. They all depicted Stina Hansson in various degrees of undress. She was sitting on a couch with bare torso, posing extremely nineteen-fifties-ish, straight-backed and with her legs close together. On another she was lying completely naked on a shaggy sheepskin in a more daring pose. On the last pictures she had stretched out on her back on the floor with a streak of sunshine like a ribbon diagonally across her body. Her right hand was placed far down on her stomach and the tips of her fingers were touching her pubic hair.

The pictures were not exactly pornographic, they were too proper for that, but there was a tendency in that direction, a tendency that was the photographer's while the model made cautious resistance.

Malin set aside the binder and sank down on the floor, weak and nauseated. From the corner of her eye she saw Maria pull it to her and browse to the next sheet.

"It's only that one."

Malin did not answer.

"Okay," said Maria. "What do you say?"

Malin stared toward the open cabinet, but the only thing she saw were Stina Hansson's breasts. And the gesture, the exposing gesture, the arms that seemed to have made the decision to pull the shirt up in front of the camera.

It was fifteen years ago. Three years before she herself came into the picture. Henrik was a photographer. He photographed women. It was part of his job. But this was not work. She thought about the picture that had been published in *Gotlands Allehanda*, the one that was hanging on the wall down in the study. Henrik's hand around the stick-thin photo model who concealed her bare breasts behind a thin, weak arm. The almost nonexistent underpants.

"Has he . . . has he photographed you like that?" asked Maria.

Malin shook her head.

"Are you sure?"

"Yes, what the hell do you think?" said Malin sharply.

"Sorry. I was just asking."

Malin did not wish that Henrik had asked to photograph her naked. Truly not. Still she suddenly felt so jealous that her thoughts became completely cloudy. She wished she had avoided seeing those pictures. Damn. She knew she would regret it. She should have listened to Maria. She had been afraid of Stina Hansson's loving smile. Now instead she was sitting here with Stina Hansson's drop-dead gorgeous breasts on her retina.

36.

There was singing in Fredrik's head, he could not describe it any other way. It was neither a tone nor a voice. Yet he experienced it as a song.

It was seven thirty in the evening. He was standing among the fruit trees on the back side of the house. He ended up there sometimes, stood watching the overgrown crowns, considering how they should be pruned, branch by branch, twig by twig, but seldom took out a saw to do anything about it. It was more a kind of meditation, a puzzle for his brain.

There was singing in his head. At first it frightened him, but he had soon calmed down, thought it was "in his head," not in his head. True, he had experienced some strange phenomena during the time he had been on medical leave. On one occasion, several months after the accident, the surroundings had suddenly started rocking and the visual impressions had been distorted like in a funhouse mirror.

He had gone to the ER, thought that now it was over. But the doctor explained that it was simply the brain resuming its original form. When the brain has been subjected to pressure for a time, sooner or later, when the pressure is gone, it will bend back. In connection with that, a kind of wave movement arises in the brain which can give rise to quite unpredictable experiences, in Fredrik's case the strange visual impressions. He had returned home, relieved but also with some tricky thoughts buzzing in his head.

What was it really that he experienced as *me?* Were ego and personality the same thing? If he changed did he then become a different person, or just different? And everything he saw around him, was it possible to know what that really was? Or did he have to be content with his experience of the surrounding world, which apparently could change from one moment to the next? All that was needed was a little wave movement in the brain.

He had talked with Ninni about it. She said he sounded like something out of the arts pages from the 1980s. He hadn't become any wiser because of it, but he had decided to try to stop thinking about it. Better to observe the treetops.

And the song that now slowly subsided had nothing to do with the accident, he was sure of that. He was healthy. He had papers to prove it. From a whole team of doctors.

Ninni was moving through the kitchen, on the other side of the window glass that reflected the foliage with the still not-quite-ripe fruit. She stopped and looked out toward the garden, as if she sensed him observing her. She caught sight of him, waved, and went on, disappearing into another room where he could no longer see her.

The song subsided completely and he was surprised by a strong feeling of happiness. He was happy because he could stand there in his garden. Because he had Ninni. And because he had Simon and Joakim. The happiness he felt was a lightness difficult to describe. It swept forth like a wind through the trees. He felt quietly euphoric.

Then came a whiff of hog manure from the neighbor, bringing him back down to earth.

37

Malin loaded the shopping cart with vegetables. At this time of year the produce case was full of organic and locally grown. It was not just that it was right, the vegetables on Gotland were also the best in the country. This was due to a large extent, of course, to the location, Sweden's best cultivation zone, but also that there were quite a few farmers who really cared. Even if one of the biggest producers went to jail for toxic dumping some years ago, there were also many who chose to farm organically.

Maria was at home with Ellen and Axel. It was nice to be able to shop in peace and quiet, without stress, without children tugging at her. Malin realized that Ellen would have to go back to school, but she hated the thought of dragging her there again. She had had time to consider a number of more or less impossible alternatives. Should they change schools? Would that help or would everyone soon know that the girl who had been kidnapped from the Fårösund school had transferred to the school in Slite or Visby or . . . It wouldn't work anyway. Not unless the whole family moved and then they might as well go back to Stockholm. Sometimes she thought that would be best, at other moments the very thought felt like a defeat.

Malin pushed the shopping cart out to the parking lot with her bags. She opened the back hatch, stowed away the groceries, and politely returned the cart to the neat row outside the entrance.

It was only when she had started the car and backed out of the parking space that she caught sight of Stina Hansson. She was just getting into her white Toyota at the other end of the asphalt lot and started it up just as quickly as that time outside the school. Had she even put on her seat belt? Had she caught sight of Malin, was that why she was in such a hurry?

The rest was instinct. When the white car rolled out from its parking space and headed toward the exit she quickly put the gear selector in drive and stepped on the gas. She had to keep to the left, dangerously close to the parked cars to get there ahead of Stina Hansson, but it worked. She jammed on the brakes with the SUV at a diagonal, right in front of the exit. A sharp sound of metal scraping against metal cut across the parking lot and the SUV jerked sideways.

Malin quickly unbuckled her seat belt and jumped out of the SUV. She rounded it in back and rushed over toward Stina Hansson's Toyota.

She struck her fist on the white car body.

"You damn well leave my family alone, do you understand? You damn well leave us alone."

Malin's throat ached after the outburst. Stina Hansson stared terrified at her through the side window. A little splash of saliva had stuck to the glass.

September 3

I'm caught here—in what was us. I do think that everything will work out. Because it can't feel this way and have it just be me. It's impossible. But then come the short flashes of something different. Violent blows that say I'm wrong. That I sit here like an idiot with my messed-up feelings and you don't care at all about what I feel, if I live or die, if I kill myself or just lie down somewhere and rot. And you get that pained expression—that you want to be somewhere else. I'm just something that's in the way, something you would prefer to throw away. And that burrows its way deep inside. I'm afraid then because I don't know how I'll manage—I hardly know how I will put up with waiting for everything to be all right, that you will understand, gather courage or whatever it is you need to do, that time will convince you that you must take the step and come back. That it will be you and me. I hardly know how I will bear to wait for that—how I will stand it if I'm wrong. I'm not wrong, I know I'm not wrong, but I'm saying if. Then I get afraid and only think about death. My death, your death. I know that these are just bad, ugly fantasies that come over me when those flashes come. Flashes—like short bursts of lightning, yes, but there are flashes of darkness, when the black gets so compact that there is no other side, no way out, no hope. Maybe it's just a silly cliché that hope is the last thing that abandons us. But if that is true then those dark flashes are the end, because there is no hope, no continuation. The darkness is so dense, it is earth, denser than earth. Like black, congealed formalin and I'm floating in it. Caught, incapacitated—I have reached the end. This is total loneliness.

Should I try to kill myself? Again. Cut open my veins. A knife. Can I do that, cut myself apart? It's nice to think about, but can I do it?

A knife. I will kill you. An ugly fantasy. I could never harm you. But I want to free myself. The thought liberates me.

Have you been down? Sometimes I think that you are completely different inside. That you have never been tormented by your feelings. That it's so easy for you. That you've already forgotten me.

38.

Malin studied the carefully arranged red beet carpaccio that the blond, talkative waiter set down on the table in front of her. The last evening light filtered in through the high windows of Friheten facing toward Donners Place. They had gotten one of the two tables on the little raised platform next to the windows. Malin sat turned in toward the restaurant with a view of the patrons a half-flight down and the darkness in the bar.

Henrik raised his glass, and his eyebrows. The candles on the table glistened in the wineglass.

"Cheers," he said quietly.

It felt nice to have him home again. Extremely nice. Even though Stina Hansson's perfect breasts were dancing before the wineglass. They were sharing a glass of Sauvignon blanc with the appetizer. Henrik could not drink more than that. He would be driving.

It was Maria who suggested they should take the opportunity to go out when she was there and could take care of the kids. Malin's very first thought was that she didn't want to leave them, not even with Maria, but then she changed her mind. Maybe it was just the sort of thing they needed. Some time to themselves.

Henrik told about the days in Barcelona. Long and intensive, but not without enjoyment.

"It's so typical," he said. "First they're as tough as nails in negotiations, then they send along three people who don't fill any function at all and book everyone in business class and of course we have to go off to some legendary restaurant that takes an hour to get to by taxi. Fun, but they could have held down the costs and paid me a little better instead."

"You don't appear to be suffering," said Malin.

Henrik laughed.

"It was great, but it's crazy. You never cease to be surprised by this advertising world."

"Do you regret it?"

"Regret it? No. What do you mean?"

Yes, what did she mean? Fårö. Her. The children. That he had dropped his dream, or changed dream, or whatever it was he had done. Everything that picture of him and the almost-naked model and the over-the-hill Elvis impersonator stood for.

She had not said anything about the pictures she found in the negative cabinet. Not about what had happened in the parking lot outside ICA, either.

Fredrik Broman had called her up the following day to tell her that Stina Hansson had reported the incident. Threat and negligence in traffic. It was hard to deny. He was not the one running the investigation, Fredrik explained, but he wanted to advise Malin to let them run the investigation of the incident at the school and keep as far away as possible from any possible suspects. Malin had asked whether he knew anything more about Stina Hansson's report, but he only said that she would be called in for questioning.

There was at least one witness, she could figure that out for herself. There were people in the parking lot. They would obviously testify to the Gotland native's advantage, whatever had happened. Fucking banana republic. It was good luck anyway that the police who were investigating what had happened to Ellen were not all from Gotland, then she would really have gotten paranoid.

She reached out her hand and took a big gulp from the glass. She should have told Henrik. She tried to make herself believe that she hadn't had time, but that wasn't true. Not really.

"What's going on?" Henrik asked.

Malin reached for the cell phone.

"I'm just going to make a quick call to Maria," she said.

"Again?"

"I want to hear that everything's okay."

She had called from the car, on the way to Visby, but that must have been an hour ago.

The phone rang, but no one answered. Finally the voice mail started.

"Strange," said Malin. "She doesn't answer."

"Maybe she's in the john," Henrik suggested. "Try in five minutes."

"I'll just try the landline."

He did not protest, but she knew what he was thinking. Malin got no answer on the home phone, either.

"They must be outside," said Henrik.

"But it's almost dark."

"Malin, take it easy now," he pleaded. "Call again in a little while."

She took a deep breath and set the cell phone down on the table.

"You're right, but . . ."

"I get that this is tough," he said. "I think it's tough, too. But we have to pull ourselves together. Otherwise this is going to make us completely nuts in the end. The children don't do well, either, if we're getting ourselves upset all the time."

"I know, I know," she said, becoming aware of a slight panting in her own voice. "I'll call again in ten minutes. Fifteen."

She speared a piece of red beet on her fork and chewed it slowly. It was hard. She had completely lost her appetite.

Henrik fished for something in the inside pocket of his jacket, which he had hung on the chair alongside.

"Look at this," he said with a broad smile, holding up a white plastic card.

Malin did not understand. It looked like some kind of membership card. Only when Henrik handed it to her did she see Wisby Hotel's logo on the card. A key card.

"Know what I mean, know what I mean?" Henrik said with a smile.

She was flattered, happy, and actually a little turned on. But also worried.

"What do you mean, are we going to spend the night?"

She noticed that it was not really the response Henrik had been hoping for, but he exerted himself.

"Not necessarily. A couple of hours is enough for me."

"Okay," she said, trying to sound flirtatious, but she could not think of anything except that those ten minutes she had promised to leave the cell phone alone should pass.

Somehow Malin managed to eat up most of the appetizer. The waiter cleared the table and came in with a glass of red wine that she had ordered earlier and a mineral water for Henrik.

Twelve minutes had passed. She had been obedient, she thought, and picked up the cell phone. She tried Maria's cell first. The phone rang, but no one answered. Without looking up she went over to favorites and selected the home number. It rang, but no one answered.

"No one answers there, either."

Henrik looked anxiously at her and that made her even more worried.

"Someone ought to answer somewhere, don't you think?" she said. "Ellen always answers our phone."

"They're probably outside," said Henrik vaguely, sneaking a glance out the window toward the darkening sky.

It didn't sound especially convincing.

Malin tried to think. No answer in almost fifteen minutes. What could they be up to? No matter how she thought about it she could not come up with any explanation. Maria was aware, of course, of what had happened, the whole situation. She understood that she had to be available.

"I'll wait five more minutes, then, then . . ."

Her mouth was completely dry, she reached for Henrik's glass and took a gulp of mineral water. Her stomach ached. She would not be able to eat another bite until she got hold of Maria.

They sat silently looking at each other with an occasional nervous sidelong glance into the restaurant or out the window. Malin fingered the napkin on her lap as Henrik's cell phone signaled a message. Malin straightened up, leaned tensely across the table while he fished the cell phone out of his pocket.

He shook his head.

"It's the assistant who's going to be there tomorrow."

Malin could not bear to just sit there. It wouldn't do.

"I'll call one more time. If I don't get an answer we're going home."

Henrik did not protest.

Malin went through the same procedure as before. Maria's cell, then the home phone. No answer.

She stood up abruptly.

"We're going."

Once she had made the decision everything suddenly became extremely serious. Her legs felt heavy, her mouth was dry despite the water just moments ago. Panic was lying in wait.

Henrik got up and looked for the waiter to pay. Malin waited by the exit, saw the waiter make an anxious face and say something to Henrik. He talked on and on and gestured, seemed to never be done. Couldn't he keep quiet and just take payment? Just that would take an eternity, back and forth with credit card, receipts . . . but suddenly Henrik raised his hand in thanks and left.

"They'll send a bill," he explained as he came up to her.

It took them no more than a minute to walk to the car, which they had parked on Hamnplan.

"I'll call the police," said Malin when she had shut the door.

"Maybe that's just as well," said Henrik, subdued.

He backed out of the parking spot and drove south to go around the inner city. It would take too long to work their way through the labyrinth of alleys.

Malin hesitated with her thumb on CALL as she entered 911. She would end up with an operator who did not know the background at all, she would have to make a long-winded, complicated explanation and certainly get a skeptical reception from that person who, in the worst case, was not even on Gotland.

She deleted the three numbers and instead looked for Fredrik Broman's number, which she had saved in the phone.

What should she do if he didn't answer? Then she would be forced to go through 911. She counted the rings. Three, four . . .

Soon the voice mail would start up.

"Fredrik Broman."

Thank God. After quickly saying who she was, Malin let the words pour forth.

"Henrik and I are in Visby, my sister is at home with the kids, but we don't get an answer on any of the phones."

He immediately understood her worry and promised to see to it that a patrol car drove up.

"But it will take awhile before they are there," he said. "You don't have a neighbor who can go over and knock on the door? Then we'll have a quicker sense of the situation."

"Yes, of course," she said. "I'll call and see whether they're at home."

Why hadn't she thought of that?

"Call me as soon as you know anything more," said Fredrik Broman.

Henrik drove as fast as he dared on the dark road. Malin had tried to call Bengt and Ann-Katrin, but they had not answered. There was nothing to do other than try to tough it out and hope that everything had a trivial explanation. Between Malin's repeated attempts to get hold of Maria they sat silently and listened to the grinding of the tires against the asphalt. Neither of them could get themselves to turn on the radio.

After forty minutes they were in Fårösund. The ferry was in with the boom up. A minute or two after they drove on a police car rolled on board and right after that the ramp was drawn up and the ferry departed, even though it was five minutes to the hour.

"Do you think they're on their way to our place?" said Malin, glancing backward.

"Presumably."

Good Lord, she thought, that's as far as they'd gotten?

"I'll go and ask."

Before Henrik could answer she had opened the door and was on her way out of the car. She went up to the driver's side and knocked on the window. She recognized the bald policeman at once who rolled down the window. He had been there outside the school when Ellen disappeared. Alongside him sat a female police officer with braids.

"Hi," she said. "Are you the ones who are on the way to our house?"

"That's us," Leif Knutsson confirmed.

He got out of the car and greeted her.

"You still haven't heard anything?"

"No, I keep on calling," said Malin. "I've tried the neighbors, but they're not at home."

"Okay, but then we'll drive ahead."

"That's good. We'll follow as fast as we can."

"Just drive carefully," said Leif Knutsson, with a little smile.

"Of course," she promised.

"Is there anything else we ought to know?" he asked.

"I don't think so. My sister is at home with our two children, Ellen and Axel."

"Yes, we know that," he said. "What does she look like, your sister?"

"Like me except blond," she said.

"I see, that was easy."

Malin was about to turn around and leave when she thought of something.

"Perhaps you want my key, so that you can get in if that should be necessary."

"Yes," said Knutsson a little hesitantly. "Just wait a moment."

He stuck his head in the police car and exchanged a few words with his colleague, then he was back.

"Maybe it's best that you ride with us. If you don't have anything against that?"

Malin did not need to think about it. The sooner she got home, the better. She valued every second.

"I'll just tell my husband."

The police car drove with blue lights on, but without sirens. They had rattled across the first two cattle guards. Two left. They had left Henrik far behind them. The car jumped and shook from the high speed. The headlights swept over the dark forest and the enclosed pastures, reflected suddenly in an animal's eyes.

They would soon be there. Still, she could not keep from thinking that she and Henrik got to the ferry ahead of the police. It was that far to help and rescue if you lived on Fårö. She was starting to understand more and more the older Fårö residents' attitude to the world beyond the water's edge. Here you had to rely on yourself.

Malin fingered the cell phone, but had stopped calling. She had lost count of how many times she tried before they got to the ferry. Why didn't they answer?

She tried to keep from thinking about what the reason could be, scared that her imagination would bring up something she could not handle. Instead she concentrated on the back of Leif Knutsson's neck. He had not said much during the drive from Broa. The woman, on the other hand, whose name was Gunilla Borg, had asked a number of questions about Maria, the children, and the house. She got a feeling that it was mostly to keep her in good spirits.

The third cattle guard rumbled under the tires and shortly after that the fourth.

"Now it's up on the right," said Malin.

Leif Knutsson slowed down, but the gravel still sprayed around the tires as he took the curve up toward the house. The big pile of timber was outlined against the still-not-completely-black sky.

His colleague made a radio hail and said to someone who responded with a numerical code that they were at the address. Leif Knutsson stopped right across from the gate, next to Malin's Honda. He turned around and asked her to wait in the car while they went down to the house.

Malin could only nod, felt that her throat was paralyzed, and mutely handed over the key. Leif Knutsson took it and winked at her with both eyes. This would probably work out.

As the police officers opened the doors and got out, she heard music from a distance. Before they closed, Malin was able to recognize the artist. Rihanna, one of Maria's favorites.

She watched as Gunilla Borg released something from her belt and the next moment the ground in front of her and her police colleague was lit up by a cold light. Malin slid closer to the door and stared out the window toward the house, but could see no more than the upper half of the bottom floor. The police and the beam of light disappeared below the rise and soon it was only their heads and shoulders that stuck up.

She wanted to rush out and follow them; she wanted to stay sitting there; she wanted to hide. Were the doors locked?

Her head was rocking, light and heavy at the same time. She leaned her forehead against the window, vaguely heard bass tones from the music. Then a light came closer. She stared out into the evening. It was Leif Knutsson who had come back up the slope. He waved to her. For her? Should she come? Yes, it appeared that way.

She quickly opened the car door and got out, pointed to herself with a questioning expression. Leif waved again. Malin hurried over and opened the gate. At the same moment she heard the familiar engine sound of the Mercedes SUV from the road below, but continued toward the house.

She had not gone far before she caught sight of Maria, who was talking with the other police officer. And the children? Why weren't the children there? She ran down to the house with pounding heart and stopped in front of Maria.

There they were. Axel and Ellen sat perched on the lowest branches in one of the apple trees. They caught sight of her and Ellen jumped down from her branch and came running. Axel took it a little more carefully. For him it was farther down to the ground, although the branch was up just as high. Malin wanted to hurry over and help him when she saw how he uncertainly sought a foothold, but she was prevented by Ellen, who was already clinging to her leg.

The music was booming from speakers that were set out on a little table outside one of the windows. Maria held her hand in front of her mouth in an unhappy gesture.

"Do you think we can turn that down a little?" Leif Knutsson said as he came up to them.

"Sure, of course," said Maria, waving her hands nervously.

She looked at Malin with big regretful eyes.

"Forgive me, I'm so sorry, forgive me. I don't know what I was thinking. We've been outside playing and I set out the speakers to . . . well, so we could have a little music. Forgive me, Malin. You must have been completely—"

Leif Knutsson had clearly had enough of Rihanna. He went into the house himself, and after a little while the music stopped.

"I didn't bring the cell phone out, but I don't understand that I didn't hear anything. The window is open, after all."

Maria pointed at the living room window, which was propped open with the hasp. But the phone was in the study and the music no doubt took care of the rest.

Now Axel had wriggled down from the tree and came toward her with outstretched arms. She leaned down and lifted him up. He looked tired. She did not know what she should think about Maria's blunder. Mostly she was just happy that everything was as it should be, even if she was a little embarrassed in front of the police.

She heard steps in the grass. Henrik approached with a big question etched on his face. He looked at Malin and the kids, the police, and his sister-in-law.

"Everything's okay," said Malin.

Henrik furrowed his brow, did not really understand.

"Everything's okay," Malin repeated. "Maria didn't hear the phone."

Henrik's facial features smoothed out and he smiled with relief.

Maria had turned to the police officers.

"I'm so sorry, truly . . . I don't know what to say. Forgive me. I can't even bear to think that you drove all the way from Visby."

"It's no problem," said Leif Knutsson. "The most important thing is that you're all safe and sound."

39

It took awhile before they could go to bed, but at last they were lying there, side by side in the Fårö darkness and the Fårö silence. The alarm was on, the misunderstandings explained and apologies made.

Henrik turned on his side. Malin felt four fingertips against her hip. The light touch was like a cautious question. They had not made love since they came home from vacation. That was almost two weeks now. Henrik had not been at home, of course, for some of that time.

The four fingertips became a hand stroking her belly. Malin felt desire coming. There were a lot of things moving around in her head, an unusually large number of negative thoughts. Worry, paranoia, irritation. Not sexy at all. But the desire came anyway, heavy and demanding, almost a little unwelcome. She reached out her hand and felt that he was already hard. She slowly moved her hand as she wriggled out of her underpants with the other. Henrik was panting against her neck. When he stuck his tongue in her ear, such a strong shudder passed through her body that she was forced to turn her head aside.

It only took a few minutes from the fingers on the hip until he came. But that didn't matter. She had come, too. It was more discharge than drawn-out pleasure they needed.

In the new, more relaxed silence Malin told that she had forced Stina Hansson off the road outside the ICA in Fårösund. And that Stina reported her. Presumably she would have to pay a fine. It was most likely she would have to pay a fine.

"But what the hell," said Henrik, lying silently a long time in the darkness.

"Say something then," said Malin.

He took a deep breath.

"We have to hope you don't end up in prison."

"Prison," she said, as if it was a bad joke.

Then the ridicule did a U-turn, was transformed into something black and heavy that was dragging her down. Prison? She had not even come close to the thought. Fredrik Broman had not said anything about punishment at all. She had figured out for herself that she would have to pay a fine. But prison?

"What the hell were you thinking?" said Henrik.

"I don't know, I—"

"That's not exactly the smartest thing you could have done after moving here from Stockholm," he said drily.

She felt a sudden flash of anger.

"Thanks so fucking much."

It was as if he was putting himself on their side. The Gotlanders. Pointing her out as an outsider. As if it was him and Gotland against her, not him and her against the rest of the world. She turned on the lamp on the nightstand and sat up in bed.

"I found your old porno photos of her," she blurted out.

She could not help it.

"Who? Of who do you mean?"

Henrik sounded completely uncomprehending, as if he was the most innocent person in the whole world. "Now I'm not really following you."

"Yes, who the hell is it we're talking about?" she hissed.

He blinked at the light with a sleepy look.

Malin jumped out of bed and stomped off into the sitting room, without caring whether she woke Maria, and came back with the contact sheet. She threw it on Henrik's cover. He picked it up and looked at it.

"I see. And?" he said.

Malin almost choked, could not get out the words.

"Is that why you rammed Stina's car? Because I took pictures of her naked fifteen years ago?"

She was unable to answer that. As he was saying it she realized that maybe he was right.

"Calm down now," he said with a gentle look in his eyes. "Come to bed."

She did as he said, pulled the cover up over her legs, sat with her arms crossed and her head leaning against the wall. He placed a hand on her legs, on top of the cover. She decided to keep silent until she was sure she could open her mouth without having another outburst.

Henrik said something about the pictures, that it started with Stina pulling up her shirt in jest in the car. Malin could not keep from listening, but actually she did not want to hear Henrik talk about Stina at all. She did not like her name in his mouth. It did not please her that he only said her first name. It sounded so familiar.

At last the fury and the jealousy subsided anyway. Out of pure exhaustion, if nothing else. It had been a long day full of emotions.

"I could talk with her," said Henrik. "If that's okay with you, of course."

"Talk with her? What do you mean?"

It was hardly okay. She felt how everything was speeding up again just when she had started to settle down.

"Yes, about the report. Maybe she could consider withdrawing it. We'll have to pay for the damage to the car, of course."

"I don't have the energy to think about it now," she said. "We'll talk about it tomorrow."

She turned off the light. What would Henrik have to do to get Stina Hansson to withdraw the report? Sleep with her?

40

Göran Eide stepped into Fredrik's office and stopped just inside the doorway. Considering the size of the room, there weren't that many alternatives.

"What's really going on with that Malin Andersson?"

More than a week had passed since an unknown woman had lured Ellen Andersson Kjellander into her car, and it felt as if the investigation was going backward.

"First that woman in Fårösund she went after . . . What was her name?" Göran continued, extending an encouraging palm toward Fredrik.

"Stina Hansson."

"Exactly. In the parking lot. And then the false alarm yesterday. Is she in the process of freaking out?"

"It wouldn't be all that strange if she was," said Fredrik.

They had not been able to give Malin Andersson any reassuring news. The IP number in Uppsala pointed away from the island, toward something more complicated than an old girlfriend or family grudge. It could, of course, be a smoke screen, but that seemed farfetched.

"I'm getting a little worried that this will degenerate into some kind of personal vendetta," said Göran. "On incorrect grounds, besides."

"Malin Andersson sounded very contrite when I talked with her," said Fredrik. "I don't think it's going to escalate."

"Well, I hope you're right."

Göran crossed his arms and looked thoughtfully at him.

"How's it going? Do you really have nothing?"

Nothing, thought Fredrik, that seemed unnecessarily harsh. You never really have nothing.

"Everyone that we have had reason to suspect either has an alibi or can be removed for other reasons."

Göran Eide emitted a tired little hum.

"And what do you think, if you were to guess a little?"

Fredrik rolled his chair back a foot or two and put his right leg over the left.

"Henrik Kjellander's oldest sister, Elisabet Vogler, seems to be one tough lady, and her husband and relatives would surely lie to back her up if that were so. And there is some kind of motive, with the inheritance dispute and old peculiarities. But I have a hard time believing that she would do something as stupid as abduct Ellen. The risk that some witness would recognize her or that Ellen could point her out is much too great. To me it doesn't fit."

"No, not to me, either."

"Then there is the lead to Uppsala."

"Yes, what's happening there?"

"The lead to the public library produced nothing. The house on Fårö must have been booked with a private computer via the wireless network and you log onto that with the library's own password. Then we have produced lists of cars rented by women from Uppsala in the days before and after Ellen was kidnapped."

"And?" said Göran.

"The ones we've managed to get hold of we've been able to rule out."

"The mental hospital? They don't have any crazies up there? On Fårö, that is."

"No, no one who matches the description. Not the behavior, either, for that matter."

"And the mainland hasn't let out any crazies?" Göran asked.

"Well then," said Fredrik with a hint of a laugh. "But they're still on the mainland."

Göran stood silent a little while, staring out into space, fingering the reading glasses he had stuck in the chest pocket of the short-sleeved shirt.

"Surveillance cameras," he said. "Maybe it's too late, but in any case it's worth a try. The bank where the rent for the house was paid must have cameras. The train station in Uppsala the hours around the booking. Get Henrik Kjellander and Malin Andersson to look through that, if there are any left."

Fredrik wrote *surveillance cameras?* on his pad. The thought had already flashed past when he got the news about the computer at the Uppsala public library, but he had let it go. The investigation did not really have that weight, he thought. Was that a wrong assessment?

"We'll have to take everything one more time, broader and deeper," said Göran before he left Fredrik alone in the office.

Fredrik looked out the window, trying to find a loose end to tug on: The perpetrator books the house on Fårö from a computer in Uppsala and gives an address in Gothenburg. She, if she was alone, had demonstrably been in Uppsala on the fourth of June. Presumably not just to book the house, even if that could not be ruled out.

They had checked train reservations, but had not managed to sift out anything to go further with. Tens of thousands of people commuted between Stockholm and Uppsala every day and the tickets could be bought with cash on board. It was easy to travel without leaving any traces.

He would make an attempt with the last tenants again, the retired couple from Gothenburg. He could not keep from thinking that there must be a connection. Even if a vague one.

Gothenburg, Uppsala, Fårö. Three coordinates. It wasn't much to go on, but at the same time it felt as if they ought to be able to triangulate out the perpetrator if they only pushed the right buttons.

41

The terminal at Visby Airport was a low, plain building, no larger than a normal-sized day care center. Henrik dropped off the model, the makeup artist, and the advertising director outside the entry and they rolled off waving with their bags full of clothes, makeup, and props. They were booked on Gotland Air's last departure at 6:55 P.M. and were arriving just in time to check in.

Henrik felt mildly euphoric as he slowly rolled out from the airport area between the fences of freshly cut juniper. It had been one of those divinely inspired workdays when already after the first exposures he felt that the photos would turn out really great. Certain days it was just that way, that you knew.

There were two Swedish haute couture dresses to shoot, and the newspaper's AD was looking for majestic but severe. A little Lars Norén meets Louis XIV. "But with a heart and a twist?" Henrik had responded. The AD laughed and then added seriously: "No, no heart."

They had taken the first picture by the stone pillars in Holmhällar and the others in the afternoon light far out on Gotland's southernmost spit. No more than a few stones sticking up out of the sea. He had used medium format to make sure of the material sense in stone and fabric and to get proper draw in the dark sea in the background. The contrast between cloth, stone, and sea should bring out the various materials even more.

Henrik brought along an assistant from Hemse Folk High School. It was hard to keep an assistant on Fårö, and besides he couldn't really afford it right now, but he had worked up a network of students at the folk high school and in Visby who could work a day or two now and then. He got the makeup artist to help out with one of the reflex screens, too. It had gone well. There were some people who balked at having to do those types of services, thought it was unprofessional, but fortunately they were the exception. Henrik had a hard time understanding that kind of whining. They were just standing there alongside staring ninety percent of the time anyway.

Actually they could just as well have taken the pictures on Fårö, but the AD had insisted on south Gotland because she had been there herself and could visualize it. And Henrik saw no reason to be obstinate. When they packed up the equipment the sun was hanging right above the horizon.

That Maria had come down had in a way been a blessing. If it hadn't been for her he would not have been able to do the job in Barcelona. But it was also stressful for him having her in the vicinity. He was not sure that Maria understood that. In any event, it didn't seem like it. And they had not talked about it.

Malin had not said anything more about them not being able to keep living in the house. It was typical of her to react so drastically. In the first place, it was not because she was afraid. It was just her way. Action. As certain as she was one day that an alarm was the solution to their problems, the next day she was just as certain that they had to check into a hotel. Problems were solved by buying something or doing something—change. Hard to say that there was anything wrong with that; on the contrary, that she was so energetic was one of the reasons he had fallen for her. But sometimes you needed to sit down and think things through, too. Have a goal a little farther ahead than tomorrow.

And they had a few things to think about. Debts, interest, leasing agreements, and an extremely shaky market. Deep down he was sure that it would work out. That it was heavy right now was more lack of flow than anything else. Sure there were times when he could think that they shouldn't have taken on so much at one time. Additions, renovations, new studio lights, the slightly expensive second car, and all that. On the other hand, it was important to hold your head high. It was part of the industry. Success breeds success. It wouldn't do to be content with shabby.

Sometimes he missed the years between photography school and Ellen's birth. Not really so that he longed to be back, but he sometimes missed the lightheartedness. The years when he flew around between Stockholm and Los Angeles and a half-dozen other big cities, without really being sure of where he actually lived and not caring. Everything just flowed. He earned a lot of money, even if it was mostly eaten up by expenses. He felt eternal in those years. He was young, strong, successful, and that was how it would remain, always. An illusion, of course, but a nice feeling to live in. When the everyday routine got too dreary he would glide into the memory of that time, like a kind of meditation, and come back to reality strengthened by a dose of the carefree life of an operator.

Henrik had arrived in Fårösund and cruised down the hill toward the ferry landing. It was almost fifteen minutes until the seven-thirty ferry. He stopped in front of the white stop line, first in the priority line, and turned off the engine. He undid the seat belt, stretched, and yawned.

Without his intending it, Stina Hansson showed up in his mind. He tried to push her aside, but the more he exerted himself the more she held on. He could not understand how Malin could be jealous of her. Okay, the pictures, but that was ages ago. He had run into her a couple of times in Fårösund and it had just felt strange. There was something about her . . . He got an unhealthy sense.

When he thought back on it, he could not remember how he happened to take those pictures. Was he the one who encouraged Stina to pose naked for him, or was she the one who, completely unprovoked, had pulled up her top in the car?

From Broa to Kalbjerga Henrik did not meet a single car. It was just him, the growing darkness, and the road lit up by the headlights of his SUV. And the yellow signs with odd farm names that creaked in the darkness at irregular intervals. He shook his head and mumbled a question to himself about what he was really doing on this God-forsaken little island. But there was a laugh in his question. Partly he was laughing at himself, partly out of sheer cheerfulness. He liked it here. For some almost incomprehensible reason.

If someone had told him fifteen years ago that he would be living on Fårö he probably would have laughed a lot louder and more crudely. But deep down he would have been afraid. Was that why he had moved there? To overcome the fear?

The last stretch up the hill and he was there; soon he was backing in alongside Malin's black Honda. He took the camera bags from the backseat before he locked the car. The rest of the equipment could wait until tomorrow.

He pushed open the gate with his back, squeezed through with the heavy bags, and continued down the slope. Only as he approached the house through the gray-blue twilight did it strike him that not a single light was on.

He quickened his pace. The grass rustled faintly against his shoes and the shoulder bag chafed against his hip. He stopped at the steps and put down the other bag while he searched for his keys. It was completely silent around him. No wind in the treetops, no restless sea whispering at a distance, no birds, not even the sound of a tractor.

He took out the jingling key ring and put it in the lock, only to discover that the door was unlocked. He opened the door with the keys still in the lock and took a step in. A heavy, strange odor struck him. He could not place it. It was not perfume, not an unpleasant cooking smell, not cleanser.

He fumbled for the light switch behind the jackets on the hooks to the left. The ceiling light dispelled the dark and at the same moment the sight threw itself on him like an aggressive animal.

There was blood everywhere. It was as if someone had painted it over his eyeballs. Drawn a brush with blood over his face. It forced its way into his nose, into his mouth. The odor, the taste. Everything was red. He even heard blood.

42

On legs that did not feel like they belonged to him Henrik staggered up to Malin and fell down on his knees beside her, uncertain whether it was deliberate or because his legs gave way.

He did not know what to do. His hands were shaking above the bloody head, next to the face he did not recognize. She was not moving. The body that was wearing Malin's clothes was lying completely still, spilled out across the floor. He forced his hand down to her neck, tried to feel for the pulse. How did you do that? Cardiopulmonary resuscitation. What were you supposed to do? Didn't he know that? He turned his head to the right. Axel. In the kitchen. On the floor in front of the stove. His head was so different. Pressed in, splintery, bloody.

The paralysis spread from his legs up through his body. Nausea grew from his belly out into his chest and it became hard to breathe. He crept slowly toward Axel while at the same time he tried to get his cell phone out of his pocket. He fell down on his side, hurt his elbow. He did everything backward. Crawled ahead. The blood. It was weighing him down. Smelled like iron and animal. Axel. His little, little head. He had to help him. Rescue him. He had to wake that absent gaze to life.

His thumb glided across the glass surface of the cell phone, smeared it. His hand was red with blood. From where? It was everywhere. Trembling he managed to enter the three digits.

"They're dead," was the first thing he said when he got a response. "Or, I don't know . . . There's blood everywhere. Someone has—"

The man on the other end wanted a name and address.

"It's my wife and son," he heard himself say, and was surprised that he could even talk.

The blood was smeared between his fingers.

The voice was nagging about an address. What was it? The number on the mailbox that he always turned at. He said his own name and Kalbjerga and Fårö. Wasn't that enough? Yes, that was enough. But the voice wanted to know more. What had happened? How many were injured, and in what way? Who were they?

"But you have to send an ambulance . . . an ambulance helicopter. They're dying . . ."

He stammered out the words between tears and irregular breathing.

"Try to take it easy," said the voice. "I've already sent the alarm, but the more I know, the better we can help you."

"Okay, okay," he whispered against the glass surface sticky with blood, and tried to breathe more calmly.

"If we start with who this concerns," said the voice.

"It's my wife, Malin Andersson, and my son, Axel."

He was forced to break off and breathe panting a while, as if the short sentence had been a hundred-yard dash.

"You have to hurry," he whimpered. "There must be a helicopter?"

"How old is the boy?" said the voice.

"Five."

"And how is he injured?"

"I don't know . . . His head. He's . . . been struck on the head . . . it . . ."

"And your wife? How is she injured?"

"Same thing, her head . . ."

"Okay, you'll get help as soon as possible, but it will take a while, so it's important that you do what you can to help them. Can you see whether they're breathing?"

Henrik's voice broke in a gurgling fit of crying when he tried to answer. How did it look if someone was breathing?

"Henrik," said the voice on the other end.

He was startled by his name. Did not remember that he had said what his name was.

"Henrik, are you there?"

"Yes," he said hoarsely.

"I'm going to transfer you to a nurse now. She will help you and give you instructions. Do you understand what I'm saying?"

"Yes," he said. "I understand."

But he did not understand. His eyes ran restlessly between Malin and Axel. He had to save them. He had to save them now.

Ellen, why wasn't Ellen there? Why hadn't Malin locked the door?

"Ellen," he screamed.

No one answered.

"Ellen!"

43.

Göran's name glowed from the display on Fredrik's cell phone. It was 8:11 P.M. The time of the call already gave away that the matter was serious. His tone of voice said the rest.

"Things seem to have gone badly up on Fårö."

"In Kalbjerga?" said Fredrik, although he knew the answer.

"Yes. Malin Andersson and one of the children are severely injured. Maybe dead. Two persons are missing."

"Henrik Kjellander and the other child?"

"No, he was the one who found them. The daughter is missing. And Malin's sister."

There was silence for a moment. The words that were hanging in the air but not expressed were just as obvious as if they were physically hanging there. At least for Fredrik.

They should have seen this. If they had done a better job perhaps they could have prevented . . .

"Call me when you leave Visby so that we can coordinate the ferry," said Göran.

The call was interrupted.

There had been something heavy in Göran's voice. He was usually dry and efficient in these kinds of situations, but this time something else came through.

Fredrik closed his eyes for the image of Malin and little Axel that appeared in his mind. It disappeared, only to be replaced by the family portrait with the eyes poked out. It was as if an old-fashioned slide projector had started up there.

He went into the living room and told Ninni that he had to go.

"Something seems to have happened with the family up on Fårö," he said vaguely.

"The ones with the daughter who disappeared from school?"

"Yes."

"Oh dear," was all she said, looking at him.

He was glad that no one was suggesting that an unexpected call out late in the evening would be too much for him. Neither Göran nor Ninni.

"Be careful," she said.

He put on his shoes and jacket and hurried out to the car. As he rolled out of the yard he peeked up toward Simon's room where the lamp was on over the desk. He pictured him, alone in front of the computer. Then he thought about Joakim far away in Stockholm. What was he doing right now? Was he at home with his girlfriend? Was he out in the city or sitting on the subway? Fredrik had no idea.

Then he pushed all thoughts about his own family aside, closed them in behind a watertight bulkhead, and tried to prepare himself for what was waiting. Severely injured. Maybe dead.

44

Henrik did as the nurse instructed and as he vaguely remembered from some lifesaving course long ago. The little chest heaved carefully every time he blew. He did not dare put too much force into it. Then Malin. Breath after breath.

"Ellen!"

He screamed himself hoarse between exhalations.

And then, like a miracle, voices outside. Steps.

"Ellen!"

"Daddy," was heard from far away.

Ellen. She was alive.

"Henrik, it's okay. We're out here."

Maria this time. Henrik flew up from the floor and hurried out the door, which he left open behind him. They were only a few steps from the stairs.

"Wait! Wait out here!" he roared uncontrollably, even though it had just gone through his head that he should be calm and collected, not frighten them.

Maria and Ellen stopped abruptly, stood with bathrobes flapping and stared at him.

"There's, there's," he stammered, not knowing how he should explain.

For a moment he thought about saying something in English, but the next moment the idea seemed completely bizarre.

Maria's eyes were wide open. Terror and doubt reshaped her pale face to one he had never seen before.

Henrik looked firmly at her.

"Stay here with Ellen."

He was actually able to make his voice more or less normal.

"You have to stay out here."

He turned abruptly and rushed back in with a strange happiness rushing through his body. Ellen. She was alive and uninjured. A quick glance as he passed the hall mirror. He was covered with blood. His hands, shirt front, face. His mouth was smeared with dark red, sticky blood. He felt Maria's eyes behind him, as if they could go right through the wall. She must think he's gone crazy, that he killed them, or that he himself was injured. He didn't care which. It didn't matter. The only thing that was important was that she did not come in with Ellen, that he made sure Ellen avoided seeing this.

He sank down on his knees next to Axel. Must continue. Leaned over and pinched his nose. The cell phone he had set down on the floor buzzed. He could make out the voice's whispering from the speaker, but not what it said. He could not take it now. Not yet. First he had to blow.

He had been alone with them so long, alone in the house with the blood and the bodies, alone with the nurse's voice. He had listened to the voice, blown air into Axel's lungs and pressed with his hands on the little chest. The voice had been his rescue, the voice would guide him while he woke them to life again.

Alone in the dark he had struggled against death, soiled with blood, sometimes a break to scream for Ellen. For every endless minute that passed a distant reasonableness had pressed an ever colder hand around his heart. Said that it was too late.

He heard the sound of a car outside. It stopped abruptly. A door opened and closed again. It was silent for a moment, then a strange voice. He heard the words "nurse" and "rescue service." That she was from Skär. He had not struggled in vain. Now came the rescue. Now the one who would put everything right had come.

Everything would work out.

45

Fredrik was standing with a few of his closest associates outside the wide-open front door to the house in Kalbjerga. The hall was bathed in light. The whole house was lit up and some twenty people were either in or outside the building.

The middle-aged woman in red-yellow reflector jacket with the word DOCTOR in capital letters on the back got up from her kneeling position by the side of the blood-covered little boy. She had thick, platinum blond hair cut short and was not much more than five foot four inches tall. She looked around among the tall policemen who, with the exception of the technician, were waiting in the doorway. She seemed uncertain who she should turn to.

"Yes?" said Göran Eide to help put her on the right track.

"There's nothing to do," she said. "They've been dead for several hours."

She looked tired, her forehead full of worried wrinkles.

"Can you say how many?"

"Well," said the doctor, turning quickly toward the dead again. "That's not really my department," she continued after thinking a moment, "but three or four hours, at a rough estimate."

She stroked her forehead with her jacket sleeve.

"And the cause of death?" asked Göran.

The doctor blinked as if she thought the question was superfluous, but quickly realized the technical side of the matter.

"There are head injuries, of course," she said. "But it will take an autopsy to determine whether the immediate cause of death is due to loss of blood or that the brain damage caused vital bodily functions to stop."

Fredrik turned quickly and stared out into the darkness; he felt an unpleasant stabbing sensation in his legs. It was not the blood-spattered walls, the two dead bodies or their crushed heads that upset him. It was the doctor's words that surprisingly took him out to Östergarnsholme.

He fell along the cliff, or more correctly stated, he saw himself fall. He tumbled along and remained lying on the shore while the waves broke only a few feet away. Splashed foam over him and the dead man under him. He saw something he had never seen before. A fantasy obviously. He had been unconscious, of course. There was nothing to remember.

Fredrik took a few deep breaths and heard the doctor continue behind his back.

"They have been struck repeatedly with a hard, heavy weapon. What kind of weapon she can probably say better than me."

Fredrik assumed it was Eva the doctor was referring to with the last comment.

"The woman has fractures on her arms and hands," the doctor continued.

"Defensive injuries." He heard Eva Karlén's voice.

He turned in toward the hall again and stuck his head in between Gustav and Göran.

"Yes," said the doctor. "I guess there's not much more I can do here."

She was part of the helicopter team. They had arrived at the same time as Fredrik and Gustav and the other colleagues from investigation and landed right across the road down by the mailboxes. Since the duty officer had taken the alarm at two minutes past eight ferry traffic had been closed for everything except the emergency response traffic. The first ferry had shipped over an ambulance and two patrol cars. The ambulance personnel, just like the nurse from Skär that the emergency response service had sent in advance, realized that they had arrived too late. They decided not to move the bodies.

"The perpetrator must under any circumstances still be on Gotland," said Göran. "She can't possibly have caught either a flight or the boat."

He turned toward the on-scene incident commander who was standing ten feet away along with Leif Knutsson.

"We'll have to keep track of the departures tomorrow morning," he said and got a confirming nod in response.

Göran turned again to the doctor.

"It would be good if you could take a look at the father of the child. He doesn't seem to be doing too well."

"Of course, I didn't know that he was here."

"I'll go with you," said Göran.

Fredrik and Gustav stepped to the side so the doctor could go past.

"And you wait there," said Eva Karlén superfluously to them as they took a step forward again.

She was surely irritated about all the running around, he could understand that, even if rescue and safety had to go first. The ambulance personnel, the nurse, and the doctor had been in the hall, besides two colleagues from the uniformed police to secure the rest of the house. That was seven people, including Karlén herself.

"What do you think about the weapon?" said Gustav.

"Some kind of tool. An ordinary carpenter's hammer is a qualified guess."

Eva had taken out a camera and started photographing the bodies, but also the room. She covered floors and walls bit by bit so that in principle she could re-create the hall by means of the pictures.

"Both of them got ten or twenty blows. It's hard to count with all the blood."

Fredrik and Gustav looked at each other, silent. Fredrik knew exactly what thoughts were going through Gustav's head. Ten or twenty blows. A little boy, five years old. Who does something like that?

Fredrik turned toward the hall and the bodies again. Bodies. Dead. Victims. It was a little easier to think about them like that. But this time they were more. Once before he had stood in front of a murder victim that he knew. But in all other cases they had started as just bodies. Blank pieces of paper that would get a name and personality in pace with the progress of the investigation.

It was harder to defend yourself when they already had all that. When he had talked with them, heard their worried questions, seen them smile and laugh.

Axel Andersson Kjellander was lying in the kitchen with his head in front of the stove and his legs pointed toward the hall. Everything around him was bloody. He was bloody. His head, arms, likewise the light green T-shirt and black soccer shorts that ended mid-thigh. His eyes were open, but his gaze was hidden under all the blood.

Where did the fury come from, the glowing hatred that burst all barriers? Could it even be explained in words like hate and fury, which after all belonged to a description of a normal, if extremely pressured psyche? Fredrik tried to picture it, or rather imagine himself in it. One blow he could understand, perhaps even two, at a grown person, but the rest?

The room reeked heavily of blood. A few flies were buzzing in there, settling down on the bodies and walking around in jerky hops.

"I have a pretty clear picture of what happened," said Eva while she was working her way in toward the room with the camera. "The doorbell rings. The woman goes and opens it."

Malin, thought Fredrik. Malin Andersson goes and opens the door.

"Considering the background it must have been someone she recognized, or in any case did not perceive as dangerous."

Don't you perceive almost everyone as not dangerous? thought Fredrik. Not dangerous in the sense that you don't expect them to pull out a hammer and strike you twenty times on the head with it.

"The person who rang the doorbell must have taken out the tool more or less immediately, we can call it the hammer for the time being, and gone on the attack," Eva continued. "The woman tried to defend herself, but the bones in her wrists and one forearm were crushed and then she basically had no chance. I can't decide in what order the injuries occurred, but presumably the first blow against the head already made her too groggy to flee. If you look at the blood splashes around the head you can see that several of the blows, perhaps even the majority of them, must have hit when she was already lying down."

Fredrik could only note that Eva's description seemed to tally. Blood had splashed across the floor in several directions from Malin's head, even up on the wall.

"The boy either followed the woman when she went to open the door, or else was lured out into the hall by the commotion." Eva picked up the thread again. "When the perpetrator felt done with the woman, or however you want to put it, she went after the boy. He received roughly as many blows as his mother, but has no defensive injuries."

Eva lowered the camera and walked slowly back to the front door. She was moving in a narrow area in the middle of the room that she had marked.

"Everything must have happened extremely fast," she said. "I can imagine that the perpetrator was not inside the house more than thirty seconds, a minute max."

"So you think that she, or he, was only in the hall?" asked Gustav.

"It's too soon to say for sure," said Eva. "But reasonably there ought to have been blood tracks on the floor if the perpetrator had gone in, considering how it looks here in the hall."

Certainly the floor surface was covered with spattered blood or blood from bleeding. There were several bloody shoe impressions on the clean surfaces, hopefully some of them would turn out to belong to the perpetrator when impressions from the ambulance personnel and others who had been in the hall had been sifted out.

When Fredrik let his gaze glide across the hall floor, he suddenly sensed something between the fingers in Malin's clenched hand.

"She has something in her hand," he said.

Eva crouched down next to Malin Andersson's dead body and carefully loosened the four fingers.

"Hair," she said.

In the palm of the dead woman's hand was a large wad of blond hair.

46.

The steel plate rumbled under the wheels of the police van as it rolled on board. Henrik looked out over the sound for a moment. The glow from the ferry landing's streetlights were reflected in the surface of the water, and to the north and south the beacons of the ship channel were blinking.

Boarding the ferry knowing that Malin and Axel were still in the bloody hall in Kalbjerga, that was . . . a boundary, he thought sluggishly. He passed a line that made it definitive. The nightmare finally became reality.

Thoughts were moving slowly and the panic he ought to feel wandered back and forth impatiently, locked into a dark little room in an unknown place inside him. It must be the pill he got from the doctor. A light sedative, she said as she handed over the little white capsule, still enclosed in its packaging. Henrik had pressed it out in his hand and they both realized at the same time that there was no water to wash it down with. After briefly asking around, one of the emergency medical technicians had come with a mug of water. Henrik put the tablet on his tongue and swallowed it. Maria has also been offered a pill but declined.

They were sitting in the backseat of the police van with Ellen between them, Henrik with his arm around Ellen. Maria stared out the windshield, Ellen looked down at her lap. None of them said anything.

They had not said a word since one of the police officers closed the door on them and the van started moving.

He wondered what Ellen was thinking, what she understood. She had been full of questions that got inadequate answers and had finally fallen silent. That something dramatic had happened must be obvious, but what did she think? What fantasies were flying around in her head? The questions had to get better answers, but how would that happen? How could he tell Ellen what he barely allowed himself to think? The bodies in the hall. Axel's little boy's body. Like a doll. Like a discarded, bloody doll. Henrik had been alone with them so long. So alone with the dead. He closed his eyes and squeezed the padding of the backseat with his right hand. Ellen let out a plaintive sound and he realized that he had squeezed her shoulder just as hard with his left hand. He stroked her shoulder and mumbled an apology.

Henrik had fought against death. First alone, then pinning his hopes on the nurse from Fårö who had come equipped solely with her goodwill. Then, when she had given up, his hope had been awakened again by the sound of the helicopter. Now it was for real, he had thought. Now the ones who could fix everything had arrived. Emergency response, acute care, transport to the country's best specialists. Whoosh, whoosh, whoosh through the air. There came the rescue. Finally it would be right. An end to his own fumbling over bloody bodies. An end to local nurses and powerless ambulance personnel. Here came the real pros, the rescue from the air with adrenaline syringes and drip and . . .

Then hope died. Even before the helicopter hit the ground. It was just a reflex, a feeling without any anchoring whatsoever in reality.

He did not remember how he got out of the house, but suddenly he found himself out in the garden with Ellen and Maria. There were several others there. Police officers. An ambulance. Two policemen took him heavy-handedly aside, demanded that he show identification, asked questions. He was a confused man in bloodstained clothes at a crime scene. For a few dizzying seconds he was a suspected murderer.

His calling for Ellen echoed in his memory. She was all he had left now. Was that really so?

The police van drove slowly ahead and stopped in front of the gate at what was the forward end of the ferry at the moment. Immediately behind them followed the ambulance with the paramedics who had not been able to do anything. They had to get back to Visby of course, couldn't stand and wait in Kalbjerga for nothing. Had to be available for others. For those who could still be saved.

Their bodies rocked sideways in a common movement as the ferry put out from Broa and started its journey across the dark sound.

47.

Sara Oskarsson had been waiting in the Harbor Hotel reception area for almost twenty minutes. She was starting to get tired of staring at the ceiling fixture above her and the blue linoleum floor between her feet and wondered whether it really was the best way to use her time. Then finally Henrik Kjellander came through the door accompanied by his daughter, his sister-in-law, and the officer who was assigned to protect them.

Sara stood up, nodded to the officer, and then extended her hand to Henrik Kjellander.

"Hi."

"Hi," said Henrik in a subdued voice.

He was holding Ellen by the hand.

Sara reached out her hand to Maria Andersson.

"My name is Sara Oskarsson and I'm a detective inspector with the police in Visby."

Maria took her hand and gave it a brief squeeze.

"Maria Andersson."

"I'm truly sorry," Sara continued. "I understand that this must be difficult, but I have to ask a few questions. If that's okay?"

"Yes," said Maria, sneaking a glance at Ellen. "Yes, that will be fine."

"Do you want to go to the room for now?" the officer asked Henrik. Henrik looked questioningly at Maria. She raised her eyes. She looked tired, the whites of her eyes were more gray than white.

"You two go ahead."

"You can bring her to the room later," the officer said to Sara.

"Of course."

The receptionist took out two key cards and handed them to Sara's colleague. He took them and went with Henrik and Ellen. He had not said what room they were going to.

"Shall we sit down over there?" Sara suggested.

She pointed to four tubular armchairs covered in blue cotton fabric that were in an out-of-the-way corner of reception.

Maria went there without saying anything, flopping down on the closest chair. Sara sat down across from her.

"I want you to tell me what happened from the time you left your sister's house earlier this evening until you came back."

Maria looked down briefly, sucked on her lips, and looked up again.

"I asked Ellen if she wanted to go down and have an evening dip after dinner, and she wanted to. I asked . . ."

Maria fell silent, sat a little while with her mouth wide open, but then started up again.

"I asked Malin if it was too late, but she thought it was okay, for Ellen anyway. She and Axel would stay home. Well . . . we left, that is, we rode our bikes."

"What time was it then?"

Maria wrinkled her nose a couple of times, as if she could smell her way to the time.

"Six thirty I would think. About that. It was a little late as I said, but Ellen really wanted to."

Sara nodded and made a note.

"About six thirty."

"Yes."

"And then? You took off on your bikes?"

"Yes, we biked down to the shore. We stayed a little longer than we intended. The water was so warm."

"So how were you dressed? That is, when you took off on your bikes?" asked Sara.

"Bathrobes. Both of us had bathrobes and swimsuits underneath."

"Did you see anyone on the road, or did you see anyone at the shore?"

"No," said Maria, hooking two fingers in the neckline of her avocado-green T-shirt.

"You didn't notice anything else?"

"No."

"No car that was parked anywhere?"

"No," said Maria as she inhaled.

She crossed her arms.

"What was it like later, when you came back?"

Maria coughed.

"Well, Henrik came rushing out, screaming that we had to wait. I didn't understand a thing, he—"

She interrupted herself and lowered her voice.

"He was completely covered in blood and . . ."

The gray eyes suddenly became even darker. Sara could see how something seemed to close off inside her and Maria sighed deeply.

"Is that enough? I don't think I can take any more."

"Just one more question: Do you know what time it was when you came back?"

Maria sighed again.

"I would guess right after eight. Ten past maybe."

"Did you take your cell phone with you to the shore?" asked Sara, well aware that this was yet another question and that she was pressuring Maria.

"No," said Maria. She stood up. "Now . . ."

"Of course, forgive me," said Sara. "That will do. We'll have to continue later."

Sara showed her police badge to the receptionist, a young, dark-haired woman in a burgundy-red jacket, and asked for the room number.

"Room number fourteen. It's at the far end to the left."

She pointed in the direction that the officer had just gone with Henrik and Ellen.

When they came to the corridor, the policeman was already sitting outside the hotel room door. He raised a hand to show that he saw them. Sara didn't actually need to accompany her any farther, but went to the room with Maria anyway. Before they parted she turned to Sara.

"If Ellen and I hadn't gone swimming, what would have happened then, do you think? Would Malin and Axel still be alive, or would we be dead, too?"

48.

It was late before Fredrik could drive back to Visby and from there farther south. It was only a few hours before dawn when he entered the house. Everyone was asleep. No one heard him.

He locked the door and turned in toward the hall, remained standing, and looked at the jackets on the hooks to the right, shoes in a row below. No blood here, no dead bodies, just an ordinary hall.

He took a few steps forward and looked into the kitchen. No dead boy in front of the stove. Only their ordinary kitchen with a carelessly cleaned counter and kitchen table cluttered with magazines, papers, and boring mail that no one bothered to open.

Henrik Kjellander's kitchen had also been an ordinary kitchen until a few hours ago.

Fredrik went slowly up the stairs. The evening's events were hard to shake off. What he had seen in Kalbjerga combined two cases that he had a hard time coming to terms with. Violence against children and unprovoked violence that affected regular people. However unusual it was, it had a capacity to make everyday life fragile and unreliable.

He stopped by Simon's door. It was closed. He hesitated a moment, but then pushed down the handle and opened the door enough to be able to stick his head in. One of the hinges creaked. Simon mumbled something and moved in his sleep. He was tall, hardly seemed to fit in the bed where he was outstretched, would soon be taller than Fredrik.

The years with small children had seemed endless when they were going on. Now they were over. Many times he had longed for that, thought it would be a liberation. Be spared the endless minding and driving around, be spared slushy overalls, spilled-on clothes, sudden angry outbursts, and relentless refusal to perform the simplest little chores. Now he was no longer so certain.

He slowly closed the door and slipped in to Ninni.

"Hi, is that you?" she mumbled barely audibly in the darkness.

"Hi, how's it going?" he whispered.

He waited for an answer, but realized that she had already fallen back asleep. A little disappointed, he undressed. As soon as he crawled down into the bed beside her, he felt that he did not need to lie there sleepless after all.

49

It was six thirty in the morning. Henrik looked out over the harbor terminal. The Destination Gotland ferry was docked at the pier. The upper half of the side of the white vessel was lit up by the morning sun, the lower half in shadow from the cliff. The first cars had already started lining up in the many rows. Several rolled up to the gray-and-apricot check-in booths where three sleepy young people had just sat down in front of their computers.

Henrik saw police officers stopping the cars and looking in through the windows, searching for a blond woman in a white car who yesterday evening had killed . . .

He stopped the thought, tried to send it off in a different direction, tried to just see what was in front of his nose. But it was hard considering what was going on outside the hotel windows. They must not have thought about that when they decided to put them right there.

He turned his back toward the windows. Looked at Ellen, who was still lying in bed under the light blue cover. She was sleeping. Miraculously enough. Looking at Ellen both helped and made everything worse. She was still there, Ellen was still there, he thought. That was life, everything was not over. That was big, actually. Then he thought about her pain, her loss.

Henrik closed his eyes and sat down on one of the chairs that belonged to the gray-brown sofa group. The room was large. A white-stained door led to another room where Maria was sleeping. Or lying awake and staring. It was quiet anyway in there. A kind of suite in all its simplicity. Something that suggested that they would be there awhile. Family room, it said in the folder on the desk. A family room for half a family. A police officer standing guard outside the door.

The room was decorated in white and blue. There were the kinds of things that are usually found in hotel rooms, plus a small kitchenette in one corner. Above the bed hung a framed color photograph of windblown pines on one of the island's beaches. All of it far away, seen through a thin curtain that only existed in his head. He had slept a couple of hours after taking a sleeping pill.

Henrik ran his hands over the chair's upholstery. He did not know who he was right now. What would he be without the sleeping pill and the sedative they had given him? He was given three tablets in a small bottle. To take as needed. Who would he be? Exactly what would he feel? It was as if there were different floors inside him and right now he was moving on one of the middle levels, without the possibility of seeing down to the ground floor. At the same time something told him that it wasn't possible to live there. The air was poisonous, impossible to breathe.

He looked out at the sky, which was light gray. Perhaps because it was early in the morning. Perhaps because it was cloudy. Perhaps because that was how he saw the world. He could not decide which. Or was there actually a real curtain hanging in front of the windows? He wanted to get up and feel, but remained seated.

50.

Saturday morning. Fredrik did not feel completely present. His eyes were cloudy and the back of his head heavy as lead.

He was not the only one who was tired. It was noticeable from their movements as they sat down. But there was also an eagerness to get going, to make progress. Sara jabbed at her notepad with the back of her pen, and Ove rubbed his face with both palms, like a delayed morning washup. Gustav was sitting leaned over the table and conversing in a low voice with Leif Knutsson, who was sitting two seats away.

At eight o'clock sharp, Göran started to go through the state of the investigation, standing in front by the whiteboard. His eyes looked uncommonly dark, more black than blue.

"Henrik Kjellander's information has been checked with the witnesses and times for connection with cell phone masts, and everything he said checks out, so we can remove him. He drove home from a photo shoot down at Sudret by way of Visby. There he dropped three people off at the airport about six thirty, which all three have confirmed. It also tallies with information from Gotland Air's check-in. Henrik then took the seven thirty ferry from Fårösund. SOS Alarm took his call at seven fifty-seven, so we can expect that he was parking his car in Kalbjerga a few minutes before that."

Göran wrote down the set times on the whiteboard, which so far was blank, except for two portraits, one of Malin Andersson and one of her son, Axel.

"The closest neighbor, Ann-Katrin Wedin, says that she saw two individuals bicycle past dressed in bathrobes, an adult and a child, sometime between six twenty-five and six thirty. She was sure of the time because she usually turns on the TV when she comes home from work. She leaves it on in the background with *Evening Magazine* on TV4. When the local news starts at six thirty she sits down and watches. And the two in bathrobes had bicycled past a minute or two before the news started. The witness thought she recognized the child as Ellen Andersson but was unsure when she didn't recognize the grown woman as Malin Andersson. We can probably assume that it was Maria and Ellen she saw. Neither Ann-Katrin Wedin nor her husband Bengt made any other observations of individuals or vehicles during the evening."

Göran wrote these times down, too, and then browsed in his papers while his eyebrows glided higher and higher up on his forehead.

"I know that we've questioned the ferry personnel, they usually keep good track of the Fårö residents, but it doesn't seem as though we've got that information."

There was a throat clearing from Leif Knutsson, who was sitting all the way over by the opposite short wall.

"I was the one who questioned him," he said with his arms crossed over his uniform shirt.

"Okay, then you can inform us," said Göran.

"Olle Holt navigated the ferry yesterday. He went on at fifteen hundred hours and was still on duty when we ordered the stop. He was a little difficult, but finally spit out the Fårö people he thought had left the island between the seven ten trip and the stop. I'm sure he keeps track of every car, but you know how they are up there."

There was silent nodding around the table. The Fårö residents were not known for cooperating with the police. There were even rumors going around that ferry personnel called and warned people when there was a police car on deck. Fredrik doubted if that rumor applied any longer, but it had certainly been true at one time.

"This concerns three ferries on which the perpetrator could have left Fårö," continued Knutsson. "Besides Fårö residents, Olle Holt remembered a little red sports car, a Mazda, a smaller white car with some kind of streamer in the rear window. He was a little uncertain there. It could have been some kind of detail on the car. And finally two older Volvo station wagons about which he did not remember any details. Then, of course, there could have been more that he forgot."

"Thanks, then we'll get that into the system, too," said Göran. "Holt couldn't say which trip the white car was on board?"

"No, unfortunately," said Knutsson.

"Too bad they don't record on the surveillance cameras," said Ove.

"Exactly," said Göran and looked at Fredrik. "How did it go with the surveillance cameras in Uppsala? Did we have any luck there?"

He concluded with a little grimace that suggested that he did not count on any positive news.

"No," said Fredrik. "We were too late. The information no longer exists. I've asked the Uppsala police to check whether there might be any other cameras on the road between the station and the library, but it's probably the same thing there."

Göran hummed disappointedly and turned to Eva Karlén, who sat closest to his right.

"What do we have from the crime scene?"

Eva adjusted the band that held her hair together at her neck, even though it wasn't necessary.

"The shoe print from the hall seems to hold. Most likely it comes from the perpetrator, but I want to have someone else double-check. It's from the front half of the shoe. Unfortunately it has glided in step so it's not possible to determine the size exactly, but about size seven or eight. I'll try to find out what kind of shoe. Unfortunately, the wad of hair Malin had in her hand lacked roots, but I've sent it to the forensics lab for shampoo profile and hopefully mitochondrial DNA."

Eva continued to report on findings and observations in the hall at the house in Kalbjerga. She seemed to have everything in her head, didn't even need to glance at the papers.

"There are no traces of dragging in the blood around the bodies, which for one thing indicates that the victims had been unconscious or in any event incapable of moving once they landed on the floor, and for another that the perpetrator did not try to move or turn over the bodies."

"Is it possible to say anything more about the perpetrator based on the injuries?" asked Göran. "Height, for example?"

Eva shook her head and shut her eyes briefly.

"No. It's much too messy. It's not possible to see that sort of thing now. The medical examiner will certainly be able to, but not until the bodies have been cleaned of blood. He should have been here now, by the way, but there's an airline strike."

"Good timing," said Sara.

"Yes, I know," said Eva, rolling her eyes.

"One thing I don't get is why Malin Andersson even opens the door," Gustav broke in. "I mean with everything that's happened, the alarm they installed . . . Shouldn't she have been more watchful?"

"A conceivable explanation is that she knew the perpetrator," said Göran.

"The perpetrator may have her own key," said Fredrik.

The others turned inquiringly toward him.

"If we imagine that it is the same person who is behind everything that has happened so far, the damage, the threats, and that someone lured Ellen away from the school, then the perpetrator has had access to keys during the time she rented the house and was able to make copies."

"They installed an alarm, but didn't change the locks? Yes, of course it can be that way," said Sara, making a face.

"In any event, the lock is not manipulated in any way," said Eva. "Either the perpetrator got in with a key or else Malin opened the door."

"Or forgot to lock," Ove added.

Everyone in the room looked at him.

"I know, not likely, but we can't rule it out."

Göran pointed at the times he had written on the whiteboard.

"The perpetrator struck some time between six twenty-five and seven fifty-five. If we weigh in the doctor's assessment it's most probable that the murders occurred closer to six twenty-five. Assuming that the time is not random, the perpetrator must have waited for a moment when Malin would be alone in the house. She or he presumably enters the house shortly after Maria and Ellen have taken off down to the beach. In other words, the perpetrator must have kept herself hidden somewhere where she or he could observe the house."

"From the south you have a good view of the house from a long distance," Eva pointed out. "She could have parked behind the pile of timber down by the mailboxes, for example. From there you can see the front door and the parking area without being seen yourself."

Fredrik leaned slightly over the table.

"Isn't that a slightly strange time of day if you are hoping that the intended victim should be home alone?" he said. "The chance, or the risk, is pretty great, on the contrary, that someone suddenly comes home, as Henrik did. Perhaps she was only there to observe them and then the opportunity presented itself."

"Yes," Göran agreed. "Unfortunately there's not much about this that's unambiguous. Because the previous threats were directed against the whole family we can't be certain that the perpetrator was out to kill just Malin. Perhaps she or he simply went after those who happened to be home."

"It's just this thing with the child that feels so unpleasant," said Gustav. "Why would she attack the child? It really seems as if she wants to get at all of them."

"So she isn't satisfied yet, do you mean?" said Ove.

"That can't be ruled out."

Göran grasped the back support on the chair he had so far not sat down in.

"Okay," he said, "time to summarize. We are going to get in lists of names from those who have checked the ferry. The airplane isn't going due to the strike, as we've already discussed. We have to go through the whole passenger list, naturally, but we will get a compilation of blond women traveling alone that we will prioritize. Even if I think that this perpetrator is a little too intelligent to leave on the first morning ferry. If she is still on the island and not from here, she must have gone somewhere, so we'll check hotels, hostels, campgrounds, etc. Considering what we said about keys to the house it may even be worth checking up on the former owner."

"Wasn't it Ingmar Bergman?" said Ove. "He doesn't feel that relevant."

"There was someone in between," said Fredrik. "Some colleague of Henrik Kjellander, I believe."

"That makes it even more interesting," said Göran. "Will you take that?"

Fredrik nodded.

"Interviews with Stina Hansson and Henrik Kjellander's sisters have highest priority. Ellen Andersson could not point out Stina Hansson, but we have to recall that this may involve several perpetrators and crimes that don't necessarily have to be connected to each other."

"Or that Ellen was uncertain or didn't dare identify her," Sara added. "That has happened before."

"Exactly," said Göran. "So Stina Hansson is relevant to the highest degree. Fredrik and Gustav, you'll take that interview."

They nodded in response.

"And Sara and Ove will take the sisters on Fårö. The sisters' father must also be questioned."

Sara and Ove nodded in turn.

"No known lunatics came up in connection with Ellen and the school, but they must be checked again, too," said Göran, pointing at Leif Knutsson. "We have to keep all doors open. Maybe it's not a woman we're after this time at all."

He looked out over his detective inspectors and those who came from the uniformed police.

"So does everyone know what they're doing?"

There was nodding around the room and one or two were already starting to stand up.

"Good," said Göran. "Let's get going."

51

Fredrik had been right. Stina Hansson's kitchen was lighter and more pleasant in the mornings when the sunshine came in through the foliage on the big trees.

She looked more tired and paler than the last time he was there. Her hair was unwashed and the V-neck top was wrinkled.

"Are you still on sick leave?" he asked.

"No. You could have asked the ones who were here last night," she said, looking at Fredrik and Gustav through narrowed eyes.

"May we come in?" said Fredrik.

"Sure," she said, in a voice that sounded heavy and resigned.

In the bathroom the cat was pawing in the litter box. They sat down at the kitchen table in the same places as during the interview the week before, Gustav on the chair where Sara had sat. Fredrik felt his head starting to wake up, but his body was still putting up resistance. Ever since the accident he had been careful about sleep. He had no idea how he would cope with hard work and little sleep. At a guess, badly.

"So you were working yesterday?" he said.

"Yes. You could have asked the ones who were here last night that, too," said Stina Hansson.

She concealed a wide yawn behind her hand. It seemed like it would never end.

"But I'm asking you now," he said. "That's how this works."

He felt the irritation lying in wait, but so far he sounded calm and collected.

"Okay," she said simply, and curled up in the chair.

"Are you cold?" he said, mostly to compensate in case he had seemed unfriendly just now after all.

"No, it's okay."

He smiled briefly at her.

"When did you come home yesterday?"

"Four thirty, I think. I got off a little early."

"Any particular reason?"

"We didn't have that much to do, so I took the opportunity to leave early."

"But you're not completely sure of the time?"

"Not exactly. But around four thirty."

She was holding hard onto her upper arms, as if she was embracing herself. It really looked like she was cold.

"Was there anyone who saw you come home, a neighbor in the building or on the street?"

"Not as far as I know, but you can always—"

She stopped; she had already been told.

"We'll ask the neighbors," said Fredrik. "But if you know whether anyone has seen you it will go a lot smoother."

She nodded. The sun struck her face from the side and made her close the eye nearest to the window almost completely.

"Were you on Fårö yesterday?" Fredrik continued.

"No."

"You went straight home from work?"

"Yes."

"And later in the evening, you didn't go out then?"

"No."

Stina released the hold on her upper arms and leaned forward a little.

"She ran into me in the parking lot. I reported her. She didn't seem to be in her right mind. I don't know what got into her. But . . ."

She looked at Fredrik, then at Gustav, as if that was something they ought to understand.

"But what?" said Fredrik.

"But this is something completely different. I don't understand why anyone . . . I haven't been able to sleep all night. Not since they were here. I don't think anyone has been able to sleep all night. And it's really hard that the police come here as soon as something happens. You wonder what people are thinking."

"Your neighbors never seem to notice when you come home, so maybe they don't notice us, either?" said Gustav.

Stina Hansson glared at him. Two pink patches flared up on her pale cheeks.

"I was together with Henrik fifteen years ago. What of it? And okay, I followed the car a week or two ago because I wanted to talk with him."

She panted out the words in a trembling, agitated voice.

"And I'm blond and have a white car, like it says in the newspaper, that's what you're searching for."

She giggled abruptly and shook her head.

"It's so silly, you don't even notice it. Huh?"

Her voice seized up and she suddenly started crying. Her body bobbed on the chair and she hacked out sobs.

"Stina," Fredrik started.

She waved one hand defensively in his direction as if he had tried to touch her. The crying jag increased in strength like a rain shower that turns into a downpour.

Fredrik looked quickly at Gustav. It was a strong reaction. Experience had taught him that closeness to death could trigger the most varied reactions in people. Sometimes it had to do with their relationship to the deceased, but it could just as easily be death itself that struck something in them. Some closed up and seemed cold, some broke down, others became exaggeratedly pleasant and energetic. It was tempting to draw conclusions, but they would most likely be incorrect.

"I want you to leave," she said furiously between sobs.

For a moment Fredrik felt awkward, both as a person and a policeman. Should they bring her in? If Stina Hansson was the perpetrator, perhaps she was about to break down completely. There would be a risk that she would kill herself.

"Go," she almost screamed. She showed no sign of calming down.

"Stina. We can't go when you are so upset."

"Yes, you can," she said stubbornly, hiding her eyes behind her right hand.

Fredrik became more and more certain that they would have to take her along to Visby.

They sat silently at the table while Stina sniffled behind her hand. Fredrik wished he had Sara with him.

"Stina," said Gustav. "We can't just leave. You understand that, don't you?"

She removed her hand, but looked down at her lap. The crying quieted a little, but did not stop completely.

"You think it's going to be one way," she said, "but then suddenly half your life is over and you're still standing there staring toward the future. Do you understand?"

She looked up at them for a moment. Stina Hansson was only thirty-five. She ought to still have time, but Fredrik understood what she meant. He thought so anyway.

"It's as if life is turning on its own axis and suddenly everything has changed even though you're still standing in the same place," she said quietly.

Now her voice was fragile.

"It's like night and day. Suddenly everything is too late."

52

Elisabet Vogler looked challengingly at Sara Oskarsson and Ove Gahnström after closing the front door behind her.

Sara observed Elisabet while she tried to find the right words.

"I don't know if the rumor got here before us, but Malin Andersson, wife of your half brother Henrik Kjellander, was found dead in her home yesterday evening. Her son, Axel, was also found dead in the house. I'm sorry."

Elisabet Vogler blinked when Sara mentioned the boy, but otherwise stood mutely without batting an eye.

It was a strange situation. During their entire lives, the siblings had only met face-to-face at a funeral and were fighting over an inheritance at the moment. Even so, Sara felt that she had to show some kind of sympathy.

"Thanks." Elisabet finally found herself.

She already had her hand on the door handle as if the whole thing was over for her. A breeze made the leaves rustle in the dry maples.

"Yes," said Ove, "we have a few questions. Is it okay if we come in for a moment?"

Elisabet laughed as if Ove had just said something funny. She looked at him without saying anything, her head lowered slightly and pulled back as if she was studying something peculiar.

An uncomfortable silence ensued that was finally broken when Elisabet Vogler pushed down the door handle.

"Okay, okay, come in then."

Elisabet showed them into a large, light kitchen immediately to the left of the entrance hall.

"Be my guest," said Elisabet Vogler, making it sound like the opposite.

With an outstretched hand she showed them to a long oak table that was placed along the two windows toward the farmyard. On the table were two pewter candlesticks and over it a lamp was hanging with two white-glass shades.

"Where were you yesterday between six o'clock and eight o'clock in the evening?" Ove began the interview when they had settled down at the table.

He sat heavy and imperturbable in the chair across from Elisabet. The shirt that peeked out under a beige cotton jacket bulged the buttons over his stomach. He had his notebook out and both arms on the table.

' "So I'm a murderer now?" Elisabet Vogler exclaimed. "I killed my sister-in-law? Is that what you mean?"

"We are following up on everyone who has any relationship to the family and who was on Fårö at the time of the crime. This is routine."

"I had no relationship to any of them," said Elisabet.

"A formal relationship is sufficient," said Ove patiently.

Sara had to exert herself to remain neutral. She was annoyed by Elisabet Vogler's condescending manner. But there was something else there, too, more nervous than self-assured.

"So, between six o'clock and eight o'clock?" Ove repeated when Elisabet did not say anything.

"Yes," she sighed. "I was home then."

She put her chin in the air and looked at him with her light blue eyes. Sara could not help thinking that despite her dissociative manner she was extremely naked. She had an appearance that did not conceal much.

"Was there anyone else at home then?"

"Yes, at that time of day, of course. The children and my husband were all at home."

Elisabet turned her head away and looked out the window. A high, persistent sound forced its way in to them. It sounded like a fan on a silo.

Ove appeared to be thinking about his next question when the door opened and Ernst Vogler came into the kitchen. He stopped abruptly at the threshold and looked at Ove and Sara, adjusted his blue jeans jacket with two large hands.

Sara stood up, greeted him, and introduced Ove. The man reluctantly took her hand, squeezed it hard and quickly, and then Ove's.

"Ernst Vogler," he said.

"We need to ask you a few questions, too," said Sara. She could easily imagine that Ernst Vogler would have preferred being addressed as Mr. Vogler.

"Now?" he said. "I don't know if I have time for that."

Sara cleared her throat.

"It would be nice if you could take the time," she tried politely.

"Can you come back this afternoon, around four?" he said, striding farther into the kitchen and reaching for a thermos that was on the counter.

He set it down with a disappointed look.

"This concerns a murder case, so you'll just have to answer. Otherwise we can ask the questions in Visby."

Sara was tired of the whining resistance.

Ernst Vogler opened his eyes wide. For a moment it looked like he was thinking about lashing out at her, but then he gave up.

"Then let's do it now," he said simply.

"Where were you between six and eight o'clock last evening?" she asked.

"I was here at home," he said. "That is, in my house next door."

He pointed out the window with a slightly bent hand.

"And Elisabet was here, too," he continued without anyone having asked. "I saw when she came."

Elisabet did not bat an eye.

"And when was that?" Sara asked.

"Just past five. Then she was home the whole evening."

Sara turned toward Ove, who in turn looked out over the farmyard.

"You have a number of cars here," he said. "Which one did Elisabet use yesterday?"

"It was the Volvo, the silver-colored one there," said Ernst Vogler,
pointing out the window. "The one between the pickup and the white
one."

53.

Stina Hansson had been worried about her cat, would absolutely not
go anywhere before she was sure that someone would take care of the
cat. It was a little strange, as if she expected to be gone a long time. Or
was it simply a way to put up resistance?

Fredrik got hold of a neighbor who promised to feed the cat and
then they could send Stina off with a patrol car that was on its way back
to Visby.

They divided up the apartment between them. Gustav took the living room and bedroom while Fredrik took the bathroom, hall, and
kitchen.

The cramped bathroom with mottled gray floor tiles and bright
yellow glazed tile on the lower half of the walls truly reeked of cat.
Stina ought to think about changing the litter a little more often if she
was so concerned about her pet.

Fredrik put all the shampoo bottles in a bag, in case a shampoo
analysis of the tuft of hair from Malin's hand would be relevant. He
went through the medicine cabinet, without finding anything more revealing than a tube of salve for fungus that had expired several years
ago. He packed all the contents of the laundry basket in a paper bag

and screwed out the filter on the small washing machine that was
squeezed to the left of the door. It was just as well to do it thoroughly
while they had the chance.

He continued by going through the pockets of the outerwear hanging in the hall and was scratching in the clutter in the top drawer of the
hall bureau when Gustav called from the living room.

"What did you say?" he called back.

"Come and look at this," Gustav shouted.

With a few quick steps Fredrik was in the living room. Gustav stood
leaning over a thin white cardboard box with the cover in one gloved
hand and a photograph in the other.

"Here," he said, handing it over to Fredrik.

The black-and-white photograph depicted Stina Hansson. She was
lying nude on the floor with her fingers wedged into her pubic hair.
The picture was a few years old, it was apparent.

"Okay, that was daring, but . . ."

This was one side of the job he still sometimes felt uncomfortable
about. Rooting in people's most private hiding places. But he assumed
that Gustav had not called him in so that they could drool over Stina
Hansson's naked body.

"Check the back side."

Fredrik turned the picture over. It was stamped with Henrik Kjellander after a copyright symbol and an address in Stockholm.

"Okay," said Fredrik.

"There are more here," said Gustav, handing over two more pictures.

They also depicted Stina Hansson more or less without clothes. In
one she was sitting in an armchair, in another in a car with her top
pulled up over her breasts. There were also four faded Polaroids in the
carton. In those she was dressed, and in one of them together with
Henrik. His arm was stretched out toward the camera and ended in a
black shadow along one edge. Fredrik presumed that Henrik himself

had been holding the camera and aimed it at Stina and himself. Both of them were smiling broadly. Stina looked happy.

"We'll take these along," said Fredrik. "But most people probably save old pictures, especially if it's a famous photographer who took them."

"I'd like to know when they were taken," said Gustav.

Fredrik looked for a date marking on the pictures, but did not find one.

"We might as well continue with this," said Fredrik.

He pointed at the big shelf loaded with books, binders, and magazine holders.

They went through the shelf from either end. Fredrik browsed through grades, proof of employment, account statements, but also old class lists, a twenty-nine-year-old certificate from swimming school and a number of photographs that did not tell him anything. They worked intensively for almost an hour without making more than a few scattered comments.

"That took time," said Gustav when they were finally done with the shelf without having found anything else worth confiscating.

"Yes, she seems to save everything," said Fredrik.

"May indicate someone who has some difficulty letting go of the past," said Gustav.

"Christmas Eve for the amateur psychologist."

Gustav laughed curtly.

"In any case, there's more in the bedroom. I'll continue there."

Fredrik went into the kitchen. Maybe there was something in what Gustav had said anyway, he thought, as he picked up a bundle of magazines from the far end of the kitchen table. There was a feeling he himself had the first time he met Stina Hansson. Under the seemingly healthy surface there seemed to be a person who sat at home watching over something. Perhaps old memories? Old love? What she said today did not exactly contradict that thought.

He picked up the magazine on top and shook it over the table, then continued with magazine after magazine. When he was halfway through the pile five or six loose pages suddenly fell down on the tabletop. Fredrik immediately recognized the woman smiling toward him from a picture on the topmost sheet. Vegetables, fruit, and a can of Greek olive oil were beautifully arranged on the marble counter in front of her.

54.

Alma Vogler lived near the sea. You could sense the sea even if it was concealed by a few sparse rows of pine trees. It was there as a smell, something cool and fresh in the air and a quiet swelling against the stones of the shore. The house must have been built in recent years. It looked modern and deliberate with black wooden panels, large windows, and an unpainted metal roof. Both foreign and Fårö at the same time.

"I just can't understand it," said Alma. "Here on Fårö. It's so awful."

Sara did not need to convey any news of the deaths. Alma Vogler started talking about the murders even before Sara and Ove managed to say hello.

"I didn't know Malin and Axel," Alma continued. "I've only met Malin one time, at Mother's funeral—"

She interrupted herself and lowered her eyes.

"But even if I didn't know them, they are related in some way. And Henrik—"

She interrupted herself again and looked in the direction of the sea that was so present, but not visible.

Yes, thought Sara, how was it really with Henrik?

They asked to come in. Alma suggested the living room. The kitchen was one big mess, she said. Sara and Ove sat down on a firm black felt couch, and Alma sat across from them in an armchair. She sat far out on the cushion, attentively leaning forward with her forearms supported against her knees.

"Where were you between six and eight o'clock yesterday evening?" said Sara.

Alma looked up toward the wall, somewhere above Ove's and Sara's heads, while she answered.

"We had dinner at five thirty, all of us, that is, Krister and I and the kids. Then I mostly sat in front of the TV. Krister was out working on his car for a while."

"So all of you were at home the whole evening?"

"The kids were over at the neighbors, right after dinner, but Krister and I were home."

"But you were in here and he was outside?"

"Yes, but that was only for a short time and right outside," she said with a gesture toward the window.

"How did you find out that Malin and Axel Andersson had been murdered?" asked Sara.

Alma's eyes narrowed when she heard the word.

"It can't be anyone from here who did it," she said, squinting at Sara. "It must be some complete lunatic, right?"

Sara did not answer, but noted that "lunatic" and "stranger" were synonymous.

Alma looked at her in confusion for a while, but then remembered the question.

"Excuse me. It was Elisabet who called. Although then she didn't know what had happened. Just that there was something going on with helicopters and police and that presumably someone had been killed."

"What time was that?"

"Right after ten."

"Do you know how Elisabet found out about it?" asked Sara.

"Someone phoned her. I don't remember who."

Sara turned over a new page in her notepad and looked out the high windows that reached almost all the way from floor to ceiling. You could actually see glimpses of blue between the trees.

"Was it you who built the house?" she asked.

"No."

Alma looked toward the windows, too.

"But it was practically new when we bought it. The family that built it lived here less than a year. They weren't from here. They probably didn't feel at home."

"It's nice. Extremely modern."

"Yes. The old stone houses have their charm, but I prefer this."

Alma cleared her throat briefly. She was presumably starting to wonder what Sara was after with her questions. Sara changed track.

"When did you find out that Henrik was your half brother?"

The question did not appear to come as a surprise. Alma barely reacted. Possibly she shrank a little in the armchair.

"Mother told Elisabet when she was eighteen and Elisabet told me, of course. Mother didn't want us to find out about it only after she died. Then that sort of thing comes out, with inheritance and such."

"Yes, that's the way it is, of course," said Sara.

"I actually wrote to Henrik once when I was sixteen. It was maybe six months after Mother told. But I never got an answer. I don't even know if he ever got the letter."

"Did you talk about it later? I mean the whole arrangement that Henrik grew up with his grandmother. Well, your grandmother, too, of course."

Alma slid backward in the armchair.

"No, that's not something anyone talks with Dad about."

"Not with your mother, either, when she was alive?"

"I asked a few times about what really happened, but Mother never really answered. Just something to the effect that it was different at that time, but I never really understood. That was in the seventies . . ."

Alma turned toward Ove Gahnström, as if she wanted to assure herself that he was listening, too, even though he had not said a thing since they sat down.

"I think it was extremely painful for her," she said. "It must have been."

"And Henrik?" asked Sara. "Didn't he ever try to make contact with you and Elisabet, or your mother?"

"No, not with us anyway. And if he was in touch with Mother that wasn't anything we heard about. I think he turned his back on everything, as if he wanted to show that he didn't need this place. He lived in Los Angeles for a while. He talked about that at the funeral. As I said before, I probably would have done the same."

Ove pointed toward the windows and the light that flooded in from the south.

"You practically have a waterfront lot here," he said.

"Yes," Alma admitted. "But the trees there aren't on my lot, so there isn't any sea view."

"That can't be cheap here on Fårö?" he continued.

"No," said Alma with a perplexed crease between her eyebrows. "Actually it's a depopulated area, but the summer visitors jack up the prices."

"But you got help to buy the house in connection with your father turning over the farm to Elisabet, is that correct?"

"Yes?"

The crease between her eyebrows had deepened and was joined by several wrinkles on her forehead.

"Was it your mother's inheritance from your grandmother that paid for the house?"

Alma's smile froze a little.

"I don't know exactly how they resolved that."

55

Maria was standing in front of Henrik wrapped in the hotel's blue-and-white–striped cover, looking at him with half-closed eyes. She had slept a long time. She must have taken two of those tablets they got from the doctor.

He didn't want to sleep. He never wanted to sleep again. He wanted to keep watch. Over Ellen, over himself, and over Malin and Axel. He would become a new person, a different person. A knight who never slept, who fed on air and lived for his daughter and the memory of his son, the memory of his woman. Malin and Axel. The ones who would never return.

He would be like the shores of Fårö. He would be sea, wind, and stone. He was already halfway there and the reasonable voice that whispered that he was going crazy was getting weaker and weaker.

"You have to tell me that this happened, otherwise I'll think I've been dreaming," said Maria hoarsely.

Her voice disturbed him in his almost euphoric sorrow. Maria was struggling to keep her eyes open. They were pulsing toward him, now narrow slits, now a black demanding gaze.

He kept silent.

"You have to tell me that this happened," she said again, coming a few steps closer to him.

Henrik glanced over his shoulder. Ellen was sitting in front of the TV but he had no idea whether she was following the program or simply sitting and staring into the screen with her ears on full alert.

He took a step toward Maria so that they were standing very close to each other.

"It did—" he started, but then his voice got stuck in a rasping resistance.

He took a couple of deep breaths and tried again.

"It did happen."

The blinking eyes became quiet.

"It did happen," he repeated. "They're gone."

He couldn't take any more. No more than that was needed.

He saw how Maria's eyes became glassy. Then the tears ran over.
Sobbing and struggling for air she raised her arms toward him. The
cover she had held firmly with her hands fell to the floor. She looked
like a helpless, confused child who had woken up from a nightmare.
She threw her arms around him and pressed her head against his chest.
He held her and felt how the crying made her skull hop against his
chest.

It did not feel very knightly, standing there holding onto his half-
naked sister-in-law in a medium-class hotel with a view of Visby harbor, but it would have been even less knightly not to do it.

How could they have ended up so wrong? Were they bad people,
unscrupulous? He wanted to ask Maria, but realized that this was not
the right moment to talk about it. Time had come to an end. He looked
out over the sea. There was always an end, even though you imagined
the opposite. Now he was there.

September 5

*I know that I'm an idiot who fritters my days away thinking about you. I
return to the best memories and to the ones that hurt the most. Which often
are one and the same. Remembering the best almost hurts more than remembering the worst.*

The first time you made me come, and I am swept away, don't understand what is happening to me. It's like the first time ever, my own experimenting thirteen-year-old fingers under the covers, and I think that something is wrong, that the world is ending, that I'm going to die.

The first time you come into me and, moaning, you whisper my name.

Then your closed face when you've said that there's no point in continuing. As if it were some damned law of nature that we can't be together. The worried wrinkle between your eyes as if I'm only a nuisance. An obstacle on the road. A road to a goal that I'm not part of.

Stubbornly I return there. The worst that causes pain and the best that causes even more pain. Stubbornly.

Now the drugs don't work. They just make you worse. I mortify myself, but I get no closer to God—ha ha.

I come to the fantasies. When I fantasize it's never about you, only about me. Always the same: that I am hanging in a big tree outside your house so that I'm the first thing you catch sight of when you come out in the morning. And if I'm feeling really bad: that I'm lying in a black plastic sack on the floor in the trash room and cutting up my arms. I cut deep into the arteries along the forearms, not amateurishly right across the wrists. In a couple of minutes I'm dead. There is no way back. Not even if a neighbor happened to come in right then to throw out the trash is there any chance for me. I am irretrievably lost. So nice not to feel anymore. And I have made it as easy as possible for those who will clean up after me. Did not even get blood on the floor.

I am ashamed. Don't believe for a moment that I am not ashamed of these thoughts.

56

Fredrik entered the interview room. It was in the middle of the corridor with direct connection to the jail. Stina Hansson was already waiting in the room along with the attorney who had been called in for her. Roger Lindell was one of Gotland's most experienced criminal defense attorneys. He was approaching sixty but there was still more blond than gray on his head. The closely trimmed full beard that decorated his powerful jaw was gray and red. He was dressed in a dark blue suit and a light blue shirt that was open at the neck.

Göran had held an initial interview with Stina Hansson as soon as she arrived in Visby. He had explained that on reasonable cause she was a suspect in the murders of Malin and Axel Andersson. She denied the crime.

Fredrik greeted Stina Hansson and Roger Lindell and set down the bundle of papers he had brought with him. He noticed how Stina Hansson's eyes widened when she caught sight of the black-and-white pictures that happened to end up at the top of the pile.

"What? Were . . . where did you . . ."

She looked at him with flaming cheeks.

Fredrik cursed his carelessness. It was poor tactics to let her see the pictures this soon.

He tried to repair the damage by turning the bundle with the nude photos and papers upside down. Besides the printouts from Malin's food blog, he had found printouts from GotlandsResor's presentation of Henrik and Malin's house and from Henrik's own website. In addition two newspaper clippings: the interview with Malin and Henrik in

Gotlands Allehanda and a feature about the Kalbjerga house in *Elle Decor.*

"Did you search my apartment?"

The thought seemed to be completely foreign to her.

"We have conducted a house search, that's correct. Where investigations of serious crimes are concerned, unfortunately normal consideration has to take a backseat."

"But I have nothing to do with this crime," she said in a shaky voice.

"That's what you say, but there is a good deal that suggests the opposite."

Stina Hansson abruptly opened her mouth but could not get out a protest. She stared right into Fredrik's shirtfront with wild eyes.

"I would like to know what you were doing on the fourth of June."

"The fourth of June," she repeated. "Why is that? That was three months ago."

"Yes. And I would like to know what you were doing that day."

She still looked doubtful, as if he was toying with her.

"The fourth of June . . . what day of the week was that?"

"It was a Thursday," said Fredrik.

"I see," she said hesitantly and looked away. "I guess I was working."

"According to your employer you took the day off."

The indifferent expression disappeared.

"Exactly, it was then. It's not so easy to keep track of every single day after the fact like this," she said quickly.

"No, of course not," said Fredrik. "But on that particular Thursday you were off work."

"Yes, Friday, too."

"Why was that?"

"No particular reason. I just felt like it. I'd been working a lot and the weather was nice, so I decided from one day to another. We have a few people who can come in if someone gets sick, so that was no problem."

"From one day to another? What does that mean exactly?"

"Mean?" said Stina.

Fredrik sensed hostility in her voice.

"I mean, when exactly did you decide to take the day off?"

"The day before. And that was when I asked Gabriella. My boss, that is."

"So you got a long four-day weekend," Fredrik noted.

Stina nodded.

"What did you do during this time off?"

She thought about it.

"On Thursday I was at the beach a couple of hours."

"Wasn't it cold in the water?"

"I didn't swim. But it was a very nice day. I lay there and read, brought coffee with me."

"But there can't have been many people there?" said Fredrik.

"No, I was probably alone, as I recall. Maybe someone walked past."

"Anyone you know?"

"No."

No one who could say that she really had been there, thought Fredrik.

"Were you at the beach in Fårösund?" he asked.

"No, it was in Valleviken."

"I see. That's a ways to go."

"It's not really that far," said Stina. "And I did have the day off."

"And the rest of the day?"

"I didn't do that much. I think I did some shopping on the way home, then I made dinner and kept on reading. I had a book I was really into."

"What book was that?"

"What do you mean?"

Why didn't she just answer the question? Did she need time to think of a title?

"You said that you were really into it. Then you must remember what book it was, right?"

"*The Ice Princess* by Camilla Läckberg," she said curtly.

That was probably what everyone in Sweden was reading, so it could be true, but less convincing for just that reason. If he were to ask what it was about. No, she could have read it on the train to Uppsala. Her "What do you mean?" was more interesting than a reference to the plot. He let it go.

"But on the way home from the beach you did some shopping. Or you're not sure of that, either?"

"Yes, I did some shopping."

Stina coughed and looked at the mirror glass into the adjacent room. "Is someone sitting in there?" she said with a nod toward the mirror.

"No," Fredrik said truthfully.

Stina sighed quietly and briefly met his gaze before she looked away in another direction. Fredrik steered her back to the interview.

"Where did you shop?"

"At the Bungehall grocery store," she said.

"Did you pay cash or with a card?"

"Uh . . . cash, I think."

"So you spent all of Thursday by yourself?"

"Yes."

"What about on Friday, did you see anyone then?"

"No, not exactly. Probably said hello to someone on the street. On Saturday I visited a friend and had coffee."

"Have you been in Uppsala at any time?"

She was silent for a moment, but then shook her head.

"No."

"You have no connection there? Relatives or friends who live there?"

"No. Maybe I know a few people who studied there, but no one who still lives there."

"Maybe, or do you?" he said.

"I know a few."

"Can I get their names?"

Stina gave Fredrik names and addresses, which he wrote down. Her tone of voice suggested that she thought this was a little silly. There was a short pause while Fredrik wrote down the last address. The ballpoint pen rustled faintly against the paper.

"May I go home when this is over?" Stina asked.

Suddenly she sounded anxious.

"You know that you've been taken into custody, Stina. Göran Eide explained to you what that entails, didn't he?"

Her eyes became glassy, but she blinked it away.

"Yes, yes," she said.

"In any event, I'll soon be done with the interview," he said, smiling at her.

He reached for the printouts he brought with him and spread them out across the table.

"These are from Malin Andersson's food blog and from Henrik Kjellander's website."

He pushed forward another paper along with the clippings from *Gotlands Allehanda* and *Elle Interior*.

"And this is from GotlandsResor. The page where their house is presented. The article from *Gotlands Allehanda* was printed in August. All of it was found at your home."

Fredrik fell silent and waited for a reaction. Stina did not say anything. Her eyes moved slowly between the pages.

"You have collected a good deal of material on Malin and Henrik."

Stina swallowed.

"Is it the case that you've thought quite a bit about Henrik and about how he was doing with Malin and his family on Fårö?"

Stina looked at page after page as if she was seeing them for the first time.

"Is that so?" Fredrik tried again. "What do you really think about this?"

He nodded at the pictures.

Stina Hansson leaned slowly over the table and hid her face in her hands as if she did not want to see any more. Roger Lindell briefly met Fredrik's eyes before he turned toward his client.

"Stina? If you want we can break off the interview," he said.

"No," she mumbled from behind her hands.

She relaxed her palms, supported her forehead against her fingertips.

"Do you think I'm nuts?" she said. "Maybe I am. I don't know," she mumbled from behind her hands.

Fredrik was uncertain whether she had turned to him or to her attorney, but then decided that it was to him.

"Was it not the case that you were in Uppsala that Thursday you were off? You were there and visited someone and then you got the idea to rent Henrik's house, which you had seen on the Internet. Or had you already planned it before you went there?"

She must have because her name was not on the ferry passenger list.

Stina Hansson peeked out from between her hands and let them slowly sink down to the table.

"What? Was that why you asked about Uppsala?"

"Stina. Tell us now."

"There's nothing to tell. I have nothing to do with this. I know I don't have an alibi, but I live alone and I don't have many friends. Excuse me, but that's my life."

She sighed heavily and turned away, but suddenly turned back again when she met her own gaze in the mirror glass.

"Stina," said Fredrik. "You've been together with Henrik Kjellander, you have no alibi for the fourth of June when Henrik's house was booked in Uppsala, you have been observed outside Axel's day care . . ."

"I've explained that."

"You have no alibi for the day when Ellen was taken away from the school, but by chance you were at home in Fårösund that day. You are blond, have a white car, and you have no alibi for the evening when Malin and Axel were murdered, your shoe size is seven and a half, which matches the print in the hall . . ."

He pushed the bundle of papers to the middle of the table.

"And you have snooped in Henrik's and Malin's lives and preserve old memories, pictures of you and Henrik together."

Stina looked silently at the pile of pictures and clippings. There was twitching below her left eye.

"That's a strong chain of circumstantial evidence. Don't you think so?" said Fredrik.

"You don't have to answer that," said Lindell.

He leaned toward Fredrik.

"This is a chain of circumstantial evidence, but that's also all it is. There is not a single piece of technical evidence or a witness statement that points to Stina."

"The shoe print," Fredrik reminded him.

"The size possibly agrees, but Stina doesn't own any shoes with soles that match the print, you know that. And Ellen Andersson could not point her out during the lineup."

Fredrik did not answer. He had no desire to sit and debate with the attorney. Too many things were missing to be able to go to court, he realized that, as well, but the investigation of Stina Hansson had only begun.

57

After Fredrik turned Stina Hansson over to the jail guard, he took a break and bought a mineral water and an apple. He took a couple of large gulps on the way to his office and tried to collect himself for the next interview. He was starting to feel that he had been going all day. That he had slept too little.

There was something in what the attorney said. There was no technical evidence, not one witness. Considering how many circumstances there were that spoke against Stina Hansson, it was almost strange that they had not found any concrete evidence.

Fredrik sank down behind his desk, leaned back, and closed his eyes. After a minute he had fallen asleep. He dreamt that he was back in Stina Hansson's apartment, rooting through the medicine cabinet, pulling out drawers, bagging up dirty laundry.

He woke up with a jerk and looked toward the doorway with a guilty conscience. No one there. He looked at the clock. He could not have slept more than a couple of minutes.

Energized from his brief nap, Fredrik reached for the bottle and emptied it. He set it down on the table and caught sight of Stina's printouts from Malin Andersson's food blog. He had searched for potential perpetrators in the comments field of the blog posts, but what was there to say that the worst comments weren't already edited out even before they appeared on the site?

He inserted his card into the reader and brought the computer to life. He searched online for a switchboard number for Coop, picked up the phone, and dialed the number. After some wrangling he got hold of a website technician. He quickly explained what he was looking for

and was transferred again. A saucy melody invaded the receiver while
he waited.

The melody stopped and he got a response from Anna Jones, who
spoke in a barely noticeable British accent. He explained once again
what this concerned.

"Yes," she said, "we sift out comments that are obviously unpleasant or have no connection to the content on the site."

"So those comments are never published at all?" Fredrik asked.

"No, it's just me or someone else in the office who sees them. We
have to approve everything before it goes up on the website."

"Are they saved? I would like to see everything that has been removed during the past year."

"Yikes, that can be quite a bit."

"Really? Has there been a lot of that sort of thing on Malin's
pages?"

"Well, not specifically on hers. The Internet is full of them. Unpleasant is probably just the first name. But it's kind of like the name
of the game."

"Okay, but you can produce them?"

"Absolutely, no problem. In general they aren't even deleted, it's just
that they are never published. But I have to compile them. If I can have
an e-mail address?"

Fredrik gave Anna his e-mail address and thanked her for the help.
He hung up and looked at the clock on the computer. He would have
time to give Göran a brief summary before it was time for the interview with Henrik Kjellander.

"That business with Coop is good," said Göran. "Stina Hansson has
been a frequent visitor to Malin's Table."

He got up from his chair, continuing his reasoning while he stretched
his back and slowly moved toward the other end of the room.

"At the same time, there's something that bothers me. It's over fifteen years since Henrik Kjellander. Seriously speaking . . ."

Göran stopped by the big, refrigerator-like safe that was in the corner diagonally from the desk. He turned around and looked at Fredrik.

"I agree."

"Provided that they haven't—" Göran began.

"Started something again?" Fredrik interjected when Göran delayed the continuation.

"Exactly."

Göran eagerly took a step forward.

"Last spring, or maybe a couple of years ago when Henrik came back. A little affair on the side. Strong emotions were brought to life in Stina, but for Henrik it's just a little sidetrack."

"It's a good idea."

"Pressure him about that. People can keep quiet for the longest time about infidelities, but in this case . . . If you hang Stina Hansson out as a conceivable perpetrator, he ought to talk if there's anything to tell."

"Can we get her held in remand?"

"Peter seems certain. Plenty of circumstantial evidence, and considering the nature of the crime, the escalation from threat to murder, it is conceivable that in the worst case the perpetrator may murder again."

"But that is a circular argument: You have to be guilty to be dangerous."

"Yes, but Peter is counting on the judge overlooking that in this case."

Fredrik frowned.

"You don't seem convinced."

"Well," he said, "I just see that this can crack and if it does we'll basically be left empty-handed."

"True. We don't have to get too caught up about Stina Hansson. Pressure Kjellander about her, but it is also important that we find out as much as possible about him and Malin. Dig deep and wide. There may be something that both he and we have missed."

* * *

Fredrik had chosen the bigger room at the end of the investigation group's corridor, considering that it was more pleasant than the little room next to reception. At first he intended to hold the interview at the hotel, but Henrik himself wanted to come to the police station.

Henrik looked pale and dogged, his face swollen by too little sleep. His hair was tangled with old hair gel.

"How is Ellen doing?"

"I don't know," said Henrik quietly.

He looked down at the table.

"I understand how hard it must be to answer questions now," said Fredrik. "I'll try to keep this as brief as possible."

Henrik raised his head from his hand and looked at Fredrik.

"Thanks."

"There will quite certainly be more interviews, but for the moment there are only a few questions."

Henrik trembled.

"What is it?" asked Fredrik.

"I've hardly slept a wink," said Henrik. "Despite the sleeping pills. I . . . I'm a little groggy. . . ."

He closed his eyes and sat quite still, leaning forward slightly. Fredrik almost thought he had fallen asleep.

"Henrik?"

He slowly opened his eyes and reached out the palm of one hand in a kind of inviting gesture.

"Of course."

Was there any point at all in holding an interview under these circumstances? Fredrik got a definite feeling that Henrik could say just about anything. Even if his eyes were open and he answered when addressed, he hardly seemed conscious.

"Stina Hansson," said Fredrik.

Henrik Kjellander's eyes widened a little.

"You had a relationship when Stina lived in Stockholm."

"Yes. It ended fifteen years ago."

"You haven't had any contact since then?"

"No."

"Not at all?"

"I've run into her in Fårösund a few times."

Henrik seemed uninterested in the subject.

"It's not the case that she or you made contact since you moved back?" asked Fredrik.

"No."

"If that is the case, it's important that we find out."

Henrik tried to change position in the chair, but the end result was that he remained sitting the same way as before, slightly collapsed.

"Why is that important?"

Fredrik hesitated, but decided to put his cards on the table.

"There are a number of concurrent factors that indicate that Stina Hansson could be the perpetrator."

"Stina?"

"I'm not saying that's the case," Fredrik emphasized, "but it is a possibility."

"Not Stina," mumbled Henrik.

He looked away and shook his head. Fredrik thought that he saw a little smile.

"What we don't understand is why in that case she would have done it. But if the two of you, in one way or another, have started a relationship again, that could be an explanation."

"What the hell," said Henrik, looking doubtfully at Fredrik. "You don't think I've been having an affair with Stina, do you?"

"I am forced to ask."

"Okay."

He didn't even bother to deny it again. Fredrik believed him.

"I need help with another matter," he said.

Henrik nodded, almost like a drunk who promises without meaning it.

"I want you to make a list of all your customer contacts and all your personal contacts in the past year."

"Personal? You mean people I've gotten to know? Or do you mean all?"

"No, new acquaintances. And write down all the trips you've taken, where you stayed, who you saw."

"All of them?" said Henrik skeptically.

"Everyone you can recall that you have had some kind of contact with that has been more extensive than just saying hi. The kind you've worked together with. Someone you met at a party and sat and talked with. Tradesmen who've been in the house on Fårö. The car dealer you bought your car from."

"That was two years ago," said Henrik.

"Okay, forget about him for now. But you understand the principle."

"Sure," said Henrik, swaying a little on the chair.

"Maybe it's easier if we do it together," said Fredrik. "If we go through your calendar, your invoices and credit card statements. That's usually a good support for your memory."

"Now?" said Henrik.

"Maybe you need a good night's sleep first?"

Henrik did not answer. He turned his head away and coughed.

"What do you think?" said Fredrik.

"That will have to wait," said Henrik.

"Before you get to sleep, you mean?"

"Yes."

"We can talk with the doctor. You must have something so you can sleep properly."

Fredrik was a little ashamed that his concern about Henrik was mainly about getting him in good enough condition that he could hold a reasonable interview.

"I don't want to," mumbled Henrik.

Fredrik froze. Had he pressured him? No, hardly.

"You don't want to continue?"

"I don't want to sleep."

Fredrik forced back a paternal smile.

"You have to sleep. It's important."

Henrik did not answer. He had fixed his gaze on the room's long, narrow windows that sat high up under the ceiling.

"Do you want to go back to the hotel?" asked Fredrik.

"I don't want to sleep," Henrik repeated.

He seemed more confused than Fredrik realized at first. It was not really possible to continue.

"Do you need anything from Fårö to be able to do such a review?" he asked anyway.

Henrik seemed to think for a while; perhaps he needed time to even understand what Fredrik was getting at.

"The computer," he said.

"Okay, we can arrange that. Anything else?"

Henrik sat silently.

"Then we'll see about getting the computer here. If there is anything else you think of that you need, then give me a call."

Henrik nodded.

"I don't have all the information, but you can talk with my agent, too," he said. "She keeps track."

"Where can I get hold of her?" asked Fredrik.

Without answering, Henrik stuck his hand down in his back pocket and pulled out his iPhone. He fixed his gaze on the display and browsed through the menus with his right index finger. Then his arm suddenly fell downward as if it slid off an invisible table edge. Henrik lost his grip on the phone. It fell to the floor, bounced once, and slid slowly buzzing away across the linoleum.

58

Fredrik turned over an unused page on the notepad and searched for the number to Henrik Kjellander's agent.

"Drake Agency, Janna Drake," an energetic yet slightly veiled voice answered on the first signal.

Fredrik introduced himself and explained why he was calling.

"Yes, good Lord, I heard that yesterday," said Janna Drake. "That's completely insane. Henrik is one of those we've worked with the longest. He's . . . well, he's a good person, professional, easy to deal with. You're always happy to work with him. And then this. It's—"

She sighed into the phone.

"Do you know who did it?"

"I need your help with some information," said Fredrik.

"Of course, anything you ask for. I'll do all I can."

Fredrik started by asking about a list of Henrik's clients during the past year. Names, contact information, and a brief description of the assignment.

"I'll compile that," she said. "You'll have it within half an hour."

"Do you know Henrik personally, too?" Fredrik asked.

"Well, yes," she said. "That depends on what you mean. Sometimes we socialize outside work, we've been working together a long time, but mostly it's through work. I'll be at some dinner with Henrik and Malin—"

She fell silent and continued a bit more hesitantly.

"A few times a year maybe. And they'll be at our place. On that level."

"So you're not that familiar with his circle of acquaintances?"

"No, but many of them are photographers, I know them through work. But I know who you could talk with. Thomas Bark. He's one of Henrik's best friends. They've known each other a really long time."

"All the way from Gotland?" asked Fredrik.

"No," she said, "not that far back, but I think they went to the photography school together and that was seventeen years ago."

Janna gave Fredrik Thomas Bark's cell phone and work numbers.

"He probably knows Henrik's friends pretty well."

"Did you know Malin?" asked Fredrik.

"Yes, I did. It's completely incomprehensible . . . Completely incomprehensible. I mean, does this sort of thing happen here? You're a policeman. You must know."

"Not really. It's extremely unusual."

"That makes it even more incomprehensible. Who would want . . . And Axel."

Janna's voice became shaky.

"How were things between Henrik and Malin?" said Fredrik.

"They were good. They were always so sweet together. I think they were doing fine."

"Even since they moved to Gotland?"

"It seemed that way, but of course it's hard for me to say."

Fredrik felt satisfied with Janna Drake for the moment. He thanked her and said that perhaps he would get back to her later.

He immediately dialed the number for Thomas Bark. It rang a long time. Finally someone picked up the receiver at the other end, but without saying anything. Instead he heard a conversation going on in the room. Something about who should do what when and the name Fransson was repeated several times.

"Yes, hello," one of the voices said at last, a little irritated.

"Is this Thomas Bark?"

"Yes, excuse me, it's me," said Thomas Bark, putting on a polite telephone voice.

"My name is Fredrik Broman and I'm calling from the police in Visby. I need to ask you a few questions."

"Oh hell. I understand."

Fredrik heard Thomas Bark breathing into the phone.

"You are a close friend of Henrik Kjellander, is that correct?"

"That's correct. I understood that was what you wanted to ask about. I heard—"

"Have you talked with Henrik?"

"No. I haven't had a chance to call." Thomas concluded with a slight cough.

"Or for whatever reason."

There was complete silence on the line.

"Are you still there?"

"Yes, I'm here. I . . . To be completely honest I don't know what I should say. This is really awful. What do you say?"

Fredrik realized after a brief silence that the question was sincere, not rhetorical.

"I don't think it's that important what you say," he said.

Thomas Bark mumbled something into the receiver.

"Excuse me?"

"You have a point there," said Thomas Bark, more intelligibly. "Is there anyone with him now? I mean some friend or relative?"

"He's with a relative."

"Okay, that's good."

There was a scraping on the line.

"Hello?"

"Yes, I'm still here."

"Have you and Henrik maintained contact even after he moved to Gotland?"

"Yes, absolutely. We don't see each other as often, of course, but Henrik is in town at least once a month and I've been down to Fårö three or four times for sure. It doesn't take long to fly down and, well . . ."

"How were things between him and Malin? I assume that he tells you about such things?"

Bark cleared his throat.

"You don't suspect Henrik of this, do you?"

"No, he's been ruled out."

"Well, that's good."

There was silence on the line.

"Malin and Henrik?" said Fredrik.

"A pretty big question. You can't be a little more precise?"

Answering that kind of question is not really that tricky, thought Fredrik.

"Were they doing okay, or has Henrik mentioned any problems during the past six months or year?"

"They were doing really well, I would say. Then they've been together a pretty long time and have two kids. A long relationship always has its ups and downs. But on the whole . . ."

"No real problems, you mean?"

"No."

"Henrik hasn't said anything about any relationships with other women?"

A brief silence before Bark answered with a question.

"You mean if he had something going on the side?"

"Yes."

"Why would that be interesting?"

"One thought we are working on is that the murderer may have been driven by jealousy."

"If you ask me, I think it seems to be pure madness."

"It might be that way, too, of course," Fredrik admitted. "But it's still more likely that somehow or another this has a connection to Henrik or Malin."

"Yes, of course," mumbled Thomas.

"Are you aware of whether he had any other relationships, short-term or longer?"

"No."

"He never talked about any such thing?"

"No, I can't say that he did."

"You don't sound completely sure."

"Well, I'm thinking about whether he hinted at anything, but . . . No."

"And no names came up that could be interesting in such a context, even if he didn't say anything concrete about them?"

"I don't know, no . . . that is, there are an awful lot of names spinning around in our industry. Models, people from magazines, stylists, makeup artists . . . But nothing that . . ."

He clearly had difficulty finding the words.

"Not in that way," he decided at last.

"So you mean that you haven't had any boy talk about photo models or other women?"

Thomas Bark laughed.

"Sure, that has happened, but that sort of thing doesn't mean anything."

"Stina Hansson, does that name say anything to you?"

Bark thought a moment.

"No. Or wait. That was one of Henrik's girlfriends . . . well, a hell of a long time ago."

"One of Henrik's girlfriends?"

"Yes, he probably had one or two before he met Malin."

"It doesn't sound as if it was a particularly steady relationship. Between Stina and Henrik, I mean."

"That I don't really know. I have the idea that they lived together awhile, so it must have been somewhat steady."

"But you haven't heard the name since then?"

"No."

"And you don't know whether Henrik saw her recently?"

"He . . ."

Thomas Bark interrupted himself and had a new tone in his voice when he continued.

"Do you mean she's the one who did it, this Stina? That sounds completely crazy."

"Stina is one of many leads we are working on. It doesn't mean that she's guilty."

"But you're looking for a jealous ex?"

"That's one angle."

"I see, do such things happen? It sounds like a movie."

"It happens. But you're right. That a woman, as it appears to be in this case, murders out of jealousy is extremely uncommon. Most often it's men. But as I said, we don't even know if that's how it fits together."

"No, I understand."

Fredrik could hear Thomas Bark's breathing on the line.

"I see, well then, was there anything else?"

"You never answered the question of whether Henrik had seen her since he moved back to Gotland."

"No, exactly, exactly. Now as far as I know. He hasn't mentioned her."

"Okay, then I won't disturb you any longer."

"It's no problem."

"Yes, just one last question," said Fredrik. "Henrik has not mentioned any other conflicts, anyone he's had a falling out with, quarreled with about a job or about money?"

"No, not that sort of thing, either. Henrik is not a guy who gets into trouble. He always works hard to do his best. If there's ever any trouble you can be very sure that he met up with a real asshole."

"But no one like that has shown up this year?"

"Not that I know about."

Fredrik thanked him and hung up. He had not found out much. Practically speaking nothing. But he had a definite feeling that he had not been told everything.

Ninni heard the front door open and shouted a hi out toward the hall. There was a muffled hi back, then silence while Fredrik untied his shoes.

"You're home really late."

She got no answer. She saw Fredrik pass the doorway like a shadow before she heard his steps on the stairs, heavy but steady. They continued across the floor upstairs. The creaking of the floorboards was clearly heard through the ceiling. Then there was silence. Ninni pricked her ears. She thought he was on his way into Simon's room, but it was completely silent up there.

Ninni looked at the pile of papers lying in front of her on the table. She thought she would be done with them this evening, but had not made it more than halfway. The TV had stayed on a little too long.

It was simpler with ordinary tests. When the students wrote essays in English it sometimes got so complicated that in the end the submitted papers contained more red pen than pencil. Ninni mostly felt like a butcher out for some poor young person's self-confidence and desire to learn. But many were also extremely advanced. Whatever the average skills in the country might be, there were a number of Swedish children who were very good at English, that couldn't be denied.

It was ten minutes to eleven. It was high time to nag Simon into bed. She gathered up the essays in a neat pile, the uncorrected ones on top, stood, and went upstairs.

"Fredrik," she called halfway up the stairs.

No answer.

When she came into the bedroom he was lying stretched out across the bed with his clothes on, his face turned toward the wall.

"Fredrik?"

For a moment she was scared. Then she saw that he was breathing. He was probably just worn-out. Completely-worn out, clearly. How tired were you if you didn't even have the energy to stop and say hi properly? And he had driven home from Visby. A forty-five-minute drive, alone in the car, verging on unconscious.

59

Several new pictures had come up on the whiteboard in the window-less conference room, but two of them in particular attracted Fredrik's attention. They depicted two heads. It was not hard to understand whose, even if the hair had been shaved off and the skin on the skulls was turned down over the faces. Only splinters remained of the upper parts of the crania. In several places the bone was crushed and pressed in, and the holes were of the same size and shape as a hammerhead.

Fredrik's own head was ringing, just like the other evening in the garden. He turned his eyes away from the macabre images. The sound was imaginary, created in his head just like the memory of how he fell out at Östergarnsholme. The memory that could not possibly be a memory. He peeked at the pictures from the corner of his eye and wondered how having them posted would help them solve the crime.

It was two and a half days since SOS Alarm had taken the call from Henrik Kjellander. The lineup was not really the same as over the weekend. Gustav was missing, as was Eva Karlén.

Fredrik leaned closer to Sara and asked if she had seen Gustav.

"He's not coming in today."

"Is he sick?"

"Family reasons."

The test results. Was it today they would get the news? Fredrik was not certain. He fingered his cell phone and wondered whether he should call, but realized that he would not have time before the meeting. Besides, calling would probably only be a disturbance. Better to call this evening. Or maybe tomorrow, if Gustav was still not back at work.

He looked at the whiteboard again. Of the other pictures that had been put up, five were from the crime scene, four were enlarged passport photos that depicted Stina Hansson and Henrik Kjellander's half sisters on Fårö and their father.

"Okay, let's get going, with a little luck we'll have a crime-scene technician here, too," said Göran, setting his glasses down on the tabletop.

He pointed at the passport picture on the whiteboard that depicted Stina Hansson.

"Hansson is still behind bars, held for homicide. There are remand hearings tomorrow. We still have no technical evidence, but there's a lot that suggests that it's her. Besides, she's the woman without an alibi. So far we have not managed to find any person or circumstance that can support that she has been where she says she's been, neither when the Kalbjerga house was booked in Uppsala or at the time of the murders."

Peter Klint nodded at Göran, raising one index finger in the air.

"And that is exactly why we have to keep working," he said. "Find a witness who may have seen her, talked with her, anything at all that can refute or confirm the information she's given us. She was a little wobbly on a few points during the interview, but no worse than if she simply didn't remember."

The prosecutor slowly ran his gaze over the police officers in the room as he spoke.

"If what Stina Hansson says is true, reasonably there ought to be something that can link her to her home at a certain point in time, an Internet connection, a cell phone or landline call, a neighbor who heard flushing in the pipes. Something. On the other hand, if she is not telling the truth she can not possibly have been in Uppsala to book and pay for the house, then also have been in the house, taken Ellen Kjellander with her in the car from the school, and committed the murders without having been seen or left a single trace on any of those occasions. And someone ought to have seen her car on Fårö. At the time of the murders it was dented on one fender and easy to identify. Someone has definitely seen it, but not made the connection."

Göran turned back to the pictures on the board.

"Our other cluster of possible murderers is the three Voglers. All of them have alibis, of course, but these three and the sisters' husbands give each other alibis back and forth. There is a motive."

Again Peter Klint's eyebrows went up and his finger in the air.

"We've talked about that inheritance before. I don't think Henrik Kjellander has much of a case, in purely legal terms."

Göran rubbed his forehead thoughtfully.

"In any event, the Voglers' alibis must be checked carefully. As long as we haven't found any outsider who can support their alibis they will remain as case files."

Göran picked his glasses up from the table.

"What else do we have?" he said while he put them on.

He quickly browsed through his notes.

"Exactly! The former owner of the house. How did that go?"

He looked at Fredrik.

"He was at work until seven fifteen on Friday. There were a dozen associates who could confirm that. I've spoken with two of them. Otherwise he said he gave Henrik all the keys at the closing."

"Then we can remove him," said Göran, lowering his eyes toward his papers.

"The passenger lists have not produced anything really interesting so far. We will continue to check the departures. Destination Gotland's personnel will note the license plate numbers of vehicles with blond women traveling alone. I hope that works as it should. Hotels and hostels have given a few leads that have been followed up, but nothing hot there, either."

He turned over the paper.

"I guess I'll take the technical aspects that I'm aware of, because

Eva isn't here. The shoe that left the print in the hall is a Vans brand. That's a simple cloth shoe without laces with a rubber edge around it. We haven't found any shoes of that type in the house search of Stina Hansson. In asking around among coworkers, friends, and neighbors, no one has reported having seen her in such shoes, either."

Göran interrupted himself briefly, pulled out his chair, and sat down for the first time during the meeting.

"Eva has secured a print on the log pile down by the mailboxes. It's presumably from the same kind of shoe, but it's a very poor print. It indicates, anyway, that Eva was right in her assumption that the murderer hid there while keeping an eye on the house. We've got the shampoo profile on the wad of hair. It shows that the hair may have come from Stina Hansson, but as you know that doesn't count as technical evidence in court. We'll have to wait and see if they can produce DNA, but that will take another few days."

The door to the room opened and everyone turned in that direction. Eva came in with a green plastic folder in her hand.

"Sorry I'm late," she said, catching her breath.

She had evidently hurried up the stairs.

"I just went through the technical findings," said Göran. "Do you have anything new?"

"Yes, I have something interesting here," she said, holding up the folder. "A picture of the perpetrator."

There was total silence in the room. Everyone watched as Eva took a printout on shiny photo paper from the folder and handed it over to Göran. The head of the squad inspected the picture and then handed it on to the prosecutor.

"I got a tip that a number of alarms with cameras have an internal control function," Eva related while Klint inspected the picture. "Even if the alarm is not activated, the cameras take a still picture once a minute that is stored in the memory, but which are then deleted, or rather written over, when the alarm is activated and starts storing video images. There is no function on the menu to display these images, but with a little support from the manufacturer I've managed to extract them."

"Is this the only one you produced?" he asked.

"No," said Eva, "but the only one that shows the perpetrator."

"So now we have an exact time," said Göran. "I assume that you've checked that the alarm's clock was right?"

"I've done that," said Eva with a smile.

Fredrik got the picture after the prosecutor. In the bottom right-hand corner the date and time were indicated: 18:36:23. The picture covered the whole hall with the front door farthest away in the picture. In the middle of the picture someone in a light jacket or sweatshirt with a hood was seen leaning over Malin Andersson. The hood on the jacket was pulled up. It was not possible to see any of the hair or face, but it was quite obviously a woman. The shoulders were narrow, the hips broader, and in the forward-leaning position the rear end had a form that Fredrik at least had never seen on a man. The color reproduction was poor and leaned sharply in the blue-violet direction. Presumably the jacket, or sweatshirt, was light gray or possibly pink. On the back it said NYU in big letters. The person in the picture had both arms in front of her, so probably it had been taken just when a blow struck Malin Andersson's head.

"Bring in Henrik Kjellander for questioning," said Klint. "Maybe he knows who it is."

Fredrik handed the picture over to Sara. He had a hard time taking his eyes from it. Far out on the left-hand edge of the picture the head of a little boy was visible and a pair of terrified, wide-open eyes.

60

Henrik Kjellander pushed back his hair with a hand that was clearly shaking. It was as if the seriousness in the room had affected him before they even said why they had asked him to come in.

Fredrik was again sitting in front of Henrik in the big interview room at the far end of the corridor, this time along with Sara Oskarsson. Henrik appeared to be feeling a little better than on Saturday, or at least seemed more present, which was not necessarily the same thing.

Fredrik set the green plastic folder out on the table with the printed-out photo from the surveillance camera upside down.

"We have a picture we want to show you," said Fredrik.

Henrik looked worriedly at the folder under Fredrik's hand.

"Is it a suspect?" he said.

"The picture comes from one of the cameras that are connected to the alarm in the house."

Henrik looked at Fredrik with surprise. It was evident that he did not really understand how it all fit together and Fredrik explained the situation with the control function that Eva Karlén had discovered.

"I see, so . . . what does it show?"

"The picture shows the perpetrator."

Henrik gave a start, almost jumping backward in the chair.

"The one who . . . You're quite sure of that?"

"Yes, there is no doubt that this is the perpetrator," said Fredrik. "But the person in the picture has his or her back turned toward the camera. It's not possible to identify him or her. Or in any case, we can't. We thought that possibly you could help us."

Henrik raised his hand as if to push back his hair again, but the movement stopped level with his forehead without his fingers touching his hair.

"The picture was taken while the crime was committed," Sara clarified. "We understand that it may be extremely hard for you to look at this. You don't see much of Malin in the picture, but even so . . . And, of course, it's up to you whether you want to look at it."

"Up to me?" said Henrik.

He took a deep breath and audibly exhaled through his nose.

"Do I have any choice, I mean . . ."

He fell silent and looked first at Sara and then at Fredrik.

"This may be decisive," said Sara.

Henrik forced a tight smile and cleared his throat.

"Okay," he said. "It's just as well to get it over with."

Fredrik nodded, took out the picture, and placed it in front of Henrik.

"But," he said immediately and then abruptly fell silent.

He looked up at Fredrik and Sara, then at the picture again.

"But that's . . . that's Maria. Or I think it's her sweatshirt. I don't get it. It can't be Maria, can it?"

No, it could not be Maria, thought Fredrik, they had already ruled her out. It could not be her. Assuming that the neighbor's information was correct.

Henrik laughed.

"Or what? This is absurd. It's impossible."

He reached out his hand and carefully brushed the picture as if the touch could reveal something more.

"It just can't be her," he said again.

"You're sure that this is her sweatshirt?" said Sara.

"Yes," he said with clear certainty. "She's been wearing it ever since she got here. It doesn't show very well on the picture, but it's pink . . . those letters . . . yes, that's it. There's a zipper in front."

But if it wasn't Maria in the picture, thought Fredrik, why did the murderer have her sweatshirt on?

"When did you last see her wear the sweatshirt?"

"No," Henrik screamed loudly.

Both Fredrik and Sara recoiled from the sudden outburst.

"No, no, no," whimpered Henrik.

He leaned over the table and tenderly stroked his fingers over the left edge of the picture, right next to his son's staring eyes.

"No, no, no."

His eyes filled with tears and despair cut into Henrik's words.

"He's alive. Look, he's alive."

61.

Fifteen minutes later Fredrik and Sara were standing in Göran Eide's office. The sky had turned cloudy above the courtyard's glass covering. The roof lighting formed shadows on their faces.

"It can't be Maria Andersson," said Fredrik. "The picture was taken at six thirty-six and Ann-Katrin Wedin saw Maria and Ellen pass before the Channel 4 local news had started. She's quite sure of that."

"You've double-checked it?"

"Yes."

Eva had checked the alarm's time indicator yet again. Fredrik had called and questioned the neighbor once more to rule out any possible mistake. Sara had even checked with TV4 that the program truly had been broadcast at the scheduled time.

"The perpetrator may have put on the sweatshirt to conceal her own clothes," Göran suggested.

"Or to get Malin Andersson to think it was Maria who had come back," said Fredrik. "That could explain how she got in."

Sara picked up the picture, which was lying on Göran's desk.

"But then she must have been certain that it was Maria's sweatshirt."

"We can forget about the motive right now," said Göran. "We have a picture of a sweatshirt that, if it's not burned up, is probably lying in a trash barrel or wastebasket somewhere here on Gotland. Or possibly tossed by a road somewhere. The perpetrator must have taken it with her in her car, otherwise we would have found it. And she can hardly have risked keeping it in the car very long."

"If we find it that may be the key that connects the perpetrator with Malin and Axel," said Sara.

"I'll go to the media with it, so maybe we'll get a little help," said Göran. "You can question Maria and try to get some clarity in how the perpetrator may have acquired the sweatshirt."

He reached for the picture that Sara was holding and put it back in the folder.

"The garbage in Stina Hansson's building has been checked," he said. "Nothing there."

He drummed with irritation against the desk with his index and middle finger.

"If it's Stina Hansson or one of the half sisters, we're going to be able to prove it sooner or later, I'm sure of that. But if it's someone else this is moving much too slow."

Fredrik agreed. They were holding one person, but that track was not being developed. They had to go further. With Stina Hansson or someone else.

"I've talked with Peter and we've decided to arrange a meeting on Fårö," said Göran. "At the community center. Today is too late, but tomorrow evening at seven o'clock. We will draw on every conceivable contact and set up posters. We have to get them to tell what they know. Someone must have seen something, that's just how it is."

"Is it really true, that business that Fårö residents are so bad at co-operating with the police?" Sara asked.

"As long as it concerns testifying against other Fårö residents, yes,"

said Göran and smiled back. "On Fårö and in När they're the tricki-
est. All old policemen on Gotland know that."

Maria Andersson sat completely mute and observed the picture that
Fredrik had set out on the table. The blood vessels were clearly visible
under the thin skin below her eyes and her hair was flat and heavy on her
head. She had set her hands on either side of the picture, lightly clenched.

"What do you say?" said Sara at last.

Maria looked up, blinked a couple of times.

"Huh?"

Maria turned her eyes toward Fredrik, as if she was pleading for
help.

"Isn't that your sweatshirt?" said Sara, pointing at the picture with
a white ballpoint pen.

Maria looked at the picture.

"I have a sweatshirt like that, I do have, but . . ."

"According to Henrik you were wearing it on Friday morning," said
Sara.

Maria opened her mouth and closed it again without saying anything. She was reminiscent of a fish on dry land.

"It must be your sweatshirt, right? It can't very likely be a coincidence," Sara pressed on.

She looked up, met Sara's gaze.

"Do you think it's me? That I killed Malin? And——"

Maria silently shook her head.

"We just want to know how the murderer happens to have your
sweatshirt on."

"I don't know. How should I know that?"

She shook her head, but then her hands flew up in the air.

"Wait," she said. "Wait now."

She waved her hands defensively toward them, as if to gain time and
space to think.

"It's true that I was wearing it the morning when Henrik left. Then we were outside. It got hot in the sun when I was running around in the garden with Ellen and Axel. I took off the sweatshirt and hung it on a chair. I must have left it there when we went in. Then we changed into swimsuits and put bathrobes on, so then I didn't think about it."

"So you think that the sweatshirt was still hanging on the chair and that the murderer put it on before she went into the house."

"Yes, it must have happened like that."

She looked in distress at the picture that depicted her sister's final seconds in life.

Yes, thought Fredrik. That was no doubt the simple explanation. For a brief moment, just like Henrik Kjellander, he had thought that Maria might be the murderer, however strange that seemed. But she had neither opportunity nor motive.

62.

Before the day's end there was one more setback. The technical investigation of Stina Hansson's car produced nothing that could bind her to the murders or in any other way prove that she had been in the house in Kalbjerga. Fredrik wondered whether Klint really could get her remanded.

He got away earlier than the day before and was at home in time to see the news. They included the sweatshirt in their story about the Fårö murders.

"How are you?" said Ninni when he had turned off the TV.

"Good."

"You seemed completely absent over the weekend."

"I know," he said. "There were some long days."

Ninni looked at him as if she expected something more.

"What?"

"No, nothing."

Fredrik got up and went into the kitchen.

"There's food in the fridge. I didn't know when you would be coming so I put it in there."

"Thanks. I'll see if I can manage to warm it up."

He opened the refrigerator door.

"Is it the casserole dish with the blue cover?" he called.

"You don't have to shout. I'm here." She had followed him out into the kitchen. "Yes, it is."

He took out the plastic dish and raised the lid. Mashed potatoes, Salisbury steak, and green peas. An unusually light Salisbury steak.

"Veal burger?"

"Yes."

"Advanced."

He turned on the oven and transferred the food to an ovenproof glass dish. While the food heated, he went up to Simon. For once he was not sitting in front of the computer. He was semi-inclined on the bed and writing with barely legible letters on a piece of notebook paper with dotted lines.

Fredrik decided not to offer any sententious advice about the advantage of sitting at a desk when you write. It was not that easy to keep quiet, but he succeeded.

"What are you doing?" he asked.

"Religion."

"We can look through it later."

"Sure."

When Fredrik came back, Ninni was still sitting in the kitchen, browsing through the newspaper. She put it aside as Fredrik set out the food and sat down.

"I saw some pictures today, of the ones who were murdered up there," he said.

Ninni wrinkled her nose.

"Ugh."

"Yes, exactly. I thought it was really unpleasant."

"Yes."

"Although I don't always think that. True, they were autopsy pictures . . ."

"But stop. Do you have to talk about that when we're eating?"

"So what? I'm the one who's eating, not you."

"But I think it's horrid," said Ninni.

Fredrik took a big bite of the veal burger. Perhaps it wasn't possible to explain to someone who wasn't a police officer. Not even to Ninni. The point was not that it was horrid. The point was that he normally didn't react to pictures of dead, mutilated people. Looking at that sort of thing was part of his job. It was a means to achieve a goal. Just as well to forget it.

"Listen," he said instead.

"Yes."

"Gustav told me something the other day. It was . . ."

He hesitated. Should he say this?

"What was it?"

A curious gleam had already been lit in Ninni's eyes, so he no longer had any choice.

"It was in confidence, but I must be able to tell you, I assume. But just so it doesn't go any further . . ."

"Was it about Lena? That she might have MS?"

Fredrik stopped in midmotion, lowered his fork again.

"You knew that?"

"Yes, Lena called a week or two ago."

"I see," he said.

Of course. How could he be so dense to think that the ladies hadn't already talked with each other.

"I should have called him. They were going to get the test results today. Or have you talked with Lena?"

"No."

"Maybe better to wait until tomorrow. Or what do you think?"

"Yes, maybe so."

Ninni looked at him seriously. He set his silverware down on the plate. He understood what she was thinking about. It was easy for her to imagine what it must be like for Gustav and Lena right now. She had been there herself. Waited for news, waited for improvements that no one knew for sure would come.

"Maybe it's nothing," he said. "It may actually be that simple."

"Yes, that's true," she said, forcing herself to smile.

63.

The white stone building created an austere, determined impression in its setting in front of a forested area a few hundred feet from the sea. It had been built out at an angle and the windows had broad frames in faded brown that were on the same level as the façade.

The rain had poured down all the way from Visby. So close to the sea, it came in gusts with the wind and whipped against the side of the car. Fredrik, Sara, and Göran hurried into the community center. Even though it was not far, Fredrik still felt the dampness settle into his clothes.

Fredrik wiped away a few drops of water from his forehead and looked around the meeting hall. It was fifteen minutes before the appointed time, but three people had already sat down in the chairs that had been set out. In the next-to-last row. All three were in their sixties. Hopefully this was a good sign. They were all worried that the bad weather would cause many to stay home.

Two colleagues were already there, Gunilla Borg and Leif Knuts-son. They had driven up an hour or two ago to help out with the practical aspects. Three plainclothes and two in uniform; Göran did not want more there, considering the less-than-positive attitude of Fårö residents toward the police.

The rain was rushing off the edge of the roof and fell with a clear patter down into the narrow ditch that had been formed along the long sides of the building. The sound of cars rolling onto the yard broke through the rain and soon murmuring voices were heard outside. The door opened and wet rubber boots squeaked against the floor.

He had still not called Gustav, it struck Fredrik. He had to call. It was the second day he was gone from work. He looked at the clock. Now it was too late. He could not call and then interrupt in the middle because the meeting was starting. But then, afterward, he promised himself. This could not take more than half an hour, possibly an hour depending on how it developed.

"Strange price setting," said Sara.

She pointed to a slip of paper on the bulletin board. Fredrik looked closer. It was a price list for renting out the community center: Five hundred fifty kronor per day. For large parties two thousand kronor for three days.

"Maybe they clear the tables hard at the wedding receptions. A lot of shrinkage," Fredrik whispered.

On the bulletin board there were also old clippings from Bergman Week and Fårö's potato dumpling championship. The same individual had taken home the title three years in a row. Most recently he had tucked away twenty-one dumplings.

Ten minutes later everyone was seated in front of the little stage and Göran started the meeting after a brief introduction by the chairman of the local historical society—a move that might possibly lend him a little more legitimacy among the Fårö residents. Fredrik counted fifty-seven persons. Not too bad with a population of around five hundred and fifty. The majority were over fifty, but there were also a couple of teenagers among those assembled. Like at any lecture, in other words. Göran briefly talked about the Andersson Kjellander family, mentioned the background of escalating threats, without going into too many details. He then explained that the purpose of the meeting was to gather as many observations as possible for the time between six and eight last Friday evening. Who had been where, what cars had been out on the roads. Everything was of interest. A sound that someone heard was enough. A car starting, a scream, voices, footsteps. And this applied not only to the area around Kalbjerga, but all of Fårö. The idea was then that the police would piece together all the information, in the hope of discovering something new.

"So I really encourage all of you to get in touch with us," he said, starting to approach the end of his speech. "It's fine to talk with one of my associates right now . . ."

With his hand he indicated Fredrik and his three other colleagues scattered around the room.

"But you will also be given information about where you can call or send e-mail. It's also possible to leave information anonymously if you prefer."

For a short time there was complete silence in the hall, as if Göran had said something indecent. He was about to thank them for coming when a gray-haired woman in a red jacket raised her hand.

"Yes, excuse me," said Göran. "If you have any questions I'll be happy to answer them. Yes?"

He reached out his hand toward the woman in an inviting gesture.

"This here person who murdered them in Kalbjerga, can he get it in his head to strike at someone else, too?"

Göran smiled amiably at her.

"We have no reason to believe that. As I said, we are starting on the assumption that a series of incidents led up to the murders. There was a reason that the perpetrator attacked these particular individuals."

"What was the reason?" said the woman.

"Unfortunately I can't go into that," said Göran.

Because we don't know, thought Fredrik.

Several others raised their hands. Most of the questions concerned the investigation in such a way that Göran chose not to answer them. Because he could not or because it was inappropriate.

That took up about ten minutes, then no more hands were seen. Göran thanked them. Murmuring and scraping of chairs quickly took over the hall. On the way out everyone got a piece of paper with telephone numbers and e-mail addresses. A few stopped to lament or more generally comment on what had happened on Friday evening. No one came forward to make a witness statement.

"That went just great," said Fredrik to Leif Knutsson as the last ones were on their way out the door.

Leif folded up the papers that were left over and put them in his pocket.

"What did you expect? It's obvious that no one will say anything now," he said with a grin. "Wait until tomorrow. Then maybe."

On the way out to the car Fredrik happened to think about Gustav again. He had to call, it could not be helped that the others had to wait for him. He excused himself and went back in. A few from the historical society were still there, occupied with something out in the kitchen. He took out his cell phone and scrolled to Gustav's number.

It rang a long time, but finally there was an answer.

"Hi," he said. "It's Fredrik."

"Yes, hi there," said Gustav.

Fredrik tried to interpret the tone of voice, but it was impossible. He thought at first it sounded paralyzed by despair, then neutrally relaxed.

"How are you doing?" he asked.

"I'm fine."

"And Lena. Have you . . . I assumed you've—"

"Yes," said Gustav, and disappeared for a couple of seconds.

Fredrik heard him coughing away from the phone.

"Yes, we were there yesterday. It was a little much for Lena. That was why I stayed home today, too."

A little much? What did that mean?

"But everything's fine. She's healthy," said Gustav quickly.

"Is that true?" said Fredrik, relieved.

"Yes. She'll go for some follow-up in a year, to be on the safe side. But, yes, she's healthy."

"That's great," said Fredrik.

"Yes, it was . . ."

He heard how Gustav swallowed.

"Lena is happy, of course," he continued, "but you know . . . Well, sudden changes and that. If I didn't know better I would think she was a little shattered."

"It's probably the tension," said Fredrik.

"Yes."

"That was really nice to hear anyway."

He looked out the window toward the parking lot.

"Listen, we're up on Fårö and they're waiting for me in the car."

Now it was not as hard to break off, when the news was positive.

"Okay," said Gustav.

"But give my best to Lena. Will you be in tomorrow?"

"Yes, I will. Count on it."

64

On Wednesday the information from Fårö started to drip in, just as Leif Knutsson had predicted. Drip was probably just the right description, thought Fredrik. It was not a steady stream of witnesses that yesterday's meeting had called forth.

"We've received an interesting finding from the medical examiner." Göran started the morning meeting.

Tests from the wounds on Malin Andersson's head had been shown to contain residual chemicals. These were very small residues, but it was possible to determine that it was detergent. A conceivable explanation was that the hammer that had been used as the murder weapon had been stored somewhere where there were also packages of detergent and that some of the contents had spilled out. The detergent could also have come in contact with the hammer when it was transported to the scene of the crime.

Eva Karlén would send the detergent that was in Stina Hansson's apartment to the forensic lab for a comparative analysis.

Sara got the task of following up and coordinating the tips from Fårö. Fredrik would try to organize the material he had gathered with the help of Janna Drake and the calendar information in Henrik Kjellander's computer.

When he logged onto his own computer after the meeting he had an e-mail from Coop. He opened the file that was attached and brought up the never-published blog comments from the past year. There were hundreds.

He copied the document and started going through the comments on the screen, erasing those that did not seem interesting. Those who questioned Malin Andersson's competence as a cook, or "food in-spirer," which was the official title on the website, and were not overly aggressive were removed first. Not overly aggressive meant in this case that they were only sprinkled with the most common swear words and an occasional sexual reference in a more neutral context. After that he removed pure nonsense, such as scattered invectives without context, for example: "Crap!, Cunt, Whore!!!" What was left was still a long but nevertheless manageable collection of more hateful comments. The majority ended with something sexually aggressive that described more or less in detail what the sender wanted to do with Malin. Comments such as "You should be penalty-fucked with an unvarnished baseball bat" were among the more benign. There were also a few that were not blatantly aggressive, but which nonetheless aroused Fredrik's interest because they were about Henrik. Especially one: "Tonight it's me and Henrik. Tonight I'm the one he wants. I want you to know that."

The ill will and envy that seethed in the comments made him uneasy. He understood why Malin's employer thought she should avoid reading them. That was probably wise. But also frightening that in a way they were there, but yet not. Like a clenched fist everyone ignored.

When he was done he forwarded the document to Eva Karlén. She got to take the next step with the Internet service providers.

Fredrik got up and went over to the window. It had stopped raining, but the dampness was hanging in the air. It was one of those depressing gray days that autumn on Gotland sometimes had to offer. Dark-gray sky, low clouds, fog and dampness. The surrounding world was rubbed out, disappeared into a faintly lit haze. It was hard not to be affected.

He stretched his arms high above his head, felt how his muscles tensed. He yawned and went back to the desk.

Henrik had traveled a lot. It was not that easy to chart everything. There were notes in the computer's calendar, but not always. There were booking confirmations for airline tickets and hotels in the e-mail program's inbox and in those cases where the client took care of the bookings that information was included in the material the agent sent over.

Fredrik printed out a large portion of the material to more easily get an overview and be able to sort the trips in chronological order. Henrik had been in Stockholm sixteen times, in Copenhagen five times, and there were scattered trips besides to Capetown, New York, Milan, and Östersund. Combined it added up to sixty-four travel days. That was quite a bit for a father of small children who had just enticed his family to an isolated house on a not-exactly easily accessible island in the middle of the Baltic. How had it worked?

Sara's voice interrupted his musings.

"I think we have something."

Fredrik looked up from the desk, which at this point was completely covered by printouts from various airlines and hotels.

"What is it?"

"One witness is certain she saw Alma Vogler drive past the ICA store at twenty past six on Friday evening."

Fredrik rolled back a little from the desk and turned the chair toward Sara.

"And she's sure of that? She really saw Alma, not just the car?"

"She is certain," said Sara. "She was standing only a couple of feet from the road."

Fredrik straightened up.

"So Alma was lying. What the hell was she thinking?"

"You wonder."

"What do we do?" said Fredrik.

"Klint wants us to bring her in."

65

The day disappeared into the grayness. It was as if time stopped. It became silent; the damp crept into the houses and settled into your clothes. A soundless, invisible rain.

Alma Vogler looked small and crushed sitting across from Sara and Fredrik. She had had an hour and a half to herself to think, in the backseat of a police car on the way through the gray weather.

"If you have questions I could just as well have answered them at home," said Alma. "I don't understand why I have to come along to Visby."

But there was no protest. Her voice was weak and bewildered. She had on a pair of jeans and a natural white wool sweater that fit tight around her body. It made her look fragile.

"You were not at home on Friday between six and eight," said Sara.

Alma's gaze wandered.

"I may have been mistaken by a few minutes," she said.

Sara sat quietly and waited, but Alma did not continue.

"Exactly when were you at home then, do you think?" asked Sara.

"I don't know. You don't go and look at the clock all the time when you're at home, do you?"

She looked imploringly at Sara and quickly glanced at Fredrik.

"I thought I was at home between six and eight. I must have arrived a little later."

It hardly sounded like Alma believed what she was saying herself. Sara looked down at the report she had brought with her to the interview, marked a line with her finger.

"But here in the interview last Saturday you say that you had dinner at five thirty. Do you mean that you left the house after dinner and came back later, or is it not true that you had dinner then?"

Alma Vogler breathed heavily through her nose and made a gesture as if she was trying to grasp something in the air.

"Perhaps I didn't express myself that clearly."

"At twenty past six on Friday you drove past Nyström's, the ICA store on Fårö," said Sara. "You were driving north, so even if you would have turned in somewhere and returned right after, you can't very well have been home before quarter to seven."

Alma looked unhappily at Sara. Fredrik leaned a few inches forward.

"But it does seem strange that you only would have driven to the store and turned around," he said. "And it wasn't to shop, was it?"

"No," Alma let out.

"No, because the store was closed, of course," he said. "On the other hand, if you continue in the direction you were headed and turn left at Eke, you can get to Kalbjerga that way, too."

"Okay," said Alma, sighing heavily. "You're right. I was not at home. I went over to Elisabet's."

"Were you on your way to her place when you passed the store?"

"Yes."

"And that version Elisabet can, of course, confirm?" said Fredrik. "The former was attested to by your husband. If you have several alternative alibis perhaps we can take them all at once."

He rested his forearms on the table and looked inquisitively at her.

"No, she can't. She wasn't home."

She sounded more definite now. If this was the truth, it meant that Elisabet had lied, too. All of them had lied. Elisabet, Alma, their husbands, their father Ernst Vogler . . .

"We thought it was simplest. That we said we were at home. There would just be a lot of trouble otherwise."

In contrast to what it had become now, thought Fredrik, but looked at her without saying anything.

"We have nothing to do with that," said Alma, her voice rising in pitch.

"So when did you get to Elisabet's?" said Sara. "Six thirty?"

"Something like that," said Alma, lowering her voice.

"And she wasn't home then?"

"No, exactly."

"Not Ernst, either?" asked Sara.

"Yes, he was there. Elisabet had gone to Skär to look after the lambs. They have lambs there."

"But still you all agreed to say that everyone was at home between six and eight? Elisabet with you, and you with her?"

"Yes."

Sara turned toward Fredrik.

"I think we'll take a break."

He nodded.

"Maybe they did it together, Alma and Elisabet. Or whatever combination of these five," said Göran. "Now everything is open."

"We'll have to get a DNA sample," said Ove.

"Hmm, we will," said Göran, "but we don't have any good DNA to compare with."

"There is still a blond person with shoe size seven or eight who has been in the house," said Fredrik. "One of the men may be involved, of course, but if these are the guilty parties then it's one of the sisters who was holding the hammer."

"What is there to say that there can't have been two in the house," said Ove. "Maybe one of them didn't leave any prints."

Göran moaned and went back and sat down at the desk.

"Let's calm down a little," he said with his back turned to them. "We'll start by bringing in Elisabet, then we'll see what she has to say

about the matter. I'm sure you have other things to keep busy with for
the time being."

They looked at each other and withdrew from Göran's office.
Fredrik thought about his desk and all the papers covering it.

66.

The sea had vanished in the fog. The footbridges from the terminal to
the gangways were also consumed, halfway.

Henrik sat in the armchair with the uncomfortably high arm support and looked out over the harbor area. The hotel room seemed to
have shrunk after the latest interview with the police. He would not
be able to stand it there much longer. If he didn't have to take Ellen
into consideration he would already have started throwing things
around, or curled up in a ball on the floor, or simply escaped from there.

Something had changed between him and Maria without his understanding how it had happened. It was nothing they had said or
done, but it was still so obvious. The closeness that existed between
them, and which they both could have found a little consolation in,
had been transformed into something else. It was as if they no longer
knew how they should behave toward each other. Maria mostly stayed
in the little bedroom. Ellen moved between them, unknowing, but
hardly without noticing the changed atmosphere.

It was as if Malin's dead gaze could see everything. It drilled right
into their secret. Axel, too, was staring at him. What he could brush
off before as a stupid but nonetheless meaningless escapade had been
transformed into something rotten and loathsome. The first few days
he had been too shocked to even reflect on it, but then it had come
crawling and grown bigger and bigger. Did Maria feel the same? He

thought so. He thought he could see it in her eyes that turned away, that no longer sought his. Or was he the one who was avoiding hers? The dead knew everything. Saw everything.

For a fraction of a second he had actually believed that Maria could have killed them. Just when Fredrik Broman had set out the picture and he recognized the sweatshirt. As soon as he really thought about it he could never believe anything like that. But that had been a terrifyingly dark fraction of a second.

67.

It was Sara's own idea that she should be alone in the interview room with Elisabet Vogler. Perhaps it would get her to open up. With two police officers in the room Elisabet would feel pressured and the more pressure she felt, the more she would hide behind her dissociative manner and stay on her high horse. That was the theory at least. Göran had said okay. Ove and Fredrik had taken seats behind the mirror in the technology room.

Elisabet Vogler was her usual self from Sara's meeting with her at home a few days earlier. She did not look the least bit upset. But Sara had not expected her to be, either.

"Why did you say you were at home between six and eight on Friday when you weren't?" Sara began the interview.

She deliberately avoided the word "lie."

"I thought it was simplest that way," answered Elisabet Vogler.

She sat away from the table with her hands clasped and resting on one leg. Sara felt how easy it would have been to spit out something sarcastic. But she was not there to comment on Elisabet Vogler's decision.

"Whose idea was it that you would stick to that version?" she asked instead.

"I don't actually remember who suggested it, but it was a joint decision."

From Elisabet it sounded as if she was accounting for a decision on the building committee rather than explaining why she had lied about her alibi in a murder investigation.

"So what were you doing between six and eight?" asked Sara.

Elisabet took a dramatically deep breath before she answered.

"I checked on the lambs. We have lambs up by Skär."

"When did you leave home?"

"Around six."

"And when were you back?"

"Around seven."

"How long were you with the lambs before you drove back?"

"Well, I don't know exactly, but at a guess half an hour."

They had test-driven the stretch between Elisabet Vogler's home and the pasture where the lambs were. If you kept to the speed limit it took twelve minutes to drive. That tallied pretty well. They had also test-driven the road between Elisabet Vogler's home and Kalbjerga by way of Eke. That took fourteen minutes. That also fit pretty well. Especially if you added time for getting rid of bloody clothes and shoes.

"Is there anyone who can confirm this information?" Sara asked.

"Not that I know of. But there seem to be those who keep track of Alma. Maybe there is someone who has seen me, too."

Elisabet smiled curtly.

"Thanks," said Sara. "Then I don't have anything else to ask you right now."

Elisabet was about to stand up, but Sara stopped her.

"You can sit here awhile. I'll be back soon."

"You can't exactly say that I got her to open up," she said to Fredrik and Ove out in the corridor.

"Maybe she doesn't have anything else to say," Ove suggested, scratching his chin with a blunt finger.

"An apology would have been in order. If this is true then it's so fucking dense . . ."

The irritation Sara had held back in the interview room was coming out.

"How much time have we wasted on those two?"

"Perhaps you should have tried to pressure her about the inheritance?" said Fredrik.

"No. I have to have something concrete to work with."

Sara left them outside the technology room and hurried over to Göran's office.

"I have to speak with Klint," he said when Sara reported on the interview. "If it were up to me I would release her. We can't have both Stina Hansson and Elisabet Vogler held for the same crime. And I believe more in Stina as a murderer than this lady. But we'll do a house search and then we'll see what the DNA sample can produce when we get the results from that wad of hair."

"I would like to make another attempt with Ellen," said Sara. "If the father goes along with it. Some detail may come up. Now that we have something to compare with, I mean."

"That's a good idea. Do it down at the hotel."

The papers were sorted, the desk liberated from the white patchwork quilt. Fredrik instead had a bundle of letter-sized papers in chronological order in front of him. He was transferring the information to a list on the computer that he could then sort by various parameters such as date, place, and person.

Many of the trips he had been able to check off with Janna Drake. She had given him names of companies and individuals not shown by the bookings she sent over first. But certain trips he would be forced to go through together with Henrik Kjellander.

The review of Henrik's travels had produced a long list of names.

There were employees at advertising agencies, editors at magazines, models, makeup artists, stylists, assistants, and sometimes representatives of the companies that engaged the advertising agencies who in turn engaged Henrik.

Fredrik decided to first look at recurring names and places. There was nothing obvious, but he was more likely to find something interesting close at hand. During the sixteen trips to Stockholm, Henrik had stayed at a hotel once. Fredrik assumed he had stayed with relatives or friends, for example with Thomas Bark, on the other occasions.

He called Hotel Lydmar in Stockholm and the Old Theater Hotel in Östersund and asked them to send over guest lists for the nights Henrik Kjellander had stayed with them. He also called Hotel St. Petri in Copenhagen, the same hotel all five trips, and asked about their guest lists. The other hotels around the world he left for the national investigation bureau. They knew better what threads to pull on, but it would surely take time, in any event, with Capetown and New York. Italy was part of the EU. That ought to go quicker. At least in theory.

Fredrik let his eyes run across the names on the screen. The list was exhaustingly long even now. With the guest lists from the hotels it would be multiplied.

When the phone rang a few minutes later it was a welcome break. He saw that the call was internal.

"Yes, Fredrik," he answered.

It was Anna, one of the radio operators.

"I have a man down at Storsudret on the line. He's calling about a break-in at a summer cottage."

"Yes?" said Fredrik.

He assumed that there was a good explanation for why she wanted to transfer the call to him. She knew that he was not working on break-ins at summer cottages. Especially not when a double murder had just happened on Fårö.

"It sounds like it could be something," said Anna.

"Okay, connect him."

There was a snapping on the phone.

"Hello?" a voice said. It sounded like it belonged to a man roughly Fredrik's own age.

"Police department, Fredrik Broman."

"Hello, my name is Markus Bergvall. Well, it happens that I am a neighbor to some people who have a summer cottage down on Storsudret, Larsson is their name."

Bergvall took a breath and continued.

"Now I happened to see that there was someone there last Friday . . . Or to make a long story short . . ."

Thanks, thought Fredrik.

"I went past the cottage today again and then I discovered that someone had broken a window. So I went in to see what had happened, if there was anything stolen or such."

"Did you go in through the window?" asked Fredrik.

"No," said Bergvall, sounding a little amused. "No, no, I have a key. They leave a key with me in case anything comes up."

"I understand."

"Nothing seemed to be missing, but someone had lit a fire in the stove, there were ashes and soot spilled out on the floor in front of the stove, and in the kitchen there were several bowls pulled out. I went in there and thought about putting things away, just so that the things wouldn't be in the way when they come down next time, and then I saw that there were some strands of hair in the kitchen."

Fredrik reached for a pen.

"Yes?"

"I don't know if I'm letting my imagination run wild, but I thought about those murders on Fårö. That was last Friday and I thought that maybe the one who did it hid here and cut off or dyed their hair. Well, in order not to be recognized."

"I understand."

"It's a bit unusual to break in someplace and dye your hair. If you don't have a good reason, I mean."

"When last Friday did you see that someone was there?"

"It was pretty late. Sometime after ten o'clock."

"Exactly what was it you saw?"

"I saw a car. I didn't recognize it, but they fly down sometimes on the weekends—the Larssons, that is—and then they rent a car from that Micke's Car Rental; he rents used cars."

"What kind of car was it?"

"It was a Volvo. A station wagon. The Larssons have a Volvo, too, but this was as I said an older model. Larssons' is new."

"Do you remember what color?"

"It was pretty dark, so it was hard to see. But some dark color anyway."

"Was that all you saw?"

"Yes, that was all," said Bergvall.

He coughed away a trembling in his vocal cords.

"It was late, so I didn't want to disturb anyone. Then I went past on Saturday, too, thought I would go in and say hello, but then there was no one there."

"But you didn't notice then that the window was broken?"

"No, I didn't go onto the property. That was only today. I thought it was strange that someone had been there for just one night. And then I've been following these murders. You get a little worried and suspicious."

"I think it's best that we drive down and look a little more closely at that cottage. Where is it?"

"It's right by the water. You drive past Vamlingbo church, then turn left toward Nore and continue as far as you can toward the water, and then to the right."

"Then I know exactly."

All too well, thought Fredrik.

"Can you meet me there—"

He took a quick glance at the clock on the computer.

"At twelve thirty?"

"Sure," said Markus Bergvall.

"But don't go in again. Not even on the property."

"No, I see."

"No one may go in. Not even Larsson himself if he happens to show up."

"No, of course."

Fredrik went over to Göran and briefly summarized what he had just found out.

"Worth checking," said Göran. "Older Volvo. Wasn't that what Holt on the Fårö ferry had seen?"

"Two older Volvos, a red Mazda sports car, and a smaller white car of unknown make."

"That works out with the time, too. Damn. If this tallies, that rules out both Stina Hansson and the sisters on Fårö."

"I know, one step forward and two steps backward. But that remains to be seen."

"The sooner we know, the better. Drive down with Eva so she can go through the cottage properly. You can take her car."

"I'll probably take my own," said Fredrik. "You never know how long she needs to stay."

There was the limit. To Nore in the same car as Eva Karlén.

"Yes, I won't get involved in that, it was just a suggestion," said Göran.

The hell it was, thought Fredrik.

68

Sara walked down to the hotel. She took the route through Österport and along Hästgatan. The Kränku tea shop still attracted aimless Visby strollers who stopped to inspect the cans of tea inside the shop. The summer season was not quite over yet. Sara turned left onto St. Hansgatan. Maybe she should have driven anyway. She had hoped that a quick walk would energize her, but the damp, gray weather made her mostly tired and a little dull. It felt like her soul was shriveling up.

The hotel where Henrik Kjellander, Maria Andersson, and Ellen were quartered was halfway up the cliff above the ferry terminal. They were staying next door to the old prison, which had been renovated into a hostel. She wondered whether they felt safe there with a police officer on guard outside the door or if, on the contrary, they felt a little like they were in prison. Locked in, watched. If they even thought along those lines at all. Perhaps the shock and sorrow overshadowed everything else.

A police constable with a crew cut and long legs was sitting on a chair outside the room looking bored.

"Maria really wants to go out and get some exercise. I thought we could take the opportunity while you're here. If that's okay with you, that is?" he asked.

"Sure, that will be fine," said Sara.

He knocked on the door and opened from outside after he got a response from Henrik. That was the arrangement.

"Hi," said Sara, shaking hands. "How are you doing?"

Henrik Kjellander shrugged his shoulders. There was a tray with three dirty plates on the narrow desk over by the window. A suitcase was open on the bed, the clothes in it in disarray.

"It is what it is," he said. "What can I say?"

He took a couple of steps into the room. Sara followed.

A voice mumbled hello behind her back. She turned around in time to see Maria Andersson slink out the door. She turned back toward Henrik. An embarrassed smile twitched on his face.

"I see. How shall we do this?" he said.

Sara looked around the room.

"Is Ellen in there?" she asked, pointing toward the bedroom door.

"Yes."

"We'll have to check with Ellen, to see what she thinks."

"Okay."

Sara went up to the bedroom door, which was open but pushed shut. She opened it carefully, turned around, and saw that Henrik remained where he was.

"Are you coming?"

"Well," said Henrik, "I thought . . ."

"You should be there, too."

Sara continued into the room. Ellen sat on the made bed with a miniature game of Chinese checkers on her lap. The pieces were set out in all six homes. It seemed more like she was playing with the game than that she had been playing it with Maria.

"Hi, Ellen," said Sara.

Ellen looked up from the board.

"Hi."

"You remember me, don't you?"

Ellen nodded with slow, exaggerated head movements.

"That's good. I was thinking that you and me and your daddy could talk awhile."

Ellen looked at Sara, perplexed.

"Shall we sit down in the other room, or do you want to stay in here?"

"Here," said Ellen.

"Good, then that's what we'll do."

Sara moved the only chair in the room over to the bed and sat down on it. Henrik sank down in a crouch a little ways from them.

"You can bring in a chair if you want," said Sara to him.

"This is fine."

He leaned back so that he could support himself against the wall.

"Is that your game of Chinese checkers?" Sara asked Ellen.

"It's a fox-and-geese game," said Ellen, squeezing along the edge of the playing area with her fingers.

"That's true," said Sara. "I saw wrong."

She asked a little more about the fox-and-geese game, then they talked awhile about the ferries outside the windows before she guided the conversation to the day when the lady in the car had stopped outside the school and Ellen rode with her.

Ellen looked a little sulky.

"Could you tell about that?"

"What do you mean, tell?" said Ellen.

"What it was like. What you talked about."

Ellen sighed.

"What do you mean, that I got gum, played on her DS, and then I had to walk the whole way back to school?" she said in a single exhalation while she rocked her head from side to side.

"Yes, that's exactly what I would like to hear about."

Ellen chattered her teeth in her closed mouth.

"She was going to buy a kitten, but then she didn't find her way to the ferry."

"A kitten from Fårö?"

Ellen kicked herself farther back up on the bed. She fingered the game. Some of the red and black pieces came loose and fell down on the bedspread.

"One time when I was on the ferry with Daddy he forgot his camera, so we had to drive back and get it. Daddy was really angry. He shouted really loud. Damn it! Goddamn it! That's what he shouted."

"What happened then?" said Sara neutrally.

"I got scared and started to cry," said Ellen.

She looked furtively and appeared as if she didn't really want to tell this. Then she suddenly brightened up and continued.

"But then Daddy stopped the car and said that I wasn't the one he was angry at."

Sara heard how Henrik changed position behind her.

"Then did it feel better?" asked Sara.

"Yes."

"It's easy to get scared when someone gets angry," said Sara, smiling at Ellen. "It can seem a little scary."

"Yes."

"I get scared sometimes, too, when people get angry."

Ellen giggled. "No," she said. "Police officers don't get scared, do they?"

"Do you think police officers can't be scared?"

"No. They're brave."

"Yes, you're right about that," said Sara. "Sometimes you have to be brave. But I think it's good to be a little scared of things, too, sometimes. If you're never scared, you can't be brave. Have you thought about that? You're brave if you do something, even though you think it's a little scary."

Ellen stretched her neck and leaned over toward Sara.

"Then I've been brave," she said satisfied.

"When was that?"

"When I started school in Fårösund."

"That was brave," said Sara. "It's usually a little scary when you're going to do new things."

Ellen thought about it with a sly expression.

"And when I blew bubbles at swimming lessons."

"You see," said Sara happily. "You've done lots of brave things."

Ellen sank back and lowered her eyes toward the fox-and-geese game.

Something moved outside the window. A white wall of steel plate appeared out of the fog. The M/S *Gotland* came out of nowhere. From a distance the rumbling of the engines could be heard as the ferry maneuvered in toward the pier.

"At first she looked pretty, but not the whole time," said Ellen.

Was she talking about the woman in the car now? thought Sara. Or about her teacher? Or a classmate?

"I thought at first that she was a girl, but then a lady."

Sara waited. Ellen noticed one of the game pieces that had come loose, picked it up, and put it into place.

"It was kind of chapped here."

She scratched on her cheek with her index finger.

"Chapped?" said Sara.

"Yes. Here."

Ellen pressed with her finger against her cheek so that the skin turned white around the fingertip. Then she looked up toward the window and slid quickly down from the bed.

Chapped? Dry skin, a scab, or what?

"Now they're opening for the cars," said Ellen.

M/S *Gotland*'s bow ports slid up. Soon the load of cars and trucks would crawl along at a snail's pace out of the innards of the ferry.

Sara understood that the moment was past.

69

Fredrik could see the equipment van in the rearview mirror. In front of the van, the light gravel road; behind it, the fog like a wall. They were in the middle of the pine forest south of Vamlingbo, would soon pass the house in Nore where he had lived during that period when he and Eva . . . He was unsure what he should call it. Dated? Had an affair? Slept with each other?

The big stone barn emerged first out of the fog, then the house. It was the first time he had driven past since that summer. He looked at the house and, instead of the feared surge of nostalgia, had a surprising experience of time as passed. He still remembered how burningly urgent it had been for him to be with Eva those months, urgent enough that he would turn his whole life upside down, but he could not feel it. What had been so important, so vibrantly strong, was now only a then. History.

He wondered what Eva would feel when she drove past.

Five minutes later, Fredrik caught sight of a man in boots, brown corduroy pants, and a thin black jacket. He was waiting along the narrow, rough road. Behind him, to the left in among pines and scrubby alders, a small cottage with black-painted wood panels and dark green corners was visible.

Fredrik stopped and rolled down the window.

"Markus Bergvall?"

"Yes."

Fredrik got out of the car and shook hands. Bergvall had medium-blond hair and gray-blue eyes, a pair of steel-rimmed eyeglasses on a cord around his neck.

"Is this the house?" said Fredrik, pointing toward the cottage.

"Yes, that's Larsson's cottage."

The house was practically on the beach. It was a small weekend cabin, one hundred and thirty square feet at most, and appeared to be built in the forties or fifties. To the left of the house was a brown-glazed garden shed of considerably later vintage. The location was unique. There were not many houses so close to the shoreline this far south.

"We'll just wait for the technician," said Fredrik.

The last stretch of road was barely passable. Eva had fallen behind. Or else it was Fredrik who drove away from her when he stepped on the gas a little more outside the house in Nore.

As soon as Eva had arrived and unpacked they went over to the cottage. The surf was indolent and subdued out in the fog. It was not possible to see more than a narrow strip of sea beyond the stony beach.

"Whose place is this?" asked Eva.

"A family from Stockholm," Bergvall answered. "A woman from here in Vamlingbo owned it until a couple years ago, but she was alone and couldn't keep it."

On the side toward the sea the house had a veranda where the owner had stacked garden furniture and a couple of large plastic tubs. Eva stepped up on the veranda and rested her heavy bag against the railing.

"And the Stockholm family?" she said.

"Kalle and Sofia Larsson. They have two children. It's probably a little cramped for them here, but there are other things that compensate."

"What do they do?"

"He works for some newspaper, but now I'm not sure whether it was *Aftonbladet* or *Expressen*."

What a surprise, thought Fredrik. Storsudret, a refuge for the media elite.

Markus Bergvall unlocked the green, flaking front door and let them in.

"You'll have to wait outside," said Eva when Bergvall was about to follow them.

Fredrik stopped in the doorway and looked around. The cottage consisted of a sleeping loft, a little workroom, and a main room with an open red-brick fireplace in the middle. Besides a flat-screen TV over which someone had hung a linen cloth as dust protection, nothing in the house was more modern than the seventies. It must be the former owner's things that were still there.

"I'll start with the kitchen," said Eva.

She took out a flashlight and shone it on the counter.

"Nothing on the counter."

She investigated the cupboards and searched the floor in front of the counter.

"There's some hair here. Pretty long," she said. "Not so easy to clean without running water."

She studied the finding more closely with the help of an ordinary magnifying glass.

"It adds up that someone has cut their hair. The question is, where did the rest of the hair go?"

"Incinerated?" Fredrik guessed.

"Maybe. Doesn't matter too much. There's enough hair to compare with the find from Kalbjerga, but you can check the garbage."

She looked up toward Markus Bergvall, who was standing right behind Fredrik.

"Is there a garbage can?"

"Two of them. They're behind the garden shed."

"We'll go out and look, so Eva can work in peace in here," said Fredrik.

He closed the door behind them and looked south along the shore. It could not be more than a couple of miles to Gotland's southernmost point where Henrik Kjellander had been taking photographs only an hour or so before the murders. If those strands of hair turned out to come from the murderer that would be a strange coincidence. In that case, the murderer and Henrik Kjellander had driven in opposite directions across the island and in a way changed places. It was very possible that Henrik encountered the murderer on his way home.

"That was the one that was broken," said Markus Bergvall.

He pointed to one of the windows on the veranda.

"It's barely visible now, but I closed it and wedged a twig so that it wouldn't glide up."

Fredrik went closer. There were break marks by the lower hasp, both on the window casement and sill, but as Bergvall pointed out it was not something you would notice at a distance.

"So when you came here was the window standing open?"

"Yes, but no more than a hand's width."

They continued over to the garden shed.

"Do they really have waste collection down here?" Fredrik asked.

"No," Bergvall smiled. "They don't drive down here. You have to take the garbage to the crossroads where you turned off the last stretch. They usually leave them up there in the summer, but now they've shut down for the season."

There was a black and a brown can behind the shed, one for compost and one for incineration. Both were empty.

Fredrik asked a few more questions about the Larsson family, got their home address and telephone number, then excused himself and went back into the house.

Eva was done in the kitchen. She had spread out a plastic cover in front of the fireplace and was scooping the ashes into a plastic bag.

"How's it going?"

"Someone burned clothing here," she said without interrupting her work.

"Are you sure?"

"Quite sure. There are cloth fibers in the ash. And look in there."

She turned around and pointed toward a smaller bag of brown paper that was on the floor behind her back.

Fredrik went over and picked up the bag after having removed his shoes. He carefully opened it. At the bottom of the bag were several sooty, small metal objects.

"What are they?"

"I'm quite sure they're rivets, the kind that sit around the pockets on jeans. And the larger ring-shaped objects are two eyelets."

"Eyelets?"

"That are used in clothes to reinforce holes. For example, where a cord runs in a hooded sweatshirt."

"Was there a cord on Maria Andersson's sweatshirt?"

"Don't know, but there usually are on that kind of sweatshirt. We'll have to check that."

Fredrik silently observed the small objects in the bag, then closed it and set it down.

"Let's say this is the perpetrator. Isn't it a bit strange to go to this place in particular?"

Eva finished her work in the fireplace by vacuuming up the last remnants of soot.

"No, why is that?" she said. "It's isolated, it's a long way to the nearest neighbor."

"Sure, in that way it's perfect. But to take off here . . . You saw yourself what the road looks like. To even expect to find a house out here . . ."

"You mean she must have known that it was here?"

"Yes."

Eva turned off the vacuum cleaner. The muffled roar from the motor turned into a brief growl before it became silent.

"If you're right, perhaps it's possible to find her by way of the owner of the cabin, or one of the neighbors."

Fredrik nodded toward the kitchen.

"How long will it take to get an answer to the strands of hair?"

"A microscopic comparison won't take long. But even if it matches it won't hold up in court."

"Right now I don't care about the law. I just want to know if this may be what we think it is."

70.

When Fredrik woke up on Thursday only a quick glance at the blind was needed to see that the fog was gone. The sun drew a shadow image of the window bars on the stiff, pale yellow fabric.

He pulled on his bathrobe, went into the kitchen, and filled the coffeemaker. He could not help thinking about the cabin by the sea. What would have happened if Bergvall had not been so curious, and imaginative besides, to connect the break-in and the strands of hair with the murders? Presumably nothing. He would have cleaned away the traces without thinking any more about it.

Fredrik took a quick shower, shaved, and got dressed. In the short distance to the mailbox and back he thought about whether it had all been planned from the start: driving to the cabin to burn the clothes and dye her hair. Or if the perpetrator had panicked, suddenly felt that she had to change her appearance, happened to think of the cabin, bought hair dye, and drove there.

He called Kalle Larsson, took a chance on *Expressen*, but it turned out that he worked at *Aftonbladet*. There were many people, of course, who knew about the family's summer place, but none that Kalle Larsson could connect with Henrik Kjellander or Malin Andersson.

If it hadn't been for the burned-up clothes Fredrik could have imagined other explanations, but now he had a hard time seeing that it wouldn't have a connection with the murders. Someone breaks into a cabin roughly three-and-a-half hours after the murders, burns clothes, including a garment that could be Maria Andersson's sweatshirt, cuts her hair, and presumably dyes it. Eva had found traces of chemicals in one of the tubs that indicated the latter. That could not be a coincidence.

When he came in with the newspaper, Ninni was standing by the counter pouring a cup of coffee. He tossed the newspaper onto the table, aware that he would not have time to read it. He had browsed through the day's article on the Fårö murders on the way back from the mailbox. That would have to do.

"You haven't forgotten that Joakim is coming tomorrow, have you?" said Ninni.

"Not now that you've reminded me."

"But I assume we aren't going to see much of you?"

"Probably not, but I'll find time to see him. If he's not going into Visby and partying every night."

"There is that risk."

He looked disappointed.

"Murder is murder," said Ninni, sitting down at the table.

Fredrik looked at the kitchen clock. The one that was always five minutes slow, even though he moved it ahead every Saturday.

"I have to leave."

Fredrik had just made it back to his office after the morning's review when they were called to a meeting again. The forensic lab had sent a report: The strands of hair that were found in the summer cabin could come from the same head as the wad of hair that Malin Andersson had held in a firm grasp even after death.

"Because Eva has found fingerprints on the broken window, this may be the technical evidence we've been missing," said Peter Klint.

"Although now we no longer have a suspect," said Fredrik.

"No, the fingerprints are not Stina Hansson's of course. We probably shouldn't completely rule her out, but it's no longer defensible to keep her in custody."

"Pity," said Ove, who stood with his arms crossed inside the door. "She seemed like the perfect perpetrator for this case."

"Well, that's how it is, anyway," said Göran. "Now we'll have to start over."

He took off his glasses with a sudden movement and turned to Fredrik.

"Do we have the guest lists from the hotels?"

"Yes, they arrived yesterday. But they weren't that urgent before Bergvall and the cabin turned up."

"And then we have Kjellander's other contacts. The ones you got from his agent in Stockholm. There must be quite a few?"

Göran did not wait for the answer. He squeezed his glasses back over his nose and looked around among his associates.

"We'll have to divide this up so we pick up the pace. It may be worth questioning the journalist who owns the cabin about who has been there to visit."

"The accountant," said Fredrik.

"What?"

"He's an accountant, not a journalist. Although he does work at *Aftonbladet*."

"Okay," said Göran. "The accountant. Whatever, even if he couldn't connect any of his guests to Henrik Kjellander or Malin Andersson we can't miss that possibility."

"There is another person I think we might be able to get something out of," said Fredrik. "Thomas Bark. He's known Henrik since student days and they are still close friends."

"But haven't you already questioned him? That didn't produce very much, as I recall."

Göran sounded uninterested.

"No, but I got a sense that he was holding back something."

"Yes?"

"I asked if he knew whether Kjellander had any relationships on the side. He maintained that was not the case, but I got a feeling that he knew something that he didn't want to tell. I pressured him about Stina Hansson, but now, of course, we're searching for someone else."

"You mean you want to question him in person?"

"Yes, I think it might produce something," said Fredrik.

Göran rubbed the top of his bald head. He looked moderately enthusiastic, turned questioningly to Klint.

"I say go," said Klint. "But go at him properly. Don't give up."

71.

Malin and Maria's older brother, Staffan, was surprisingly his usual self. The quick movement with his hand as he brushed aside the dark, shoulder-length hair from his face, the quick, slightly nervous way of moving. It was only the gaze that was different. It did not move around curiously like it usually did, but instead was lost in something else beyond the room.

"We could have stayed at the same hotel, but I didn't think about that when I made the reservation," he said, adjusting his jeans shirt, which had mother-of-pearl snap fasteners.

Staffan had reserved a room for his mother and himself at Wisby Hotel, a ten-minute walk from the hotel where Henrik, Maria, and Ellen were staying.

Ewy was like a different person. This happy, talkative, almost professionally pleasant woman was silent and resolute. The summer tan had taken on a grayish tone and she moved stiffly and slowly as if she had aged twenty years overnight. She hugged them, hard but somehow absent.

Henrik had a hard time meeting her eyes. Staffan's were easier, but that was because they had been such good friends. Somehow that got the upper hand.

He found himself thinking they *had been* friends. As if it was over now. Henrik knew that, but not Staffan. It was not because Malin and Axel were dead, but instead because of that other thing. What would tear what was left of this family apart if it ever came out.

Ewy took a few hesitant steps up to the desk. She put her hands on the back of the chair and tried to turn the chair out toward the room, struggled and failed. Staffan hurried over and helped her. Henrik stood where he was as if paralyzed. He ought to have been more attentive, should have . . . Ewy sat down stiffly. She set her bag on the floor and looked around the room.

"How long are they thinking the three of you should stay here?" she said in a voice emptied of all joy.

Henrik turned completely cold. He felt a scratching in his throat. He coughed a couple of times with a croaking sound. It was something about the words "the three of you." That he and Maria were a unit. It sounded so revealing. But perhaps she didn't mean that.

"I don't know."

When he heard his own feeble voice he realized how tired he was of being in the dreary, impersonal hotel room. All he and Ellen had brought with them from home were a few items of clothing. Things they hadn't even packed themselves. It was as if his world was dissolved into different time axes that were moving at completely different rates. It was ten seconds since he had opened the outside door to the bloody hall in Kalbjerga. It was a month ago, at least, since the police placed them at the hotel by the harbor.

"I'll go home with you tomorrow," said Maria.

Henrik and Maria had not talked about it, but when she said that it felt completely obvious. This was not her place. She had a life somewhere else, only happened to still be here.

"I see, yes, of course," said Ewy.

Henrik did not understand what she meant by that and didn't intend to try to understand, either.

Staffan mumbled something about the flight, occupied with Ellen. Staffan's niece climbed steadily up his legs while he held firmly onto her hands. She made a backward somersault and landed with a dull thud on the soft hotel room carpet. That was something she always wanted to do with just Staffan. Because she was so small for her age it still went well.

Henrik lost himself for a moment in their play. What would he do without Ellen? What if she and Maria had not gone down to swim? Think if both Axel and Ellen . . . He closed his eyes hard.

"But it must be monotonous for the girl, don't you think?" said Ewy.

Henrik opened his eyes and turned toward his mother-in-law.

"I'll try to arrange an apartment," he said. "Or else the police can arrange that. And bring a few of Ellen's things here."

"Have they said anything about the house?"

When he heard Ewy gather her fragile, joyless voice and ask the practical questions he thought that she shouldn't have to go through that. That she ought to be able to lie down and close her eyes and keep silent, which presumably is what she wanted to do most of all. Plucky, thought Henrik. A word you seldom use.

"I'm sure they'll be done with the house soon. But perhaps you don't even want to—"

She made a little movement with her mouth as if she wanted to take back the question.

"I don't know," said Henrik heavily. "I really don't know. But you're right of course. We can't go on living here."

Ewy reached for the purse and took out a tin of throat lozenges. She put a lozenge in her mouth and then extended the tin in the direction of Ellen. After a slight hesitation Ellen went up to her grandmother and started fishing for a lozenge.

"You can take the whole tin," said Ewy.

She smiled tenderly at Ellen and then looked at Henrik again.

"There are a lot of things we ought to talk about, but I don't know where to start."

She turned the lozenge in her mouth with a faint smacking. Staffan suggested that they should go with them over to their hotel so they could drop off their bags and then they could have lunch at the hotel. If the policeman outside had no objections?

Henrik had a hard time imagining that he could consume more than a glass of water in the company of Maria, Ewy, and Staffan. He would be forced to tighten his inner straitjacket to the bursting point not to scream all the secrets right out.

No, that was not true. He would not say a word. Ever. They would have to torture him first. But it felt as if he was about to fall apart. That something could leak out, against his will. The policeman who was assigned to protect them had no objection, but to be on the safe side made a call to his superior at the police station.

They took the upper street. Henrik did not know whether that was because it was closer or because it should somehow be better. Safer. Did they really need to be protected? The police no doubt knew what they were doing, he assumed, but he had a hard time feeling threatened. The picture of Malin and Axel, battered and bloody, overshadowed all else. There was no room for dark fantasies about what could happen to them. The worst had already happened.

The wheels on Staffan's carry-on bag rattled across the cobblestones as they passed through Skansporten's rugged gray limestone arch. Ewy looked quickly up toward the tower ruin alongside the gate opening. Henrik took a couple of deep breaths and fixed his gaze somewhere at the end of the street. He felt dizzy. Apart from climbing into a car and being driven to the police station, this was the first time in five days he had left the hotel. They had walked around in the Harbor Hotel's back courtyard. Like prisoners. Perhaps they could have taken a walk outside if they wanted. He had not thought to ask.

Ellen was holding his hand. Staffan, Ewy, and Maria walked in a row ahead of them. Order was restored. The Andersson family by themselves and then his own semi-family. The police officer came last.

When they came into the dark, stone-paved lobby of Wisby Hotel and Henrik saw the walkway that connected the hotel with Friheten it was as if he lost all control of his legs.

They got so close. The restaurant. He and Malin. The key card in his pocket, which would be a surprise. Maria at home with the kids.

On sheer will he took three swaying steps up to the nearest couch and sat down with a clumsy motion.

"What is it?" asked Staffan with a worried frown.

"I can't eat lunch here," he whispered. "I—"

His mouth was dry; he had a hard time saying the words.

"Malin and I . . ." he said, trying to turn around with a gesture toward the restaurant.

"We'll go somewhere else," said Staffan, leaning over and placing a hand on Henrik's shoulder. "Or would you rather go back?"

"No. Not back," Henrik mumbled and felt how the hand burned against his shoulder.

"We'll just quickly check in, then we'll go," said Staffan.

He rolled away with the bag to reception, leaving a cold hollow in Henrik's shoulder. Maria went with Ewy up to the reception counter and Ellen sat down beside him on the couch. He heard their voices. Their names. The scraping of a pen against paper.

After an eternity they were done. Staffan and Ewy could, of course, not suggest any place to eat. That became Henrik's task. Why should they eat? It seemed absurd that they should sit together and eat food. But even grieving people have to eat. Perhaps it was the only thing grieving families could do together. Cling to the practical things. Survival. Sleep. Food.

He took them to Bakfickan, the little fish restaurant by the church ruin on the main square. Henrik used to eat there when he was in Visby.

The staff recognized him. He noticed how the waiter looked startled as they came in, uncertain how to greet them.

They were early. The little restaurant was empty and they got a table by the window to the left. There were only a small number of tables in the tiled former butcher shop.

"You're welcome to eat with us," said Staffan to the policeman.

"Thanks, but it's better if I wait outside," he answered.

After a quick glance around the place he went back out.

Strangely enough, Henrik could eat when they got their food. All of the grilled salmon and some potatoes. Over coffee, Ewy started talking about the funeral. She would prefer for Malin and Axel to be buried on the mainland. That was her personal wish. But she thought that Henrik should decide. If he preferred Gotland she would not object.

"But that depends, of course, on what you intend to do now."

Henrik looked at her perplexed.

"If you intend to stay here. It would feel wrong if . . ."

She stole a glance at Ellen and searched for a suitable formulation.

"If they're buried here and you and Ellen move home later . . . or, I mean . . . back to Stockholm. Then they'll be alone here."

"No, it's true. That would be strange."

He promised to think it over carefully. Staffan had no opinion. He left the whole decision to Henrik. Maria simply mumbled a "no, no, sure," and nodded at him.

Henrik had actually not given it a thought before. Fantasies about the burial itself had forced themselves on him, but they had played out in an unknown church that he had not connected to any particular place.

He visualized Fårö, the church in the middle of the island. The sea that would soon be cold. The barren beaches with knotted prickly pines. Did he want Malin and Axel to rest there? Was it better if she got to return to the mainland? Return? She was already there. He lost himself in images of Malin at the coroner's office, of Malin being conveyed back in a coffin on the car deck of the Gotland ferry. How she would be left alone between the echoing metal bulkheads while all the other passengers walked away up the stairs and settled down in heated lounges.

72.

Once Klint had said yes it did not take Fredrik long to make his way from Visby to Södermalm in Stockholm. He had arranged a time with Thomas Bark in his studio in Hammarbyhamnen, but first he wanted to question Janna Drake.

The agency was housed in a typical fin-de-siècle apartment two flights up on Hornsgatan. The color scheme of the walls and woodwork was white and looked as if it had been painted yesterday. Judging by the many signs on the door, the Drake Agency shared the office with several other businesses.

Two sober, gray couches met them in the unstaffed reception area. Above the couches two poster-sized black-and-white photographs were hanging. One depicted a naked young woman on a horse, the other some laughing children in a shabby backyard in an unknown country. Two worlds. Which one was it that enticed Joakim? Fredrik didn't know.

A woman roughly the same age as Henrik Kjellander entered the room, walked quickly up to Fredrik, and extended her hand. He recognized Janna Drake's slightly hoarse voice at once.

She showed him into the room she had just come out of. Two large desks stood across from each other, edge to edge.

"You can sit there," she said, pointing to the one seat.

Fredrik pulled out the chair.

"Oops," he said when he realized he was sitting very low.

Janna Drake giggled. "There's a lever there at the side," she said.

He found a black plastic lever and managed to adjust the height.

Janna Drake did not look at all as he had expected. She was about five foot five, and her medium blond, straight hair was cut short. Her face had friendly, soft forms. Fredrik had expected a stately woman with definite features. Probably it was the name that called forth an upper-class pattern.

"How many work here?" he said, looking around the room.

"Do you mean in the whole office, or at the agency?" said Janna Drake, sitting down across from him.

"At the agency."

"Right now there are three of us. Helena, my partner, and then we have one employee, Andreas."

He already knew the names.

"But you're the one who is Henrik's agent? I mean, who has contact with his clients, manages negotiations and such?"

"Yes," she said. "We divide our photographers up between us. That's a source of security for them, but it is also good for the clients that they know, for example, who I represent. That it's not different from one time to the next. Then sometimes we fill in for one another if someone is sick or there's a lot going on with certain photographers."

"Good," Fredrik said firmly.

He did not really know what it was that was good, but was eager to interrupt. The tone suggested that a longer presentation of the Drake Agency was on its way. A sales pitch that Janna Drake presumably could supply with a sparklingly intense gaze while she thought about something else.

"You said before, when we talked on the phone, that you did not really socialize with Henrik privately," he said.

"That's correct," said Janna.

"But you have nonetheless been his agent for a really long time."

She nodded. "Over ten years."

"That's a long time. Almost as long as he's been together with Malin."

"Yes?"

Her eyes narrowed a touch and her forehead got a wrinkle, as if she did not really appreciate the parallel.

"But you didn't know him before you became his agent?"

"Yes, we were acquainted before that."

Fredrik looked at her with surprise.

"So you have socialized privately, even if you no longer do?"

"No, or . . ."

She interrupted herself with an embarrassed sigh.

"It was different then. We were younger. You went out a lot. We socialized in the same circles, met at the bar."

"Okay, I think I understand the difference."

"We were acquaintances, but not friends. It's no more difficult than that."

"Do you know if he saw other women? Other than Malin?"

"Other women?"

Janna Drake leaned slowly back and looked at him with her head at a slight angle. "What exactly do you mean?"

"I mean if he had any relationships on the side, short-term or longer."

The guarded expression on Janna Drake's face was replaced by a smile.

"You shouldn't confuse the image of the fashion photographer with the private person," she said. "If you're constantly surrounded by beautiful young women in provocative clothing it's easy for people to get a certain impression. But it's crucial to distinguish between apples and oranges."

Fredrik hated that silly fruit metaphor that people hid behind when they really wanted to say you seemed a little dense.

"You don't need to defend him," he said. "I'm out to find a murderer, not to root in Henrik Kjellander's private life. But if the way to the perpetrator goes via his private life, then I have to do that."

"And you know that?" she said in a somewhat flat voice.

"No, but that's how it usually is."

Janna Drake got up and went over to a low cabinet to the right of the door. She reached for a glass and filled it with water from a carafe. She raised the glass, but stopped.

"Excuse me," she said, turning to Fredrik. "Would you like a glass of water?"

"No, thanks, I'm fine."

She took a couple of sips and came back and sat down, holding the glass with both hands and letting it rotate slowly.

"If you're looking for something concrete I probably can't contribute. But this much I can say: that when I started working with Henrik he had a reputation for being pretty wild. As I said, that's fairly common in our industry."

"What does wild entail?" asked Fredrik.

"Well, you know, women, going out a lot. But my understanding was that this was before he met Malin. To me, Henrik has always been a decent, open person. Flirtatious perhaps, but not creepy in any way, if I may say so."

"With you as well?" Fredrik asked.

"Flirtatious? Yes, but in a social way."

"What do you mean?"

"He is extremely considerate and positive, but he hasn't hit on me."

How do you know that so definitely? thought Fredrik.

"You've never had a relationship," he said.

"Us?"

Janna Drake stared at him with mouth half open. There was no mistaking that she was surprised, almost offended. As if she was exerting herself.

"Yes," said Fredrik. "You and Henrik."

"No, not really."

"Not even a temporary—"

"But now you have to back off. If you think I would start a relationship with one of my clients. That's just crazy."

"Not a good idea, perhaps, I agree. But you're not his psychoana-
lyst, of course."

Janna set down the glass with a bang that presumably was louder
than she intended. The determined gaze turned to the side and wandered around the room.

There was not much left of the pleasant atmosphere that had started
the interview, but that was his task, to ask the uncomfortable questions.
Not considerate and positive like Henrik Kjellander, he thought.

"I'm almost done. Just one last question. What were you doing last
Friday?"

Perhaps it was just as simple as Janna Drake had already said on the
phone. She did not know Henrik Kjellander as a private person, thought
Fredrik as he stepped onto the light rail at Gullmarsplan. He himself
could say that he knew some of his colleagues really well, in the sense
that he understood more or less how they functioned. At the same time
he knew very little about what kind of lives they led. Perhaps he knew
that they were married, had children, and liked to play tennis. But not
what they brooded about at night.

Janna Drake thought anyway that he was a bastard, and she had
an alibi for Friday.

The wheels of the tram creaked against the rail as it took a long
ninety-degree curve. The cars wound out from the enclosed track area
at the subway station and came out among cars and scattered pedestri-
ans in Hammarby Sjöstad.

It was the first time he had taken the light rail down to the newly
constructed residential area. It had not been there when he left Stockholm for Gotland. Not many of the buildings, either.

He got off at Lumaparken, or Luma as the stop had concisely
been christened. Both got their name from the dirty-yellow complex

between the park and the canal, the old lightbulb factory that had been renovated into apartments. Fredrik remembered that he had skimmed through an interior decorating article about one of the new apartments. A duplex apartment full of expensive furniture.

According to the address Thomas Bark had provided, his studio should be in an industrial building with a brown sheet-metal facade, immediately to the left of the Luma factory. Fredrik found the door and came into a worn stairwell. On the second floor, at the far end of a narrow corridor, was a piece of graph paper taped up with "Thomas Bark" carelessly printed in pencil.

He knocked, heard steps, and soon the door was opened by a man with short reddish-brown hair. He gave Fredrik a pirate smile. One of his front teeth was completely gold.

"Thomas Bark?" Fredrik asked, slightly disconcerted by the eccentric row of teeth.

"Yes, that's me."

They shook hands and he was let in.

"Did you just move in?"

Thomas Bark looked at him, perplexed.

"The note on the door."

"I see, no." Thomas Bark grinned. "I like keeping a somewhat low profile."

The steel door closed behind Fredrik with a scraping sound. He followed Thomas Bark into the studio, a long, narrow room with a very high ceiling. The windows were covered by white sheeting, but daylight seeped in through a narrow slit high up where the fabric had come loose. At the far end of the room was a stand with paper backdrops in different colors. Right behind Thomas Bark was a flash tripod with a large tent-like arrangement that Fredrik guessed would reflect light in some way. The tent stood on end with a square white bottom that shone faintly.

Thomas Bark looked around the room.

"I don't really know . . . I never have any real meetings here, so I haven't arranged any good place to sit. But maybe there?"

He nodded toward a couple of office chairs in front of a counter with large computer screens.

"We can stand here," said Fredrik. "I'll try to keep this brief. But it would be nice if there was a little more light."

Thomas Bark's face was almost entirely in shadow.

"Of course."

He quickly found a switch and three rows of fluorescent lights started flickering in the ceiling. The darkness was swept away. It almost made his eyes hurt. Fredrik squinted toward Thomas Bark, who was dressed in a black T-shirt and a pair of baggy black pants with large pockets on the outside of the legs. He was approximately the same height as Fredrik and had a pair of round tortoise-shell eyeglasses that matched his hair color.

"Better?" asked Thomas Bark, scratching himself nervously on the neck.

"Yes," said Fredrik.

"Okay . . ." said Thomas lingeringly, with a little coughing laugh at the end of the word.

"I was on Hornsgatan and spoke with Henrik's agent, Janna Drake, just now. She's your agent, too, isn't she?"

"Yes."

"Do you know whether she and Henrik have ever had a relationship?"

Thomas Bark's eyes widened. He seemed both surprised and a little amused.

"Did you ask Janna about that?"

"Yes, but I got a feeling that I didn't get a completely honest answer."

Thomas looked away.

"I can imagine that."

"Have they?"

"Relationship is saying a lot, but . . . Uh, it's guaranteed completely uninteresting to . . . well, for what happened . . ."

Thomas Bark picked up a lens from a small table on wheels right behind him. He screwed off the lens cap on one end, viewed the lens, screwed the cap back on again.

"There is nothing that has to do with Henrik Kjellander that is uninteresting for this investigation. It's that simple."

Bark laughed drily and shrugged his shoulders.

"Okay, if you say so . . ."

He set down the lens.

"They had sex on the bar at PA."

It was Fredrik's turn to look surprised.

"But it was after closing and it was a really long time ago. They were like twenty-two, or something like that."

"But so they did have a relationship?"

"No. It was never more than that bar counter."

"And you're certain that they haven't had a relationship later, either?"

"As sure as I can be," said Thomas. "Both Janna and Henrik stick firmly to not mixing work and personal life. Like I said, this was years before she started the agency. And Henrik has never been involved with assistants or photo models. Not the ones he worked with anyway."

"But with others?"

"Did I say that?"

Fredrik looked quietly at Thomas Bark. "Perhaps we should sit down anyway?"

Thomas sighed and looked away again self-consciously.

"Exactly what is it you want to know?"

"I want you to answer my questions honestly and frankly. Perhaps you have received confidences from Henrik that you don't want to breach. I can understand that. But this concerns a murder investigation. You can't expect the ordinary rules of the game to apply then. Or perhaps you don't agree with that?"

"Yes, yes, of course."

"I think that the person who killed Malin and Axel is someone who

is or has been in Henrik's vicinity in recent years, or possibly someone
who in turn is close to that person."

"Jealousy. You said that last time."

"Yes."

Thomas Bark rubbed his chin with his hand.

"So . . ."

He cleared his throat, stood silently, cleared his throat again.

"Damn . . ."

"What?" said Fredrik.

"Well, it's like this," Thomas Bark began.

He sounded more definite now.

"The only reason I'm telling you this is because the situation is what
it is. I doubt that it will help you at all, but . . ."

"In this situation it is definitely wrong to hold back anything you
know," said Fredrik.

"I found this out in the greatest confidence. I would be grateful if
you kept where you got this from to yourself."

"I can't promise that."

Thomas Bark sighed quietly.

"Henrik had a relationship with Maria."

For a moment the floor rocked under Fredrik. Did he mean Maria
Andersson?

"Malin's sister?"

"Yes."

"You mean a sexual relationship?"

"Yes," said Thomas Bark reluctantly.

It almost sounded as if he was the one who was the sinner.

Fredrik thought of the image of the perpetrator. The pink sweatshirt. But they had gotten to the bottom of all that. Maria could not
possibly have anything to do with the murders.

"When did this relationship go on?"

"It didn't last very long. I think it started some time before Malin
and Henrik moved to Gotland, a couple of months before, maybe.

Then they met now and then for the first six months after they moved, but not that often, as you understand."

"Who was it who ended it?"

"It was probably a joint decision. You can understand that yourself. It couldn't be more wrong. But it was something that happened and . . . well, I guess they couldn't help it. Maria and Malin were so tight, Maria was always around and I guess something started up between her and Henrik."

"It sounds as if there were strong emotions involved?"

"Maybe, but it was completely unsustainable. They realized that themselves. They probably got a little distance to it, too, with the move."

"Did Malin know that they had a relationship?"

"No, I don't think so. Henrik should have told her. If nothing else I would have noticed something. I mean, there would be consequences if Malin had found out."

A reasonable assumption that there would have been consequences. But was it so certain that Bark would have noticed something? That depended entirely on when Malin found out. If she even did find out.

It was high time to have another talk with Henrik Kjellander.

73.

It was late in the afternoon when Fredrik was picked up at the airport. He had slept almost all the way from Bromma and felt rested and energetic as he hurried up the stairs to the criminal investigation department.

The door to Göran Eide's office stood open and he heard Sara's voice from inside.

"Welcome to Gotland," Göran greeted him. "What a fucking mess this has become."

"Yes, you can say that."

"By the way, have you seen this?"

Göran turned and reached for a copy of *Aftonbladet* that was on top of the bookshelf behind him. He opened to a double spread and set the newspaper on the table.

Under the headline "The Ex-Girlfriend: I Didn't Kill Them!" was a large color photo of Stina Hansson by the ferry terminal in Fårösund. Fårö could be glimpsed in the background.

Fredrik pulled the newspaper to him. He had left the tabloid unread on the plane in favor of his nap. He quickly skimmed the story. Stina Hansson averred her innocence and told about her relationship to Henrik Kjellander, who in the text was referred to as "the famous fashion photographer." She was open-handed with personal details and admitted that she had taken it hard when the relationship ended, but explained that it was a long time ago and that she would never have harmed Henrik or his family. She experienced it as incredibly unpleasant to be a suspect, which is why it was important for her to cooperate in the interview. At the same time she claimed to understand that the police had to investigate anyone with a connection to Henrik.

"I don't get that people go along with that sort of thing," said Sara.

"She clearly felt a need to be exonerated publicly," said Fredrik. "That's understandable."

"The question is whether it helps," said Sara.

Göran folded up the newspaper and set it back on the shelf.

"Sara has produced a couple of names from the hotel lists that we think are interesting. I suggest that you confront Henrik Kjellander with them."

"I see, who are they?" asked Fredrik.

When Göran turned the hotels over to Sara, he thought it was nice to be rid of them. Better a couple of interviews in Stockholm than tedious browsing through reservation lists. But now he got an irritating sense that he had been in the wrong place.

"Sara can brief you on the way," said Göran. "Show Kjellander the rest of the lists and ask whether there are any other names he recognizes."

Henrik Kjellander was at the Wisby Hotel with Malin Andersson's family. At first he was unwilling to show up for an interview out of consideration for the family, but he had to give in. Fredrik and Sara took a car to the hotel. Sara drove.

"There are two names that recur on the lists and which are possible to link to Henrik," Sara began as they rolled out of the garage. "One is Agnes Lind, twenty-six-year-old Stockholm resident who was Henrik's assistant before he moved to Gotland. She was along on all five Copenhagen trips, stays at St. Petri just as many nights as Henrik. She was also in Östersund. On the other hand, not checked in at Lydmar in Stockholm, but that's not so strange."

Sara stopped for a red light and looked impatiently up at the traffic signal.

"Was she there as an assistant?"

"Yes, according to the information you got from the agent, she stepped in as assistant on those trips."

"And the other foreign trips?"

"No, then he evidently hired assistants on site."

"She's an assistant, but you think she may be something more?"

"It's a possibility anyway. If you can stray with your sister-in-law you can probably sleep with your assistant. I don't believe a word about that Bark's talk of separating work and personal life."

"Maybe Bark believed it."

"Possibly."

"Okay, the other name," said Fredrik.

The light turned red at Österväg, but Sara kept going anyway.

"A Marte Astrup from Copenhagen, editor at Danish *Elle* who

Henrik worked for on three of the trips. She was checked in at the hotel on all three occasions."

"But she lives in Copenhagen?"

"Yes. I checked her address. She lives a little outside the city, but not that far outside."

"It's just those two that stuck out?"

"There are more names that recur on the same hotel nights as Henrik, but no one I can connect with him. I hope he can help us with that."

A young woman with blazing red hair occupied the faux mahogany reception booth. Her name was Jenny, according to the oval nameplate. Sara asked for Henrik Kjellander. Jenny smiled and picked up a receiver. At first she seemed to have someone else on the line, then apparently Henrik after she had waited briefly.

"Yes, I'll tell them that," she said into the receiver and hung up. "He's coming down," she said to Sara with a broad smile.

Fredrik thought that he could never handle a job where you were forced to smile all the time, but perhaps that was something you could learn.

He looked around the hotel lobby.

"Should we take him up to the station anyway? We can't really sit here."

"Wait," said Sara.

She showed her police badge to the receptionist and explained why they were there.

"There doesn't happen to be a conference room available where we can sit for half an hour?"

"I'll see."

Jenny quickly turned on her computer and returned with a smiling reply.

"Yes, there is a room that you can use. You'll get a key, it's simplest that way."

She tinkered with something behind the counter and handed over a white key card.

"Thanks, that was nice," said Sara.

Just then Fredrik caught sight of Henrik. He came into the lobby from the illuminated corridor that led over to the elevators.

The conference room could hold about twelve people, so they sat down around the short end of the white-painted table. The walls were pastel green and the lighting gave a strong but almost shadowless light, just like in the police station conference room.

Sara set the guest lists out on the table.

"Can you look through these names and say if there are any you recognize?"

Henrik pulled the pile of papers to him.

"St. Petri," he mumbled. "Okay, sure."

He put his index finger on the top line, let it run downward. He stopped almost at once.

"Marte Astrup, she was at the shoot."

He looked up at Sara and Fredrik.

"You can probably tell us more," said Sara.

"Of course. She's the fashion editor for Danish *Elle*. She's the client for these jobs, and she was there at all the shoots along with Susanne, the magazine's art director. I have plenty of leeway, but they have certain basic ideas they want to look after. Different magazines have different ways of presenting fashion."

"Marte Astrup lives in Copenhagen, right?" said Sara.

"Yes."

"Why didn't she go home, instead of spending the night at the hotel?"

Henrik looked at them as if he thought the question was strange.

"I don't really know. I think the magazines do that sometimes as a little bonus. Usually you gather at the hotel or somewhere else and have dinner after the day's work, the ones from out of town, that is, and then one of the clients is often there."

"But the AD didn't spend the night. Wasn't she there at the hotel?"

"Yes, but I think she was not far from home. Or else she wanted to go home. I don't know."

"Okay, let's continue," said Sara.

Henrik read on and turned pages.

"This guy I know. David Pilgren. He's a photographer, too. I actually didn't know that he was there. Never saw him. Do you want to know something about him, too?"

"We can skip him for the time being," said Sara, but made note of the name.

Henrik continued scanning the lists. As expected, he also pointed out Agnes Lind, but that was it. That was everyone he recognized.

"None of these women you mentioned, Marte, Susanne, and Agnes, may have had reason to want to injure you or your family?"

"No," he answered at once. "No, why is that?"

He looked at them dumbfounded.

"Not at all?" asked Sara.

"No. Do you suspect something like that?"

Henrik suddenly looked worried, as if he had missed something.

"None of these women are anything more to you than customers and colleagues?"

It took awhile before he understood the drift of the question.

"What? Do you think I've been together with any of them? Good Lord, then I think I would have said so. I mean, you have asked me to tell about old girlfriends. Didn't you?"

"We thought that perhaps you had made an exception for new girlfriends," said Fredrik.

Henrik stared at him.

"What?"

"You never told about Maria."

It was as if Henrik froze to ice behind the table. He did not move so much as a little finger, was not even capable of turning his eyes away.

"We know about your relationship with Maria. We know that you haven't told everything." Sara developed Fredrik's assertion.

Henrik slowly opened his mouth.

"Uh . . ." he began.

He clenched his hands and slowly the paralysis was broken.

"Did Maria tell you?"

Sara did not answer. Henrik looked at them, one at a time.

"That's not something I want to talk about. And that's been over for almost two years. Maria . . . you know that she can't have anything to do with this. You do know that."

"Now we know that," said Sara.

Henrik sank back in the chair with a deep sigh.

"You have to help us, Henrik. If it is the case that you've had a relationship with any of these women, or any other woman, is there anyone you can imagine who wants to get revenge for having been rejected, or because of jealousy, or . . . ? You're the only one who can know."

Sara nailed him with her gaze. He shook his head.

"Is that completely certain? This is important. It may be what we need to solve this."

"There is no one," he said.

They thanked Henrik for taking the time and watched him disappear toward the elevators. Somewhere in a room in the hotel his daughter was waiting along with Maria and the rest of Malin Andersson's family.

How did you go on after having suffered what Henrik had? Fredrik was surprised that he was even able to stand up, that he was able to answer questions. It surely helped that he had his daughter. To be forced to go on, in some way. But still. A relationship with Malin's sister. And now Malin was dead.

* * *

"I don't understand this guy," said Sara when they had come up onto
Söderväg. "Why hasn't he said anything? Because he thought it was
awkward? His wife and son have been murdered."

"Exactly," said Fredrik.

"Yes, the guy seems to be a total pile of shit."

"That's not what I meant."

Sara glanced at him inquisitively while they drove through the
roundabout.

"His wife and son were murdered less than a week ago," said
Fredrik. "Presumably he may not even be thinking clearly. He's
taking sleeping pills but can't sleep."

"But he does want us to solve this anyway? If it was me . . ."

"If it was you, you would think like a cop because you are a cop.
We can't expect him to do that."

"Whatever," said Sara. "If it was me I wouldn't have slept with my
brother-in-law anyway, so the comparison is meaningless."

Fredrik did not answer. They drove on in silence the rest of the way.

"We'll have to check them anyway, the assistant and that Danish
woman," said Sara as they got out of the car in the garage.

74.

Fredrik looked out the living room window toward the light on the
neighbor's farmyard, the one that was never turned off, and the bluish
shimmer from the fly catcher in the barn. He wondered why they left the
farmyard light on all night. Was it so that the darkness would not be as
dense around them when the day was over and they had crept down into
their beds? Would it keep burglars away? Murderers? It was hardly so
that they could rush out to the animals at three o'clock in the morning

without having to turn on a switch. He saw them everywhere out in the country, lighting up the farmyards when no one was awake.

"How is it going?" said Ninni, turning off the TV.

"Oh, it's fine," he said.

"You've hardly said a word since you came home."

He looked at her with surprise.

"I haven't?" He must have. He had asked Simon about school, he had . . .

"How is it going really?"

"The investigation?"

"Yes."

"Right now it's at a standstill. But don't say that."

Ninni smiled. "They're asking about it a lot at school."

"The children or the teachers?"

"Both the children and my colleagues. It's really funny. The children ask flat out, but in the teachers' lounge it's more like they bring up the subject and hope I'll chime in."

"So what do you say?"

"That I don't know any more than they do."

"Are they satisfied with that?"

"Most are."

Ninni was perhaps right that he had not said much that evening. His thoughts were constantly making their way back to Malin and Axel Andersson in the house on Fårö. Stina Hansson, who they had been forced to release. Who probably had nothing to do with the case, but who still had something to do with the case. A woman who Henrik Kjellander had left behind many years ago, but who could not really forget him. In some way he was still in her, as a defeat, as a hope that would never be fulfilled.

Was the murderer still on the island, or had she gone home already over the weekend, with a new hairdo and in a car that they weren't searching for? On the Sunday afternoon ferry with more than a thousand passengers and a sold-out car deck?

"Hello!" Ninni called. "Now you're doing it again."

"Sorry."

He moved next to her.

"Are you trying to compensate now?" she said.

"Thanks for the encouragement."

"Sorry." Ninni put her hand in front of her mouth.

"I'm starting to doubt that we'll find her. Maybe this doesn't hang together at all the way we think it does."

He furtively stroked his hand across her leg.

"A week has passed. We have almost nothing. This doesn't add up. A murder like this should more or less solve itself. That's why I'm starting to think that maybe this isn't even that kind of murder."

"What if it is that Stina Hansson after all, the woman who was in the newspaper?" said Ninni.

Fredrik shook his head.

It could not possibly be Stina Hansson. Provided that they hadn't been led astray by the traces in the cabin. If it was some common thief who broke in and thought it was a good idea to dye her hair and burn up a few clothes . . . No, that was far too unlikely. And if it had been an ordinary thief Eva should have gotten a hit on the fingerprints she found on the window.

"Shall we go to bed?" asked Ninni.

He looked at her. Had he held out the prospect of something by stroking her leg? Or was she just tired?

75

The plane left at eight thirty. Henrik imagined that he could have seen it lift off if he stuck his head out the window and looked northward. But that was probably not true.

Only he and Ellen were left now. The air in their little hotel apartment was suddenly easier to breathe. But in the lightness there was also absence and loss.

As long as Maria had been there a kind of impossible possibility was in the air. A tension, however nauseating, shitty, and forbidden it was, nonetheless said that there was something there that meant something. That there was at least a distant echo of love.

Disgusting, Maria had said when he told her that the police knew. Was that true? He could not bear to think about it. He only knew that no one would forgive them if they found out.

It was just him and Ellen. It was easier to breathe, but he had never felt so alone in his entire life. It was easy and heavy at the same time. It was as if it blew right through him and nothing mattered. But in the light transparency there were also threatening dark gray eddies of something quite different. Perhaps that was just what loneliness was. The lightest and the heaviest we have to bear. Or else he was simply going crazy from sorrow and shame and the side effects of the sleeping pills.

He looked at Ellen and tried to convince himself that he had a daughter he had to do everything for. He had to live for her. He had to be there for Ellen, he had to, even if he felt completely incapable.

This morning he had been able to think for the first time about Malin and Axel like they were when they were alive. Before he had only been able to see their dead bodies, their unseeing eyes, just as they waited for him when he came home to Kalbjerga a week ago. Now he had managed to think past that, could see Axel's little head with shining eyes and glistening white teeth when he raised him up toward the ceiling and quickly lowered him toward the floor again so that he was choking with delight mixed with terror. He could see Malin in the garden, in the car, in the kitchen, in front of the TV, in bed in the morning, always the first one up, everywhere, always there.

Always.

Ellen came up to him and mutely dried his tears with her hand. It almost hurt more to see them living than dead. He'd had so much. More than he was worth.

He put his arms around Ellen and hugged her carefully.

"Ellen," he said.

She hummed in response. He took hold of her arms and looked at her seriously.

"Shall we go home?"

She nodded with lips squeezed together.

"Do you want that?"

She nodded again.

"Then that's what we'll do," he said, hugging her again.

76.

Summer was back. Not just the sun, like yesterday. Now the heat had returned, too. Sara was sitting with the phone between her shoulder and her ear as Fredrik came into the office. She made a gesture with her hand that he interpreted to mean that she would be done soon.

Sara had settled into her office in a completely different way than he had. Pictures of friends and relatives on the bulletin board. In a vase on the table was a fabric rose that she got from her colleagues on her last birthday. On the wall was a poster depicting Jodie Foster with pistol drawn in her role as FBI agent Clarice Starling. It had caused Lennart Svensson to crack a joke about dykes, although out of earshot of Sara. On the bulletin board Sara had also pinned up a picture of herself. It was a clipping from *GA*: Visby's first half-marathon, where Sara placed high up, right after the elite.

The only time Fredrik had been mentioned in the paper was when he fell off the cliff at Östergarnsholme. That was not something he wanted to show off.

Sara hung up and let the cheap ballpoint pen fall down among the notes on the desk.

"Marte Astrup has an alibi for the night of the murder. She left work in Copenhagen at quarter to six."

She could in other words not have been captured on an image in a surveillance camera on Fårö fifty-one minutes later.

"Have you got hold of Agnes Lind?" asked Sara.

"Yes," said Fredrik. "She was at the Cadier Bar at the Grand Hotel together with two girlfriends sipping a drink for a hundred and fifty-six kronor."

"Did she say that? What it cost?"

"Yes. Perhaps she thought it seemed more convincing."

"Good memory."

"I think I would remember that price, too. In any case, both of the girlfriends confirmed it."

Like so many times before, he could have commented that people took being suspected of murder much more lightly than being asked about who they had slept with.

"So the hotels were a blank," said Sara.

"Looks like it."

* * *

When Fredrik came back to his office a message was waiting from Eva Karlén. The words in the subject line made him quickly click it open: Coop, IP addresses.

It was a tidy list with five columns. At the far left the date and time when the comment was made, then the blog comment itself, after that the IP number and Internet operator, and then finally the name and address of the person who was concealed behind the number. Or more correctly, the one who had signed an agreement with the Internet service provider. Eva had sorted the list by mailing address.

Fredrik started with A and scrolled farther down. Approximately half of the senders had written from an address that belonged to a company or institution.

Was that the kind of thing people did on their coffee breaks nowadays? Wrote hateful posts to someone who with every good intention had suggested what they might have for dinner?

Many comments came from Gotland, not completely surprising. A good number from computers at the library. Did this mean that people who wrote hateful blog comments were bitter people who could not afford their own computer and Internet connection, or were they students who eased up the pressures of studying by sending off a few sexist comments? Or were they simply careful not to be identifiable? If he himself, for some obscure reason, were to get the idea to write vulgarities on the Internet he would definitely not do it from his home computer, that much was certain.

He searched further. There was one comment he was particularly curious about, but because the list was arranged by addresses and could not be re-sorted he had to go through everything. "Tonight it's me and Henrik."

He scrolled further. Hemse, Jönköping . . . And there it was. "Tonight I'm the one he wants. I want you to know that."

The comment was made at 5:18 P.M. on November 16 of last year. The IP number belonged to Hotel St. Petri in Copenhagen.

Fredrik reached out a finger and followed the row from left to right across the screen to be certain that he had not jumped between the rows. Same result. Hotel St. Petri in Copenhagen.

"I'll be damned," he whispered toward the screen.

Then he pushed print, got up, and looked for the folder with the guest lists from the hotels. He pulled out the ones that concerned St. Petri and quickly browsed through them. The first trip, October 4–7. He set them aside. The second trip, not that one, either, it was also October. But there, the third trip, November 16–18. The comment had been written when Henrik was checked into the hotel. Likewise Marte Astrup and Agnes Lind.

Who had written it?

Agnes Lind? The one who had been sitting at the Cadier Bar having drinks for a hundred fifty-six kronor when someone was taking a hammer to the heads of Malin and Axel Andersson? Fredrik felt how his energy drained away. It could be that simple. This did not need to have anything at all to do with the murders.

He tried to pull himself together. There was no reason to lose heart. Wasn't it time for a little lift now? It could be another guest at the hotel, or someone who worked there.

He scrolled to Agnes Lind's number in the telephone's log and called.

"Hi, this is Fredrik Broman, who just called, excuse me for disturbing you again."

"It's no problem. Was there something else?"

She sounded more curious than anything.

"Yes, I have a question that concerns the time period November 16 to 18, the third time you were with Henrik Kjellander in Copenhagen last fall."

"Yes?"

"Did you write a post on Malin Andersson's food blog from the hotel computer on the sixteenth?"

"No," she said, chirping out a laugh.

"Why is that so funny?"

"No, I guess it's not. But I don't do blog comments. I'm on Facebook and that, but . . . It's probably just teenagers and mental cases who write blog comments."

"Really?"

"Mainly."

"Are you quite sure you didn't? It's extremely important that I find out if that's the case. It may have significance for this investigation, but if you were the one who wrote it . . . well, then we can eliminate that."

"What does that comment say actually?" said Agnes.

"Do I need to tell you that for you to know whether or not you wrote it?"

"I haven't written anything on Malin's blog," she said adamantly. "I was just wondering."

"Is there anyone else who was at the hotel you can imagine may have written a post on Malin's blog that day?"

"No idea. But that depends on what it says."

"I can't reveal that, but it was not a friendly comment, if I may say so, on the contrary."

"Hmm, no, no idea."

Fredrik thought a moment. It was not certain that what was in the comment was true, but the one who wrote it must have known that Henrik was at the hotel and written it for the purpose of making Malin feel bad or to sow discord between Malin and Henrik.

"Was there anything else?" Agnes Lind asked.

She no longer sounded curious.

"Was there anyone else with you at the hotel that day? Besides Marte Astrup."

Agnes was forced to think a moment.

"No, not on the sixteenth. Then it was just the three of us. The day after, two Danish models were with us and had a drink, but they left early."

"You're quite certain that they weren't along on the sixteenth?"

"Yes, because we didn't shoot anything then. We were just prepping."

"Prepping?"

"Setting things up."

"Okay."

He probably wouldn't get any further with this. The receiver felt warm against his ear. He changed hands.

"What was it like on the two previous occasions? Were there others in your party then? Or did you meet anyone at the hotel?"

"Don't think so," said Agnes hesitantly. "Or yes, the first time we met a girl in the bar. We started talking and then she moved with us when we sat down at a table."

"You and her started talking?"

"No, it was probably more all of us. I don't know."

"Who was it who suggested that she should join you?"

"I think it was Henrik, but it was more something that just happened, even if maybe he was the one who said something like . . ." She paused.

"I don't really know how it went."

"Was it the first evening you were at the hotel, or was it later?"

"Uh . . . it was probably the first. Yes, it was."

"Do you remember her name?"

Agnes hesitated slightly before answering.

"No, I actually have no idea."

Fredrik concealed his disappointment. The strange woman in the hotel bar seemed to be about to disappear before she even got a name.

"Did she tell anything about herself?" he asked.

"I think she said she was a journalist. At *Sydsvenskan*, it must have been. She was writing about something in Copenhagen. That was why she was there."

"And you're sure about *Sydsvenskan*?"

"Yes."

It immediately looked better. If it was true that she worked at *Sydsvenska Dagbladet* it shouldn't be that hard to track her down.

"What did she look like?" he asked.

"Well, that was almost a year ago . . . She was blond, I remember that much, medium height, maybe a little shorter. She was slender, good-looking."

"Medium height, what does that mean to you?"

"About five-foot-five, maybe a little more."

"And her hairstyle? You said blond, but . . ."

"Yes, blond hair approximately to her shoulders, as I recall it anyway. Straight, simple."

"How did she talk? Did you notice any dialect?"

"No, nothing in particular."

"If you were to guess her age?"

"Thirty. About that."

"Thanks, I think that's enough," said Fredrik. "But it is possible that I'll call again."

"Sure, no problem," said Agnes.

He hung up.

The question was whether he should start with the newspaper or with Henrik Kjellander. Henrik might know the woman's name, even if Agnes did not. But why hadn't he already mentioned her, in that case?

Fredrik decided on the newspaper. After being transferred several times and waiting on the line for a while he got an answer.

"Hannes Wiklander." Someone answered who sounded as if he had just been chased up to the phone.

"My name is Fredrik Broman and I'm calling from the police in Visby," said Fredrik. "I have a few questions about a person who I believe may have worked for you."

"I see, who is that?"

"The problem is that I don't have a name. But I have a description and know a little about what she worked on."

"What does this concern?" asked Wiklander.

"This person showed up peripherally in an investigation. I just need to check off a few details."

"So, what investigation?" said Hannes Wiklander.

"Unfortunately I can't answer that," said Fredrik.

"Does this have to do with the Fårö murders?"

Fredrik remained silent.

"Yes, I was just guessing," said Wiklander.

"Can we take my questions now?" said Fredrik.

"Yes, of course. Go ahead."

"So this concerns a woman, about thirty, blond shoulder-length hair, medium height."

"That's a very general description."

"She was in Copenhagen on the fourth of October working on an assignment. About what, I don't know."

"Okay, that makes it a little easier."

"If you're uncertain you can give me several names, then I'll have to investigate it further."

"So far I don't have any names at all," said Wiklander. "But if you can wait a little I'll check. Or can I call you?"

"That will be fine."

Fredrik gave him the number.

"But it's important, so I would be grateful if you can do it as soon as possible."

"I'll do it as soon as I've hung up," Wiklander assured him.

"Thanks."

Fredrik hung up and imagined how someone at the newspaper editorial office immediately demanded Wiklander's attention. He was dragged into a discussion of some type, whatever it might be, the kind of thing you discuss at newspaper editorial offices, and the nameless employee who had been in Copenhagen was soon forgotten.

The unknown journalist was obviously someone Henrik Kjellander had not wanted to tell about. Or possibly forgotten. But the blog comment? That was made six weeks later. Who had made it?

He looked at the phone, silent on the table. Should he speak with Henrik anyway? See how he reacted to the date. November sixteenth. He could call from his cell phone so that he didn't block the line for Wiklander. He got no further before Göran was standing in the doorway.

"Kjellander is moving back to Fårö," he said.

"I see. When is that?"

"Now."

"Can we protect him there?"

"He doesn't want any protection."

Göran looked at him almost expectantly, as if he wanted something in return. Surprise? A conclusion?

"But it's not even sanitized there. He can't—"

Then the phone rang. Göran showed with a gesture that Fredrik should take it.

"Just so you know," he said and disappeared into the corridor.

Fredrik answered. It was Wiklander.

"Listen, I've checked and it must have been Katja Nyberg. She was the only one doing a job in Copenhagen on October fourth and she matches your description well. I've taken out her folder. She left at the end of January."

"Why did she leave?"

"She had a temporary position."

Hannes Wiklander coughed. Fredrik could hear the sound of a ringing telephone that no one answered.

"Did Katja Nyberg cover Copenhagen?" he asked.

"Cover is saying a lot. But she did a number of jobs there. We get a lot from Copenhagen, as you understand."

"Yes."

Fredrik had not reflected on that before, but of course that's how it must be.

"Can you fax over the contents of that personnel file?" he said.

"Of course. Anything else I can do?"

"What was she like as a person? Could you try to describe her?"

"Well, she was . . ."

Wiklander had to think a moment.

"She was pleasant, a bit serious, but still easy to make contact with. I think she was appreciated by her colleagues. Actually you would probably get a better answer from one of them. As boss you have a certain distance."

"How was she as a journalist?"

"I guess she was . . ."

He continued.

"She was capable, that I can say, but no star. She was a little uneven."

"From day to day, or how so?" asked Fredrik.

"No. She started extremely ambitiously during the summer and fall, but then it was as if she went soft. There were several temporary positions that ran out at the end of January. A few we needed to extend until April and I had Katja as a conceivable name, but then . . . I don't know what happened, but there was something."

"But it was nothing specific?" said Fredrik.

"No. She seemed tired, not really on the ball. Maybe there was something in her personal life, or something mental. I really don't know."

Three minutes later Fredrik held the fax in his hand. Pity that not everyone he dealt with was as efficient as Hannes Wiklander.

The fax consisted of four pages. The first was a form from the newspaper human resources department with Katja Nyberg's personal information. The other three pages were the application to the temporary position with attached CV.

In 2005 she had earned her degree from the journalism school in Gothenburg.

77

"Here she is, Katja Nyberg."

Fredrik set the passport photo on Sara's desk.

The woman in the picture had shoulder-length blond hair, sad eyes, and a broad mouth with full lips.

"No chapped skin on the cheek," said Sara.

"The passport is three years old."

For the moment there were things that interested him more than skin complaints.

"She was born in Gävle in 1978. She moves to Uppsala with her parents in 1993 and then to Gothenburg in 2001 to study. And finally to Malmö where she now lives. Uppsala, Gothenburg, and then the hotel in Copenhagen. Where she demonstrably has met Henrik Kjellander."

Fredrik was trying to keep a cool head, but there was too much that matched. This could really be something.

"Look here."

He unfolded the map of Gothenburg he had brought with him and set it down on the desk.

"Here is the journalism school, or JMG as it seems to be called now," he said and pointed.

He moved his finger to a different part of the city.

"Katja Nyberg lived here on Kommendörsgatan while she was studying in Gothenburg. Say that she took the streetcar to the university, got off here at Kaptensgatan, that's the nearest stop."

Fredrik follows the streetcar line with his index finger.

"In that case every day she went past . . ."

He let his finger come down on the map with a tapping sound.

"Prinsgatan 8!"

"The last tenant in Kalbjerga," said Sara and looked up from the map. "The fake address."

She let her eyes glide over the map again.

"But she also passes thirty or more other streets."

"I know. I would have been more satisfied, too, if it was in the neighboring block. But this is not chance," he said, throwing out his hand toward the map.

"There seems to be one coincidence too many, I agree with that, but . . ."

Sara took her eyes off the map, not looking really convinced.

"These are big cities, a lot of people could fit this."

"She was at St. Petri. She met Henrik in the bar."

"Take it easy, I just mean that it would be good to have something more."

"Look at this," said Fredrik impatiently.

He set out the information from the tax authorities and the insurance office.

"She has had extremely uneven income, even after her education. Besides the temporary position at *Sydsvenska Dagbladet* she has only had one other journalist job. Otherwise she has worked for a staffing agency. Maybe not so strange in itself, but she has also had several longer medical leaves. After the second year at JMG she interrupted her studies for six months."

"Maybe the interruption in studies coincides with the sick leave," said Sara.

She started looking through the papers from the insurance office.

"Yes, look at this!"

She turned the paper so that Fredrik could read it and pointed at one of the lines.

"She was on sick leave two months during the year she had a break in her studies."

"You see," he said.

"Although this is only circumstantial evidence and hardly that. It would be better if we could prove that she was in Uppsala on the fourth of June."

"Yes, but we can't question her parents before we—"

He interrupted himself.

"What is it?" asked Sara.

"Damn," he said. "Why didn't I think of that?"

He was already on his way out the door.

"Think about what?" Sara called after him.

Fredrik hurried into his office and grabbed the phone. He called *Sydsvenska Dagbladet* and asked to speak with Hannes Wiklander. He waited impatiently and listened to a desolate snapping on the phone. After a long minute the receptionist came back.

"He's not answering. You can have his cell phone number if it's urgent."

Fredrik thought about it.

"Can you connect me to the payroll office?" he asked instead.

There he got a response. It took the woman on the other end twenty seconds to pull out Katja Nyberg's travel expense account from November sixteenth. The destination was Copenhagen.

It was Katja Nyberg who wrote the comment on Malin Andersson's blog.

78.

Göran stood up behind the desk when Fredrik and Sara were far enough along in their story that he could understand the importance of it.

"Now you'll have to tell it to Klint," he said. "Then we'll see if we should bring her in."

They hurried over to the prosecutor, found him in his office, and told the whole story again, unfolded the map of Gothenburg.

"And how would this fit together, do you think?" said Klint, rocking backward in his chair. "How do you see it?"

Fredrik looked at Sara, who nodded that he should respond.

"Rather simple," he started. "Katja Nyberg meets Henrik at St. Petri; either they start a relationship, or else it's just something she wants. Let's say that they do. Henrik soon gets tired of it, or realizes that it's not a good idea, but for Katja Nyberg it gets much bigger. He is forced to make it clear to her that he is not interested, not in that way. He has children and has no intent of leaving Malin."

"So far an ordinary extramarital affair," said Klint, adjusting the watch on his left wrist.

"Yes. Exactly what happens with Katja Nyberg later, I don't know, I can't make a diagnosis, but for some reason she can't let go. She finds Henrik Kjellander's house on GotlandsResor's website, maybe she's looking to rent something else on Fårö, to be near him, maybe see him, get him to change his mind. But now she gets in sight of his house and gets a different idea. She chooses a street in Gothenburg from memory, searches for an existing family on the street, creates a Gmail address, and rents the house. At that point maybe she doesn't even know why. And then, well, you know what happens then. The threats, Ellen, and finally the murders."

Peter Klint looked worriedly at them.

"Shouldn't Henrik have said something?"

"He kept quiet about Malin's sister," said Fredrik.

"Yes, but when that thing about Maria came out in the open he ought to have had the sense to tell about this, too. If it really is as you believe."

"So what do we do?" said Sara.

Peter Klint thought a moment and then tipped his chair forward. That was clearly the decision-making position.

"Find out as much as you can about Katja Nyberg until . . ."

He looked at the clock.

"Shall we say five?"

"You don't think this is enough?" said Fredrik.

Peter Klint got a sharp crease between his eyebrows.

"I want to do this in the right order. We should get to the bottom with this woman, but before we bring her in I want to know more. Okay?"

"Okay."

They got up and Fredrik folded the map.

"And then you have to question Kjellander."

It was twenty to three; in other words, they had over two hours to work with. Fredrik and Sara quickly divided up the work between them and Fredrik ended up with Henrik.

Henrik was in the car when he got hold of him.

"It's a little hard to talk right now," he said. "I'm sitting here with Ellen."

"I understand," said Fredrik.

"I'm on my way to Fårö."

"I heard that you had decided to move home."

Ellen's voice was heard in the background. Henrik asked her to wait.

"It wasn't good for Ellen at that hotel. Not for me, either. It was like sitting in jail. Don't be offended. I know that you tried to arrange everything for the best and I'm grateful for that, but we simply had to get out of there."

"No, I understand but—"

"Listen, can I call you when I get there?" said Henrik politely but a little stressed.

Fredrik considered whether he should say something about Nyberg or wait. He decided to mention her anyway.

"We have to talk about Katja Nyberg."

"I see?" said Henrik lingeringly.

"We think that you met her in Copenhagen on the fourth of October. At the hotel."

Henrik did not answer. Fredrik could hear engine sounds and the sound of tires against asphalt. "Is that true?"

"Yes, it's true. But listen, I have to hang up now. I'll have to call you when I get there."

79.

Henrik slowed down and inched the final bit up to where Malin's Honda was still parked. It was three o'clock in the afternoon and the sky was covered by a thin layer of clouds. The gravel cracked under the rough tires of the SUV.

One of the police officers who worked with the crime-scene investigation had driven the Mercedes down to Visby for him. Fredrik Broman had been considerate enough to ask whether he needed his car. Henrik thought that sooner or later he probably would. He hadn't intended to stay in Visby forever.

"Mommy's car," said Ellen in a pitiful voice.

Henrik had stopped completely. He reached out a hand and carefully stroked her across the head.

"Yes," he said.

He listened to the rough rumbling of the engine under the hood and looked down toward the house. It was the same. Yet he got the feeling of a summer house that had been closed up for the winter. Things put away in the garden, locked up.

He put the car in reverse, backed in beside the Honda, and turned off the engine. They remained sitting without moving, silent. He listened for sounds, something to fix his attention on, but heard nothing. Realized at last that he was the one who would have to break the paralysis.

"Shall we get out?" he said, pulling the key out of the ignition.

"Okay," said Ellen, opening the door on her side.

Henrik got out of the car and took the groceries and the bag of clothes and other belongings they had with them at the hotel, carrying them in one hand. He locked the car and took Ellen by his free hand. He had to let go of her to open the gate, squeezing through with what he was carrying and closing it behind them.

Katja Nyberg? The woman at St. Petri? Did Fredrik Broman mean that they were investigating her? It sounded completely nuts. Would it continue like this? Would they hunt out every woman he had ever looked at, turn his whole life inside out?

He tried to picture Katja Nyberg here at Fårö, but it didn't work. She was a woman in a bar in a hotel in another country.

He looked toward the edge of the forest, saw how it darkened where the trees got denser. He heard in the distance the call of a bird. He knew nothing about birds, thought it sounded like a call from someone who had been abandoned deep in the forest.

Had he made the right decision? Maybe they should have left the island instead, chosen a completely different place. Maybe he had already made the wrong decision two years ago, when they decided to buy the house.

"Daddy?"

Ellen looked at him inquiringly. He smiled at her, squeezed her hand, and continued down toward the house.

He felt a growing discomfort as they got closer, but it was not fear. He squeezed Ellen's hand. It helped a little, made it so that he didn't collapse, anyway. He had not believed that it would be like this to lose someone. He had not believed that he would feel so terribly alone.

Henrik asked Ellen to wait at the bottom of the steps while he took out the key and unlocked the front door. He opened it carefully and looked in.

The hall and kitchen bore no trace of what had happened. The only thing that betrayed what had played out there was the feeling of vacuum. The hall was empty. Clothes, shoes, umbrellas and shoe horns, and all imaginable accessories that had been hanging on hooks, put away on shelves, or simply tossed somewhere were gone.

Henrik did not know where they had gone. Some of it the crime-scene technicians had surely taken care of, but the rest? Had the cleaning company thrown it away?

He tried to convince himself that it didn't matter. He turned around and waved Ellen to him.

"Come in," he said.

He tried to take a few bold steps into the house even though his legs felt uncertain and his heart was pounding hard in his chest. He did not want to transfer his emotions to Ellen. The room meant nothing to her and he really wanted it to stay that way. She knew nothing. Not about that.

"Take off your shoes," he admonished her when she was on her way in across the newly scrubbed floor.

It was almost strange how clean and innocent the room seemed. How had they gone about it? The walls shone white. Had they re-painted them? He sniffed the air. It did not smell like paint.

Ellen got out of her shoes and Henrik turned around and closed the door. He turned the lock, went over to the alarm's control panel, which had been placed at the back of the wardrobe closet so it was concealed from the entry, and activated the cameras. He quickly shifted between the three cameras to assure himself that they worked. The gate and road up by the parking area, the stairs outside the door, and the hall.

Henrik continued into the kitchen and set the grocery bag down on the table. Let it stay there. He looked around the kitchen and again got a feeling that he had come to a summer cabin that had stood empty over the winter. That he and Ellen had made a little outing to the country, were staying in someone else's house. A house that for some inexplicable reason was full of their personal belongings.

He heard a couple of thuds from the living room and went there.

Ellen had laid down on her back on the couch with the red jeans jacket on. Henrik sat down beside her and placed a hand on her lower leg.

CDs, DVDs, magazines in a careless pile on the coffee table, toys on the floor, a sweater across a chair, three glass candleholders with burned-down candle stubs. Outside the window the lilacs rocked from a gust of wind.

"Are you hungry?" he asked.

Ellen shook her head.

These everyday practicalities felt good. Eating. Sleeping. Taking off your shoes in the hall. Brushing your teeth. That was the sort of thing that held life together.

For a long time he had done his best to think the opposite. The everyday routines, trivial details, were the sort of thing that drained life of joy. For that reason it was important to always keep yourself in motion, always think creatively, always be open to adventure. Anything at all so that you wouldn't be standing there with the dental floss and the yogurt and feel . . . ordinary.

And the thought was not completely wrong, keeping the drive forward, but he had stopped being afraid of the everyday, of those practical trivial things. Right now that was all he had. If he could build up a kind of everyday existence of sandwiches and sorting laundry he would be the world's happiest person. No, that was not true. Not the world's. Not even happy. Happy was a foreign word. But he could be a functioning person. Feel that he was alive, that he had the right to live and that he could look ahead. He tried to convince himself that it was okay. As a person it was right to want to survive.

It was already five o'clock. They had gathered in the smaller conference room: Fredrik, Sara, Göran Eide, and the prosecutor.

Fredrik had contacted the doctor who put Katja Nyberg on sick leave when she was a student.

"The doctor had no recollection of her, but that's not so strange," he said. "It was more than six years ago. He found the medical record anyway. 'Depression in connection with separation.'"

"Interesting combination," said Sara.

Peter Klint nodded silently. Fredrik continued.

"'According to the patient's description, with a tendency to manic periods. Prescribe Zoloft. Return visit in four weeks.' Katja Nyberg came to the return visit. Apparently it was mostly to fine-tune the dosing of medication. Then she had no more contact with the doctor."

"So she herself broke off the treatment?" said Göran.

"That's probably how it has to be interpreted."

"I checked with the staffing agency in Malmö that was on her CV," Sara continued. "Nyberg quit there when she got the temporary job at *Sydsvenskan*. Then she got in touch again last spring. Because almost a year had passed since she last worked for them they decided that she should come in for an interview on the fourteenth of April. But Nyberg never showed up."

"It sounds like something happened during the spring," said Göran. "First she loses interest in her job, misses the extension of the temporary position, plans to go back to the staffing agency, but never shows up at the interview."

"She decides to make contact with Henrik Kjellander, but instead it ends with her renting his house," Sara filled in.

"How did it go with Kjellander?" Klint asked. "What did he say about Nyberg?"

"He confirmed that he met her at the hotel on the fourth of October, but we haven't managed to have a real interview."

"But he confirmed that they had a relationship?" said Klint.

"Only that they had met. He was in the car with his daughter. They've gone back to Fårö."

"He has to be questioned properly."

"Sure, but he never called back and I've tried to reach him."

"No, no, I understand," said Klint.

"Do you have anything else?" asked Göran. "Have you checked her phone?"

"The cell phone number in her personal information for *Sydsvenskan* hasn't been used since February."

"Has she called Kjellander?"

"No, but Kjellander has called her. One time, on the twenty-third of October."

"Three days before Henrik makes the second trip to Copenhagen," Fredrik pointed out.

"Yes, and according to the connections she has also been in Copenhagen on the twenty-sixth of October, besides the fourth of October and sixteenth of November that we already know about."

They looked at Klint.

"Doesn't seem like there's that much to discuss," he said. "We'll have to ask Malmö to bring her in."

And who is she, grinning in Aftonbladet? *An old whore who sucked you off fifteen years ago.*

The long hair that she should trim. The puffy cheeks that say she should diet. The silly smile with her head at an angle. The neck that ought to be snapped.

Why her? How could you let her into your life for a whole year, but turn your back on me after a couple of nights?

Do you understand what I've done for you? Do you understand how you fulfilled me? No, you don't understand, you don't know. If you did you would be here. It can't be this strong, this intense, without it meaning something. Meaning everything. It must be there in you, too. It can't just be me. That's what I think.

Then I think that I've misunderstood everything. That you aren't worth it. That you are an evil damned egotist who never cared about anyone other than yourself. Then I want to kill you. Erase you from this fucking earth. And I could do it. You know I can.

But then I calm down and then I love you again. I wish I could let it go. I've tried to kill myself for your sake. I've taken pills for your sake. I've killed for your sake. I've tried to stop loving you. But it doesn't work. Not more than a minute or two. When I want to kill you.

And then her. Why not me, may I ask? Why a mediocre woman with her head at an angle? Sometimes I wish they would come here and take my picture and tell my story. Not because I care about those newspapers, not because I want my picture there, but so that everyone would know. I want the world to know how much I love you. How much you love me.

You can't have forgotten how you moaned out my name as if your life depended on it. I haven't forgotten. Oh my God, you are so beautiful . . . you are so beautiful. Don't those words ring in your ears, too? They ring in mine.

Every morning when I wake up. Every night when I go to bed. Every hour, every minute.

If you hear them you must know that it's true. It's not the kind of thing you just say. It's not possible to just say. Not like that.

81.

"Hi, this is Alma Vogler, your sister."

Henrik turned completely cold. At the same time he felt the cell phone getting damp in his hand.

"Yes?" was all he could force out.

He went over to one of the windows, looked toward the barn and the pile of timber that was visible behind it. It was calm and quiet.

"I am truly sorry about what happened," said Alma.

It was like a bolt of lightning in Henrik's head. For a moment he thought Alma was apologizing. But of course it wasn't like that. She was expressing sympathy.

"The whole thing is just terrible. You truly have my condolences," she said, confirming his thought.

"Thank you," he managed to say.

He moved the cell phone over to his left hand and wiped the other against his pants leg.

He noticed how Alma braced herself on the other end, by breathing in.

"I want you to know that I am thinking about you and Ellen. And that I think it's sad that it's been the way it has between you and us."

Alma paused. Henrik did not know what to say. Was she expecting him to say something?

"I truly understand that it's hard for you to accept that. Truly. But I want you to know it."

She paused again. He heard her swallow.

"I speak for myself, I guess I have to say. This is not something I've talked about with Elisabet and Dad."

A small, careful point of warmth sprang up in Henrik's belly. What affected him was not so much the words but the nervous flutter in Alma's voice. It must have been a big step for her to make this call.

"I understand," he said quietly.

"We are siblings after all," she said.

Anger flared up in him. Siblings. Bring that up now after half a lifetime. He felt the edges of the cell phone as his grasp hardened. He never should have come back. He had turned his back on them, just as they had turned their backs on him. He didn't need them. He didn't need Gotland. The whole world had been at his feet. Yet he had come back. Like some kind of wretched beggar.

But the fury subsided. The little word "sibling" drilled through the bitterness. A hand was being extended toward him. It was tempting to take it. But should they really get off so easy?

"Yes," he said quietly, "I accept that."

"Perhaps this sounds strange to you, but I would like for us to meet. Right now perhaps is not the right moment, or maybe it is. I don't know. But . . . well, you can think about it."

He had spoken with Alma at the funeral. He could not say that he liked her, far too much bitterness and anger had stood in the way, but even so she had seemed . . . okay.

"Yes, of course," he said without being sure exactly what that meant.

"There is so much I would like to ask you about," said Alma with a kind of uncertain tenderness.

Alma Vogler, your sister.

"Why not," he said. "When I've got things a little more organized. I don't really know when we can move back to the house."

He didn't know why he lied, it just came out. He didn't want to reveal that they were back.

"No, I understand that."

"But then, sure."

They exchanged a few fumbling words about Fårö, if he would be able to do his work from there now when he was alone. He didn't know. True, he was thinking a lot about how he could survive, but in a much more immediate way. Day to day, hour to hour.

They said good-bye and he ended the call.

Alma Vogler, your sister.

The little point of warmth suddenly grew to a claw that tore in his chest. His heart stood still. He could almost not breathe. Would he always be a little boy in Fårösund?

Henrik fought back the pain, took a couple of deep breaths. He had to manage this for Ellen's sake. That had become a mantra without substance, but he continued to repeat it to himself. He had to manage this for Ellen's sake.

He turned toward the room, thought about how it would be to have a family. A sibling who came to Sunday dinner.

Then he got scared. How did it happen that she called right now? Did she already know he was there?

82.

It had rained during the night. The streets in Visby were still wet. When Fredrik got out of the car he had to make detours around big puddles that reflected the blue, cloud-strewn sky. There was a damp spray from the tires on the traffic driving past on Norra Hansegatan.

As he came up to the department, he caught sight of Göran's back en route to the conference room and hurried to catch up with him.

"Has Malmö gotten hold of her?"

"No," said Göran, shaking his head. "But they have questioned the woman she rents a room from. I'll cover the rest in there."

Fredrik followed Göran into the meeting. He was last to arrive and slid down on a vacant chair next to Gustav. Ove and Sara did not notice him. Ove was in the middle of a story and both of them were concentrating on Ove's hands, which he was holding out in front of him with the fingertips against the table. Like a chubby little fence.

Göran set his cell phone on the table.

"Malmö has questioned Sonja Krstic, from whom Katja Nyberg rents a room," he began. "Nyberg came back from a trip last Monday, with a new haircut and new hair color."

For a moment there was total silence in the room. They looked at each other.

"She took off again the day before yesterday without saying where she was going," Göran continued.

"Sounds like she's run off," said Ove.

"A search warrant for her was put out yesterday evening. We'll have to check credit card and bank accounts. If she's bought tickets, made any major withdrawals, et cetera. Will you do that?"

Ove held up his right hand as confirmation.

"Krstic also reported that Nyberg does not seem to have been feeling very well recently and that she's been worried about her," Göran continued. "One night not long ago she found her almost unconscious in the bathroom. Nyberg apologized afterward and said that she had been out at a bar and was treated to drinks and got way too drunk. Nyberg also hinted that she suspected that someone had spiked the drinks in some way, but Krstic had a feeling the whole story with the drinks was made up and that Nyberg herself had taken something. Drugs or some medicine. Was there anything else?"

Göran stroked his wrist across his forehead while he searched his memory.

"No, I guess that was all," he said. "Besides the incident in the bathroom, Krstic has not had any problems with her tenant. She says that she and Nyberg have gone out together a couple of times, but that they still stayed more as superficial acquaintants. The past few months Nyberg has kept more and more to herself."

Göran had a few questions that he could not answer and it was noticeable that he wanted to get the meeting over with.

"Malmö will provide technicians, but we'll go there and question Krstic and look more closely at the apartment itself. Fredrik, Sara: you have the whole picture, you'll take the next available flight."

Sara seized her notepad as if she intended to dash off to the airport before the meeting was over.

"We know that Nyberg does not have her own car, she must have borrowed or rented one. Maybe Krstic knows. We'll check the car rental agencies in the meantime."

Göran looked at the watch with the yellowed watch face that he wore on his left wrist.

"Gustav, you can take the mother, Hillevi Nyberg," he continued. "If Katja Nyberg is already in flight we have more to gain than to lose. Malmö got Nyberg's current cell phone number from Sonja Krstic. Maybe we can locate her that way."

Sara and Fredrik sat squeezed into the little coffee bar between the store and the departure hall at Bromma Airport. Sara took the opportunity to send a text. The barista set a double espresso down in front of Fredrik, who looked up and said thanks before again being absorbed by the tabloid. They had scrutinized the coverage of the "Fårö murders" on the way up to Bromma, traded newspapers halfway, so there must be something else that caught his interest.

This was the second weekend in a row that was lost to Sara. She did not complain, you didn't do that where murder was concerned. Besides, she really wanted to be here. She had been there from the very beginning, sat at home with Malin and Henrik, held that awful picture in her hand. It felt right that she got to be there when they opened the door to the perpetrator's home.

Micke had dismissed her apologies, it was clear that it didn't matter. He would manage. And of course he did, he was an adult. But it couldn't be much fun sitting alone in Visby where he didn't know a single person besides Sara. For the second weekend in a row. He had gone there to see her, after all. What if he got tired and stayed home next weekend?

Her cell phone buzzed. She looked at the display. It was from Micke: "Just had breakfast. Thought about taking a walk in town. See if I can find some trendy clothes at the wool boutique."

Sara laughed to herself, evidently loud enough to get Fredrik to look up from the newspaper and give her an inquisitive look.

Sara wrote a response, a crude joke about sheep and female sex organs. She regretted it when she saw it on the display. It was a bit too crude, only modestly funny besides. She deleted it and wrote instead that he should be careful not to get an overdose of estrogen.

In the loudspeakers of the departure hall they were announcing the flight to Malmö. She nudged Fredrik.

"It's time."

The airport was in a no-man's-land halfway between Malmö and Ystad. Håkan Täll, one of Malmö's crime-scene technicians, was waiting for them with a car outside the terminal.

The car was unmarked and Täll was not holding a sign with their names, yet Fredrik realized at once that he was there to meet them. He had parked in the no stopping zone and stood waiting calmly with his arms crossed a few feet from the car, as if he had a right to. He appeared to be forty at most and was wearing glasses with thick, black bows that seemed one size too big. His hair was cut short at about the same length as his close-cut beard.

He greeted Sara and Fredrik and opened the door to the passenger side for Sara. You could plainly hear that he was a native of Skåne.

They got into the car. Fredrik had to open his own door. Täll started and pulled out from the sidewalk. It did not take long before they were surrounded by forest.

"It will take about twenty minutes to get there, I would say," he said.

On the way into Malmö they told Täll about the murders in Kalb-jerga and what had preceded them, and what they knew about Katja Nyberg. Täll seemed familiar with north Gotland. "We were in Ihreviken during the summers when I was little," he explained. "We rented a house there. Must have been seven summers." He looked at Sara, then quickly backward at Fredrik.

"But you're not really Gotlanders, right?"

"No," said Sara. "Both of us are from Stockholm."

"The others don't want to leave the island. That's why they sent us," said Fredrik.

He saw Täll grin in the rearview mirror.

They were approaching Malmö, passed under the shopping center in Rosengård that was like a bridge over the road.

"What do you know about this Krstic, or however it's pronounced?" said Håkan Täll, pronouncing the name with a hard *k* at the end.

Fredrik assumed that it would be with *sh*, but said nothing.

"She came here from Yugoslavia nineteen years ago," Sara said. "She works at a travel agency and has had Nyberg as a tenant since last summer. Nothing in the register."

"But on Nyberg?"

"No, not on her, either."

Håkan Täll slowed down and parked by the curb.

"Here it is."

Spånehusvägen 41 was a three-story yellow-brown brick building across from a school. On both sides were similar buildings from different periods. Some were simple functional row houses, others from the 1910s or '20s.

They were expected. Sonja Krstic quickly opened the door. She met them with dark, friendly eyes and extended her hand.

"Hi, Sonja."

"Fredrik."

He shook her hand and stepped into the apartment, which smelled of roses. Håkan Täll put on a pair of blue shoe protectors and a pair of protective gloves.

"Håkan is going to look at Katja's room, so we can talk in the meantime," said Fredrik.

"As you like," said Sonja in perfect Swedish. "Katja's room is over here."

She showed them over to a walnut veneer door that their Malmö colleagues had sealed when they had been there in the morning. Håkan Täll carefully broke the seal so as not to scratch the door frame and pushed down the black Bakelite handle.

"Do you want to take a quick check before I start?" he said, looking at them.

"Sure," said Sara. "In case you intend to make a mess."

Täll stepped aside and they went into the room. It was sparsely furnished with a bed with a flowery bedspread, a white nightstand, and a small desk with a laptop computer. To the right inside the door was a large armchair with white cotton fabric that Katja clearly used as a closet. It was covered with clothes in a single heap. A lot of green, black, and striped. All the furniture appeared to come from IKEA.

"Is this your furniture?" Sara asked Sonja.

"Yes," she said from out in the hall. "Everything except the ceiling lamp. Katja bought that."

She stuck in one hand and turned on the ceiling light.

Fredrik looked up. The lamp was five-armed and the plastic light globes were shaped like simple upturned flower petals.

The room made him gloomy. A home of 130 square feet, with another person's rejected furniture. Who was it who lived here? What had gone wrong? What had made her so totally incapable of handling her disappointments that she had to kill? Was there an explanation or was it simply an unfortunate lack in the brain of some neurotransmitter with a silly little name?

But the majority of depressed, bitter people did not kill. Possibly themselves, not others. What made Katja Nyberg in particular cross the line?

"You have to look at this."

Sara stood at the desk and pointed at a white card that was pinned on the wall next to some yellow Post-it notes.

Fredrik went up to the desk. The card she had pointed at was a note card from Hotel St. Petri in Copenhagen. The hotel's name was in blue in the top left corner. In the middle of the card was a message in pencil. He was forced to lean over to be able to read the faint text: *See you this evening?* The brief message was signed *H.*

83.

Henrik came to life slowly on the living room couch. Ellen had fallen asleep first, tired and soft beside him. He sat up abruptly when he realized that Ellen was no longer there. He looked around, heard her steps out in the hall.

The next moment a fragment from his dream made him understand what had woken him. The doorbell.

"Ellen, wait!"

He got up from the couch and was out in the conspicuously desolate hall in three long steps. Ellen had stopped a few feet from the door. She looked at him in terror.

"There's no danger."

He tried to make his voice gentle and soothing, despite his agitation. "Come here."

He reached out his hand to her. She tiptoed over to him with lowered head.

"There's no danger, I said."

He glanced quickly at the door.

"Forgive me for shouting."

He lifted up her chin with a bent index finger. She met his eyes.

"Come."

He pulled her with him over to the alarm control panel at the back of the wardrobe closet, raised the protective cover on the display, and browsed forward to the camera by the front door.

"What are you doing?" said Ellen.

The picture on the screen was disturbingly like the picture that the police had shown him. There was an explanation for that, of course, he tried to convince himself. It was taken with the same type of camera and stored in the same system.

He observed his sister glancing uncertainly toward the windows in the living room. She was there. She was standing outside and had rung the doorbell.

"Ellen."

"Yes."

"If you go up to your room awhile I'll come soon."

Ellen protested. She did not want to.

"Yes, but please do as I say now. You can sit and draw or something."

Ellen sighed.

"Do as I say now, okay? I'll be there soon."

Henrik guided her toward the stairs. She obeyed but went up with dramatically lingering steps.

"Okay, go now." He hurried her.

When he saw that she had gone up, he went over to the door. His hand hesitated at the lock. Was he doing the right thing now? Maybe it was simpler to pretend that he hadn't heard and let her leave. Then he decided, turned the lock, and opened.

Alma smiled broadly at him.

"Hi."

"Hi," he said, considerably more guarded.

She shivered.

"It's colder than I thought."

Did she want to come in?

"Sorry to stop by like this but . . ."

Her hands slipped in under her open jacket.

"It's okay," he said.

She looked so friendly, he thought. The blond hair with a little natural wave, the open face. She seemed so innocent somehow. It was strange to be standing in front of her at such a short distance. At the funeral it had been different. Then there had been lots of people around them the whole time. Now it was just the two of them.

"I brought something with me," she said, stepping down from the stoop.

"I see, what is it?"

"It's simplest if you come with."

She looked more serious now, took another few steps away.

Henrik hesitated a little and cast a glance toward the stairs.

"Sure," he said. "I'll just put on my shoes."

He went after a pair of jodhpurs that he knew were in the closet outside the bathroom, mostly because that was quickest, and pulled on the jacket he had tossed aside on one of the kitchen chairs. He stepped out on the stairs and locked the door behind him.

Alma looked at him and started walking up the rise.

"It's in the car."

He felt unreal as he walked there a little behind her. She was moving agilely, walking with one hand inside her jacket and the other swinging in time with the rapid steps. The rainclouds had scattered and a pale blue, slightly hazy sky was arched over them. He coughed and thought that it echoed far away across the deserted landscape. There was a cold wind, she was right about that.

Alma turned around now and then and smiled at him. The last bit up toward the gate she walked backward. As if she wanted to be sure that he was following.

She stopped and held open the gate, but he signaled to her to go ahead.

"How did you know that I was back?" he said panting slightly with his hand on the rough unpainted wood.

She laughed.

"Here everyone knows everything about everybody."

He tried to work out what that meant in practice. Was it Ann-Katrin Wedin who had seen there were lights on and could not refrain from calling a few girlfriends? That would be enough, he assumed, so that soon the whole island would know.

Alma stopped behind a white Saab that was parked beside his red SUV. He took a few steps in her direction. The gravel scraped roughly under the soles of his shoes.

"I was thinking about what happened," she said, "and that you had decided to come back. I don't know if you intend to stay, or what plans you have, but—"

She opened the rear hatch and started unfolding a blanket that was in the otherwise-empty baggage compartment. Henrik approached another few steps, but recoiled when he saw the shotgun. Alma picked it up and turned around.

An icy chill quickly spread in him and he almost started shaking. Had the police misunderstood everything?

84.

Sonja Krstic's kitchen was newly renovated. Cupboards of gloomy gray laminate and a kitchen counter of something that was supposed to look like wood but wasn't.

The old, slanting oak table and the romantic curtain arrangement with tulle and lace valances were a glaring contrast. In jeans and a simple white blouse Sonja Krstic did not look like a lace valance type of person, thought Fredrik from his seat opposite her. Not like a gray laminate type of person, either, for that matter.

The flowers in the window were simple green plants, so the aroma of roses must come from another room, if she was not using perfumed cleanser.

"We thought we should concentrate on the time period from the middle of August until today," he said.

"Has she done something? This seems really serious," said Sonja Krstic with a nod in the direction of what was going on in her tenant's room.

"We don't know for sure yet. But that's why we're here, to find out whether she may have done what she is suspected of."

"So she is suspected of something?" said Sonja. "I mean, she is my tenant. If she is suspected of a crime I want to know what it is."

She looked at Fredrik, her eyebrows furrowed with worry. He understood.

"Unfortunately I can't talk about that," said Fredrik. "As long as a suspect is not indicted we have an obligation of confidentiality. But we have flown here from Gotland to question you and look at Katja's room. . . ."

He fell silent and let Sonja draw her own conclusions. Perhaps he was imagining things, but he thought she turned pale.

"Oh my God, what has she done?"

"She is a suspect," he reminded her. "If she were to be guilty of this crime there is still no reason to believe that she would want to do anything to you. But if she comes back here it is important that you contact the Malmö police via nine-one-one. If she makes contact in some other way you can call me directly."

Fredrik handed over a business card that Sonja looked at quickly and then set down on the table alongside a fruit bowl with a single lemon.

"But can't you contact me? I mean, if she has done something—"

"We'll be in touch if there's anything you need to know," said Sara.

That was a vague promise, but Sonja seemed content anyway.

"So," said Fredrik. "From the middle of August and on, have you been at home here during that entire time?"

"Yes."

"And can you tell us when Katja has been here, if we start around the middle of August and go forward?"

Sonja Krstic looked at a wall calendar that was hanging alongside the refrigerator.

"I have to think about it."

She got up and fetched the calendar, browsed back one page to August.

"Hmm . . ."

Her head was hanging over the calendar.

"She was gone awhile here somewhere," said Sonja, circling in the weeks between the tenth and the thirtieth of August.

She moved her finger between a few different dates and hummed to herself.

"Yes, now I know, it must have been this week, the seventeenth to the twenty-third. She came back on Saturday. I remember that. I was out with some people from work on Friday. It was the first time after vacation that we were out."

"So she came back on Saturday the twenty-second?" said Fredrik.

"Yes. She was gone that week. It is possible that she left already over the weekend, but it may have been on Monday, too," she answered.

"But definitely between Monday and Saturday, perhaps longer, and at the longest from Saturday to Saturday? Is that what you mean?"

"That's exactly what I mean," said Sonja Krstic.

"Where was she during that time?"

"She said she was going to visit friends. Some in Gothenburg, maybe in Stockholm."

"Did she say who?"

"No. She didn't mention any names. She said that she wanted to improve a little, that it might just as easily turn out completely different. She was eager to see something new."

"Did she mention any places she was interested in going to?"

"No. Or we talked about it a little in general, but that was probably mostly me carrying on. I work in the travel industry."

"Do you remember what places came up?"

"Yes, it was probably places like Österlen, Koster, Gotland, the High Coast . . ."

"Was there anything Katja reacted to in particular?"

"No, not as I recall. No more than anything else."

"How was she going to travel?" said Fredrik. "Did she have access to a car?"

"I think she rented one."

"Did she usually do that?"

"Sometimes, but she also borrowed. She has borrowed my car a few times when she was only going to be gone a day or two, but this was, of course, a bit longer."

"When did she last borrow your car?"

"Sometime last spring. The end of March, I believe."

They continued to go through the time from the twenty-second of August until today. Sonja could not pinpoint the date exactly, but Katja Nyberg had been gone a couple of nights around the twenty-sixth. If she had been out of town or only spent the night somewhere else in Malmö, Sonja did not know.

"You didn't ask?" Sara wondered.

"Yes, but she said only something vague about a friend."

Then she had gone away again a week later and thus was gone until last Monday.

"Did she say anything about where she was going that time or did she just disappear?"

"No, she said she was going to visit a friend. I got a feeling that she had met a guy because she left so often, so I didn't want to keep asking. And it was apparent that she didn't want to talk about it."

Fredrik was surprised that Katja traveled so much back and forth. He had believed that she had remained on Gotland, at least between the time she rented Henrik's house and lured Ellen away. There were not that many days in between. That she went home could mean that she did not have a plan to start with, perhaps felt finished with Henrik, but then changed her mind when she came home and returned to Gotland.

"You said to our colleagues that Katja did not seem to be feeling well," he said.

"Yes, actually," Sonja Krstic said with a nod.

"Can you expand on that?"

"I did talk about when she passed out in the bathroom, are you aware of that?"

"We heard about that episode," said Sara.

"It was probably a kind of low-water mark, or whatever you want to call it. But this has been going on quite awhile. I think it started when her temporary position at *Sydsvenskan* ended. She's had a hard time getting work as a journalist, she's done a number of other things, so that job probably meant a lot to her."

"It was just that? Nothing else?"

Sonja leaned her elbows against the table and looked meditative before she answered.

"I got a feeling that it was connected to some guy, too. Last fall she said that she had met someone. She seemed really in love. She didn't say too much, but you could see it on her."

"She didn't mention any name?"

"No, but she said that she met him in Copenhagen. I think it ran out in the sand pretty quickly. She didn't say anything else about it anyway. I thought that maybe he was the one she had started seeing again, in August when she was gone so much."

85

"You're not afraid of guns, are you?"

He stared at her without answering. Alma held the shotgun aimed in his direction, but not straight at him.

"There's no danger," she said. "It's not loaded."

"Okay," he said submissively, feeling the cold slowly subsiding.

"I thought that since you're living out here all by yourself, then—" She held out the shotgun with both hands.

"But it's up to you."

She cocked her head and looked at him uncertainly.

"Do you think that was dumb?"

"Oh, no," he said. "But I've never used a shotgun."

"I can show you."

She changed her grip on the shotgun, went back to the car, and fished out a paper carton in the folds of the red blanket.

"We can go a little ways into the forest here."

Alma nodded in among the trees beyond the neighboring house. Over there the forest was denser and it was dark between the tree trunks.

"Bengt and Ann-Katrin are probably at work. We won't disturb anyone."

"Okay," he said without having thought about whether he really wanted to have a shotgun in the house.

The recoil was less than he had expected, the shots louder. There was a big difference between standing five feet from Alma when she shot and having the gun right next to his ear.

The shot tore up a big gash in the bark on the pine he had aimed at. Alma said something, but he could not hear. He was still half deaf after the shot.

"What?"

She came closer.

"How does it feel?"

"All right."

He had no idea how you talked about guns.

"You hit the target. That's the most important," she said.

She was standing so close that he could feel her breath as she talked. It was just the two of them, the struggling old Fårö pines, and the melancholy whispering of the wind in the treetops. It was so intimate. Extremely intimate with a perfect stranger who was his sister. And just before he had been the world's loneliest person. It was as if in one moment he had crossed a thirty-year vacuum. He had stepped over an endless abyss, as if it never existed.

"Isn't it kind of strange," he said.

"What is?"

"Us," he said.

Alma looked at him seriously. Her lips twitched a little as if she was searching for a word.

"Yes," she said, and fleetingly placed her hand on his upper arm.

The pines stood silently around them. He knew nothing about the woman who was standing before him, yet emotions were churning around in his chest as if she was one of the most important people in his life.

"One more time," she said, pointing at the light patch on the trunk of the tree.

Henrik raised the shotgun and fired off the second cartridge. Hit the same spot.

In the temporary deafness after the shot he thought that neither of them referred to what the shotgun and his little target practice was really about.

Shooting at a person.

Alma reached out her hand for the shotgun. He handed it over. She opened the gun, let the empty cartridges fall out on the ground, and gave it back. Henrik let it rest open on his forearm, as he had seen people do in movies. He felt a little silly, was not at all sure that was how you really did it.

Alma looked at him thoughtfully. At first he thought she was going to comment on how he was holding the gun, but she said nothing, just continued looking at him with that worried gaze.

"Is there something?"

She smiled cautiously, but then became serious again.

"Not everything is the way you think."

What did she mean? The shotgun firing? What had happened in his house? Malin and Axel? He looked at her in confusion.

"It's not that easy for me to talk about this," she said.

"About what?"

The words frightened him. What was it she was suggesting? He wanted to know now.

"Mother. You. Us."

She said it quietly, almost whispering, but it was as if every word were made of lead, sank to the bottom in him and made it impossible to get away from there. He felt dizzy.

"I don't know how much you know, but I'm quite certain that you don't—"

She interrupted herself and quickly touched his arm again.

"Grandma talked about it before she died."

She was speaking so quietly that he had a hard time hearing her.

"I don't understand. Does this have something to do with Malin and Axel? That they—"

Alma quickly shook her head.

He was relieved, but at the same time filled with a new discomfort.

Alma said something and this time he could really not interpret the words. He happened to think about Ellen. How long had he really been gone? He had only meant to go up to the parking area.

"Alma, listen . . . I have to go back."

She understood and took a deep breath.

"Daddy hit you."

He stood completely dumbfounded. The ground rocked beneath him.

Alma looked searchingly at him and he could see that she was afraid. As if he would accuse her. Perhaps hit back.

"Hit me? But I was only—"

"A little child, not much more than an infant."

"Is that true?"

"That was what she said, that he hit you. Mother didn't dare have you stay there."

"Ernst?" he managed to get out. "You mean Ernst?"

Alma nodded without averting her eyes.

"Grandma wanted to report him, but Mother begged and pleaded that she shouldn't do that."

Henrik was forced to look away. He heard what Alma was saying, but still didn't understand. Where did this truth fit into his life? Did he need it at all? He didn't want Ernst Vogler in his life.

"That was damned high-minded of her," he said with a bitter sneer she could not see.

"Love isn't always so easy to comprehend. Sometimes it makes us into the kind of people we don't want to be."

What did she know about that? He opened his mouth to protest, but when he saw her tormented eyes he stopped short. They stood quietly and looked at each other.

"I'm sorry," she said at last.

"Did he hit you, too?"

"No."

Because they were girls? Because they were his? He looked down toward the house.

"I have to get back."

"Me, too."

Alma handed over the carton of cartridges. He weighed it in his hand.

"I hope you don't need to use them," she said.

They started walking toward the house. It was not far, they had only stepped into the edge of the forest.

They stopped in front of Alma's Saab.

"Well," said Alma.

How do you say good-bye to someone you had suddenly come so close to, but didn't know at all?

"See you," he said.

"Yes."

He took a step backward. She reached out her left hand toward him and for a brief moment he took it and squeezed. It felt like an offense, but he didn't know against what.

They parted, but up by the gate he happened to think of something.

"A shotgun like this, is it legal to just have it at home? Shouldn't it be locked up?"

"You're not even allowed to have it," said Alma.

Henrik made a face.

"But you should store it somewhere where your daughter can't get at it."

Ellen, he thought. This, too, was for her sake.

86.

As soon as they ended the interview with Sonja Krstic they started going through Katja Nyberg's belongings. That didn't take long. Täll had done most of the work for them. On the desk he had set out three Polaroids he found in one of the dresser drawers. Three black-and-white pictures of

Katja Nyberg. They were slightly reminiscent of the pictures of Stina Hansson, but Nyberg had kept her clothes on.

Fredrik carefully turned them over to see whether there was anything written on the back side, a date perhaps, but the reverse sides were blank. They confiscated the pictures, as well as the correspondence card from St. Petri.

"Do you think she's run off?" said Fredrik while he put the pictures in an envelope.

"No," said Sara. "Perhaps she's gone off somewhere, just to get away for a while, but I don't think she has fled. I think she believes she has been too smart for us."

Sara ran her hand over the computer. It looked strikingly expensive compared with the meager furnishings, but that was probably because the computer was her professional instrument.

"I don't dare start this, then I'll probably get a scolding from Eva."

"No, don't do that."

"We'll take it with."

Sara leaned down and disconnected the power cord.

"Sheesh, it's really dusty back here."

She carefully brushed her gloved hands against each other. A dust bunny the size of her little finger fell to the floor.

"Excuse me, may I come in?" Sonja Krstic's voice was heard from the other side of the closed door.

"Yes, come on in," said Sara.

She opened the door before Sonja was able to.

"I've been thinking about something," said Sonja, looking doggedly at them.

"Yes?" said Sara.

"If Katja really has done something . . . Well, you're not saying anything, but . . ."

She interrupted herself, then went on.

"I think it feels uncomfortable not knowing. I've seen on TV about those murders on Gotland. But it can't very well be that, can it?"

She fingered a pendant that was hanging around her neck on a thin gold chain, let it run back and forth while she talked.

"I understand that it feels uncomfortable," said Sara. "But as Fredrik explained, all we can say is that your tenant is suspected of a serious crime."

Sonja looked back and forth at them.

"But what should I say when she comes back? I think it's—"

She took a breath and Sara took the opportunity to interrupt her.

"The important thing is that you contact the police here in Malmö. You can say to Katja that you have to go to the store, and then call from your cell phone. All you need to say is that you've been asked to make contact when Katja Nyberg comes back to this address. They know the rest."

"But—"

Sara interrupted her again.

"Do you have a toolbox?"

"Toolbox?" said Sonja Krstic.

"Yes."

Sonja looked puzzled and slightly irritated. Fredrik was following the conversation, he, too, a bit puzzled before it occurred to him why Sara was asking.

"I have some tools. Do you need something, or what?"

"I just want to look at them."

Sonja Krstic shook her head slightly and backed out of the room. Sara and Fredrik followed, watched her open a closet door at the other end of the hall.

"They're somewhere in here at the very bottom. It's a little messy."

Sara crouched down in front of the broom closet and looked into the lowest shelf.

"It's a little hard to see," she said, leaning down even more.

"I know, it's a little dark."

Sara ran her fingers over the bottom of the closet, got up, and held up her hand in the light under the ceiling lamp. Her fingers were covered with dust, dirt, and small white grains.

"Do you usually keep laundry detergent there?"

"Yes. I just ran out, but . . ."

Sara twisted her hand under the light.

"I know, it's one big mess," Sonja Krstic sighed.

It could very well be, Fredrik thought. And the hammer that killed Malin and Axel had in some way come in contact with laundry detergent.

He went to get a bag in the case he had left behind in Katja Nyberg's rented room. Sara gathered up more of the dust from the bottom of the closet and brushed it down into the bag. She folded it up, marked it, and handed it back. Then she crouched in front of the closet again and searched among the tools.

"Do you have a hammer?" she asked Sonja.

"Yes, of course."

"I can't find one."

"Yes, but wait," said Sonja Krstic, crouching down beside Sara.

Sonja pulled out a large chisel, a pincer, a staple gun. There was a heavy clatter of metal.

"Strange," she said. "It's not here."

87.

Henrik had gone through the whole house several times. The top floor, the main floor, the bedroom, the kitchen, the study. Finally he was forced to accept that there was no ideal hiding place. He put the shotgun on the top shelf in the hall closet and concealed it behind a sweater.

Alma had shown him how to detach the bolt. He could have spread out the parts in different places to be quite certain that no one would be able to use the gun. But he had quickly given up that alternative. He could easily imagine how he would fumble with the bolt and not get it in place when it was really needed.

And how would he know when it was needed? Who was he going to defend himself against? Stina? The police had thought it was her. They locked her up, but now she was out. Back in Fårösund.

Did they think it was Katja? He tried to picture Katja in the house in front of the portraits in the study. How she poked out their eyes with a pencil. Or how she crouched over the toy box and . . .

No, it was much too bizarre, much too crazy. Not to mention the thought that she could have . . . killed. This was a person he had been close to. He didn't know her all that well, he had to admit that, but she was still a regular, normal person. That much he could say.

Henrik divided the cartridges in various different hiding places. Some in the study, some in the kitchen, and a few up in the big cabinet in the sitting room. For each and every one of the hiding places various scenarios played out in his head. Also thoughts he did not want to have, but that intruded, compulsively.

When he was done he looked at the front door. Had he locked it? He could not see from where he was standing and took a couple of steps toward the door. Yes, the lock was vertical. Even so he felt compelled to go over and feel it.

Was he going crazy? Or was he crazy for having returned to the house? He turned his back to the door and went over and checked the alarm. It was working as it should. All three cameras were functioning. He closed the closet doors. He thought that one of them did not close properly. Was the shotgun touching it?

He took a step back and peered toward the closet. Did it matter? No. That one of the doors was slightly open did not make it obvious that there was a gun hidden on the top shelf. No one would notice it.

He went into the living room and sat down on the very edge of the couch. He had to pull himself together. He thought that by not taking the pills he would be more focused, but it didn't seem that way. The sleeping pills were, of course, ruled out, but the others? He would never manage this if he couldn't calm down.

He got up, went into the kitchen, and took out the pills from the cupboard to the right of the stove. The pills were almost ridiculously small. Smaller than the head of a match. Should he take one?

Ellen called from upstairs.

"Yes?" he called back.

"Can you come here?"

"I'm coming."

Not now. Not yet. Wait awhile. A few deep breaths. Focus. One more try.

"I'm coming, honey," he called again.

As he passed through the hall he could not keep from looking at the front door. The lock. What position was it in really?

88.

There were not many departures from Malmö to Bromma on Saturdays. They had to fly via Arlanda on the way back. Fredrik and Sara lined up behind a group of charter tourists returning home at the gate in terminal three when Fredrik got a call from Henrik Kjellander.

"I've been trying to reach you."

"I haven't been that easy to get hold of," Fredrik excused himself. You should have called yesterday, he thought.

"You wanted to ask me about Katja Nyberg," said Henrik.

"Yes, but I think it's best if we sit down and take a little time."

"Okay. Can you come here? It's a little hard for me to come to Visby. With Ellen, I mean."

The line was moving quickly forward. A red digital eye scanned the boarding passes.

"We'll have to see how we resolve that. Right now I'm boarding an airplane, but I'll call you as soon as I'm back in Visby. Say, in an hour? Will that work?"

"Sure."

Sara got her boarding pass scanned ahead of him.

"Good, then that's what we'll do."

"Listen . . ." said Henrik.

Fredrik handed his boarding pass to the woman in the dark blue suit and fluorescent green silk scarf. Was there a law that women who worked at airports had to wear a silk scarf?

"Do you really suspect Katja Nyberg?"

Fredrik looked around before he answered.

"More than suspect I would say. But I can't really talk about that now."

"Have you talked with her? What does she say?"

"We haven't talked with her. At the moment we don't know where she is."

"But then how can you say . . . ?"

"We are as good as certain about this."

Sara held open the door for him. He nodded in thanks and came out on the tarmac. A gust of wind made him blink involuntarily.

"I really have to go now," he said. "I'll call in an hour."

A short walk up to the plane and then they were on board.

Gotland showed up as a grayish brown strip right above the surface of the sea when Fredrik laid his head against the window and peered over the wing. Soon he could see Fårö to the left. They were flying low enough that it would be possible to interpret certain patches of color. Yellow in the sound—ferry; white and black in the middle of the island—church. He tried to find Henrik Kjellander's house, but it was too far away, fused together with the surroundings.

* * *

Before they went up to the department they carried what they had confiscated from Nyberg's room into the tech unit. Sara locked it in one of
the cabinets and let the key disappear in the slot.
The time was ten past five. Most of the day had gone to the trip
to and from Malmö. The detour through Stockholm was time-
consuming.
They went straight to Göran Eide's office, where he and Peter Klint
were waiting for them.
"Now all that remains is to find Nyberg," the head of the investigation squad said.
"Not hardly," said Sara. "We still don't have a single piece of evidence that she really has been on the island."
"There you're mistaken," said Klint. "The technicians in Malmö
have compared fingerprints from Nyberg's rented room on Spånehusvägen and fingerprints from the summer cabin down at Sudret."
"They match?"
"At least one holds up as technical evidence. Nyberg is being booked
in her absence."
"And Gustav has questioned Larsson again, the owner of the cabin,"
said Göran. "It turned out that he has an acquaintance at *Sydsvenska
Dagbladet* who was there and visited last year. Katja Nyberg must have
heard him talk about the cabin on a coffee break."
They were almost there, thought Fredrik. Göran was right, now it
was just a matter of finding her.
"It's high time to get to that interview with Kjellander," said Klint.
"Oh crud. I promised to call him."
He looked at the clock. It had been more than an hour since Henrik
called.
"I think we'll question him this evening," said Sara. "I want to
know what happened at that hotel."
Sara's words made the travel fatigue scatter. It was clear they should
do it now.

They looked at Klint.

"I can wait until tomorrow morning," said Klint. "It's up to you."

Sara turned toward Fredrik.

"What do you say?"

"Let's go. I'll call him at once."

89.

Malin smiled from the screen, standing there with vegetables, cheese, and olive oil. She was never really satisfied with that picture. Said she thought it looked like she was standing at attention. It wasn't really that bad, the picture was quite all right, but it would have been better if Henrik had done it, he knew that.

He certainly could have done it, too, if Malin had only asked. But she did not want to bring it up with Coop. And he understood that. It gave an unprofessional impression when people started dragging their married halves into work situations.

It was strange that Malin's pages were still up on the website. Hadn't they thought about that? Or had they thought about it and decided it would draw people to the site if Malin was still there?

Henrik had promised himself not to go there. Truly convinced himself not to do it. Yet here he was doing it. Manically. After every visit he decided that this was the last time. Really. He forbade himself.

You might think there would be no difference between going to that website and sitting and looking at a photograph. But there was. When he looked at a regular picture of Malin or Axel he could feel sorrow, despair, or in the best case a kind of aching nostalgia. When he went to Malin's blog, on the other hand, he was filled with a deep, night-black disappointment. He sank inexorably. He must have been there five or six times before he realized why. When he went to a site on the Internet he somehow expected that the site would be different than the last time he was there. Some news, a post, a comment, maybe even a new picture.

In some idiotic way, he could not explain it otherwise, he was hoping for a sign of life.

He looked up from the screen, out the window, but was met only by his own mirror image. He heard a car up on the road. It was driving slowly. He could hear the gravel crunching under the tires. Could it really be the police already?

He closed the lid of the computer, got up, and turned off the desk lamp. He stood quietly and listened while the trees outside the windows slowly came into view and assumed contours. The engine sound had stopped. A car door opened, then a long silence before it closed.

Henrik went out in the hall, opened the protective cover of the alarm, and activated the camera that was aimed up toward the gate. He actually saw better on the little display than he would have if he looked out the window. Just like the display on his own digital camera, it reinforced the light.

It took a moment, then a figure showed up by the gate. She stopped and looked around before she unhooked the hasp and pushed open the gate. Henrik immediately recognized her. She had done something with her hair, but there was still no doubt that it was her.

At first it was only recognition, then came something else. He noticed that his hands were trembling slightly, and in the next moment a strong feeling of fear came over him. He stared at the woman on the screen. She was not there for the first time. There was something domestic about her movements as she pushed back the gate behind her and looked down toward the house, directing her gaze right into the camera. He panted. The adrenaline was rushing in his veins.

He tried to collect his thoughts. Ellen, first and foremost. He listened for sounds from the top floor. She was asleep, but she had fallen asleep early. Sometimes she woke up again after an hour or so if she fell asleep before eight. He slipped up the stairs as quickly as possible without making them creak. He peeked into the children's room. Ellen seemed to be sound asleep. He closed the door and hurried down again.

A glance at the display. She was walking slowly down toward the house.

Henrik opened the closet, swept aside the sweater, and took out the shotgun that Alma had loaned him. Then there were the cartridges. The kitchen or the study? The kitchen was closer, but there he would be visible from outside. He chose the study, but first set the gun down on the hall floor, right next to the baseboard. Thought that it was stupid to walk around with it, stupid if she caught sight of it. She might have gone the other way around the house, of course.

He unlocked the drawer, dug out the cartridges. How many might he reasonably need? One? Two? He put two in his back pocket and held two in his hand. Took time, for some reason, to carefully close the drawer again.

The doorbell rang. A short, definite signal. Was the door really locked? Could the doorbell have woken Ellen?

He came back into the hall and leaned over for the shotgun. He noticed how his heart was pounding in his chest. His hands were shaking. Don't get stressed now. Henrik held the gun in his left hand and put the two cartridges in place. It was easy. They almost fell down into the barrels. He closed the gun, looked up toward the door, took a deep breath.

He hadn't forgotten anything, had he? He quickly looked at the gun. No, everything was the way it should be. Another deep breath. He could see her head moving outside the window in the front door.

With six controlled steps he was at the front door reaching out his right hand toward the handle. Panic struck him. What did he really intend to do? Would he even be capable of firing the gun if it became necessary? Shooting at a pine tree was one thing, shooting a person something else again. He backed into the hall, fished his cell phone out of his pocket, and entered 911. He hesitated with his thumb just above CALL. He did not have time to think, he had to decide.

He pressed his thumb against the display.

Crouching against the wall he whispered his message. His distress call. He hung up even though he had been asked not to do that. He felt stronger again.

He got up, went to the door, and turned the lock. Nudged open the door.

"Henrik," said Katja Nyberg, smiling at him.

She stepped up onto the top step, seemed not to have noticed the gun.

"Don't come any closer," he said.

90.

"Here it is," said Fredrik.

"I see it," said Sara, braking hard.

The sign popped up out of the darkness surprisingly suddenly, even though it was in the middle of a straight stretch.

Sara turned toward Kalbjerga. Soon one of the cattle guards was rattling under the wheels.

"I don't understand this guy," said Sara. "Why hasn't he ever mentioned Katja Nyberg?"

"Well," said Fredrik. "Guilt, shame? Could it be that?"

"What do you mean, guilt?" said Sara almost contemptuously.

"Haven't you ever been involved in investigations that got stuck because people kept quiet about their infidelities?"

"Yes, sure, but this is about murder. His wife, his child. Isn't that more important?"

"All the more guilt. Maybe he sees it as his fault. If he hadn't strayed with that lady in Copenhagen, this never would have happened to them."

"But even so he must want the one who did it—"

Sara interrupted herself with a frustrated sigh.

"Or else he couldn't imagine that it could be Katja and then there isn't sufficient motivation to overlook the shame," said Fredrik. "Easier to keep quiet."

"My God," Sara hissed toward the windshield. "Men. Are you all like that?"

"Thanks for that."

There was silence in the car. Fredrik thought for a moment about Eva Karlén. And the woman on the course in forensics many years ago. He would like to think that he was better, but perhaps he was no different.

"Excuse me," said Sara, "I just get so—"

She was interrupted by a call from the radio.

"General call from four-four. We have received an alarm via nine-one-one that the suspect in the murder case on Fårö is at the injured party's residence in Kalbjerga. I repeat . . ."

Fredrik and Sara quickly looked at each other and Fredrik answered as soon as the general call was finished.

"Four-four to forty-four eighty-five twenty, over," the operator's voice was heard.

"Forty-four eighty-five twenty on Fårö," Fredrik answered.

"I see that you are only a couple of miles from Kalbjerga, over."

"Yes. We're en route to question Henrik Kjellander. We're about five minutes from there, over."

"Wait, you'll get VB here, over."

There was a snap and Anna's voice was replaced by the duty officer.

"Kjellander called nine-one-one, he was certain that Katja Nyberg was outside the house. But that's all we know. The call was cut off, over."

"Have you tried to call back, over."

"We're trying now. So far no result, over."

Sara increased speed and soon they were driving twice as fast as before. The car hopped and swayed on the uneven road.

"Okay, what do we do, over." said Fredrik.

"We're sending reinforcements. Get to the house, but be extremely careful and report in as soon as you know more. If it's even slightly unclear what the situation is, wait for reinforcements, is that understood, over."

"Yes," said Fredrik. "That's understood, over."

"We've stopped the ferry so they're coming right away, but both cars are in Visby, so you'll have to count on it taking an hour from now, over."

"We'll do what we can in the meantime," said Fredrik. "End over."

The narrow road, lit up by the headlights, rushed quickly toward them. The gravel sprayed around the car and large stones struck hard against the chassis. Sara braked for a cattle guard, but increased speed again as soon as they were over.

91.

Henrik got her to sit down on one of the chairs in the bower. It had taken an eternity of more and more irritated nagging. It was as if she didn't hear what he said, or even understand. Was she deliberately misunderstanding? Was she trying to manipulate him?

To what end, in that case?

Henrik sat on the bench with the shotgun on his lap. The lamp above the stairs lit Katja up with a sharp glow. He saw every motion, while he was a shadow to her.

It irritated him that she didn't listen. He was finding it more and more difficult to keep calm. And the calm he showed was not much more than a front. He had hit that pine tree up in the forest, but that did not mean he was comfortable with a shotgun in his hands. He was not even sure he would be able to pull the trigger if something were to happen.

Katja smiled at him with a kind of inscrutable seriousness and reached out a hand. Five long, pale fingers, an upturned hand, a dead crab.

Why had she come? Was she a ticking bomb that could explode at any moment? Did she have a hammer inside her jacket? A knife? What would he do if she suddenly went on the attack? What if she was too quick, was over him before he could react. And then? Would she continue into the house, up to the top floor?

Katja moved her hand again. She could not reach him. There was too much distance between them. He observed her peculiar smile, the deceptively friendly eyes, and the right cheek with a dry patch, big as a thumbnail. She didn't have that when he met her in Copenhagen.

Chapped.

He was shaking inside. No. He was really shaking. His hands that were holding the gun jumped. Did she notice that? If he had any idea how it was done he would have liked to frisk her to see if she had a weapon on her. But he didn't intend to go near her. He didn't intend to leave the bench he was sitting on. He was convinced that any attempt to do anything other than remain sitting where he was would end badly.

He was starting to boil inside when she did not do as he said, when she pretended like he had never opened his mouth. Then he would pull the trigger at once. To escape that boiling feeling that said she was dangerous, that said that he would miss if he waited any longer, that he would drop the gun and shoot himself in the foot. Anything could go wrong.

Malin. Axel. His little Axel lying lifeless in front of the stove. Who he tried to waken from the dead. He had done everything he could, but nothing had helped.

Katja. Was it really her? The woman from St. Petri. They'd had a good time together. Why should she kill his family? He hadn't made any promises that he hadn't kept. They met in a hotel bar and had sex in a hotel room. What had she expected?

He shook off the thoughts. There was no point in trying to understand. If it really was her who had been here, who rented the house when they were away and then . . . There was no logic, no reason.

"Henrik."

He didn't like it that she said his name.

"Henrik . . ."

She rose up from the seat of the chair.

"Sit down!"

She stood up.

He stood up, too, raised the shotgun with trembling hands.

"Sit down, I said."

Around them were Malin, Axel, and Ellen. A warm summer evening in the bower. Axel rushing up and down out of the chair, could not sit still, didn't need to sit still.

And then only Katja. Everything narrowed down to that familiar face, the quiet smile that was only a mask. She had destroyed his life. He wished that she would take a step forward. Just one more step so he could shoot her. He really wanted to. He wanted her to disappear from the face of the earth. Be erased from history. He did not want her to sit in prison, perhaps tell her story in the newspaper. Become a serial without end. One day be released. Get out in twenty years. Continue living her life. While his life was destroyed.

Ellen. He had Ellen. Yes, he ought to shoot to protect Ellen. Shoot her so that Ellen would not have to worry that Katja Nyberg would ring her doorbell one day in the distant future.

One more step.

92

Sara let the car creep forward with the headlights off the last stretch and stopped halfway up the gentle slope. They got out of the car, left the doors open to make as little noise as possible. They sneaked ahead in single file, Sara first, in one of the rutted tracks.

The evening seemed lighter when the headlights were turned off. There was still a faint blue sheen over the landscape.

"There's a car there," Sara whispered over her shoulder.

Fredrik could see it, too. A Volvo alongside the two bigger cars that belonged to the household.

They stopped when they reached the gate. There was a light over the front door and in a window up toward the road. They stood stock-still and listened. Not a sound, not a movement. Had they arrived too late? Fredrik remembered the house from the night of the murders. Would this be a repeat? Dead bodies. Blood.

"I hear something."

Sara hissed out the words with her mouth right next to Fredrik's ear. "Do you hear it?"

After a moment's concentration he could hear a voice. It came from below the house.

"It sounds like Henrik," he whispered in Sara's ear.

A moment later he heard another voice. A woman's this time.

Without saying anything more, they took out their guns, released the safeties, and held them lowered to the ground. Sara signaled that they should continue through the gate. He heard the woman's voice again, but still could not see anyone as they walked carefully down toward the house.

He pointed toward the overgrown lilacs and Sara nodded.

She took a few steps to the side so that they had a gap of two or three yards between them before they went the final bit up to the bower.

Henrik was sitting closest to them. The woman sat farther in, with her back against the straggly green leaves. She looked up toward them. Her hair was shorter and the hair color different compared to the passport photo, but Fredrik recognized the broad mouth and beautifully shaped but sorrowful eyes.

The strong lamp above the front door cast a hard light over them, but also left large sections in deep shadow.

"Henrik," said Fredrik.

If it hadn't been for a negligible shift in his body he almost would have thought that Henrik had not heard him.

Fredrik sought Sara's attention for a moment to make sure they were in agreement about how to proceed. Sara nodded in the direction of Katja as confirmation.

"Henrik, it's Fredrik Broman," said Fredrik. "I'm here with Sara Oscarsson. Is everything as it should be?"

Henrik did not answer and did not turn now, either. It felt stupid to talk to the back of someone's head. The whole situation was strange. Why didn't he answer?

Sara moved a few feet forward to the right and then stopped abruptly.

"He has a gun," she said. "A shotgun."

Fredrik took a couple steps to the right, then he saw it, too. Henrik was holding it along his leg, aimed at Katja Nyberg.

He looked at Sara and again they exchanged a momentary look of mutual understanding.

"Katja," said Sara. "I want you to hold out your hands so that I can see them."

Katja started at her name and stared at Sara, who was holding her service revolver aimed at her.

"Do you understand what I'm saying? I want you to hold out your hands in front of you so that I can see them."

One of Katja's hands was resting on her lap, the other was hidden behind the chair.

"Katja. Can you do as I say?"

She remained seated, as if the words hadn't sunk in.

"Katja?"

Slowly she extended her arms.

"Good," said Sara. "Put your arms up in the air and put your hands behind your neck."

Fredrik looked at Henrik, who was following Katja's movements with his eyes. His left hand took a firmer hold on the shotgun. He raised it.

"Wait now, Henrik," said Fredrik.

He took a couple of slow steps over toward Henrik.

"We're going to end this now. Take Katja with us to Visby, make sure that she is indicted for the murders."

Fredrik had a feeling that Katja was staring at him, but he had all his focus on Henrik, did not intend to release him. He would have preferred to get Katja out first, but the bower was a dead end. Sara could not tell her to back away. The only way was forward, past Henrik.

Henrik did not let out a sound now, either, but his right hand was moving on the gun. His finger rested dangerously close to the trigger.

"Did you hear what I said, Henrik? We're going to take Katja with us. But before we do that you must put down the gun."

The seconds ticked away. Henrik kept silent, but Fredrik could see that he was listening. The words affected him. The question was, in what direction?

"We have everything under control. You don't need to worry any longer. We'll take care of Katja. You can put down the gun."

A brief glance in Fredrik's direction showed that Henrik was listening. But nothing happened. He sat there as if paralyzed.

"You know that you cannot fire that gun. If you do, you won't be let out until your daughter is grown. Ellen will have to grow up in a foster family."

Henrik breathed heavily, his head lowered a few inches.

"Henrik," said Fredrik. "For Ellen's sake if nothing else."

He could hear Henrik's breathing, then how he swallowed.

"You'll get the gun," he said hoarsely.

"Good," said Fredrik. "That's the right decision. Do as I say now. Set the gun down on the ground beside you."

Henrik took a deep breath.

"Calmly and carefully," said Fredrik. "With the butt in my direction."

Henrik changed his hold on the gun and leaned slowly to the side, setting it down on the ground.

"And then scoot it backward in my direction as far as you can."

Henrik did as Fredrik told him.

"And now?" he said tonelessly.

"Just sit there," said Fredrik.

When Henrik was settled again, Fredrik went over and set one heavy foot down on the butt of the gun. Not until then did he lean down to pick it up.

He backed away with the shotgun, holstered his own weapon, opened the shotgun, and took out the cartridges; at the same time, he kept a worried eye on Henrik.

"Henrik," he said.

"Yes?"

"I want you to get up and go over and sit on the steps."

"Okay," said Henrik.

Henrik got up and went toward the steps. When he was there he turned around toward Fredrik.

"Can I go in to Ellen?" he asked.

"Is she in the house?"

"Yes, in her room."

"Very soon," said Fredrik. "First we're going to take Katja to the car. During that time I want you to sit down on the steps, nothing else. Okay?"

Henrik sank down on the steps without saying anything else.

"Thanks," said Fredrik.

He didn't want to take any risks, did not want to give Henrik the chance to change his mind and come rushing out with a knife or some other weapon.

Fredrik went over to Katja and set the unloaded gun down in the grass.

He told her to stand up with her hands still on her head, then he took out the handcuffs and shackled her arms behind her back.

"Ready?" asked Sara.

"Yes."

He saw how she relaxed and holstered her gun. They took Katja Nyberg by either arm and led her out of the bower.

"We're going to take her up to the car, then I'll come back down," he said to Henrik.

Henrik nodded silently, and they passed him with Katja between them. No one said anything else. When they were on their way up the rise, Katja twisted her head and looked over her shoulder toward Henrik. Fredrik turned around, too. Henrik had stood up from the steps and was staring after them. The strong lamp above the door glistened in his dark eyes. Fredrik had never seen anyone look so incredibly alone.

93.

It was Monday afternoon, calm and quiet in the police station. And warm. The summer heat had come back with full force the day before. Fredrik was off all day Sunday. He had spent the day with Joakim, or to be more exact, from when he woke up at noon until Fredrik dropped him off outside the ferry terminal at three thirty.

He had asked him what type of work he would prefer if he became a photographer. Joakim grinned and said he didn't know. Fredrik told about the visit with Janna Drake and the two worlds on the wall in the entry, the children in the slums and the photo model. He could see that Joakim did not really understand what the problem was. Maybe it was only in the head of a middle-aged man born in the sixties that those two pictures were poles apart.

Fredrik let the water run from the tap in the kitchenette until it got really cold. He filled two glasses and carried them up to the interview room.

"Are you okay?" he said, looking at Henrik Kjellander, who was already waiting in the room.

Henrik met Fredrik's look with tired eyes.

"Yes, of course," he said hoarsely.

Fredrik set the glasses down on the table. Henrik thanked him, picked up his glass, and took a couple of deep gulps.

"I hardly slept last night," he said. "I don't think I've slept at all."

His voice was clearer now, maybe thanks to the water. Henrik set down the glass.

"I can't understand this. So it's really her?"

"Yes."

"You mean it was her the whole time?"

"She denies everything, but I'm certain. She is going to be convicted."

"This is damned incomprehensible."

Henrik rubbed his neck and looked down at the table.

"Why didn't you ever say anything about Katja Nyberg?"

"I couldn't imagine that . . . I never thought of her."

"You never thought of her, despite everything we talked about?"

The tone had gotten harder. He could not help it.

"Yes, yes, of course. That's not what I meant. Of course I thought of her. But I never believed—"

He fell silent, turned away from Fredrik, and took hold of the back of the chair.

"That it might be her?" Fredrik filled in.

"I know," said Henrik. "I was supposed to tell about everything, but I didn't. I didn't tell about Maria, and not about Katja Nyberg."

And perhaps there were others he didn't tell about, thought Fredrik. "Is that hard to understand?" Henrik turned back toward Fredrik. "Is it completely incomprehensible?"

"No," said Fredrik.

Fredrik let it go. He had not been asked to torment him, just to get the pieces to fit together.

"Tell me about Katja," he asked.

Henrik cleared his throat a couple of times, settled himself on the chair, and then hesitantly started.

He had met Katja Nyberg at Hotel St. Petri on the fourth of October. That was already known. She had been in Copenhagen during the day to interview a Danish politician. When she was done with the interview she went to St. Petri's bar to have a drink. Henrik arrived later along with Marte Astrup and Agnes Lind. Someone exchanged a few words with Katja, Henrik could not remember who. They started talking and later when they moved over to a table, Katja came with them. They remained sitting for several hours, then the editor and Henrik's assistant left in turn. Katja went with Henrik up to his room and spent the night. Henrik left the hotel early in the morning while Katja was still asleep, but left a note on one of the hotel's note cards—the note that was pinned up on Katja's wall at home in Malmö.

When Henrik came back to the hotel on the evening of the fifth Katja was sitting in the bar waiting. They spent that night together, too, as well as Henrik's third and last night at the hotel.

When Henrik was going to fly to Copenhagen again a few weeks later, he called Katja and asked if she had time to take the train over.

"It was an impulse. I never really thought I would see her again, but then . . . Well, now it turned out that way."

"And it was on your initiative?" said Fredrik.

"Yes. She came to the hotel, we . . . Yes, she stayed over, but . . . I guess I knew it wasn't a great idea. I told her that I was married and had children, I mean, I said that right from the start, but that I couldn't continue with a relationship on the side."

"How did she take that?"

"Fine, it seemed like. Or, maybe she got a little annoyed that first I asked her to come and then . . . But she said she understood."

"And it was on the morning of the twenty-seventh you said that?"

"Yes."

"So on that occasion you were only together for one night?"

"Yes."

"But you met again in Copenhagen?"

"No."

Fredrik tried to conceal his surprise. Who besides Katja could have written the comment on Malin's blog?

"Wasn't she at the hotel on November sixteenth?"

"Yes. She was there. But we hadn't been in touch or anything. She just showed up."

"But she must have known that you would be there?"

"Yes, of course. I must have said something about that time, too."

"So what happened?"

"I had to ask her to leave. It got a little tiresome."

"In what way?"

"She took it okay, but it was a little painful to send her away. She was disappointed, it was noticeable, but there was no big drama or anything."

"Did she try to make contact with you again after that?"

"She sent a couple of e-mails and asked if I would be going to Copenhagen anymore, or to Stockholm. She also called at some point and left a message on my cell phone. But I never answered that."

"But she never came to St. Petri again?"

"No."

"And there was nothing in what she said or wrote that was threatening? Or that you perceived as strange in any other way?"

"No," said Henrik. "Not at all."

The phone in the room rang. Fredrik excused himself.

"Yes?"

It was Sara.

"I think Ellen wants her dad now."

"Okay," said Fredrik. "Then I'll finish up here."

Henrik took the words as a sign that the last question had already been asked and got up before Fredrik had even hung up. He seemed eager to get out of there. Fredrik extended his hand.

"Thanks for coming in."

"You're welcome."

Fredrik followed Henrik and Ellen through the building and let them out on the front side. He had solved his first case since he came back into service for real. What ought to have been a simple one-person job on Fårö had turned out quite differently. He had a definite feeling that he would remember them a long time. Both the dead and those who remained.

94.

The day was mild, cloudy, and windy. The sea neither threatening nor beautiful, just gray and a little sad. Malin had often talked about nature on Fårö, how it had two sides. Today, Friday the sixteenth of October, it didn't seem to have any side at all.

Axel, was the first thing Henrik thought when he came into the light, open church sanctuary along with Ellen.

Axel.

The two caskets were at the front by the chancel. The larger casket with Malin to the left and the smaller one with Axel to the right. Henrik knew that they would be there, he knew what they would look like.

He was the one who had chosen them. Two simple white caskets with two simple wreaths of spruce. No pictures. He had said no when the woman at the funeral home asked if he wanted to have portraits on the caskets. In this context, he preferred his own internal image, a living image, rather than a frozen moment. And he wanted all the others who came to the funeral to have their own images, undisturbed.

He went down the center aisle holding Ellen by the hand, felt her small fingers moving against his, and without exerting himself, without even thinking about it, he felt Axel's even smaller fingers against his free hand. Hundreds of times Axel's little hand had slipped into his, hundreds of times, perhaps thousands, to get support, strength, consolation, or simply in search of an obvious intimacy.

With every step he took it was as though the grief stabbed a sword deeper and deeper into his chest, with every step death came ever closer and could finally whisper right into him. A cold voice that reached to the very depths of his soul. This is you. This is everyone you love. Malin, Axel, Ellen. You.

Candles were lit on the altar and alongside the caskets. Above the altar no soothing Jesus, simply God's all-seeing eye in the form of a simple sun. Without being able to take his gaze from the two caskets, he took the final steps up and sat down trembling in the front row with Ellen beside him. Maria came right after and sat down next to Ellen.

The newspapers had not missed any details. Everything would be out in the light, wide open. Names, pictures, and places. The hotel. "Here he met the murderer." They had ferreted out Agnes and Thomas. They declined to be interviewed, for which he was grateful. Not because it made any great difference. Everything was there, every miserable detail. But it meant a lot to him that they had still done what they could to protect him.

But not a single line about Maria. That had escaped them. Or possibly had not been defensible to publish. Maria remained a secret.

Ewy and Staffan sat in the pew behind Henrik. They spoke as little as possible with him. He could not blame them. In their eyes everything was his fault and maybe they were right. If he had not betrayed Malin the way he did, she and Axel would still be alive now. Betrayed. What a pleasant paraphrase for his having slept with a complete stranger in a hotel in Copenhagen. A stranger who then killed his wife and his child.

The bells started ringing, and he looked cautiously around the sanctuary. Right across the aisle, on the second pew from the chancel, sat three friends of Malin who had come down from Stockholm. Tyra had worked at Kakan, the other two, Viktoria and Måns, were old friends from high school. Behind them sat Janna, Thomas, and Agnes, and then the neighbors from Kalbjerga, Bengt and Ann-Katrin.

Two vacant pews behind them he noticed Alma. His sister.

He had not noticed her when he came in. He tried to catch her eye, but it was directed forward toward the caskets and the chancel.

The funeral would take place in Fårö church and the burial in Stockholm. Thankfully that had been easy to agree on despite the icy chill between him and Ewy and Staffan. Because they had such a hard time talking with one another they decided that Henrik would decide on the funeral arrangements and Ewy, Staffan, and Maria the burial. In the background lurked an unspoken tug-of-war about which family Malin really belonged to. The first one she had been born into, or the second one that she had formed together with him? Henrik could only hope that the struggle would remain hidden. He did not want to start a war over Malin's dead body.

Maria still talked with him. Perhaps she had a harder time judging. Between the two of them the obstacles were of a different kind. But she sat beside him. No, she sat next to Ellen. Maybe it was only for Ellen's sake.

The minister stepped up to the head end of the two caskets and began the funeral service.

"We are gathered here today to follow Malin Andersson and Axel Andersson Kjellander to their final rest. Mother and son . . ."

The minister's words, the customary ones, restored him in one stroke to the present. The funeral, death. Malin and Axel. The bodies in the caskets. Under the lids. He could not understand that they were there, under the white lids. How were they lying? What did they look like?

Ellen's hand was damp against his. The funeral attendees kept silent around him. The room was white and stripped down. A chancel with two doors to the sacristy, a pulpit in the corner. The minister's voice. She spoke about Malin and Axel. He could hear the wind outside, then a car passing on the road.

Henrik had met the minister three times to talk about the funeral, how he wanted it. But mostly they had talked about Malin and Axel. He had tried to describe them to her. She had listened, asked a question or two. It had not been difficult for him to talk about them, even if he was forced to stop sometimes because his voice got stuck or death became far too real.

The last time they met before the funeral he had talked about guilt. The thoughts that it was his fault. It couldn't be avoided. However you twisted and turned it, it was his fault, somehow.

The minister listened to him for a long time. Then she looked at him with a gaze that was both sympathetic and demanding. "I think your daughter needs you more than your guilt needs you."

Acknowledgments

Many thanks to Daniel Åhlén at the Gotland Police Department, as well as to Sune Jacobsson, formerly with the same agency, whose viewpoints I always listen to and almost always adapt to. Sometimes, however, police realism has had to take a backseat to fiction.

Many thanks also to Inger Nennesmo and Lars Rambe, who contributed medical and legal details.

The Intruder is partly inspired by true events, but all persons are fictional, as is the story in its entirety.